The GOD Maps
Volume 1

Yvette Kendall

STRAVARD®

L U X

Publishing House

Published by Stravard Lux Publishing House
StravardLux.com

ISBN: 978-0-578-45857-1 (hardback)
ISBN: 978-0-578-55380-1 (paperback)

Library of Congress Control Number: 2019904008

A special "Thank You" to my circle: Terry, Mahari, Matt, Amandilo, and Larry. I would also like to thank everyone else who has supported me with prayers, words of encouragement, and enlightening conversations.

"BEING A BETTER HUMAN BEING IS OFTEN OBSTRUCTED BY BEING HUMAN."

—YVETTE KENDALL

TABLE OF CONTENTS

FOREWORD

It's true—time is relative. Depending on the time period in which you've lived, explanations for the manifestations of the unknown would have gone into one of three categories: magic, science, or God. A wise man understands that they are all "one-in-the-same." For those who don't believe the possibilities and the steps with which you can arrive there, there is a term you may use, and that term is "science-fiction."

For those who believe and understand that everything exists at the same time, the "right now," and that we are in diligent pursuit of the "how" to get there, we have a more powerful term, and it's called "pre-faction." Pre-faction: "The state of particular knowledge, concepts, products, and/or processes before it enters into a non-fictional status." Existing in pre-faction is where you have to be in order to go places that others can barely imagine.

CHAPTER ONE

For identification purposes, you may call me "Oldso." I can't share with you who I truly am, but I belong to a recondite society that documents extraordinary world-changing events which have taken and will take place throughout the history of mankind. These events will be sealed until the future generations are intellectually, spiritually, and physically prepared to utilize this data. Reason being, the magnitude of this information will allow them to critically elevate in knowledge and thus give them the ability to transcend space and time.

We've been requested to shadow and document the complete research and experiences of Lab-J71. This report is written and told from an "Archimedean point," done with details I assembled through direct observation, research notes, and one-on-one interviews with the lab and other associated persons. Here is my report:

Located somewhere in the depths of Stromford University's research building is an undisclosed lab, where five of the brightest young minds in fringe scientific research formed an illustrious team. Together, they used their respective skills to access and dissect things that are outside the scope of human understanding.

The team members involved are as follows: Dr. Ameerah Mahar, a noted Cryptologist; DK Nero, a leader and innovator in the field of coding; Dr. Chad Peterson, one of the youngest Neuroscientists to win the Brain Research Prize; Raj Patel, MD., a pioneer in medicine and stem cell research; and finally, Lisa Kim, an Astrophysicist who holds 31 unchallenged patents and majored in mathematical physics.

One night, the team gathered together and huddled over a curious ticking machine. They have, in recent years, perfected the process of "Immaculate Existential Transitional Advancement Pairing" (IETAP). Modern technology finds have bestowed upon them the privilege of experiencing 0.00% failed attempts, which in turn has given them 100% accuracy with each and every subject that is processed.

Their positive output ratio is impeccable. Their latest upgrades have given them the ability to process mass subjects at one time, a capability for which they've long searched. Here is a taste of a day in their lab:

* * *

The phone rings and the team is informed that four people have just arrived in holding—everyone is tremendously excited. They are ready and waiting in anticipation for their guests to die.

Not far from them, hovering over computers and data machines, are several bodies in large, horizontal casket-like glass capsules with what appear to be digital locks affixed to the outsides of the enclosures. One of the five team members briskly walks to the capsules to check the numbers on the meters. She calls for the others, who by that time are already en route to view the latest data.

Peering into one of the capsules, Ameerah, the cryptologist says, "It's time to tag!" At that very moment, the body in the first capsule begins to flail, gasping for air and clawing at the glass. She quickly punches a sequence of numbers into the meter on the capsule unit and then repeats that same sequence of numbers into the computer. The input has to be exact or this death will be for nothing. She knew that this was much more than an experiment—these are people, and that meant something to her.

The subject in the capsule dies quickly, and the numbers on the meter frantically gauge up and down before suddenly locking in on a 26-digit code with dashes here and there. The group races over to another computer. A map of the galaxy is shown on its monitor, with a layover of numbers that resemble latitude and longitude coordinates peppered throughout the face of the computerized map. It has a fifth-dimension quality to it, as if you could physically step into it and experience the universe unencumbered.

Here is what we have learned about their plans thus far:

This group came together out of a similar curiosity. Where does the soul go after death? Not so much in the "esoteric" sense, but more in the "cosmic location" sense. They feel that the soul is a quantum entity that acts as the program for the computer of our brain and exists independently outside the physical body after death.

With that collective understanding, and armed with their respective skills, they developed an "astral algorithm" and locator system. Its job is to capture the soul upon leaving the body, and "tag it and track it" with a specialized biological/mechanical algorithmic software that has been created by the team. A united link is established between the abstract and the mechanical, and their software can analyze and give unlimited destination addresses to the entire universe and beyond.

The soul-tagging system is nothing short of miraculous. This process is so sensitive and distinctive in nature that its scientific implications may not be fully known for the next one thousand years. This tracking system involves the combination of extreme coding, ancient text, and decoding. This includes brainwave activity that's transcribed into a newly created mathematical language.

The final steps are to factor in personal vibrations, sound waves, magnetism, UV radiation, and nanotechnology. There are a few more processes involved, but patent protection is not a viable option for the group at the moment, so they won't disclose anything more than this. The delivery mechanism is just as complicated but has proven to be an excellent fit for all these critical components.

The glass capsules are hermetically sealed and levitate over extremely sensitive, specialized scale sensors. Once a subject dies, the weight reduces minutely (by a specific number of grams). That weight reduction informs them that the soul has separated from the body. The tagging system is automatically initiated, because they only have a matter of milliseconds to complete the process or the soul will be gone for good.

With this tracking software, the locational possibilities are endless; however, this excludes the Black Hole zone. They cannot track in the Black Hole because of its vacuum functionality. The team shared the following statement: "We have given every known and possible location in the galaxy unique and distinctive addresses in order to keep up with our subjects."

Ameerah volunteered to give me information; she has been one I have become particularly fond of. She explained it as follows:

* * *

"This program is extensive. Not only can we track the souls, but we can quantify what they are feeling or sensing, such as happiness, sadness, euphoria, or pain. Another bonus to the algorithm is that we are also aware of any instances where tagged souls are together in the same vicinity, at the same time. Our aim is to obtain the physical locations of Heaven and Hell (the Alpha & Beta).

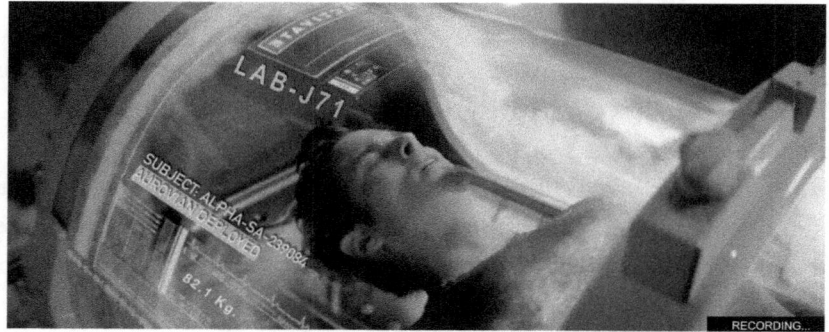
A subject in a transition capsule

"At the very least, we want to find out whether or not these souls are congregating, and what they are experiencing the moment they do meet. That should give us an agreeable consensus on where the souls could be, and if theology is applicable. This could finally end the debate of the religious status of the Bible—if it's a literal compilation of historical miraculous facts, or if it should be shelved as allegorical mythology."

* * *

This elusive data has been aptly dubbed "The GOD Maps" by the team. During their research, they came across the studies of a scientist who had engaged in the soul's functionality. He studied the soul when it was tethered to a body and when it was external to the body, to which he said the following:

"It turns out that the human brain could be similar to a 'biological computer' and that the human consciousness may be like a program run by a quantum computer within the brain. What's even more astonishing is that after someone dies, his or her soul goes back to the universe, and it does not die."

* * *

These scientists have long argued that the soul is maintained in micro-tubules of brain cells.

●

INTRODUCTORY OBSERVATION ENTRY:

Ameerah has never really been one for theatrics, but explaining the science behind her tagging system brings out her inner Rod Sterling. After she comfortably situates herself in the chair across from me, she goes into the specifics of the team's work. Before she begins to speak, she comments on how it is a privilege to speak to such a being in person. I smile and nod but am careful not to get too close to her. My presence isn't exactly compatible with an "organic."

Observing is a fixed position for me, as it is for the few others like me. Something happened a while back that has caused me to be cautious—something dreadful that I regret to this day. I had tried to mate with an organic (only once), and it resulted in a damning entity that changed the balance of life. The universe was charged a heavy price for my indiscretion.

Ameerah leans in coyly, chattering away. This isn't the time, but my curiosity gets the better of me. I let myself lightly graze the back of her hand. I barely touch her, but it's enough to sway her course.

To Ameerah, she is still in conversation with her guest, but in actuality, I give her a piece of me that will take a lifetime to digest. I will be a passenger for all her undertakings. I will go wherever she goes, and I will know what she knows. For all intents and purposes, this meeting is just a formality for the "Forever Records."

In touching her, a seed was planted for all that is to come. I am here for more than a report. My true job is done, as I have collected abundant information, but there is still much more to learn. After all, she and her team have done something spectacularly tyrannical to God. The details of this feat must be cataloged. Like they say, "The Devil is in the details," and she is about to make it plain.

I move out of her flesh and restore myself as the polite visitor with whom she is enamored. I chuckle as she continues, eyes bright and mind racing.

"Allow me to get technical, just for a moment," she says. "This will help you better understand what you will be seeing and hearing in our lab and have a foundation on why we are doing the things that we are doing. It's of central importance that you understand how the human consciousness works within the body, so you can then understand the independent power that it has outside the body.

"The stars of the show are micro-tubules. They are conveyer belts inside our cells. They move like independent tiny muscles—they operate as a computerized toy Lego set. We think that microtubules are quantum computers (computers that processes data extremely fast), as well as being the seat of human consciousness."

I sit back and ponder everything I've learned and take in what she is telling me. With an ear-to-ear grin, Ameerah continues, "Their lifestyle is quite remarkable! Allegedly, when human beings are 'clinically dead,' the microtubules in the brain lose their state of being but are still able to retain the information inside of them. Let's say the heart stops beating, the blood stops flowing, and the microtubules lose their current state of being.

"That information (or essence) within the microtubules is not destroyed—it can't be destroyed—it just distributes and dissipates into the universe. Human beings are made of energy and the facts are that energy never dies; it just transforms. If the patient is resuscitated or revived, their information/essence can go back into the microtubules in their body and the patient wakes up and says, 'I had a near-death experience.'

"On the other hand, if they're not revived, and the patient dies, it's possible that this information (essence) can exist outside the body, perhaps indefinitely, as a soul."

I already know what Ameerah is saying, but I still enjoy hearing her fawn over it all. So, what she is saying is the hard-scientific aspect of it all, but the second part is less science (so to speak) and more esoteric understanding. The team's flip side of the coin is that they tapped into the teachings of "noetic science."

Noetic science explores phenomena that do not necessarily fit conventional scientific models. It explores the "inner cosmos" of the mind (consciousness, soul, and spirit) and how it relates to the "outer cosmos" of the physical world. It explores how people come to know things or affect things that have no apparent rational explanation.

"Our focus with this belief system was with the 'after-death' communications and personal transformations, as well as how it can relate to the nature of human consciousness," Ameerah explains. "You can see how these theories became a very important form of confirmation for our work— verification that we may be on the right track. Being alive is a system of electrical currents, moving frequencies, rhythms, wavelengths, and vibrations in a balanced dance."

I want to interrupt Ameerah as she rambles on about her findings, but I can't bring myself to do it. I feel grandiose listening to a human being swim within the infancy of her knowledge. It's quite endearing to experience her celebrating her milestones and successes. Humans have no clue that our species is a privileged one. I know where God hides the rain when the sun is out to play. Despite that, I take no offense in learning how humans channel greatness (on their level).

Ameerah is a beauty for the ages with a mind that can't wait. It's funny; she was scheduled to die only moments before I arrived. I have been sent here to set her in motion. Her fate has changed paths and is suddenly of the utmost importance to the hierarchy. I need to know why she is so important to the thread. I've been told that she must go the distance and that the Book won't be complete without her.

I watch as she gleefully laughs between breaking down complex sciences "for" me. Yes, she giddily and effectively "human-splains" the hows and the whys of life to a thing that has seen the first blade of grass emerge through freshly conjured earth. I heard the first lie ever told and punished the first man who committed an abomination with another of his kind. Everything she has said is full of truth, albeit a truth whose fruit is of the poisonous tree. She will learn that wisdom has a grave for us all.

Ameerah isn't done championing her findings just yet. She has a tale from the womb and news about the perplexities of human nature. I sit as a wanting juror, hanging on to her every word. The floor is hers and she isn't shy about taking command of it.

"Even at birth, we are beckoned into this world with rhythmic contractions and a mother's involuntary movements to separate one life from the next," she continues. "Different beats create different vibrations and tones that resonate with only certain kinds of individuals. Have you ever heard someone say, 'I hate jazz music?' The jazz lovers in the room gasp in disbelief. However, it's not that they actually hate this style of music; it's simply because jazz is on a frequency that is not in harmony with their life's frequency."

I watch Ameerah in awe as her eyes grow wider and her hands begin to shake as she continues explaining her research. "Another example is when a man finds a woman attractive (when the general consensus is that this woman is unattractive)," she says. "It's because of many things, but a majority being chemistry and vibrational pulls between the two. We could go on and on with proven examples in nature, life, and science.

"However, if you begin to slow down and pay close attention, you will see exactly what we mean. If you really want to see evidence of God, then learn the language of science. What many people may not realize is that if you were able to shrink yourself down to the size of a speck of dust, enter the human body and illuminate its activity points from within, it would appear very similar to the universe, stars, and galaxies.

"Yes, our meager human bodies have a blueprint like none other. That alone should speak volumes about our designer, as all humans vibrate on different frequencies. It's important to have subjects from many different walks of life, backgrounds, and religious beliefs to study as controls. Our subjects come from different cultures, religions, ages, and genders.

"The representation of these diverse groups of people is of the utmost importance. They're a part of the human tapestry. Each group represents a different vibration that signifies an alternate path to where they will ultimately end up. Simply put, what you are determines where you'll be. It's a 'you are what you eat' type of philosophy, and our research may prove this to be overwhelmingly factual.

"Our team believes in our research so deeply that when we are in the pre-stages of death ourselves, we will ride the wave of Aurovian too. What happens after this life is unavoidable; just as we've experienced their destinies, you can experience ours. The only difference is that we may continue to be aware of the roles that we've played prior to our deaths. These risks will unquestionably earn us a unique review of our life's activities in regard to the higher entity that governs those realms.

"Your birth identity coupled with your life choices dictates your grid breakdown. It's exciting to see what that may mean for any given person on this planet in the afterlife. That's part of what this entire experiment is about—where will we end up because of our choices? Do good Christians go to Heaven? Do bad people go to Hell? Are gay people damned for all eternity? This is an equation that excludes no one, regardless of religious faction. If all goes right, we may be able to peer into a restricted existence of the final stop."

* * *

To date, the team has processed nearly 400,000 subjects. Here is the breakdown of their current (new) studies in a "master grid" form:

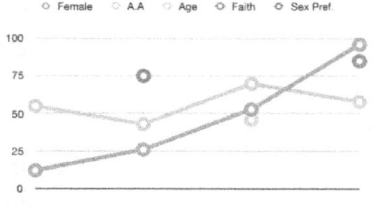

Subject name: Alpha-SA-119034
Gender: Female
Ethnic Background: African-American
Age: 46
Religion: Christian
Sexual Preference: Straight

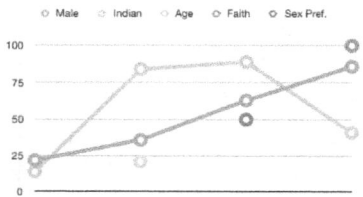

Subject name: Beta-SB-119035
Gender: Male
Ethnic Background: Indian
Age: 21
Religion: Non-Denominational.
Sexual Preference: Bi-sexual

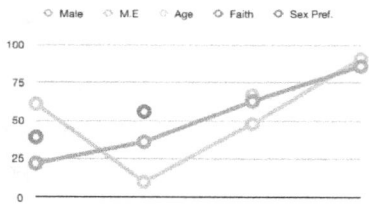

Subject name: Gamma-SC-119036:
Gender: Male
Ethnic Background: Middle Eastern
Age: 67
Religion: Muslim
Sexual Preference: Straight

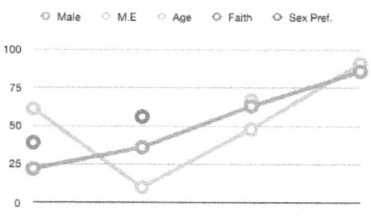

Subject name: Delta-SD-119037:
Gender: Female (transgender to male)
Ethnic Background: Caucasian
Age: 34
Religion: Atheist
Sexual Preference: Straight – Adjacent

CHAPTER TWO

INTRODUCTORY OBSERVATION ENTRY, PART 2

meerah went on to explain their tagging process. This is her account:

* * *

"Our subjects are chosen at random. We find them at hospitals, hospices, and have even found a few who were living on the streets. We don't take anyone against their will—our research is strictly voluntary. Once we have identified a subject, we sit down with them and go over the entire procedure. The subjects are generally dying from a severe illness or have had trauma that has caused irreparable damage to the quality of their lives.

"We keep in contact with their caregivers until they are near death. We then transfer them over to our facilities, where we keep them comfortable and monitored until they are ready to transcend. Our on-site physicians perform constant evaluations of the subjects so that we will know when to enclose them into the capsules. The capsules themselves are hyper-sensitive scales that can detect the slightest difference in solid weight; this apparatus will activate the next step in the procedure automatically.

"During our initial test years ago, we lost several subjects due to not understanding the timing, nor how to capture (or at least delay) the soul's transition so that it could be tagged. You would be surprised at how researching fiction and even comic books can lead to a real-life scientific breakthrough. Fantasy is nothing more than a concept that has not been put into a position to manifest. In essence, everything is real, but the question is when does science fiction = science fact?

"The more we do this type of work, the more we see God's face. We are not really discovering anything; it is God revealing Himself to the chosen few who dare to seek."

Although they're all working toward the same goals, it's not complete harmony in their camp. Their team members' belief systems are rather conflicting. They have a couple members who believe that there is a higher power. They also have an evolutionist and a fair share of undecided folks; these are the pillars in their think tank.

Having such diverse beliefs among them forces them to confront certain issues (rather intimately) that they did not have to examine before. They've learned too much to ignore certain truths, and the reality of it all has changed their minds both collectively and individually.

The science is very compelling and has changed the way they went about implementing lab processes. One of the most interesting facts that they have learned is that the heart is the first organ to form during the development of the body. An embryo is made up of only a very few cells, and each cell can get the nutrients it needs directly from its surroundings. The cells divide and multiply to form a growing ball, which becomes the heart.

A neurologist discovered a sophisticated collection of neurons in the heart organized into a small but complex nervous system. The heart's nervous system contains around 40,000 neurons called sensory neurites that communicate with the brain. They called it "the Little Brain in the Heart." It has been known for many years that memory is a distributive process. You can't localize memory to a neuron or a group of neurons in the brain. The memory itself is distributed throughout the neural system.

To sum it up, the team had to go beyond the brain when creating the coding and collecting personalized subject data. Luckily, they were able to utilize more extensive organic data. One could argue (and they have) that the zombies that appear on our favorite shows may still have their souls intact, since there is current activity in the areas where this information would be stored.

This data would be horribly corrupted and misaligned. This is an "in-lab" bet that they hoped not to win or bring about in any way. Remember this: all that you need for that perfect storm—the one that could possibly end humanity—is curiosity, ego, and access.

Now, back to the subjects. The tagging process is the most complicated procedure to explain. How do you basically arrest and then attach to thin air? That's the simplest way they are able to pose this question. It's almost like trying to pinpoint emotional pain. You can't. Emotional pain has no location. One thing that they discovered was that the more complex a thing was, that this imparted a trait all-in-of-itself, and this gave them a starting point for identification.

For instance, there are three major types of tears: basal, reflex, and psychic (triggered by emotions). All tears contain organic substances, including oils, antibodies, and enzymes, and are suspended in salt water. Different types of tears have distinct molecules. Emotional tears have protein-based hormones, including the neurotransmitter leucine enkeph-alin, which is a natural painkiller that is released when we are stressed.

The tears seen under the microscope are crystallized salt and can lead to different shapes and forms. So, even psychic tears with the same chemical composition can look very different. Different variables in the emotions of why you are moved to tears will offer very specific identifications.

With that said, part of what they do is catch variables with the changes of the sealed air in the chambers. Ameerah enthusiastically tells me the details as she continues gushing about her research:

* * *

"The data collectors can hold volumes of information, which is quickly analyzed with our state-of-the-art computer system that we've named the IDIAMTRACE-10.

"The system then creates a profile that has many components. Firstly, a soul has an 'instinctive orientation.' The team will identify this and then configure it with a mathematical crypto algorithm, vibrational coding, UV measurements, sound matching, color zoning, DNA identifiers, wavelength catchers, and so forth. Then these microscopic layers are converted into a bio-data product called 'Aurovian,' a new nano-technology.

"Aurovian are 'nanites' that have been engineered into a biological/mechanical/vibrational mist. One of these is applied by formatting the soul in a volumetric shape, and then during a custom energy blast (compliments of their own Tesla-like delivery unit), they can tag an outgoing soul with a nearly 100% accuracy.

"This product cannot freeze, burn, or be damaged when too wet or too dry. It has a stored and protected light source that cannot be absorbed by utter darkness. It can utilize the soul's aura as a source of energy; it cannot break or be crushed, it is not affected by speed or inertia, it can thrive in the atmosphere or lack of any atmosphere, and it cannot be washed or rubbed to the point of becoming cosmetically altered.

"It has a lifespan of 100 years and it can record non-stop for that same length of time. However, Aurovian can be corrupted and rendered useless if any of these units were to experience a lack of sufficient energy from its host or soul. If that energy ever dissipates or even gets redistributed, the tracker will cease functioning and will phase out.

"Another important route (but not the only one) is through the nasal passages, as to have direct access to the brain. These actions are synching at the same time while being paired with their physical computer system for tracking. The monitor is custom-made for this experience as well. It looks like a device somewhere between a crystal ball and a flat-screen television. It was made that way to accurately mimic the structure of the galaxy, planets, and stars.

"We have to map the universe and what may be behind it. This gives the feeling of being in a planetarium on a compact scale. There's a reason why Mary Shelley's *Frankenstein* stood the test of time, and it's not because it's a fascinating read. The science of the story is sound. It's missing a few key elements, but it's sound, nonetheless.

"One of the key factors we must use to identify tagged souls during their external journeys is patterns. Everything has a pattern—its personal rhythm or system. Even when you think of life (with this particular rule), you have to be aware that there is a designer; if not, the world as we know it would be as random as they come. A seed could grow an apple tree one day, and then the same seed would be able to grow rubber the next day.

"Some people are born with two eyes and a nose, and some could be born with three noses and one eye, or bones made out of sugar. The point is that there is a formidable and purposely designed system at play with life—before, during, and after. Some examples are when and where flowers grow, rain drops, and the structural design of the human body. Everything and every cell has an important function. Then comes the fact that humans are intertwined with plant life on a molecular level.

"Plants have 'blood,' which is green and called 'chlorophyll.' If you look at the structure of a chlorophyll molecule, it's very similar to a hemoglobin molecule. In fact, they are identical with one main difference. There's a metal atom in the middle of each of those molecules; in the case of a plant's chlorophyll, it is ***magnesium***. This gives it a green color. In our case, it's ***iron***, which gives our blood a red color.

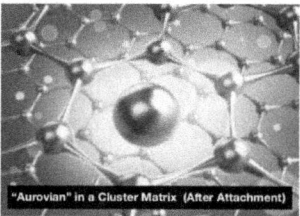
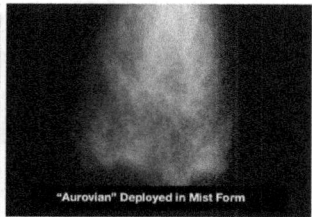

"Aurovian" in Nanite Form.   "Aurovian" in a Cluster Matrix (After Attachment)   "Aurovian" Deployed in Mist Form

"Understanding an entity's individual uniqueness allows them to track tagged souls with an ease they didn't have before. It especially helps them differentiate which tagged soul is which when they are in close proximity to one another. To be clear, they can only track their tagged souls, which is why securing as many subjects as they can is so important. Unfortunately, they cannot tag a soul that has already departed its body."

As Ameerah previously explained, one's DNA, brainwaves, and unforgiving tagging time are crucial components to the success of the process. The team believes that these key criteria are burned off during their transition, or at the very least, separated from their home subjects so quickly, to the point of confusion.

Imagine tossing a grain of sand into the existing sands on the beach and then having waves of water wash on the beach, dragging large portions of all the sand into the ocean. Now, their job would be to find "your" one grain of sand and put it back in your hand. That would be the simplest analogy to express the level of difficulty they would have to try to find and contain a random soul and then tag it to be tracked.

Timing is everything to the success of their work and having a fortress of solitude in which to conduct their experiments is even more crucial to the process.

"We try to do most of our research and tracking after the campus shuts down for the day," Ameerah continued. "However, souls don't have a schedule to adhere to and travel randomly, 24 hours a day, so we have to be here to witness and log their experiences. We have a data printout machine to provide hard-copy evidence for the times we can't be here. Reading masses of information on thousands of trackings can be daunting and unforgiving when it piles too high. So, we do our best to stay on top of it—"

————THUNDEROUS COMMOTION————

Ameerah's account ends abruptly as the walls begin to shake.

CHAPTER THREE

AMEERAH'S ACCOUNT FROM THAT NIGHT

"What the hell!" I shout out, my face crumpled in distress as my eyes bolt to the window. I see Oldso make an odd expression as I get up to check what is going on. My train of thought gets shaky as the noises outside get louder and start pounding at my skull. What was once a normally quiet quad is now filled with vapid protesters and Bible-thumbing zealots. How can anyone get work done under these conditions? We are now subjected to the repetitive chanting of "SHUT THEM DOWN! SHUT THEM DOWN!" echoing from the ground level.

Luckily, the dean of the university, Norman Rydell, is a very understanding man and a proponent of fringe science theories. He's been a key figure in making sure that the lab's research is well funded. Unfortunately, certain individuals have put a strain on our work.

There was a sixth member on the team. His name was Prof. Ron Sherman. He became highly opposed to our research and left the quad about three months ago. Before his departure, we had made other accidental discoveries (which he felt were unethical), and he couldn't say his piece without his obligatory flair for the dramatics.

He shouted at the top of his lungs (in the style of a Shakespearian monologue), "*You* know *not* what you do! This work is egregious and borderlines on the diabolical and blasphemous. I will not be a part of this chicanery. I will take my leave because God sees *ALL*!" Needless to say, we feel pretty confident (via his usual pettifoggery) that he leaked certain revelations about our work to reporters, and it has garnered us unwanted attention by many "unenlightened" individuals.

Let's just say that science is transcending, and therefore incomprehensible when viewed by the masses on a fixed scale. Not to mention that science has made great strides in the past 50 years, so much so that the world agreed to change our global calendar. They did away with the 28–31 days on any given month (out of the 12-month year) and decided that each month would be just 28 days long. With that re-arrangement, there were another 28 days to be accounted for. A thirteenth month was created with those days. We now have "*Davinuary,*" the third month of the year, named after famed scientist and Renaissance man, Leonardo Da Vinci.

Prof. Sherman is a weasel of a man and has a penchant for foolishness, but he remains one of the most sought-after professors in theoretical physics. He is a towering six-foot, four inches and dresses as if he admires an evil villain or two. Black is his signature color—even his lab coat was a pristine black gabardine fabric. It was so dark that it seemed to swallow any light that ventured near it.

We were sure to never ask him his age, but he looked to be rounding fifty years old, and whenever he spoke it was reminiscent of someone who had smoked cigarettes for the better part of his life. Oddly enough, he was the one that posed the initial question about the locations of Heaven and Hell.

The Nation
of Christian Founders

You see, he is a devout Christian and bishop of a well-known religious organization in our area: "**The Nation of Christian Founders.**" He rarely missed an opportunity to mention that our work here should be limited to curing diseases and advancing space travel—that our work would be better suited for purposes of mining other planets for precious metals and other rare findings.

In the genesis of our discoveries, he said, "There have been complaints lodged against our lab by religious groups with claims that we are trying to subvert nature and the natural process by unprecedented means."

We all found this to be a little strange because no one knew of our "true" work, not even the university in which our lab is located. As far as they knew at the time, we were working on various new innovations in science, medicine, and mathematical coding. Particularly research on extensive space travel and various product testing.

We felt that this was Prof. Sherman's way of pressuring us to back down with him not being the direct cause of it. Today, we have to think about how to move forward in the midst of the ever-growing public eye. Everyone wants to know what we're doing and why. The Church has made its presence known in a very big way.

The fanatics have reared their ugly heads as well—most of whom are novices in the world of fringe science (which we affectionately refer to as "exotic science"), as well as comic book enthusiasts. They feel a kinship and want to lend support wherever they can. Some have decided to act as makeshift security for popular hangout spots of the staff on campus. They feel like caged high-profile entertainers.

Oldso knows all of this, so I won't bore him with the details. I simply look at him with a sort of defeated half-smile and say, "The only way we can navigate within the public arena is in ridiculous disguises, lest we be mobbed for autographs or kidnapped and tortured into compliance." I look back out the window and stare off into night sky. "For now, we have to stay put. We have newly tagged souls, and we are awaiting the transmissions of their whereabouts."

THERE IS A REPORT!

I rush to look at the report as the notification shocks me out of my head. I look at it and see something strange. "Wait a moment . . . one of our tagged souls still appears to be earth-bound . . ." We have painstakingly tried to cover all of our astral travel bases (thanks to Google Earth) so we can track all of our planetary locations just as easily as we can off-planet—this includes latitude and longitude.

We quickly pull the file for Subject: Beta-SB-119035 to view his most recent address and family members' addresses. He is, in fact, at his mother's home; the tracking can be more intimate if we have a blueprint of the location. Then we can tell exactly where he is, down to the room he's in.

Visitations of home and loved ones are very common, especially in the moments following a transitioning period. The visits vary from a few minutes to several days or weeks.

Emotions appear to be strongly tethered to souls, and this makes tracking them and identifying their emotional auras effortless (in a manner of speaking). This subject will more than likely travel off-planet soon and visit the boundless destinations available to it. Then the team can learn a little more about where it goes and maybe even why.

Not all of our tagged souls are interested in Earthly visits. "Interested" might not be the best word; maybe a better term is "able." The lab has experienced three subjects who were terminally ill who decided to take their own lives in the chambers; they were monitored with the same policies and procedures. There was an eeriness with these cases (because of the manners of death).

After these events, their souls traveled to a non-specific location in space (the same exact location for all three) and remained stationary for several weeks, almost as if they were being detained (in every sense of the word). The read on each subject is inconclusive. Their energies appear to be muted, almost suspended. Those souls are emitting barely enough energy to keep the pairing system in place.

We have no way of knowing what actual experiences the souls are having; if we could, this would change the direction dramatically. The lack of activity has the lab concerned and curious. The ability to monitor auras and emotions gives us the necessary data in order to ascertain where they may be, and this sort of halt leaves us at a serious disadvantage. What we can gather paints a Picasso-like, abstract picture, which will just have to do for now.

Monitoring shifts are endless. The lab runs twenty-four hours a day. Some of us do manage to dip into our individual lives under this hectic radar. Usually, though, a trip or two home is all we can afford, other than our time spent sleeping (however long that may be). Our work is our top priority.

CHAPTER FOUR

THIS IS THEIR STORY

Ameerah (28 years old) was the resident cryptologist. She accomplished many academic accolades, but she still lived at home with her parents because she didn't see a need to leave. Her mother was a patent researcher and leaned on Ameerah a lot to assist with research and proofreading her findings. Her father worked 18-hour days and was usually found asleep on the recliner in front of a game.

Ameerah wanted to head home for the night; she had hopes of decompressing from all the commotion at the lab. The long drive from the city to the suburbs usually helped her relax and ease into thinking about the next steps of the team's operation. When she made it home, she would walk past her dad (in his second usual place on the couch) and slump into her nighttime routine. There was always a pen and a notepad on her nightstand, as well as smelling salts in a glass shaker.

Only a few people knew this, but Ameerah had a secret—cryptology was not a choice of study, but a means to save her life. She suffered from something called "vivid dream syndrome," a rare phenomenon. People who experience it have vivid, bizarre, and/or disturbing dreams. These dreams can seem hyper life-like and hard to distinguish from reality.

Once in her dreams, she could see in color, feel temperatures and textures, experience wetness and dryness, and interact with others on extraordinarily deep levels. There were little to no clues indicating that she was actually asleep. This made it nearly impossible to wake her up if she was alone.

On several occasions, she was left locked in her dream world for hours on end. One weekend, she was asleep for more than seventy-two hours while her parents were on a short vacation. Fortunately, she was able to exit her dream that day because she attempted to google something on her laptop while in the dream. Oddly enough, no information would populate.

In your dreams, you are the architect and the authority on everything; after all, you made the world yourself. So, if you google something that you don't already know, you cannot provide the answers to it. She had realized that she wasn't in the waking world and became lucid immediately. She woke to what felt like the residual effects of a bad drug binge.

This night, Ameerah was exhausted. She felt a deep sleep coming on but didn't want to worry her mom about waking her if she happened to be arrested into her dream world. Lisa Kim, her lab team member/astrophysicist (and the only other girl in the lab), lived near to her parents' house. She thought that maybe she could conjure up a believable story to explain why she would need to be monitored and awoken if necessary. It was the best that she could do on short notice. She begrudgingly made the call and prayed Lisa would keep her condition a secret if need be.

Lisa Kim was on her way home when she received the call from Ameerah. She answered her cell in her signature sterile voice, "Yes, may I help you? Oh, good evening, Ameerah. You need me to do what?... I suppose so but give me an hour. I have to meet with Savoy at a coffee shop near my house first to pick up new prototypes and samples."

Savoy Sellers was a high school buddy of Lisa's. Savoy never went to college; instead, she decided to go into the field of innovation and product development. Not having any formal education actually gave her an advantage when it came to innovating uniqueness. The team members worked in conjunction with Savoy to assist her with testing her prototypes and providing avenues to place her finished products.

On this particular night, Savoy passed government testing for an instant bulletproofing, flexible adhesive panel that she aptly named "Ballisticks."

With this product, one could bulletproof anything instantly, including one's self. The lab would definitely make good use of the samples.

As Ameerah prepared to leave the lab, trying her best to stay awake, she thought about how she'd been in the lab alone one night a few months ago, drifting off into deep thought. Being involved in the sort of research they were in made her consider her life choices and her own mortality. *Where will I go?* she thought to herself.

She looked over her shoulder, and then climbed into one of the sterilized transition capsules.

Once the capsules closed, they sealed off hermetically and no one could possibly open them from the inside. She thought it wise to prop open the lid with a wedge that was lying on the floor nearby. Ameerah had been on her feet for twenty straight hours and didn't realize how exhausted she was. Once horizontal, fatigue kicked in immediately and she drifted off into a deep, deep sleep. Within a few minutes, she was awake and aware (or so she thought).

It was warm and the sun was setting unusually fast. Before she knew it, it was nighttime. The park was full of people going about their business; ironically, no one seemed bothered by the unorthodox lapse of time. The scenery was sublime.

They were encircled by picturesque trees, lofty grass, and sparkling waters as far as the eye could see. Although it was suddenly evening, her view of the landscape was optimal. As she slowly made her way onto the path, she noticed that some of the people were glowing—not all over, but in little blue luminous patches on different parts of their bodies.

Some had the patches on their chest or arms, while others had patches on their foreheads or hands. She picked up the pace to get a closer view, and then it dawned on her—there wasn't a building or road in sight. Ameerah was beginning to get a surreal impression and instinct kicked in.

"Oh, shit! I'm asleep." She tried to wake up, but she couldn't. She began to panic as she attempted to pull herself away from this dream world.

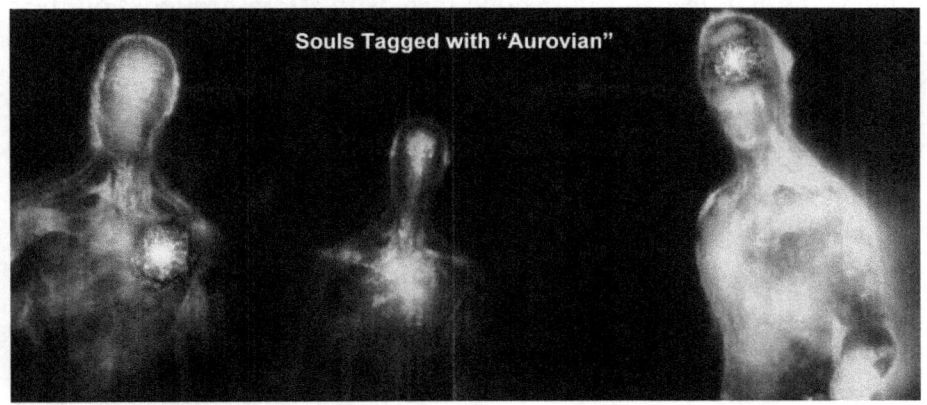

Souls Tagged with "Aurovian"

"I should have known!" she said, frantic. She was so occupied with the glowing people that she didn't notice the strange colors in the world around her. They were colors she had never seen before. There were literally no words for the spectrum presentations that were right in front of her face.

A sense of disconnection descended on Ameerah rapidly. The people in the park turned to her, smiled, and waved goodbye while she faded to black.

Ameerah's eyes open rapidly, and before she could even think, she realized she could barely breathe and was struggling for air. The wedge was gone from the capsule lid. She was sealed inside the capsule. All the air was just about depleted. She frantically looked around the room only to find that the IDIAMTRACE-10 had been turned on and was active. Ameerah was about to be tagged.

She began to sob uncontrollably and apply whatever force she could to the lid of the capsule. It was to no avail because she had no leverage or strength to push. Near her chin, she could hear the "Aurovian Mist" deploying. She screamed and kicked and then covered her mouth while she held her breath.

Just then, the room brightened up. Ameerah could hear faint tones of someone quickly punching the keys on the digitized pad outside the capsule. A hissing sound filled her ears and air rushed into her nostrils. By the time she could focus, she saw the faces of her team members, D.K.,

Simon, and Raj. Everyone just stood there with astonished looks on their faces that read "WTF!"

"How could you do something so STUPID?!" D.K. screamed as he bailed Ameerah out of the capsule. D.K. was visibly shaken. He was undoubtedly more upset than the other team members in the room, and everyone understood why. Ameerah and D.K were first cousins. Her mom and his dad were siblings . . . estranged siblings. Despite that fact, this pair of cohorts got along famously, like a brother and sister should.

Even in his anger, he made sure that she was all right. After making sure she was okay, he went in with his full reprimand of Ameerah's foolish decision to engage the Transition Capsule alone. Once she gained her composure, she sat close to D.K, close enough to mumble in his ear and call him by his awkward family nickname. "Raggedy, I think that I'm okay, but this was not a clumsy mistake or a malfunction. Someone was here and did this to me on purpose." They both sat without speaking any further. The realization was setting in that the lab and their work may be compromised.

Everyone thought it best that Ameerah head home for the night. The team needed to decompress and come to terms with what they had just experienced. Protocols must be put in place to avoid this from ever happening again. The ride home for Ameerah was one of reflection—better yet, confusion. She could recall the events in her dreams clearly, but there was a weird impression attached to them that she couldn't shake.

CHAPTER FIVE

Ameerah's issues were twofold. Along with her vivid dreams' syndrome, she also had involuntary episodes of astral-planing. The astral-planing episodes occurred during her vivid dream activities. Due to the team's penetrating research into the "Golden Coordinates," the knowledge they had uncovered stimulated her condition.

Unbeknownst to Ameerah, she had been visiting one of the Golden locations in her sleep state. She had made several trips, not realizing that that was where she had been. Her dreams were always hyper-realistic. Sometimes she recognized the landscape, and sometimes she didn't. She had always been told that dreams were real-life stressors or concerns that the mind attempted to reconcile in its sleep, but hers were a little too literal.

In actuality, her dreams were independent of her emotional worries. She was living another reality—one that could answer questions the team had been relentlessly searching for. The findings would be disruptive. She had been there. She didn't need the coordinates because she knew where it was (deep down, anyway). She walked amongst the souls as one of them.

Ameerah offered something greater than that, though—she was a living witness who could report what she'd seen, heard, and felt. The people she saw in her dreams—the people who glowed with electric blue patches—should have felt somewhat familiar to Ameerah. They glowed with blue patches on their surfaces because they were the tagged souls from the lab.

When the Aurovian mist was active and energized, a blue essence illuminated the carrier.

The souls no longer had human bodies. The nanite mist glowed on their new vestiges, wherever it was able to attach. Ameerah was truly special. She was a hybrid with "bi-plane" capabilities. If only she were cognizant of what she could do.

Snapping out of deep thought in her bedroom, Ameerah heard a door close and familiar footsteps ascending the stairs.

Knowing someone was there to check up on her, she felt an instant calm take over her mind. Now, at least she would have someone there to snatch her away from Never-Never Land if needed. As she listened to the muffled voices upstairs, she realized they were her parents. Her mom had come home, and her dad woke up from his usual sleeping position on the couch. Before long, her dad was wide awake and Ameerah could hear him practicing with his nun chucks to the beat of "Tower of Power." She winced at his vintage choice of music as she descended into her world of sleep.

●

Lisa Kim finally made it to the lot of "Pie-Fi," a favorite Internet bakery for all the local eggheads in the area. Savoy was there (early as usual) and eagerly waved Lisa into a parking spot, still sporting a patch on her right eye. Although Savoy was in her early thirties, she suffered from an elderly disease called "macular degeneration." It was a genetic disease that was causing her to slowly go blind.

Savoy often dropped hints by frequently saying, "I love my retina specialist Dr. Kohon, but it's time for a more hi-tech remedy!" So, the previous week, Raj and Lisa gave in to her not-so-subtle suggestions. They injected Savoy with nanites to cauterize the bleeding in the affected eye.

Currently, the only available remedy they had for this condition was monthly injections in her eye (below the pupil) for the rest of her life. Ugh! Needles in your eyes, while you're alert and looking at it travel to your face to puncture your eyeball—Lisa shivered just thinking about it. One would think Savoy would be ecstatic about her new procedure above anything else, but no. She was hyped about one of her new inventions. She would undoubtedly run down her entire concept, research, and development in a matter of sixty seconds or less.

Generally, Savoy's innovations were savvy but utilitarian. She was a "futurist" for sure. The lab team tested all of her innovations. They would test them out before the inventions hit the market or before she accepted any licensing offers for them. Their lab was full of her products for testing and everyday use. Savoy had a line of anti-bacterial disposable drinking cups called "Cleencups" that they swore by. It cut down on hand-to-hand contamination and helped kill the common cold in its tracks.

However, tonight was different. The information that Savoy had could benefit the lab's current research with the tagged souls and the Divinity Location(s). Savoy started out by regurgitating information that Lisa already knew.

"You can only track souls that have died in your lab and tagged with the Aurovian," she said. Lisa nodded her head up and down several times in an effort to show some level of interest with this anti-revelatory information.

Savoy continued, "What if you guys could tag the other souls that your subjects come in contact with?"

Lisa tilted her head and sat up straight. She looked at Savoy and squinted her eyes as if to say, "What are you getting at?"

Savoy went on to say that she found a way to have the nanites operating inside the Aurovian to infect other host-like energy sources. Lisa urged Savoy to keep talking.

"You wouldn't get the same beneficial data as you would with a tagged lab subject, but what you will get is a number count. Meaning that every soul your hosts comes in contact with will be 'soft-tagged,' so to speak. You guys can get a substantial census in any given location. A count that you wouldn't have otherwise had. That actually means less tagging for you to do, to identify a location."

"We can even program the Aurovian to reject other nanites once a cluster has already claimed a secondary host," Lisa added, beginning to beam. She knew this was a game changer. Without a moment to lose, she called Ameerah to cancel the overnight visit. She did, however, send out a **"CODE RED"** message and told the team to head back to the lab ASAP.

CHAPTER SIX

When all the team members made it to the lab, Savoy did her best to thoroughly explain how her process could work in theory. She threw the ball in the team's court to actualize the concept.

Several weeks later, the new batch of "viral nanites" were ready to be introduced to the Aurovian, with another added benefit. After months of tests and trials, all the science and engineering were finally complete. They then had the capabilities of having two-way communication with the tagged souls. Although the team's work was considered "top secret," they had begun the patent process for the less substantial innovations that served as a support system for the principal inventions. Nearly one hundred patents needed to be filed, and trade secrets needed to be declared.

The creation and deployment of the Aurovian was so groundbreaking and disruptive to the known scientific boundaries that "Aurovian" had earned a place on the periodic table of elements. A new category had been sanctioned especially for their innovation. Introducing the new elemental category of "Rh-Meta: for Unknown Metascience Elements."

However, they were uncomfortable about disclosing specifics at that time (because working

"Aurovian" has been added to the Periodic Table of Elements

Located in the New Elements Category:
"Rh-Meta Element" - Unknown Metascience Element

in this medium had never been done before). Also, because the learning curve was steep and unending—new information could literally reveal itself daily. Nevertheless, they did disclose the news to Dean Rydell because global validation was advantageous in order for the team to acquire much-needed funding. Keeping him in the loop was critical to their research. For now, pushing papers would have to wait. Raj was triaging a new batch of subjects, and the team was ready to prep, tag, and send fresh souls off on their journey.

Their nano-acoustics and linguistics specialist, Simon Christian, had officially joined the team. His job was to decipher and convert the sounds that they heard from the tagged-souls to a language they could understand and communicate with. What they came to realize was that souls don't communicate in a human language. They speak in a language of organic sounds and clicks.

Simon was certain he could quantify what he'd heard. He stated, "They are very similar to a cosmic Morse code. We, in turn, would speak to them in this same language, in hopes that we can learn about what they are seeing and experiencing."

The first round of tests was to send out signals to the souls that were paired with the Aurovian tagging systems. It was like a galactic ping. When that ping returned, Simon sent out one word to all the beacons: "Hello." Then they waited, but not for long. Shortly after Simon's outgoing message, his audio equipment began to chime with what sounded like whales moaning. This was followed by faint clicks, and then silence.

Simon repeated his "Hello" transmission and was met with the same reply. Ameerah and D.K were close by to document the findings. His job was to generate a coding system and sound catalog guidebook for them to work from.

This type of banter went on for several months until Simon was able to create a discernible codex to break down the language that was being spoken. The language was finally coined "*Fregodian.*" The language needed a name for the sake of categorizing and for usage in the lab. The name translated as "to free God's speech." Since no one knew the language God speaks, this revised option was what the team would use to translate the transmissions. Alternate languages to communicate with God was by no means unique.

Here on Earth, many religious people experience something called "xenoglossia." It's the spontaneous use of a language which the speaker has never heard of or learned in any natural sense. Yet, they can speak it as well as someone who has that language as a native tongue. Fregodian is no different. After a while, communication becomes very fluid.

The tagged-souls would be asked questions and would reply back in Fregodian. The data then went through a language translator and rapidly shot out lines of words, which the team analyzed in order to yield a more complete picture.

Most of the communications appeared in this manner:

Light - - - Stars - - - Fast - - - Peace - - - Full - - - High - - -Love . . . .

Depending on their questions, the results (of course) varied. Each subject responded differently as well. As their process became more efficient, the questions they asked became more particular. For example, one of them asked, "Did you meet God?"

A subject responded as follows: Here - - - Learn - - - Face - - - Hear - - - Leave . . . .

Even with this information, accuracy was still speculative, but spectacular, nonetheless. The answers were rarely "yes" or "no"; they were more explanatory in nature. They had much more educating to do as they worked on expanding the Fregodian vocabulary. Until then, tracking was the main agenda.

With all the excitement of the Fregodian language decryption, the team completely forgot about a new subject that was scheduled to arrive that day. The call light blinked for one of the team members to meet the new arrival at the front desk. Chad swiftly sprinted to the elevator and rode up to the first floor. He always jumped at the chance to welcome fresh subjects. He felt he could get a leg up on the process if he had private time with them. He chatted them (or their families) up during their short journey through the quiet stretch of hallway to Dr. Patel's triage room. Today was going to be different, though. Today would be more than they all bargained for.

What they experienced with **Subject: Echo-SE-147090** was nothing short of spectacular—an anomaly of the highest level. She came to them via the usual channels of acquisition. Her medical exam provided typical results other than the auto-immune disease from which she was suffering. She was barely 28 years old and seemed to be flawless outside of her unfortunate condition. They issued immediate physicals to all their subjects who volunteered; this was to verify that they were in fact at the end stages of their life cycle, but no other investigations beyond that point were necessary.

Subject: Echo-SE-147090 was very phlegmatic about the whole situation. They couldn't tell if she was rounding the final stages of grief (which is acceptance), or if this was her general overall demeanor. After her triage, she was placed into a capsule and their systems were then set and ready to tag her soul. All they needed her to do was let go and pass away. When the time came, no one could have predicted this—a one in a seven billion event.

Their data report communicated that there was an "attachment failure." This had never, ever happened before. They all stood in one spot as if frozen in time, their mouths gaped open and eyes wide and frenzied. How could this be? They rechecked the data ... rebooted the system ... checked the subject for lifelines. They had to do something! It appeared that they would sooner solve the mysteries of the Pyramids before they found answers to what just happened in their lab.

Raj, the medical physician, thought to go to her file and comb through her medical history and what other information he could find. One name resurfaced over and over again. Raj said to himself, *EmSigna Labs, never heard of them, but who are we to judge? After all, we do have several corpses encased in glass caskets, stashed away in the basement of a well-respected university.*

No, they were not in a position to frown upon anything. As you can imagine, EmSigna Lab's involvement made the team a little nervous about what they might unearth. In efforts to understand the misfire, they had to investigate.

When morning came, calling EmSigna Labs was the only thing on the to-do list for Raj. He picked up the lab's landline and anxiously dialed their number. Ring . . . ring . . . ring. . . . "EmSigna Labs, may I help you?"

Raj sheepishly answers with a crack in his voice, "Yes, this is Dr. Patel with Stromford University. I would like to speak to someone in Research & Development about a Miss Eve Saccarum."

His requests were met with abject silence, then the muttering of "Get Dr. Laszlo now!"

After a few moments, someone picked up the phone and said, "Ahem, I apologize for the delay, Dr. Patel. Someone will be right with you." Raj gave a quick glance to his team as if to say, "What in the world is going on?"

Suddenly, a stern-voiced man blurted out "Where is Eve? Is she okay?"

Raj responded, "Hello, Dr. Laszlo. My name is Dr. Raj Patel, I would rather not speak of this over the phone due to confidentiality concerns. Our team will come to your office and speak in person."

"Yes, of course," Dr. Laszlo replied, "I will see you here within the hour."

Chad grabbed his coat, keys, and laptop and then headed for the door, all while beckoning the team to stay with him. All they knew was that this was bigger than a random sick girl who died in their lab—much bigger. Shortly after the call, they arrived at EmSigna Labs and was directly greeted by Dr. Laszlo himself.

His one and only question was, "Where is Eve?"

The team hesitantly introduced themselves one by one for the sole purpose of easing Dr. Laszlo into somewhat of a comfort zone; they wanted to gingerly explain how they crossed paths with Eve. The conversation was tense, and he was the definition of a brooding man if they had ever seen one. Reading the room, they felt that maybe Eve was his daughter or someone he cared for deeply.

That assumption was not far off, but the details were more complexed. Eve is (was) unbeknownst to the world, the first successful human to be cloned. Dr. Laszlo and his team did this in total secrecy and Eve actually lived at their facility until one day she decided to leave without his knowledge in the middle of the night. She took nothing but the clothes on her back. Eve left a parting note that simply stated, "Born by chance to live on purpose. I love you all. Good-bye."

The reason that Eve was confined to her residence in EmSigna Labs was because her immune system rejected certain key cells during her creation process. Dr. Laszlo created a special concoction H2O mixture that flowed through her room's vents. This provided Eve with what she needed to live a long life, but without it, her immune system would turn on her and end her life.

The team excused themselves to confer with each other and grapple with what may have caused a misfire in Eve's process. The likely causality of this misfire was the lack of what we call "Carbastran." It's the essence material of which souls are comprised. By all accounts (theologically speaking), it takes two souls in order to make one soul, i.e., the mother and the father or the male and the female. The team's most educated guess was that a clone is void of that donation. Dr. Laszlo shared even more information that was very telling.

Apparently, the team did not excel in lost languages because Eve Saccarum's name literally breaks down to Eve (Life) and Saccarum (properly spelt "Saccharum," which is Latin for "Synthetic"). She was a "synthetic life." At the end of the day, Eve was intellectual property and Dr. Laszlo needed her remains back before her body was picked up for medical students to research and perform class practicals on (not to mention Eve's agreement to be an organ donor).

This could not be good for anyone. It definitely put the team's research on a more visual level. Poor Dr. Laszlo could face a whole litany of inquiries, investigations, fines, and have his medical license taken from him—and he could even face jail time. There was no time to waste. Eve had to be returned to EmSigna Labs today, and the clock was ticking (and not in the team's favor).

Lisa was the designated driver to shuttle everyone back to the lab. They all prayed to whatever entity they individually believed in that the cadaver transport had not made it to the lab before they did.

Lisa slid into the parking lot by the loading dock. White coats catapulted out of her late model Nissan like nerdy super heroes answering a call for help. When they made it to the lab, they slid to a halt. The lab's door was open, the lights were out, and the IDIAMTRACE-10 was completely shut down. Even stranger, Eve was gone and the cadaver transport guy was walking up behind them saying, "Ahhh.... I'm here to pick up a body. Where should I go?"

Ameerah, Raj, D.K., and Chad stood stone-faced and silent. D.K. broke the awkwardness long enough to apologize to the driver and offered to call him back to reschedule. Lisa had finally made it into the building, only to meet her team shadowing the entrance of the lab.

She belted out, "There is no time to waste . . . What the hell are you doing standing in the doorway?"

Ameerah replied, "Lisa, Eve is gone and transport did not take her."

Without speaking, each team member paced slowly into the lab with a precision of a black ops team. Still lingering in the air was a familiar dated scent of Drakkar Noir, an ungodly, putrid stench (if you were born any time after 1990). That meant only one thing: Prof. Ron Sherman had been there, and he had Eve.

They quickly turned the lights on and rebooted the IDIAMTRACE-10. The equipment should never be cut off; if the computer is off for a considerable amount of time, it could sever the digital tether to deployed Aurovian clusters, and Prof. Sherman knew this.

D.K. flung a chair across the room and yelled, "That dude is a HATER!"

Whenever he was angered, his urban Chicago roots made themselves known, but his superpower for coding kicked in. He opened his laptop and began hacking all the cameras in the building and any camera within a 10-block radius of the laboratory. They loved to watch him do his thing; it was otherworldly. Coding and hacking for him was a rap song regurgitating in his head. In five minutes flat, he found the proof that they needed to hopefully find Eve and get her back to Dr. Laszlo.

CHAPTER SEVEN

That angry old Bible-toting sycophant had indeed been in the lab and left with Eve in tow. When Eve was secured, they had to figure out how Prof. Sherman gained access to a lab that he became restricted from many months prior. In the past, he and his merry band of zealots had just been an irritating thorn in their sides. Now, Prof. Sherman and the Nation of Christian Founders were a problem.

They could potentially destroy the vast pioneering work the team had done, sans him. They couldn't just walk into the NCF main office and request Eve back like they were ordering a latte. No, this would have to be a stealthy mission—one worthy of a standing ovation, and time was of the essence. Prof. Sherman could not find out who—or what—Eve was.

I Spy wasn't typically their thing, but considering the circumstances, the team couldn't frown upon the unsavory in order to get the job done. Once D.K found the blueprints to the building, Ameerah handled recon on who and how many people would be in the building at that very moment. Everyone sat down and put their intellects together to structure a one-time play that had to work. Prof. Sherman would not allow a second chance.

Although Lisa Kim was dry and stern, she was beautiful and highly trained in Krav Maga. She could handle herself with ease. The team thought it best that she went in as a distraction, and the rest could handle liberating Eve. This had to be fast, and not just because of Prof. Sherman. The team didn't spare any personnel to watch the data at the lab. Literally anything could happen, and no one was there to monitor and calibrate the machines.

The team was ready, and everyone was accounted for except Lisa. Just when Ameerah was about to bellow out her name, Lisa strolled out of the changing room. Her hair was released from its normally highly constricted bun and was flowing down her back and shoulders like an onyx river. Her eyes, no longer framed with expensive spectacles, gave a mesmerizing piercing quality to her face.

Raj said, "My God. She's beautiful!"

Hidden under that cold and sterile facade was a sexy woman. After being shaken by the newfound revelation, Raj cleared his throat and wiped the sweat from his forehead and muttered with a cracking voice, "I think it's time to go!"

They took the lab's cargo van, and Lisa drove her car alone. She was to arrive first through the front door. The rest of the team headed to the rear exit near the loading dock of the NCF.

Lisa sauntered into the building and arrived gracefully at the front desk. The guard on duty looked pleasantly puzzled as to who she was and why she was there at that time of night. She began to engage him with the tried and true explanation of a troubled vehicle, but the guard offered to call a roadside service to assist. Lisa knew that she had to up her game in order to buy the time needed so that D.K. could loop the camera feed on the loading dock.

D.K. was the only person that could hear the conversation transpiring between Lisa and the guard, and what he started to hear made him blush. She somehow made her way to the guard's desk and was now straddling him in his chair. At first, he attempted to resist, but she kept saying to him, "Yes . . . Yes . . . Yes . . ." and then there was complete silence. D.K. was baffled because his heart rate was up and he wasn't sure if it was from what he heard or what he wasn't hearing.

Abruptly, Lisa's voice ordered D.K., "Loop the cameras now!"

D.K. jumped into action and notified the rest of the team that they were a go. However, D.K. could not get the images out of his mind of Lisa and the guard. Should he dare to ask what happened?

Before he could say anything, Lisa stated, "Nothing happened, by the way. It was simple. I needed to get close enough to him to administer a light sedative and put him to sleep. So, I sat on his lap facing him, and the act of agreeing with him confused him long enough for me to stick him in the neck with the sedative . . . easy!"

D.K. was silent and afraid at how she knew to do this and executed it with ease. That would have to wait until later, though, because there was an important job that needed to be done and all hands were needed on deck. The NCF was huge, and not only that, the design of the building was made like a labyrinth. It was made more for a secret society rather than an over-publicized religious organization. What were they really doing there? The feelings that the team was receiving was more the feeling of maliciousness than of spirituality.

With D.K.'s guidance, they were able to work their way deep into the bowels of the building and look through the menagerie of items and rooms that inhabited the location. To their astonishment, there was equipment there that was eerily similar to the parts necessary to make a second IDIAMTRACE-10. They knew that they had one mission for the night, but they couldn't just leave the equipment there. It was a unanimous vote. The team would find Eve and dismantle whatever nefarious deeds Prof. Sherman was planning on doing with another IDIAMTRACE-10 machine.

Part of the team remained in the equipment room while the others went on to find Eve. Lisa reminded the team that the sedative would give them two hours at best and that they would have to move quickly. Team One—to find Eve—consisted of Lisa, Ameerah, and Raj. They tiptoed down the cavernous halls, peeking in each dimly lit room to see if anything resembled a body. It was like the Smithsonian Museum down there.

"What kind of Church collects such items?" Ameerah asked.

Right at that moment, they saw a silhouette of a figure lying on a table. Raj whispered, "There she is!"

The room was cold—freezer cold. Even though Eve was deceased, they had her plugged up to EKG machines and ran an IV. They didn't have the time to assess the situation, so they snatched Eve and whatever file folders that were on a nearby table and ran. Thank God that Eve was a tiny person, because Raj was worse for wear by the time they made it to the equipment room. The team carried bundles of equipment, wires, and a dead person as best they could and high-tailed it out of there.

D.K. led them back to the loading dock. Lisa broke off to the front of the facility to move her car, and they all rallied up a block over from the NCF. Once everyone was accounted for, they sped back to the lab. There was no time to waste.

Everyone scattered when entering the lab. Raj began to examine Eve and review the file folders they found. D.K. started coding a new security system with cell phone surveillance capabilities, and Ameerah plopped down in the chair next to Lisa to review data from the IDIAMTRACE. Chad checked on the subjects that had not transitioned yet.

It took no time for Raj to figure out what Prof. Sherman and his cronies were trying to do. Although the Professor was familiar with the IDIAMTRACE machine, he was not learned in how to create and operate the Aurovian. He was trying to extract residue of the Aurovian from Eve, not realizing that there was nothing "attached" in her case. If there was nothing attached, the Aurovian would die off instantly because there would be no energy source (soul) to leech on.

Today, the team won, but there would be a next time, and they all wanted to know what exactly Prof. Sherman was trying to do in his bigger picture. Whatever it was . . . it was not good.

After Raj examined Eve, Dr. Laszlo was the first person he called. Dr. Laszlo answer the phone almost immediately on the first ring, "Do you have her? Do you have her?"

Before he could ask a third time, Raj exclaimed, "Yes, we have her! Her condition hasn't changed."

Raj offered for Dr. Laszlo to come to the lab right away to pick up Eve so they could wash their hands of this horrible situation. On the heels following the Prof. Sherman robbery, the team was alerted of another strange activity: an unexpected development.

CHAPTER EIGHT

O ne of the tagged souls had been in a location (location address: OP-A200037..18331-509Z6691..530201) for 189 days and 15 hours. The unit was experiencing a lot of instability (what we would consider emotions), and then suddenly, the location of the unit re-routed back to its home planet (Earth). This had never happened before. It was certainly unusual, but fortunately the team was able to track it to an accessible location.

Although this tagged soul was one of the team's verifiable subjects, the data for it was off—not off as in corrupt, but that it had been altered in some way. The only thing to compare it to would be when a document in the IOS operating system goes to another computer via email, and the document is opened by someone who has a Windows operating system. Their system would convert fonts that it doesn't recognize to fonts that it has in its existing catalog. Conversions can sacrifice imperative information into something with limited clarity.

This would force the team to decipher transcribed coding that may or may not be accurate. Basically, it was the same soul, but it now looked different. Why? A few of the team members volunteered to take on another outing—to the latitude and longitude of where the tagged soul was beaconing. Within several hours, they had deplaned and were in route to the location. With a little chicanery and quick thinking, they were able to get inside the exact location of this rouge soul, but the team wasn't prepared for what they saw. They were literally staring through a glass at a room full of newly delivered babies in some sort of labor & delivery wing.

"Is this possible?" Chad asked. "Is it possible that one of our tagged souls has just been re-issued?"

"A more spiritually-friendly word is 'Reincarnated,'" Lisa interjected.

"This explains much of the change in the data," Chad said, "If a soul has been re-assigned or re-inserted, then there is new DNA attachment, along with new brainwaves. We don't exactly know the extent of the differences or the similarities, but this is our Subject Zero."

They needed to get closer and do tests. Unfortunately, this would be next to impossible, if not completely impossible, but it had to happen. Chad pulled out his tablet with its portable tracking software. He had to grid the room so he could be sure to identify the correct infant housing the previously tagged soul. This was something they had not anticipated or planned for.

This could introduce a whole new set of complexities that they would now have to figure into their blueprints. D.K. was always there to configure new coding on the spot if necessary, but with this, he didn't know where to begin. One thing was for sure: Chad was there, and he would make certain that they got the information they needed. Chad was what is called an "excogitator." He took it upon himself to lead the charge to pin down a solution.

With his long, spindly, branch-like arms, Chad ushered them all to an unoccupied sitting area to go over the facts. He quickly wrote down their questions and solidified a method by which to get the answers they needed. They had to compare the new broadcasting data to the previous data for this reallocated soul unit.

It had to be cataloged and accessed. The previous soul unit was female but had now inserted itself into a male infant. This somewhat explained the skewed data. The alteration was comparable to putting unleaded low octane gasoline into an expensive car that should only use high octane premium gasoline. It will still run but it will not perform the way that it should.

A surly voice interrupted Chad from completing his current task. Lisa tossed out a "vibrational theory" regarding homosexuals and transgender individuals, feeling that they were or are born gay. Lisa, with her designer bifocals tightly affixed to her face, asked, "Is it possible that the multitude of the LGBTQ communities are experiencing a 'soul re-allocation' experience at birth? For those who were not stimulated into that lifestyle, curious, or hopping onto a fad-promoted bandwagon, might this be a cause? If you would allow me the floor for a moment, to remind you of our research on vibrations, we may all arrive at a unanimous conclusion to a more pressing question."

She began to explain as if she were speaking to freshman students on the first day of school. "One of the most perplexing issues that humans deal with day to day are questions of race," she said. "Why do we have the many different types of races and nationalities, and why do our differences promote conflict? Ironically, we have discovered some answers through this amazing experiment.

"Research has provided that the many races of people (at least on Earth) are a result of different vibrations. Essentially, we are the physical products of various levels of complexed 'bass and treble,' if you will. We have a rare benefit of which our team can boast, and that is, our experiments dictate that time is irrelevant. Why? Because of the medium we work with.

"Galactic travel happens in real Earth-calculated time for our subjects, and we are able to reap the rewards of endless travel to unknown locations via our ghostly host. If I were to travel to the moon, it may take one calendar year (or more), but if a soul decides to go there, it could take a matter of minutes. Luckily, we can log distances and reference locations. When we encounter uncharted territories during the travels of tagged souls, our trackers map those sites for us to incorporate into our Galaxy Map. Those locations are coded and given an in-house name and interstellar address for our tracking purposes.

"Back to my point," she continued, "We have known this individual personally, when she was alive and human. We know her life's specs and her sexual orientation. We can track her every move and 'she' has chosen, out of all the people in the world, to re-construct in a masculine entity. If this child decides to be gay, bi-sexual, or trans, he will surely feel that he was born that way because all the evidence (in this case, at least) is showing that he was born that way.

"Why? Because your personal vibrational energy keeps its integrity no matter the vessel it lands in. It's in a woman's nature to be a woman, and it's in a man's nature to be a man." Lisa abruptly exited her statements as quickly as she entered them and took a seat in a nearby chair.

There was nothing more that could be done at the moment. Chad lurked off to the nurse's station to gather whatever information he could on the child and its parents, and then they all made their way back to the airport to go home. After all, it would be years before any usable data would be available to study. Upon their return home, the entire team met up (including Savoy Sellers and Simon Christian) to go over all the events that had taken place and what was to be done about Prof. Sherman.

Their first responsibility was to designate one team member to track and log the tagged souls on a daily basis, another team member to strictly maintain communications and grow the Fregodian vocabulary, and two team members to process and activate new subjects. The remaining team members were to plan and implement a defense method against Prof. Sherman and the NCF. With the introduction of being able to listen and speak directly to the tagged souls, they were one step closer to identifying the Alpha & Beta locations.

So far, they had logged thousands of souls in five different locations. The souls tended to do a fair bit of traveling before they settled down into any one location. Once the travels ceased for a long period of time, they settled in a highly populated location. The team then gave more attention to their emotional states.

Three out of the five locations that are frequented by the souls had been categorized as "Gamut Locations." This was because the souls tend to spend short amounts of time there. It could be weeks or several months, and their emotional experiences would be all over the place, and the soul chatter would mean that high quantities of information was being shared.

The last two locations they had gone to, thus far, were places where souls would go to and stay permanently. However, a single soul never visited both. The team tentatively labeled those two locations as the "Alpha & Beta Golden Coordinates." They didn't know for sure what these destinations were. The souls could be unpredictable and could change at a moment's notice. The team needed a more definite way to calculate and verify the more populated and stable locations.

The team's theory on this was that after death, the "soul travels" could be related to an education or verification of what their living beliefs were. For instance, if one was an Atheist, Buddhist, or Christian for that matter, he may go somewhere and encounter an entity to share with him the truths of what the Higher Power is. The locations and the lengths of time that they stay could be how much knowledge needs to be imparted before they move on to their final destination.

CHAPTER NINE

With so much sensitive information being shuffled around the lab, D.K. spent much of his time literally air-gapping the facility to protect intellectual property from seeping out and blocking prying eyes from peeking in. Ever since the team rescued Eve, the presence of the NCF protesters had grown from a few shouters to hundreds. Prof. Sherman was apparently pissed, but what could he do? Call the police and report a theft of a body that he stole in the first place?

That would be complicated to explain at best. All he could do was plot his next attack. Whatever his plans were, one of them that the team knew for sure was to make their work a public spectacle. The last thing they needed was the government sniffing around and asking questions that they weren't ready to answer. The amount of work that the team needed to catch up on was colossal, but they could not help but feel a sense of doom and gloom lingering over the lab with Prof. Sherman and his minions in play.

Savoy Sellers decided to assist Ameerah with tracking the souls. This portion of the team's research ignited a fire in Savoy that enabled her to think on a higher level of scientific innovation. She had a signature tick when she had an innovative breakthrough. She would count out words she would hear in the room into fives and tap them off with her fingertips. Then she would stretch her open hand and fingers out in a fan until she felt her joints pull.

For example, a desk over, Chad asked Raj "Can we do that later?" Savoy picked up on the five-word question, repeated it to herself, and counted each word out by tapping her fingers on the table. If the question had been four or six words, she would have rejected it and searched for a five-word opportunity.

As odd as that was, once she was done with her ritual, she would spout out something fantastic. She stood straight up out of her seat, like a rocket ship lifting off into orbit, and blurted out, "Can we give the nanites eyes?"

The entire room stopped in motion as if they were frozen in time. Savoy quickly offered an explanation of her question: "I'm thinking that since the nanites have an unlimited power source and they are mechanical and currently have audio, why not give them video, too?"

The team seemed to shrink a little more with every word Savoy spoke. How could they have overlooked something so crucial, so obvious? Yes, the advancements were possible, very possible.

This additional upgrade changed everything. Not only could they track the souls, but they could also hear and see what the souls were hearing and seeing (in real time). The very thought of this was inconceivable, unthinkable, unimaginable, and just beyond belief. The utter ramifications made them all pause. They questioned, "Should we dare do this? Who are we to spy on God?"

Ameerah's small voice sounded off in the room. "My mother always told me, 'If you put science under a microscope, you'll find God there.' God gave us Science, and for that matter, we *are* science. Look, guys, this is who we are and that's what we're doing." After her speech, there was no doubt that their research was moving forward.

The tech development for visual capabilities would take months to create. Nanites were millionths of a millimeter in size, so attaching cameras to them was complicated enough; in addition to that, there would be microscopic satellites to incorporate as well. The distance would be too great to rely on the satellites alone near the Earth's atmosphere. Earth's satellites would be paramount in relaying any wayward signals that they might catch from the nanites back to the lab.

The change in direction put a hold on accepting new subjects in the lab, so the team was surprised when the front desk rang to inform them of a visitor.

"Professor Sherman and his party would like to be admitted to the lower level. What would you like for me to do?" the woman at the front desk asked.

Chad stuttered, with a puzzled look on his face, "P-P-Party?!?!"

"I'll handle this," Ameerah said, darting out of the lab top-speed, coupled with Lisa and D.K. flanking each side of her.

When the trio reached the front desk area, there was "Dude-Ella Deville" in all his glory. Ameerah stood in the presence of Prof. Sherman and his party, thinking to herself, *We need a new receptionist.* She had grotesquely understated the magnitude of people crammed into the lobby, eagerly anticipating a meeting with the team. Ameerah took a quick scan of the room and tallied at least 30 people, the majority of whom were wearing all black suits. It looked like a scene from a new installment of *Men in Black.*

Lisa nudged Ameerah to snap her back into focus so that she could get the inquisition started. She asked, "How may we help you, Prof. Sherman?"

With a surly look on his face, he began to shake his head with parental displeasure and said, "My dear, certainly you know why we're here." He then slithered very closely to Ameerah and whispered in her ear, "The matter of theft will have to wait for now but know this: I'm no one to toy with!"

Prof. Sherman jerked away from her and openly proclaimed the reason for his visit: "The NCF and I are here to start an official investigation into the dangerous and unethical activities that your lab instigates without remorse every day. We speak on the behalf of the religious organizations under the Christianity umbrella, as well as several of the family members who have left loved ones in your care and have never seen nor heard from them since."

The team stood there in shock. While they listened to his soliloquy, Ameerah thought about how Prof. Sherman was an integral part of starting their research; it was founded on his curiosities (and his alone) combined with their scientific prowess. It was true that Prof. Sherman did complain about ethics once they started to make progress, but he stayed, even after they tagged over one thousand souls. He finally left when they found strong evidential possibilities of heavenly and consequential physical planes.

Prof. Sherman was afraid of something that they could find out, but what was it? Now that Ameerah realized that the old codger was operating out of fear, she relaxed and demanded to have their complaints/concerns put in writing and for them to be delivered to the team's attorney's office. Before she fired a round of declarations of her own, she stared him squarely in the face. She wanted to look right at him when she berated his fragile ego.

"You are the scourge of this lab and the entire scientific community," she said, "Not only are you a coward, but you are a petty thief as well, with secrets of your own to hide. These secrets will soon come to light. We have done no wrong and will continue to move forward with our work, not just in spite of you, but because of you." Her last statements were to demand a "cease and desist" for any visits from the NCF or anyone associated with them.

She went on to say that their lab would be filing an order of protection from Prof. Sherman and the NCF immediately. Prof. Sherman clutched his non-existent pearls, scowled, and ushered his mob to the nearest exit to evacuate the premises forthwith.

D.K. folded his arms across his chest and plainly stated, "What an ass."

The elevator ride down to the lab was a quiet one. Ameerah had to compartmentalize this situation with Prof. Sherman and get back to work on tagging the souls and assisting in outfitting the nanites with cameras. When they arrived back in the lab, Lisa spoke with Chad and Raj privately in the supply room. After a few moments, they emerged with questioning looks on their faces.

Raj cleared his throat to get the attention of the room and made an unpopular suggestion. "Might it be better if we all moved into the lab? At least until we complete this portion of the project?"

Everyone looked around the room hoping to see a glimpse of contentment is someone's (anyone's) face. The thought of it was not a fan favorite, but they knew that it was the best thing to do.

Chad was excited because he had been tasked with setting up the new website for the lab. They had to ensure a constant stream of hospice subjects and he needed everyone's input. Ameerah was not so thrilled because of her unknown sleeping condition. Her only relief was that she previously disclosed her complications to Lisa and hopefully she could rely on Lisa to help her, if the occasion should arise.

It was going to be a tight fit. They had sleeping quarters near the kitchen, but there were only four army-style bunk beds. With their extended team staying in that little space, things might get intense. Savoy suggested running out and picking up a few sleeping bags and other supplies to make their time in the lab a little smoother.

Ameerah pulled Lisa aside and reiterated her situation. With all of the craziness to deal with, Lisa had totally forgotten about what Ameerah asked her to do months before.

Lisa said, "This could be a problem, and to be quite frank, hard to hide. I think you should just tell everybody. What's the worst that could happen?"

Reluctantly, Ameerah agreed. After everyone returned and got settled, they did their last checks and runs of the systems for the second shift.

Ameerah called another meeting to apprise the team of her issues. They sat and listened attentively, but before she could wrap up, Raj interrupted her and asked if that was what had happened the day they had to rescue her from the capsule. Ameerah's face turned red. Lisa and Savoy squinted their eyes in confusion because the people "in-the-know" neglected to tell everyone of such an important event. Ameerah grumbled, "yes," under her breath and prayed that the conversation would end, but it didn't. They wanted to know what was in her dream that kept her from waking up. She wasn't eager to share, but she did.

She thought it best to start from the beginning of what she could remember, and oddly enough Raj took notes of every word she spoke. He asked an awkward but fair question: "How many times have you fallen asleep in the capsules?"

With her head hanging low, Ameerah answered, "Five or six times."

The entire room seemed to gasp at the same time. Raj pounced into action like a lion on a slow-moving gazelle.

"Ameerah, I have to examine you immediately! If there is an off-chance that you may have Aurovian in your system and that you are co-existing with that brand of nanites, we must know. You could be the very first living subject directly inoculated with tracking nanites on an intact soul."

"Question . . ." he continued, "is it possible that you may have expired in the capsule during one of your sleeping episodes and somehow, in some way, were revived by someone or something? In any case, currently you're 'Alive' and your soul is intact and may have Aurovian permanently affixed to it. We have no idea how the Aurovian will behave inside a living, functioning organism with Level 1 direct exposure."

Raj ceased his scientific rambling and instead began inflicting Ameerah with various forms of testing—blood work, urine analysis, EKG, CT Scan, and several more invasive procedures that she wouldn't wish on her worst enemy.

That night, all she wanted to do was sleep. She didn't care about being stuck in her dream world tonight. Maybe it was the safest place she could be. They slept in shifts while the others continued to work the lab. Luckily, Ameerah was named to the group that was able to rest in that time slot. However, to make matters worse, Raj administered a sedative to her so that she could be set firmly in her dream world.

Raj wanted her to embrace her dreams and not break the connection by trying to fight and exit them, and that is exactly what she did. That way he could interview Ameerah about what she encountered during her sleep. The drugs amplified Ameerah's dreams and the hyper-realism effects saturated her senses so much that she surrendered to her environment.

This time, things were different. She was not in that surreal park with glistening waters and trees that pulsated with the wind. She was in a dark and somber place filled with the shadows of people. Some were moaning, their words inaudible. She could hear sobbing and screams in the distance. She felt scared and sorry. The air was so thick that it was almost gelatinous to the touch, and it stunk of rot. Ameerah opened her mouth to speak and only sorrowful moans escaped from her lips.

She looked around at the shadowy figures and several of them turned and made eye contact with her. When they did, a familiar image revealed itself on their bodies; the glowing blue patches illuminated them. They began to stretch out their arms, point their fingers at Ameerah, and scream an ungodly noise. As they pointed and screeched, she looked to see where they were pointing. She looked down at her torso and noticed that she was glowing with a blue patch too.

The closer they came, the more malodorous it got. The few that reached her first began to spit on her, and their saliva was like acid resin; it stuck to her skin while it ate through her flesh. The decay was instantaneous, as she held up her hands to ward off the globs of tar-like mucus. She cried out and struggled to rub the blue stain serving as a bulls-eye off.

All attempts caused it to glow even brighter. The flock of black figures took noticed and swiftly quickened their pace in her direction. As they neared her, all she could do was cry out and close her eyes.

She was jolted awake. It happened just like this before: looking up at her team surrounded by a blinding light. Ameerah was inconsolable. She could barely talk about what she had experienced in her dream. Raj and D.K. did their best to calm her long enough to get her to open up about her ordeal. It took hours to obtain the details, but Raj was certain that her dreams were being powered by the Aurovian, and that she was serving as a conduit to the very planes that all souls travel to.

Most importantly, her dreams verified that Ameerah's soul was tagged as well. Although they were waiting for the official results of her tests, the findings wouldn't really surprise anyone in the lab. One thing was for sure: Ameerah was now listed as a subject of the team's research. **Subject Named: Pathway-SP1-000-001.**

CHAPTER TEN

"Aurovian 3.0" took months to perfect, but the team was ready to deploy the mist. It was a nervous time for the team because the initial test runs did not go well. Transmissions were fuzzy at best and beyond that, the visuals projected nothing discernible. The audio functions were fine but that still left the team with the task of deciphering the Fregodian.

A crop of new subjects was fresh in the lab, and depending on their stages of severity, the team would be able to administer the 3.0 batch sometime that evening. Expediting results was not part of their work. It all depended on the soul's circumstances; that would determine how long it could be before visual proof would be established.

While they waited for the deaths to occur, D.K. went off by himself to the control room to review videotapes of the lab over the past twenty-four months. He had a suspicious feeling that unauthorized person(s) might have been in the lab on one or more occasion (specifically while Ameerah was having a sleeping episode in the capsules). He wouldn't be able to view all the footage in one night, but he was certain that the culprits would reveal themselves on film.

By the time D.K. exited the control room, it was morning and two successful tags with the Aurovian 3.0 were complete. Simon, the linguistics and acoustics specialist, was monitoring the audio of the recent tags and had turned up the volume when D.K walked into the room. Everyone gathered to marvel at the same wails and systematic clicks. They were timed together like the chorus of a song.

They were astonished that these newly tagged souls spoke the same Fregodian language that they heard for the first time months earlier (what the team called soul chatter). It's true: God does have a language, and it's stored in the soul—a language of the universe that was and would always be. If the team could comprehensively catalog the Fregodian and assign characters to the utterings they recorded, then it's possible that communication with the Higher Power could transform.

Prayers might manifest on greater scales, and humans might be able to sense God on a more tangible scale. Just imagine what could be learned from their research. Knowing these truths would shine a brighter light on what they understood aliens to be. Every movie about aliens (that has substance and credibility) depicts interstellar speech and communications with sounds that are very similar to the "soul chatterings" that they'd recorded.

Raj ran everything over in his mind: *Could it be that we have a closer origin to God than humans do? Could it be that out of all of God's creations, that we were the only beings that He has endowed with souls, hence our special importance to Him? We literally have "The Creator" within the creation! What we perceive to be aliens observing us, experimenting on us, and mating with us could be other models of God's creations that simply do not have souls.*

Maybe they sense our uniqueness and envy the favoritism shown to our kind. With their vantage point and advanced scientific capabilities, their investigation, experimentation, and mating almost seem to be the most natural thing to do. How best to obtain a soul than to be a part of creating a hybrid of one via a child with our unsuspecting species? As far as we know, angels don't have souls, nor do creatures that belong to the animal species, and the deliberations are still out on otherworldly beings.

We are made in "His" image (so the Good Book says), the very essence of our souls could be luminous shards of "His" DNA. This changes the perspective quite a bit...

Raj sat quietly, deep in thought. He couldn't help but wonder what Prof. Sherman was doing with components for the IDIAMTRACE-10 machine. He remembered that they grabbed stacks of files in the frenzy of trying to exit the building.

Raj littered the conference room's tables with all the file folders and began to read through them one by one. Many of the folders belonged to the lab, and at some point, he returned here and took them. The other folders are schematics for their tracking machine but with unusual additions. He had incorporated a capsule with an IDIAMTRACE-10-like system.

He even spoke of inducing people into a deep sleep state and then administering low doses of Aurovian, only to chemically bring them back from the deep sleep state, but it didn't say why. He needed to share this with the team but not just yet. He decided to sneak back into the NCF alone and find the pieces of the puzzle to give a clear and concise report. However, he did need the help of one particular team member whose skills were perfect for the job.

●

Ameerah had been away from her typical duties ever since the traumatizing dream event. She spent most of her time in the lab with Simon listening to and logging the communications from the tagged souls. Somehow the haunting sounds soothed her like ambient noise. Although she barely slept, she was calm and busied herself with whatever she could find to do in the lab that didn't involve being near the active Aurovian mist.

The audio receptor was processing large amounts of communications, and Simon had the translations down to a science. The veteran tagged souls had an awareness of the teaching relationship with the lab. So much so, in fact, that they began to offer a tremendous amount of intelligence that the team didn't even know to inquire about. For instance, the astonishing revelations about human fingerprints.

Each one of us is born with a unique set of fingerprints, no two people (out of billions, past or present) have the same. Before now, scientists weren't exactly sure what purpose fingerprints served, but thanks to the knowledge of tagged souls, there may be an answer. Fingerprints may have a higher purpose. The recent communications offered shocking news to the team: not only do our fingerprints have corresponding points that intersect with the wave patterns of our brain's gray matter, but fingerprints contain embedded coding.

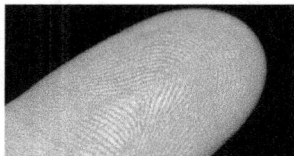

Each groove, wave, and curve of our fingerprints contains vital information that can be released once paired with the proper receiver and amplified vibrations.

The patterns and ridges have data much like a vinyl record. Given the proper apparatus, vital information can be revealed that may unlock untold knowledge—possibly the purpose of one's life path, to the exact date of their death. Each one of us has specialized encrypted hieroglyphics that's scored onto our fingertips and toes.

Speaking of records, the team took their research one step further and mapped the grooves in each of their fingerprints. They fashioned a laser that ran in the recesses of each groove to read the exact depths and contours. They then assigned musical notes to their maps. The short but beautiful songs were overwhelming. Just to know that their humanism had theme music showed that the creation of mankind was no happenstance.

Humans are intricate designs with a purpose.

Ameerah thought about the genius of God. How, if you looked closely enough, you could find out who a person was because "He" holds back nothing. *This is a profound discovery that speaks volumes about who we intrinsically are. What about the songs of people who do evil deeds? I'm certain that the Professor's song will prove to be a vile and sepsis symphony, assaulting melodies as they rise to an open ear.*

This also reminds us that in the Bible, and especially the Quran, scripture requires that you be barefoot when praying or in the presence of God. To be conservative, they require that you not wear shoes on sacred ground. Ameerah mulled all this over in her mind. *Knowing that socks are a more modern-day invention, stating "bare feet" makes more sense. Posturing in the right place with bare hands and bare feet may be paramount to the great unlocking. There is much more learning to be done, but what a great find to know that our digits may actually be the key.*

* * *

Ameerah felt that she was being briefed in a high-level security meeting. She wanted to give it another day before she resumed her work with the pre-tags. Being near the transition capsules made her feel uneasy. The more she could do to busy herself, the less she'd think of her sad reality. Ameerah briefly made eye contact with D.K. He smiled at her while moving from across the room, but before he could head in her direction, Raj was in his path asking, "Can we talk for a moment?"

D.K. replied, "Sure, I guess," with a questioning expression on his face.

"I need your help," Raj said, "I plan to go back to the NCF on a cloak and dagger mission. The Professor is up to no good, and I have to look a little deeper into the tombs of the building. Are you in?"

D.K. pursed his lips and bobbed his head from side to side as if to say "Mmmm . . . maybe?" Suddenly, a huge grin appeared on his face like the Cheshire cat from *Alice in Wonderland*, and he slyly stated, "Never was anything great achieved without danger."

They smiled at each other and walked off to prepare a plan to get back into the NCF undetected.

Ameerah watched their exchange curiously. She was out of the loop. Everyone walked on eggshells around her, being extremely careful not to upset her. Whatever they were up to, it was probably best that she didn't know. Besides, she had other things to do. Deciphering the Fregodian was a full-time job, but first, she headed for the control room to check on something. She had overheard D.K. reviewing videos the night before and wanted to know what he was searching for.

D.K.'s stamina was impressive. He left his log book and documentation of what he was reviewing in an eight-hour timespan. He watched a whopping six months of twenty-four-hour lab surveillance videos. He was looking for Ameerah. Scanning for the times that she fell asleep in the capsules. So far there was no evidence, so she decided to pick up where he left off. Did she really want to know what happened? No . . . but for the sake of the lab, she had to find out.

It's funny what you can get accustomed to. Her eyes were trained to look at symbols, glyphs, and charts, so attempting to look at a green-tinged video, second by second for hours, was not her thing. Four hours into the viewings, she saw herself. This must have been the first time that she decided to do it. She could see herself debating on the idea and checking the capsule to make sure that all of the automation was set to manual to avoid an automatic deployment of the Aurovian. She smirked as she watched the footage. She thought, *There I go climbing my dumb ass into the transition unit.*

Viewing the tape further, everything went just as uneventful. She had taken a quick nap and woke up after a couple of hours. She screened videos for a few more hours, unconcerned, but moments into the block of footage, Ameerah saw herself again, appearing exhausted. The lab was empty, and she headed for a vacant capsule again. Nothing unusual so far. She did her practiced routine of shutting down the unit and putting it on safe mode.

She climbed in and closed her eyes for a time. She felt relieved, but wait . . . The lights went out and the video went completely dark. She continued to stare into the blackness of the lab and saw the movement of a shadowy figure by the unit she was lying in. On the audio, Ameerah could faintly hear the capsule being switched on, which activated the bright lights on the unit's keypad.

There was just enough illumination to see who it was that turned the machine on. Peering out of the darkness was Professor Sherman. If that wasn't upsetting enough, what he did next brought Ameerah to tears. Professor Sherman widened the capsule lid to acquire more access to the interior and then cupped his hands over Ameerah's nose and mouth. He held it tightly for several seconds. When he removed his hands, there was a white cloth lining his palm.

Ameerah didn't wake up after that. Watching this assault made her skin crawl, learning that he was hanging over her helpless body like a vulture.

While she was in a vegetated state, he casually removed the lab coat that she was using as a warm throw and began to slowly unbutton her blouse.

She screamed, "Is he going to molest me?" She stared at the monitor with a clenched fist and tight lips.

In all his rustling around, she saw that he was having some difficulties. Ameerah was very top heavy, and the undergarments that she wore for support were more along the lines of feminine artillery rather than that of a bra. All efforts to remove her bra failed miserably, not to mention he seemed to lack the basic second base skills of a sixteen-year old boy. This perversion was not the intended reason he came, but he felt, "Why waste the opportunity?"

Even though she was livid, she found humor and said to herself, "Thank you, God, for full coverage and unfriendly underwires!"

It wasn't over yet. Her horror intensified as she watched him purposely close the capsule lid completely and deployed the Aurovian manually. He stood there chuckling and murmuring to himself until the mist subsided. He then turned the machine off, opened the lid, and placed Ameerah's lab coat back over her torso like before. Once he was done, he went about the business in which he came for in the first place.

She could faintly see him moving about the room and taking a couple of items and files. Then he backed out of the room and pulled the door up close, but not before creeping his bony fingers through the narrow space to flip the light switch back on. Then he was gone. Ameerah would not wake in the capsule for another two hours and apparently did not remember anything she had experienced. She sat in the control room chair filled with angst and despair. First, she was violated, and second, she was altered in unknown ways that would change the course of her life forever.

* * *

Raj and D.K. sat parked in a passenger van about three blocks from the NCF. They had a plan, and now it was time to execute it. Nighttime was always the best time to take advantage of the NCF's glaring weaknesses in security. Despite their breaking into undisclosed classified areas not too long ago, Prof. Sherman and his colleagues made no significant changes in the number of security officers on staff at the entrances. Once again, D.K. hacked their computer systems, but not to manipulate the cameras. This time he made an addition to the delivery roster for the nether regions of the NCF.

The simplest thing to do was to have Raj deliver mock equipment (empty crates) that required some sort of installation. Once he reached his destination in the building, he could gain access to that specific area (hopefully alone), and then he would be allowed to exit the facility, no fuss, with the crates filled with evidence. Then they would be on their way. That was the plan.

D.K. grabbed his computer and doubled-checked that their delivery was on the books, and Raj changed out of this lab gear and into the delivery uniform that they purchased earlier that day. Now, Raj was not really made for this kind of situation. He was a moderately tall man (about 5'10") and not very athletic. To be honest, his temperament leaned more to the squeamish side when threatened with violence. His resolve was strong in this case, though, because it involved someone that he cared about, and because Prof. Sherman could cause all their groundbreaking work to be nullified with his sabotage.

Raj took a deep breath and exited the rear of the passenger van. He jumped down and D.K. helped him unload the shell of crates and the dolly to wheel them in on. D.K. fitted Raj with an in-ear communication device to help him if needed. D.K. flashed his million-dollar smile and said to Raj, "Showtime," slamming the van's doors.

Raj already regretting his heroic decision: he instantly broke into a sweat, his mouth as dry as the Sahara Desert. He had to convincingly act like he delivered and installed equipment for a living. As he wheeled his cargo up the front ramp of the NCF, he thought, *No one will buy this. Shit, I don't even buy this.*

He entered the building and announced himself to the guard at the desk. "Hello, sir, I'm here with a delivery and to install it for Professor Sherman," (in his best blue-collar vernacular). He then incoherently said, "I'm from the Tech Quest Squad." D.K. was embarrassed about the cheesy name Raj conjured up for the ruse.

Raj's voice cracked at the end of his shallow statement as if he were asking a question. The guard lifted one of his eyebrows with a perplexed expression on his face in response to Raj's statement/question. He then pulled up the roster in the computer for pending deliveries. Sure enough, there was "the Tech Quest Squad" set to deliver three large parcels.

He called another guard on the radio. Raj, terrified and turning red, nervously asked, "Why are you calling for back-up?"

The guard sat straight up and aggressively replied, "Unless you know where you're going, and I'm sure that you don't, you're gonna need an escort."

Raj lowered his head in embarrassment and quickly rebounded with, "There's no need. I have done several installs here before and I remember the way."

The guard shrugged his shoulders and cancelled the escorts and sent Raj on his way. It was a good thing too because the crates barely covered the wet spot in Raj's crotch area from slightly wetting himself out of fear that he might have been found out.

CHAPTER ELEVEN

Raj made his way to the elevators uncharacteristically fast, keeping his head down and his cap's bill fixed firmly over his face like a hood. When he exited the elevator on the sub-level, he remembered the cavernous vestibule with lofty rotund ceilings. This was the very location that held loose parts and other equipment pieces that were to be used to duplicate the IDIAMTRACE-10. Everything was very dimly lit. The chamber had true gothic, dungeon-like quality to it.

He parked the crates against a wall and started down the long, vaulted hallway that was lined with doors and rooms. The only thing that was missing (to up the creep factor) were torches hanging on the walls and shadowy figures in the distance. Aiming his small flashlight, he was able to find the room where they had been building a duplicate machine. Raj couldn't help but feel that this ensuing ordeal was entirely Prof. Sherman's fault and that his overzealous nature would be the end of him.

D.K. broke the eerie silence to ask if everything was going ok. After a brief exchange, Raj switched on a light to get a closer look at what Professor Sherman has been up to. As mentioned before, the machine had a built-in cradle large enough for someone to lay in, and it also had an enclosure. Raj was still unclear as to why the unit was being combined in that way. File folders near the workings would prove to be all the answers he needed to make sense of what he was seeing.

The files also mentioned video footage with the file names listed under

Prof. Sherman's iCloud account. Raj whispered to D.K, "Can you get into Professor Sherman's accounts and pull video footage under the names 'K. Carter,' 'T. Muhammad,' 'M. Knight,' and 'D. Winchester'?'"

"Sure thing," D.K. replied, "but I think you gotta wrap it up. A group of people have pulled into the parking lot and—don't panic—one of them is Professor Sherman."

Raj went into full panic mode. In a frenzy, he began snatching the files and snapping pics with his cell phone camera. He scrambled back to the crates and dolly that he parked in the vestibule. He quickly opened the top crate and tossed the files in and hustled for the elevator. On the way out was a door he hadn't noticed on the way in because of its angle, but there was apparently another room off to the side of the elevator doors.

Resting under the emergency stairwell was a large recess that revealed a heavy metal door. Lights projected from the frame and hinges of the door. Raj wanted to inspect the room before calling for the elevator. Besides, he had to find out exactly where Prof. Sherman was. He didn't want to be in his direct path on the way out, so he used this time wisely and made advances in opening Pandora's door.

The basement of the "NCF". The tombs.

The door wasn't locked because it gave a little when Raj pressed on it, but it was heavy and resistant. An unknown force was holding the door in place. He pushed and pushed until it gave way, and he walked into an oddly huge rotund room; not only that, but the space was very, very cold.

There was a woman listless in the middle of the room, about eight feet off the ground, and completely nude. She had alabaster skin that gave off tiny bursts of colored light in various places, reminiscent of precious gems. Her lips had a bluish tinge and her eyes were completely closed. She seemed to be suspended in mid-air while stretched out like Da Vinci's "Vitruvian Man." You could feel the intense energy all around the room. She was encased in a glass sphere that spun slowly on an axis that was bolted to the floor.

It seemed as if a magnetic force kept her frozen in place. Whatever it was, it was ingenious. Her hair was the strangest of it all. Each strand was alive. A combination of translucent, iridescent, and luminescent fiber optic strands waved around aimlessly in the air. Her pubic hairs shared the same extraterrestrial properties.

She was beautiful. A true Millennial Medusa, in his mind. That same comparison reminded him that he should not be there if she decided to wake up. There was no telling how she would react.

He snapped some quick photos, took a few files from a nearby desk, and left the room. Using his girth, he shoved the door back closed as tightly as he could and headed for the elevator. Out of time and breath, he asked D.K. if it was safe for him to send for the elevator. D.K. assured him that it was, but the sooner the better. Raj frantically pushed the button and anxiously waited. He paced about, hoping that the hoist would be empty.

It came, and to his solace, it was in fact empty. Raj loaded up, calmed his demeanor, and prepped for a quick exit. When the doors opened, he gave a brisk look around and then dashed for the main entrance. He brushed by security so fast that he didn't do the obligatory sign-out. The guard shook his head back and forth and checked Tech Quest Squad off the list for the night. Raj couldn't make it back to the van fast enough. D.K. greeted him with open doors and a running engine.

They both sped off without speaking a word, saving any conversation until they were safe in their own territory. Raj did not want to disclose what he found, not just yet. He wanted to thoroughly understand what he saw (in both rooms) and what he would find in the files and in Prof. Sherman's iCloud account.

When the pair entered the lab, Ameerah, Lisa, and Simon were translating audio in a far-off corner. The group looked in their direction when the door opened and then snapped back to their work after they saw familiar faces. Everyone but Ameerah. She excused herself from the recordings and beelined to the control room. Before she could knock on the door, D.K. slid out and suspiciously asked, "What's up? Do you need something?"

Ameerah answered, "Yes," while she attempted to look over his shoulder into the control room. "What are you guys doing? Why are you sneaking around here in the dead of night? Let me in!" D.K. moved into the hallway and slammed the door behind him.

He said, "Listen. We are checking into some things and Raj doesn't want to say anything until he has a complete picture of what may be going on. I promise, if you give us a couple of hours, you will be the first person to know."

Ameerah frowned and spun away to get back to the audio files that she was working on. She was still wiped out because of the video she had watched earlier in the day of Prof. Sherman contaminating her and dreading the fact that she had to disclose yet more bad news to the team.

D.K. was relieved that she went away without a fight. He turned the knob and jumped right into Raj's face, firing off question after question about what he'd found in the NCF. Raj threw his hand in the air to silence the noise for the moment. He was reading the files that he took from those darkened rooms.

His lips moved a mile a minute while he mumbled to himself. He yanked open his laptop and started a search for the information that he found in the files. His eyes were as big as saucers as he tried to come to grips with what he was reading.

He asked D.K., "Can you pull those iCloud files for me please?"

D.K. didn't hesitate. It was the look in Raj's eyes that said to him that this was serious and to not waste any time. The files were uploaded and ready.

Raj kindly said to D.K, "You have been instrumental in retrieving these items, but I must request to listen to them alone. I'll share what I can when I'm done."

D.K. took his finger off the play button, rolled his chair back from the desk, and walked out of the room. His feelings were hurt, but he understood.

Raj emerged from the control room six hours later. This time, the entire lab waited for him around the discussion table that was adjacent to the door. He cleared his throat and shared with them what he and D.K. had done the day before. He explained, "After learning of Ameerah's possible condition and recalling the equipment and files that we found at the NCF when we rescued Eve's corpse, I was curious to find out if Prof. Sherman might be in the process of building another IDIAMTRACE-10 machine, and he is indeed."

The others looked horrified, too stunned to speak. They listened as Raj continued, "His unit will be heavily modified to allow a human subject to be inserted into the unit for attachment and guidance purposes."

"GUIDANCE PURPOSES?" Lisa screeched, her hands shaking as they attempted to remain at her side.

"Please allow me to finish," Raj replied, just as calm as he began. "His machine (in his own words and video verifications), has the ability to take pre-programmed 'Aurovian' mist and inoculate subjects who are in a coma-like state. He then sends their souls to pre-destined universal locations for a period of time. He is charging a fee for people to see their loved ones or just to visit an area that he deems as Heaven or Hell."

Raj folds his arms, his hands firmly under his arm pits as he stares at the ground. He continued, "Thankfully, we know that he doesn't have the 'Golden Coordinates,' but since he has been in our lab without our knowledge, he's learned vital information about limbo locations and other coordinates that some souls have visited. He has some files of our former clients and knows how to contact their loved ones. Taking Eve was all about his attempt to harness the Aurovian and trying to reduplicate it and alter it for his deviant means.

"He did a biopsy of Eve's nasal passages to get the nano samples that he wanted. I didn't bother to examine Eve when we got her back. I didn't think we needed to. The Professor kept her on ice. I guess we got there before he could dispose of the body; he didn't need her anymore."

Raj looked up and put his arms at his side before raising a finger and pacing, still monologuing about his findings. "Now," he said, "on to a graver concern. There was another room located in the recesses of the stair-well next to the elevator access." He carefully recounted his experience and went on to explain what he'd learned from the file he'd found.

"The phrase has come up a few times since I have been associated with this lab," he went on to say, "but it was more of a rumor, kind of like a 'scientific Unicorn.' After seeing what I saw yesterday and reading those documents, I'm here to tell you that it's no myth. It is completely real."

The faces of his teammates were still in awe, their mouths gaping and their eyes wide, as if the shock of everything was permanently stuck on their faces.

Raj's face dropped and fear shadowed his eyes, "'The Angel Particle' exists," he said, "and a sample of it is inhabiting a young woman in that room. For those who don't fully know or understand what the Angel Particle is, I will paraphrase the complex information for you. Here's an overview:

"An Angel Particle is a particle that is its own antiparticle. Scientists found the Majorana fermion via a series of lab experiments on exotic materials (Aurovian is considered an exotic material as well). These experiments resulted in the find of a lifetime: quasiparticles. The rule is if a particle should ever meet its antiparticle, the two would annihilate each other in a flash of energy.

"Researchers have been testing the facts of this scenario to find a loophole, so to speak. In the experiments, they applied electricity to stacks of superconducting materials and topological insulators in a chilled chamber. A topological insulator conducts currents along its surface (or edges) only, never through the middle. A magnet was then used to control the behavior of generated electrons as they sped along the edges of the surface. All of this was done to achieve a desired speed and configuration of what we now know as the Angel Particle.

"How is this significant? This shows proof that given the right conditions, particles and antiparticles can exist together and at the same time to create an energy like none other. A vehicle that can be used to transcend what we understand to be 'real-time reality.' The practical implications of this discovery are well in the future with potential for use in quantum computing, where it can help overcome environmental noise.

"There is one problem that has limited their development: they must be insulated from environmental noise. Prof. Sherman just may have solved that problem for them. Just imagine: a quantum computer could have many lanes and many levels of 'traffic.' The cars could hop between levels and travel in both directions at the same time, in every lane and on every level. We would need stable, armored quantum 'cars' to do this, and the Angel Particle is/are those supercars.

"Scientists have theorized that the Angel Particle could lead to a technological revolution that will make your modern-day top-of-the-line computer seem like an abacus. The discovery could have huge implications in the world of technology, especially within quantum computers, which have the potential to be HUNDREDS of MILLIONS of times more powerful than a normal computer. With all that said, the entity in the basement of the NCF is mingled with the Angel Particle and our Aurovian in a modified form.

"I don't know, as of yet, what they have created her for, but this has massive ramifications. If I had to guess, she is an IDIAMTRACE machine in the flesh. With our Aurovian in her system and the power surging through the core of her body alone, all she would need are the coordinates and she could travel interstellar distances in a flash, within her humanoid form (flesh and all). She may be the pinnacle of organic tech with a built-in galactical battery . . . deus ex particula."

CHAPTER TWELVE

L isa was the first one to speak after Raj's groundbreaking speech.
"I know that in our line of work it's frowned upon to be outraged at another cohort's work. However, Prof. Sherman has concocted an alchemical solution for trolling the afterlife. This 'Angel Particle Woman' is the augury of science."

Ameerah slowly raised her hand in the middle of the circling comments. She was going to add insult to injury with more devastating announcements. "Ahhh . . . yesterday, I viewed some old surveillance tapes of the lab and . . . I-saw-Professor-Sherman-gas-me-with-Aurovian-on-one-of-the-videos." She spat out those last few words as quickly as she could and without meeting eye contact with anyone.

The whole room let out a mixture of groans and expletives while throwing their hands in the air in disbelief.

After the mayhem calmed down, Raj stated the obvious and said, "We no longer have to wait for the test results. Now we know what we're dealing with."

The team had so many issues on their plates that they had to make a "to do" list and decide what to attack first. Ameerah's health was paramount and easily accessible, so they agreed to start there. Over the past year, everyone noticed that she developed a rash or irritation on the right side of her face.

The rash covered the area from her temple and under the eye to her lower cheek. It had a greenish tinge and almost looked like a bruise. She always refused an examination whenever Raj would offer. She was adamant that it was painless and that it would go away soon, but instead it became darker and seemed to settle in. Ameerah was still pretty young, so explaining it away as allergies, eczema, or some type of psoriasis was acceptable.

However, knowing what they did, the results of her test could shed a different light on the anomaly. Despite the drama, there was work to be done. Chad received a rather uncommon admission via Lab-J71.com earlier that day. A husband and wife by the names of David and Salina Spencer were recently involved in a bad car accident where they sustained life-threatening injuries. They were currently on life support and the prognosis was not good. Their children had decided to admit them into the lab's hospice so they could pass there.

During the telephone interview with the couple's daughter, they learned how really close the couple was. Their daughter shared, "They did everything together, even minor things like reading emails and shipping packages was a joint venture for them. They believed in helping people (at least my mom did) and they were devout Christians. This facility may be what they wanted their last offering to the world to be."

Chad admitted the Spencers that day. Dr. Patel did a full examination on both of them, and sure enough, they did not have much time. Salina Spencer had severe internal injuries, but otherwise suffered only small surface injuries. She had one weeping wound that was camouflaged by her silvery white hair.

David Spencer was a different situation. He was horribly damaged externally. There was what appeared to be gashes all over his body. Bloody gauze clogged every orifice that he owned, and that was merely the start. There was more to come for him yet. Neither one was conscious, but they laid there peacefully in wait. After sharing the couple's story with the lab, Ameerah thought of something strange. They had a huge transition unit in an on-site storage room; it was typically used for morbidly obese subjects but was too big to keep on the lab floor.

The team all pitched in to push the unit onto the floor, and when it was time, they placed Mr. & Mrs. Spencer in the capsule together. Ameerah had to rig Mrs. Spencer her own nasal sprayer (since all units only came with one) it took some doing, but she successfully installed it. The entire team encircled the unit, waiting for the vitals to worsen. The Aurovian would not deploy until the scale changed. Lisa and D.K. re-worked the weight reduction required for the Aurovian to administer.

After an hour or so, Mrs. Spencer began to decline rapidly, but her husband was still somewhat stable. Raj stroked the side of his face as he spoke, saying, "It would be a shame if they couldn't go together, and it would be a fitting end to do so."

Ameerah walked over to Raj and whispered in his ear. Whatever she said, he was totally taken aback and seemed to be lecturing her about her comment. They argued for a moment between themselves, and then Raj angrily walked away from her to the supply room.

He returned with two syringes.

Savoy asked, "Are doing what I think you're doing? Look, I don't have a dog in this fight, but this goes against not only the rules of the lab but of the law."

Ameerah stepped up and said that she would take full responsibility of what may come from whatever happened next and that she felt that it was the right thing to do. Raj, with much reservation, handed one needle to Ameerah. She went to the opposite side of the capsule and did a "1-2-3 count."

On three, Raj and Ameerah simultaneously injected the contents of the needles into their IV lines and closed the capsule's lid. The couple's pulses and breathing slowed down to a complete stop, and a high-pitched tone echoed throughout the room. Two alerts rang out in a long, familiar stream. They redlined within milliseconds of each other and the Aurovian deployed for them both, riding on their last breaths.

They left the world together, and the lab would have the pleasure of finding out if true love truly lasted forever or if it ended with the flesh. The Spencers were assigned special collating subject names because they were the first couple to die together in the lab's fringe research: **Subject: Septem-SS—532193-A and Subject: Septem-SS—532193-B**

A ping interrupted the team. It was Raj's email. Ameerah's test was back. He hurried to his computer to digest the results before he addressed the room. Before he did so, he felt that he should disclose the results to Ameerah in private first and follow-up with the team after.

Raj cautioned her by saying, "I think you should have a seat before we start."

Ameerah stood there frozen for a minute. The chair that rested behind her a few inches away caught her timbering fall, so she didn't hit the floor full-on.

He said, "To start, let's discuss the elephant in the room: you do have Aurovian in your system, as you confirmed previously, but that's not the alarming part—the amount that's inside you is what's so alarming. You have double the amount of nanites that would be involved in a single deployment. Unfortunately, you have been dosed twice."

Her face went pale white. "What does that mean?" she asked.

Raj shrugged his shoulders because he really didn't know. Ameerah was the first living human (that they knew of) to have Aurovian cohabiting in her living vessel, not to mention with levels that high.

He said, "That large a quantity gave them the notion to colonize, which is the discoloration you're experiencing on your cheek. There may even be future locations that may appear, depending on who knows what. They could be attempting to make a way to your brain to commence their natural functions, mainly because it houses the micro-tubules, and by default the soul's essence (or 'carbastran'). While we are living, our souls are kind of resting, and the energy they give off is not as strong as it is when we are deceased. The Aurovian is designed to bond with carbastran, and it will search it out at all cost."

All that was left was to share the grim results with the team. Although they were all saddened over the flagrant deeds done to Ameerah and the lab, they felt that something had to be done to help her. Chad chimed in to say that there would be no removing the nanites and that they were already idle because of the somewhat dormant activity of the soul. With further tests, maybe their idleness would prove that she could co-exist with them and have little to no negative side effects.

"Instead of looking for the negative," he said, "how about we search for the positive benefits of the Aurovian in a live subject? This exposure could possibly elevate our research."

Savoy also had a great idea. She circled back to Ameerah's tagging and her possible visitations to the Golden Coordinates. She said, "I think it would be helpful to bring in a forensic sketch artist to interview Ameerah about her dreams within the last year, and they can literally paint a vivid picture of what and who she has seen in her dreams. Then we can take that and compare it with the translations of the Fregodian and maybe get some solid answers until video returns from our last batch of subjects."

D.K. shouted out, "Savoy strikes again!" and everyone chuckled because he was right. Savoy was a quiet storm when it came to problem solving, and she had honestly earned the right to be a part of the team.

Lisa and Savoy hit the digital Rolodex in search of one distinct person for the job—it had to be the one and only John Lee Mason. The team had used John before for his exceptional skills, but he had been out of the country for the past four years. All they could do was pray that he was back on domestic soil.

Savoy dialed his number and waited for the phone to ring. After five painstaking rings, a well-spoken man with jovial mannerisms said, "Hello, what can I do you for?"

Savoy dove into her response, saying, "Hi, John, this is Savoy Sellers and I'm here with Lab-J71. We hope all is well and we wanted to toss out an opportunity to you for some work." Lisa and Savoy tag-teamed the call, explaining in detail what was needed, and shortly thereafter gave closing pleasantries and hung up the phone.

Savoy shouted, "He's in!" She regurgitated the conversation and gave everyone his itinerary so that they could prepare for his arrival. Ameerah half-heartedly smiled because she knew that meant there would have to be more rounds of induced sleep so that John would have enough material to work with.

The lab was back in full swing. The chatter was pouring in and the appointment book for new subjects was in overflow. Phone calls were screened and sent through mainly by the front desk receptionist, Carley. The only other direct line into the lab was in the subject processing room, which was private and was used strictly by the team. Imagine their surprise when the telephone rang after hours and everyone privy to that number was sitting in the same room.

"Maybe a wrong number?" Simon guessed. Ameerah shook her head. Before it could commence to a sixth ring, she reached over and picked it up.

"Hello?" she said, but it was dead silent. She said, "Hello," again and a male voice formed on the other end.

"Hello, Ameerah. I thought it high time that you and I had a coming to Jesus." It didn't take long for her to catch the familiar serpentine voice on the other end of the line. It was the fly in her ointment, Professor Sherman.

"What the hell do you want? Haven't you done enough? Stealing bodies and breaking into OUR lab, and let's not forget—you intentionally poisoned me. Yeah, after you left, we installed cameras all over this place and we have been combing through the footage. The only reason that your pathological ass is not in jail right now is because we have greater things at stake. All I have to say is this: you're doing too much and now everybody knows it, YOU FREAK!"

The line fell silent. Surely, he was taking a moment to gather his thoughts after he had been outed, not only for his breaking and entering but for his perverse nature as well.

He responded, "I guess that we both have some explaining to do. You see, I too have been heavily monitoring my lab in the NCF after my unfortunate break-in. Much to my chagrin, I observed Dr. Patel rifling through my belongings several hours ago, and that will never do.

"Your conglomeration has made an error of biblical proportions by making an enemy of the NCF. You have been warned."

Then he hung up, but before Ameerah could decompress from the call, she received a text—a text from Prof. Sherman. It plainly read: "Poison can also be the cure."

Ironically, the main line in the lab rang while she was conversing with Sherman.

Chad yelled out, "Ameerah, it's Dean Rydell."

Ameerah picked up the line and greeted the dean. To her surprise, he was not his normally pleasant self. He said, "I've just been informed of a trespassing on the grounds of the NCF by members of your team. Professor Sherman is no longer a colleague of LAB-J71 and I caution you (heavily) to refrain from interfering with his private affairs. If not, there will be consequences for your actions."

Ameerah was not used to being scolded, especially by Dean Rydell, but she complied and ended the call. She told the team about the conversation and said, "For now, let's focus on our work here in the lab. However, the Professor is still a priority because he's presenting himself to be more of a problem than a nuisance."

John arrived at the lab the next day. He was a ginormous bronze-hued, muscular man who involuntarily advertised his 6-ft-7-inch-frame at the threshold of the door. His presence commanded everyone's attention by the way he fought to get into the lab's standard-sized entrance, a doorway that typically accommodated average human beings. Once his maneuvering was complete, he greeted the smiling faces that happily anticipated his arrival.

Despite his appearance, he was relatively soft-spoken and quite intelligent. He addressed the room and finally made his way over to Ameerah, who was gingerly trying to keep her composure. She knew that his visit was all about her and she was not ready for it yet.

He pulled up a chair next to her and said, "Don't worry. I'm here to draw what you can't say." Something about the way he said that totally disarmed Ameerah and gave her a sense that she wasn't alone.

"When do you want to start?" she asked.

"There's no better time than the present," he said.

She took a deep breath and started from the beginning.

CHAPTER THIRTEEN

Professor Sherman's office was located at the very top of the NCF's Global Outreach Building. The NCF's main function was to acquire the various churches and Christian religious organizations all over the world and house them under one umbrella, much like the Vatican does for the Catholic Church. However, their structure was very much anti-scientific because of the strict belief in creationism and what not.

This fact had much more to do with Prof. Sherman leaving Lab-J71 than his own personal oppositions. What the NCF did not know was that he had continued his scientific endeavors not only on their property, but with their funding. The moves that he had made were driven by unadulterated greed and a god complex gone awry. He had been sneaking back into Lab-J71 because he left in a huff and weeks too soon. He needed copies of proprietary files in order to duplicate their work and to prey on the grieving loved ones of passed subjects.

Money was always a great motivator, but to the Professor, science was king. His inflated ego could not bear the weight of being excommunicated from mind-bending research, knowing what the team was on schedule to discover. Many months before he left the lab, he was consulting with several other scientists that were in search of the Angel Particle. He'd happened to be there the day of the discovery, and during the celebration, he elected to abscond with digital notes of how they achieved their victory.

This discovery was extremely important. The reason Sherman left

Lab-J71 was because received a hand-written note sometime before by an unknown ally, and it said, *"If* Heaven really exists, then you need to create the first physical body to touch on its firmament. The requirement to complete your research's metamorphosis will be there. If Ameerah reaches it first, then she will assume the source of power that you need. It will be hers to accept or refuse."

He then reallocated the tombs of the enormous NCF building for revamping and digitizing the organization database and communications system. Of course, this was all a cover-up for his nefarious research. Once he was able to get the Aurovian samples, he was able to reverse engineer the nanites to drive the souls rather than be passengers. The latitude and longitudes that he obtained from the lab gave him several destinations to utilize for the trips, and all he needed to do was to customize the machine to engage the clients.

The lab's previous subject files provided the rest of the information he needed. All it took was a phone call and a visit to the families, and their grieving did the rest. It took no convincing. The families of the deceased were eager to see their loved ones again.

That should have been enough, but Prof. Sherman went one step further. He offered several people the opportunity to visit a location that he had verified as Heaven, even though he had no clue where it was. In actuality, he had the coordinates to a couple random holding locations. He was making a mint—hundreds of thousands of dollars per session, but that wasn't enough. He had to supersede that lab in their efforts to find the coveted locations.

Astrid Acosto was a young lady who had been interviewed for a job at the NCF. She was responding to an ad to be the personal assistant for the director of the NCF, Professor Sherman. Although he did need an assistant, the position was never going to be filled. You see, Prof. Sherman had an affinity for young girls, and passed the time by advertising faux positions so that he could screen young girls and watch them desperately try to please him while trying to win the position.

During Astrid's appointment, he noticed something different about her. She took command of the interview and asked him questions rather than being asked. She mentioned that she had a love for science and how she had a high threshold for pain due to a genetic abnormality. She intrigued him, but on a different level, he offered her the job on the spot and asked that she return later that evening to take a tour of the entire facility. She agreed.

Later that night, Astrid arrived as promised at the front desk of the NCF. A pass with her name on it was ready and waiting for her on the desk. Security logged her in and, per instructions, walked her to the elevators and told her to push the button that was labeled "SL" for "sub-level." She did just that and the guard waved her off to descend into the guts of the building.

Professor Sherman met Astrid as she exited the elevator. You could all but see the glee on his face as the elevator doors opened. Astrid was gliding right into the spider's web. As he gave her the tour, he purposely dangled indiscriminate references over her so that she would beg for more answers. Appealing to her curiosity worked, and she was eager to learn what was in each room that they strolled by.

He explained that he was a brilliant scientist and had accepted the position at the NCF due to his dedication to God and his flock. Also, he had found a way to communicate with God directly with no interference, given the right situation. However, the problem was that he was not fit to do this—that he was physically and spiritually tainted. A woman was the only one who would be allowed to be a conduit, and she needed to be in pure standings.

"Are you pure?" he asked.

She looked at him, doe-eyed but sure of herself, and answered, "Yes, I am." She quickly went on, "I'm young but I am by no means ignorant. I answered your ad for a reason, I know who you are and what you do. I have followed your career since before you left the university and I have always wanted to work with you, to be of use to you. I held back my carnal needs and of marking my body with tattoos and piercings so that I could be pure, in hopes to meet you one day. Feel free to use me at your will."

The Professor could not have been more shocked and more pleased. He ushered her into a huge room filled with machines, examination tables, and a gargantuan glass sphere. There he explained his intentions. After a few hours of disclosing his plans, he gave her a directive: "I need you to disrobe completely. It's very important that I inspect your entire body and administer a complete physical examination, externally and internally."

Her compliance was unmatched. She did what he asked with no delays. Each exam was more invasive than the next, but no amount of poking or prodding gave her any discomfort. Her vaginal exam was done manually (without typical devices); he used his fingers as to not to disrupt the hymen (she had to remain intact). There was a necessary surgical procedure included in the discussion. Astrid was compliant yet again. She wanted to be in an optimal position to bring his vision to fruition.

When she woke up, she observed a small incision on her lower abdomen. She removed her gown to scan the rest of her body for changes or alterations. The Professor walked in coyly, smiling and salivating at the prospect. He asked for her to remain nude after the procedure because it was time to place her in the sphere. This was the moment that her life would change forever. She was to become something else.

Astrid had long dark hair and a caramel complexion that was indicative of her father's Latin background, with striking blue eyes from her American mother. She was physically fit and no more than five feet or so tall. She held on tight to the rolling staircase as the Professor pushed her to the raised glass bubble. The orb opened in a semi-sphere and she climbed in.

The Professor was not far behind her so he could close the device and start pumping the oxygen. He thought to himself that this was the first application of something that was totally theory, although sound (but still theory). He dismissed his concerns and climbed down to initiate the machines. He flipped switch after switch, and lever after lever. The orb became electrified, and he engaged the stolen Aurovian mist, administering 100 times the recommended dosage.

Inside her uterus was another tiny glass orb filled with Angel Particles. He zapped a laser directly at her midsection and the Aurovian raced to the tremendous source of energy being generated there. Astrid looked as if she was encased in water, the way her body danced and pulsated to what she was experiencing. Suddenly, a large pop burst through the air, like the cracking of a whip, and she was airborne.

Her caramel skin turned white as fresh cream and her lips graduating from rose pink to cobalt blue. Her hair—oh, her hair—turned clear as polished crystal. Each strand began to move independently, and the tips began to fade from one color of the rainbow to the next, like the aurora borealis. The Angel Particle gave her the speed and strength of a quantum computer but in human flesh. Now, it was time to see what she could do.

The Professor couldn't test her abilities until she was totally charged up. After the initial charge, the nanites would be able to feed off the base energy of her body and off of her soul. The Angel Particle made sure of that. The insulation in Astrid's uterus provided a protective layer for the Angel Orb implanted there. It mimicked the same floating environment as Astrid in her orb.

The millions of nanites running through her body generated massive amounts of energy, which fed the Angel Orb continuously. They also set up an ecosystem that effortlessly sustained its well-being. When this cycle was over, the Professor would remove her from her encasement and quantify her newly acquired skills.

CHAPTER FOURTEEN

Ameerah's session with John bordered on the ridiculous at first. He asked her questions that seemed more impulsive than educated, and that began to aggravate her. He asked her things like "What are your favorite colors?", "Do you like fluffy pillows?", and "What direction means more to you (north, south, east, or west)?" John was well known for his work, but his methods left much to be desired. She sat there mildly perturbed, but she answered his questions while he drew on his artist pad with charcoal pencils and other more vibrant colors.

She thought, *He has yet to ask me about my dreams, so what the heck could he be drawing?*

He then asked, "May I show you something?"

Ameerah shrugged her shoulders. He turned his pad around, and there was an almost identical image of her bedroom with her lying in bed, in her most comfortable position. She let out a large gasp and instantly cupped both of he hands over her mouth to suffocate the noise.

John laughed and said, "Now, will you take me seriously so that we can get some work done?"

Ameerah humbled herself and agreed. From then on, they sat in the corner while she spoke and he drew. No one intervened because of the intensity of the banter. From across the room, they could hear ramblings and the scratches of the pencils against the paper. When they were done, they had no idea how much time had lapsed, but it was more than seven hours.

Ameerah was exhausted but still afraid to go to sleep because she knew that when she was spent, that was when the dreams would come. Raj was hesitant about insisting that she sleep, but having John there to transcribe her dreams was a rarity, and the entire team wanted to take advantage of that. Her anger would be a nominal fee that Raj would have to pay for what he was about to do

Here goes nothin' he thought as he jammed a tiny needle in her neck. She turned to grab him but staggered to a chair. She was out like a light.

In retrospect, Raj should have informed D.K. about his plan because before Raj could step back away from Ameerah, D.K. instinctively dove across the table and began to deliver a vicious onslaught of blows to the doctor. By the time he was done, Raj lied there motionless and bloodied. It happened so fast that no one had a chance to react or stop the relentless retribution given to him by D.K.

"Perfect. Now we have two people unconscious," Lisa said in disgust.

The team pieced together why Raj did what he did, and that seemed to calm D.K. down. He eventually felt bad about his knee-jerk reaction. They placed Ameerah on the bottom bunk in the sleeping quarters while Raj slept off his injuries in a reclining chair in their patient lounge area. Everyone thought it best that he stayed elevated in case he was concussed.

* * *

Ameerah awoke to a narrow stream that went on for miles. It was lined with blades of grass that appeared to be communicating with each other like people talking and hugging. The water was so clear that her reflection in it was mirrored with no transparency. She dipped her hands in and every drop beaded away separately. She submerged her hands in the water again and wiped it over her face. That's when she noticed that her skin washed off like make-up and what peered from beneath it was a shimmering light.

The more she wiped, the more her skin painlessly washed away to reveal her soul and who she really was underneath. She looked up and saw other washed souls coming towards her, angrily nodding their heads from left to right, as if to say, "You don't belong here." She stood up and turned her head to look downstream, and the brightest golden light she had ever seen started to travel quickly in her direction, and out of that light, she saw a golden silhouette. It was pacing in her direction like lightning bolting directly at her.

The figure propelled from the background. Its intentions weren't clear, but she felt that its light was going to swoop her up and take her away. All she could think to do was say "Abra—" and before she could finish the word or phrase, the team abruptly woke her up.

After Ameerah gained her composure, John stepped in to take down her experience while it was fresh and still in her mental grasp. Ameerah was dumbfounded by the hyper-realistic event.

She was still in a daze and trying to digest the extreme visuals contained in her dream, but her attitude was different after this last visitation. Whatever was coming at her was an apparent iconic figure in that realm, although the inhabitants shunned her, she felt aware that the bigger concern was the imminent reckoning that she couldn't see.

The soul-tracker alarm chirped repeatedly in a cluster, which was unusual. Simon nearly forgot that he gave a distinctive alert notification when the tracking nanites achieved visuals or a certain measure of video recordings. He raced to the monitor and screamed, "Guys... Guys... Guys! You gotta see this! We have pictures!"

Everyone, including John, made their way over to the monitor, and needless to say, they were speechless. The images were from the nanites of several tagged souls. They were of three nondescript locations, meaning that the location verifications were inconclusive. The team would need hundreds of thousands of other tagged souls to corroborate these same or similar visuals and coordinates, but this was a definite breakthrough.

Visual #1:

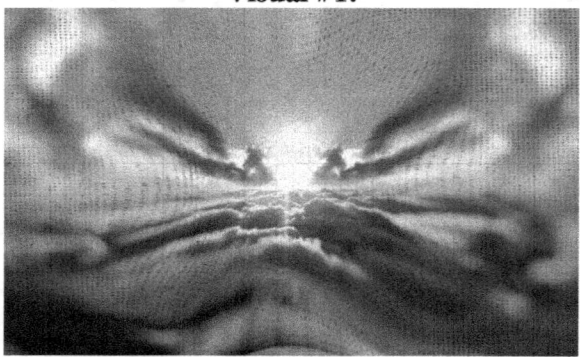

Visual #2:

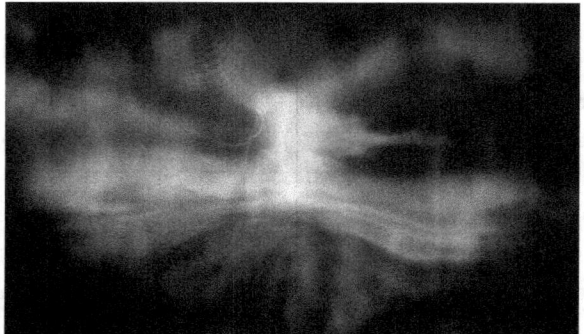

Visual #3:

The room fell silent in awe. It was so much to take in. The team didn't know exactly what the locations were, but from their coordinates they were not anywhere near the known galaxy. Even the picturesque clarity that was achieved by D.K.'s coding and programming defied all belief in what technology could do.

* * *

Back at the NCF, Professor Sherman shut off the external power that was fueling the orb holding Astrid's body. Her features had changed drastically. Her previous flowing black hair now resembled strands of lit cellophane, and her tan skin was now corpse-pale. He crept closer to view her face. At this point, he didn't know if she was alive or dead. He pried open the door of the sphere, and Astrid quickly fell to the base of the ball. Her skin was ice cold. He placed his nose at her lips to check for an exhaling breath, and there was none.

He then laid his hand over her naked breast to check for a heartbeat; nothing could be detected. He sat and cradled her on the floor. *Such a macabre beauty*, he thought. He felt the need to give her some order, so he used his fingers to comb her hair and pursed her lips closed. He wanted to remember his work in a way that bore some semblance to the thing he had in mind.

He was so preoccupied with perfecting her death pose that he didn't realize that Astrid opened her eyes and spent several moments watching him comb over her body like a voyeur. Her irises were augmented. They were no longer flat; they were as round as marbles. They had the ability to roll in all directions, even inwardly. They could roll inside the whites of her eyes like a ball in a joystick controller. She could view inside of her own body, and for good reason: her internal power source provided constant upgrades to her flesh-made machine.

Professor Sherman nearly jumped out of his skin when Astrid reached for him when his back was turned. When she tried to speak, there was a symphony of wails and clicks that bellowed out of her mouth.

"Take your time, Astrid. You are anew and there is no manual to what you are."

He helped her to her feet to check her mobility and gave her time to find her voice. It took more than a day for Astrid to speak in full sentences again and to hone back into English, which was her first language.

"Are you ready for some tests?" the Professor asked. Astrid nodded her head.

"I have programmed your source code, given you a frequency, and sent you a set of coordinates. It's the latitude and longitude for a bakery across town. I need you to go there and bring me back a flyer from their counter. Don't dawdle. If you move fast enough, no one will ever see you."

Astrid stood on her feet. Her pupils began to spin, and she was gone, leaving a static charge in the air, and even before that could cease, she was back again with a clenched wad of flyers from the bakery.

The Professor was amazed. He sent her on many more trips, each one farther than the next. Now the ultimate test was here. He sent off-planet coordinates to her and she zapped out. She was gone for more than a moment this time, and the Professor began to worry that he sent her to a place that was beyond her abilities to reach. He frantically went to the machine to track her whereabouts and to send another signal to her frequency of the latitude and longitude of the NCF's tomb's beacon.

The moment he pressed send, Astrid was back, and she looked more advanced than when she left. Now her skin was peppered with what looked like rubies, amethyst, and diamonds. Instead of being on the surface of her skin, they were sub-dermal and gave off intermittent flashed of light.

"What did you see?" he asked hungrily. Again, it took a moment to settle her voice, but when she began to speak, it was evident that she had encountered souls, and lots of them. The beauty of what Astrid had become was that she was more sophisticated than terrestrial computers.

Astrid embodied Wi-Fi technology as well. Her frequency was very resilient and structured, and her embedded radio waves were a type of electromagnetic radiation with wavelengths in the electromagnetic spectrum that were longer than infrared light. Imagine a walking and talking high-voltage tower that can give and consume its own energy—a bountiful circle that would never end.

At her foundation, she was privy to all communications that travelled these routes terrestrially or otherwise. The type of reconnaissance was unrivaled and yet to be seen in the history of the world. Who needs to spy on God when you can be one? The Professor laughed because he knew that he was light years ahead of Lab-J71.

* * *

Raj was awakened from his stupor by the loud conversations of his colleagues. He helped himself up and stumbled into the room where they were all watching a monitor and making comments.

With his eyes still adjusting to the light, his head sore from the whipping he'd taken from D.K., he asked, "What's going on?" His question got everyone's attention, and Savoy ran over to him to check on his condition.

The rest of the team followed suit, except for Ameerah and D.K. They sat unconcerned at the console, talking amongst themselves. Being the practical man that he was, it was obvious by reading the room that he needed to clear the air with the two. Raj hobbled over and began to profusely apologize to the pair and fully explain himself. He knew that his words might not have come off as conciliatory, but he moved forward anyway. He had grown to know D.K. as more of a brother than a teammate and never intended to offend him.

"Firstly, to Ameerah, I would never try to hurt you in any way. I was a bit overzealous because, despite our progress, our time is short because of what Prof. Sherman has done. I don't think you completely comprehend what this means. We are already at a disadvantage because he has key materials and insight from our lab, as well as that concoction of a life form at his disposal, and she may be able to do 100 times more than what our IDIAMTRACE-10 machine can do."

Ameerah lowered her head. He then went on to say, "D.K, brother, I'm so sorry for making you feel that your cousin was in any danger from me. You're the closest person that I have to a brother and I'm Indian," he laughed and continued, "I have several blood brothers but not one that accepts me wholly and unconditionally. So, I get the ass-whooping from you, but man, may that never happen again!"

D.K. looked up with his hazel eyes glistening. He smiled and with an outstretched hand said, "You know how we do! We all good but never forget I'm 'bout that life!"

Raj responded, "Duly noted."

They all chuckled for a moment and finished with a unified three-way hug.

"Enough of this," said Ameerah. "Come and see the new developments from the point twos. We have visuals and they are stunning."

The quality of the images was decent. There were minor distortions, but overall the team could make out the scenes laid before them. What they were able to achieve in a relatively short amount of time was spectacular. However, Raj couldn't help but wonder, *How much grander is Professor Sherman's Angel Particle Woman, and could this cause irreparable damages?*

John requested one more session with Ameerah before he completed his work in the lab. He thought it best to take her to an offsite location and ease her mind. Clients always provided more details when they were comfortable and visually stimulated. After all, she had been cooped up in the lab with six other people for days. There was no telling if that was a factor in her dreams as well. John gave her a moment to grab her things, and then they were off.

As soon as they boarded the elevator, Raj called an impromptu meeting to discuss the Angel Particle Woman. He wanted to be careful as to not alarm Ameerah in her fragile state, but he felt it prudent to talk about the monumental calamity that would befall them all. His monologue was extensively thick in scientific jargon, but the bottom line of what he had to say was, "Scientifically, Angel (what I have decided to name her) is defying the rules of nature so grotesquely that mankind will be the ones paying the exorbitantly high price for her existence."

He continued, "The other problem is that we have no idea of the depth of her abilities, nor how obsequious she is to the Professor. We are certain of his lack of morality and greed, but it's his proclivities combined with hers that is of the utmost concern. What is she able to do beyond what we have already figured out, and even greater, what is she willing to do for him?"

They all sat in somber silence. It was anybody's guess how they would acquire this information, but it had to be done.

The Professor continued to test Astrid's abilities, and every day he discovered that she could do more and more. Her tolerance for interstellar (and other plane) travel was high, and she didn't seem to tire. Her speed in which she returned from a trip vastly varied if she had not had proper time in the sphere. She was much slower after she'd been outside of it for more than ten hours of the day Astrid had to contain the energy she gave off in order to feed the Aurovian. If she didn't, it was the equivalent of a normal human being bleeding out from a severe cut or wound.

One of her skills was to emit massive levels of radiation at will, and she had the capabilities of projecting that force onto something or deploy it broadly in a certain direction. If you understand how a microwave works, you know that this kind of power can be very dangerous. She could agitate her molecules so quickly that she could cook from the inside out within seconds.

CHAPTER FIFTEEN

J ohn's idea to take Ameerah out of the lab to calm her mood proved to be a good one. He had just the place in mind for their outing. If music soothes the savage beast, then art can revitalize the soul. John had an old friend that was a talented painter, and he owned a gallery that wasn't too far from the lab. The surprise would be twofold because Matt had no idea that John was in town.

Matt Vines was an artist. His style was definitely of a modern social art vibe. He blended popular fashion with vibrant bold colors and fantastic imagery. If nothing else, Ameerah's imagination would be ignited by the deluge of whimsy in his paintings. The gallery had just opened and was completely empty. It was a perfect time to take in the beauty of his paintings and to talk with Matt without being interrupted.

As they opened the door, they were almost dizzied by the paint fumes wafting through the air and the sweet smell of a good ol' stogie fired up nearby. John crept in softly, sleekly gliding across the mahogany floors. Whoever this guy was, he had taste and a pretty nice clientele. His art was littered with commissioned tags from well-known celebrities and a red dot to boot, which indicated "paid."

An energetic voice yelled from behind them, "What?! Is that John Lee?" Matt asked.

A man with amber brown skin, a dense chiseled beard, and dazzling ice-gray eyes appeared from around a decorative pillar. The fancy fedora was a fitting piece to finish off his ensemble. He flashed the biggest smile Ameerah had ever seen. Both guys lit up when they saw each other, and within seconds they went into a ritualistic handshake and finished with a bro hug. Ameerah stood there thinking to herself, *Grown men are just boys with bigger toys.*

They took a break long enough for John to introduce Ameerah to Matt. After the pleasantries, he proudly took them on a tour of the gallery while they got up to speed. Ameerah walked ahead swiftly so the boys could chat freely. During the conversation, Matt shared that he had been engaged to be married recently but had broken off the engagement due to his fiancé's blatant unfaithfulness.

The pain was compounded by a close friend of the family taking ill and having to be put in hospice. Matt said, "He was always good to me. He treated me like a son. It hurts to know that we won't have him around anymore."

John immediately drew a connection between Matt and Ameerah's research. John knew that he would be breaking protocol if he disclosed to Matt what Ameerah's lab did, but Matt was one of his oldest and dearest friends, and he wanted to help.

John extended his arm around Matt's shoulders and said, "I get it, I really do. I know that there's nothing anyone can do to reverse this situation, but maybe Ameerah can help."

He spoke tactically about the lab and about the miraculous work they were doing. Matt didn't know how to take it. He wanted to believe his friend, but what he was saying was so far-fetched that he just couldn't. John finished by saying, "Ameerah runs the lab. She would be the best person to show you and confirm what I'm saying."

John and Matt walked up to Ameerah as she was deep in thought, gazing at a painting of a personified silverback gorilla with shiny grills on his teeth and smoking a cigar.

"How was your pow-wow?" she asked. She was half expecting to be roped into tales of women and weed form their old high school days, but instead she was taken aback by sick friends and a possible study subject for the lab. Had John been three feet shorter, Ameerah would have knocked some sense into his head.

Rather than taking the ill-tempered route, she decided to look at this situation empathetically. The scenario wasn't outside of their typical parameters, and it would give Matt some much-needed comfort. After briefly reprimanding John, Ameerah called the lab and told them to prep a unit for Matt's friend and that she would explain more when they arrived. The first challenge that Matt had to overcome was explaining that there was a "cost-free" hospice available via a harmless clinical trial.

Ameerah wanted no part of that gig. She went along for the ride in the interest of saving time, but he was going to have his hands full. Surprisingly, Matt was a natural. After a little bit of coaching, he was well-versed in educating the family on what was being offered.

Next stop was the hospice to pick up Mr. Evans. When they arrived, Mr. Evans was alone and unaware of the goings-on around him. He laid there like a discarded toy on a child's bedroom floor.

You could visually see Matt's heart sinking into his stomach. The sheer contrast of the two situations was painful, from being at Mr. Evans' home with his entire family, watching them eating and socializing, to being in a cold, sickly facility where a lowly old man was literally waiting to die all alone. It took everything out of the team to not break down in tears.

Ameerah began to race around the room and collect Mr. Evans' belongings while Matt and John disconnected whatever tube and devices that were holding him together. They sat him in a wheelchair, tossed a blanket over him, and made their way to the nearest exit.

The whole purpose of coming to the art gallery didn't even matter anymore. This was what being human was all about: being able and willing to make a difference just because it's the right thing to do. Upon exiting the elevator at the lab, it was heartwarming to see wall-to-wall white lab coats guiding the group into the door. Just like Ameerah asked, there was a transition unit prepped and waiting to receive Mr. Evans. Matt wanted to be the one to lower him into the cradle and shut the lid. Once he was done, he backed away so the formalities could be done.

Mr. Evans was not long to be with them—not at all. He began to expire shortly after arriving. The process was new to John as well, and they both stood there struggling with the complexities of what was taking place, and the surreal-ness of it all. Mr. Evans went quickly; the invisible birth of the soul cannot be seen, but it was surely felt that day. Ameerah broke the silence to give Matt a gift. She walked him over to the IDIAMTRACE-10 and pointed to Mr. Evans' soul as it ascended to the heavens.

Matt felt a peace like no other, and just at that moment, Ameerah saw the benefits of the IDIAMTRACE-10 beyond research. She would never say this to anyone, but she thought that Professor Sherman may have repurposed the nanites and their machine to do some good for the people left behind.

John Lee apologized to Ameerah and the team, but he and Matt had to go. He felt bad about veering off track and not getting Ameerah's last session in, but Raj assured him that they had more than enough renderings to move forward. Matt made sure to shake everyone's hand, and he ended his gratitude by giving Ameerah a big loving hug, and he and John went on their way.

CHAPTER SIXTEEN

Professor Sherman spent a large amount of his time at the NCF monitoring Astrid and testing her abilities. He seemed to forget that he was the head of a global organization that was in full-swing operation six days a week with an actual church service on Sunday. Although he was on the premises, he was nearly impossible to reach and even harder to find. He was ensconced in the catacombs of the NCF headquarters.

He shirked his responsibilities, so much so that the organization's investors became concerned. There was one investor that took a special interest in Professor Sherman's activities, or lack thereof. His name was Duvall Swan. Swan invested millions of his own personal capital into the NCF, mainly because of their dynamic global reach and their conservative Christian views. He was one of their largest shareholders and was very vocal about the direction of the organization.

Professor Sherman arrogantly missed several high-level meetings and it did not go unnoticed. Swan took it upon himself to delve a little deeper into the daily schedule of the appointed head of the NCF. He just felt in his bones that something wasn't right. Swan had a knack for inserting himself where he didn't belong. He exhibited delusions of grandeur, especially when he was given money (of any amount).

At times, he would say things like, "You owe me a debt that can never be repaid. Whatever money you make now or in the future, I should get a cut, because you owe me."

When confronted about his crass words, he would declare that he made the comments in jest. He wasn't the smartest man, but his paranoia made him a worthy opponent in business. Word got around the office to avoid him at all cost, lest you be haunted by his incessant ramblings and conjecture.

The story is that he made his millions from selling drugs on the mean streets of Philly, and he was subsequently arrested. He was incarcerated for 15 years in the state penitentiary where he became a reformed man. During his stay, he vowed to change his life and use his particular set of skills to serve God. He rarely discussed that time period in his life, except to say that it made him the man he was today, and he was all the better for it.

Somehow, he was able to retain his ill-gotten fortune and now used it to be the hidden hand behind the NCF. The strangest thing was that even with all the money, there were things about him that he could not fix. As stealthy as he would like to be, there was one thing hindering him.

Swan suffered from a pungent medical condition called "trimethyl-aminuria." This condition is an incredibly rare gene mutation where your body is unable to break down a key chemical compound. It's what gives fish their "fishy" smell. The trimethylaminuria compound builds up in your body and is released in your sweat, urine, breath, and semen.

So, he doesn't have the ability to sneak up on anyone, not even a houseplant—he can be identified a mile away. Unfortunately for Professor Sherman, he would soon be very familiar with this malodorous entity shadowing his every move. Kind of sad, really; the staff felt that his inability to have a personal intimate relationship was his driving force to be a consummate businessman. It would have served the Professor well to have been at those meetings because now Swan had him in his crosshairs, and he was dead set on a win.

Fifty feet below where Duvall Swan was standing, Professor Sherman was doing diagnostics on Astrid while she was resting in her orb. He began to gyrate in celebration as he read the spectacular data. Astrid's powers were far beyond what he expected, and he planned on pushing her to do more. Not that he minded, but he tried many times to clothe her, but to no avail. Despite the different materials he tested, the power that her body was giving off either would not adhere to her skin or the fabrics would instantly disintegrate.

That fact might become moot soon enough because of the high population of Aurovian in Astrid's body. They began to settle here and there (mostly around her torso and midriff) because her skin was so pale and the nanite's concentration dense; their bluish properties glowed from under her skin, to the point that it gave the appearance that she was wearing a scantily clad bodice. He was fascinated with her growth.

Astrid could do no wrong in the Professor's eyes. If anything, she was his greatest achievement. He had plans to venture to the main floor of the building. It suddenly dawned on him that he'd spent the better part of the morning and afternoon with Astrid. He hadn't eaten or drank anything since the night before.

Coincidentally, Duvall Swan was descending in the elevator in search of all the equipment his money had been purchasing. At the same time, Professor Sherman's finger was about to press the call button for the lift when the doors magically opened.

The stench proceeded Swan. Professor Sherman's face told it all when the elevator's doors opened. Swan winced with irritation. He really wished that people had more class to not embarrass others with their appalled expressions.

Swan immediately went into dialogue, "I've been looking for you. Do you have a moment?"

Sherman rolled his eyes and swept his hand in a back and forth motion, as to guide Swan back on the elevator. He reluctantly complied and they rode back up to the main floor together.

Prof. Sherman held his breath for the entire ride. Swan yammered on and on about missing meetings and accountability, and the more he spoke the more the walls closed in on Sherman. Swan's odors consumed every ounce of fresh air that was available; Prof. Sherman was to the point of turning blue. His verbal onslaught felt like it went on forever. That was one of the disadvantages of being so deep in the ground: the long trip back up.

If there was a worse punishment, he couldn't think of one. Had the elevator doors not swung open when they did, Prof. Sherman was prepared to divulge every secret he'd locked away since childhood. He was no longer hungry or thirsty—all he wanted was fresh air. Any questions that Swan had would have to be done out in an open space to dilute his odious attack.

When they reached their destination, Swan started in with a barrage of questions about the Professor's work in the basement of the building. Every time the Professor tried to answer the question, he was met with another question. The Professor felt that there was no winning this fight. The best thing for him to do was to wait until the firing ended and present his responses at that time. Swan eventually completed his rant, so the Professor gently led the conversation away from the missing meetings and expensive equipment.

He said, "I do apologize for my lack of availability. I have a sister who is very ill, and she requires my assistance in day-to-day activities. As far as the lower level goes, the equipment that you purchased is very sensitive, extremely easy to damage. For this reason, it must be secluded until it's up and running and personnel can be trained to operate it. So, you see, I'm not being evasive, just taking great care to optimize the performance of the NCF. A strategy is the key to all success; surely a man of your caliber can attest to that."

Duvall was easily swayed by compliments. It didn't matter if it was coming from a male or female. His ego had a ravenous appetite. Professor Sherman's explanations sufficed for now. Swan had been properly disarmed but closed out the conversation with one caveat.

He would continue funding for the necessary equipment if he could inspect the lower level within the next several days. The Professor's eyes grew bulbous; there was no way he could move Astrid's pod. It was bolted to the floor with a 15-foot metal beam, and there was no way to explain what the oddity was. He would have to enlist Astrid's help to pull this off. All he could do at this moment was smile sheepishly and agree.

CHAPTER SEVENTEEN

The team was back in the swing of things after John and Matt left. The mood in the lab was upbeat, despite the number of new cases in queue for transitioning. Raj still had every intention of pulling Ameerah to the side to discuss the Angel Woman in more detail. He had to make her realize the dangerous dichotomy between the work that they did with the IDIAMTRACE-10, and what Angel was able to do with her newfound abilities. Devising a plan to stop her and Professor Sherman was an obligation, not an option.

Simon and Chad had been bogged down at the monitors; visuals began pouring in all at once. Lisa circled around them like a vulture, stressing the importance of matching the right souls with the corresponding locations. Beyond receiving visuals, their final locations would be cross-referenced with their profiles. Then that information would be studied and put into the machine to obtain ratios. For instance, if they processed 2000 people with the demographics below,

:

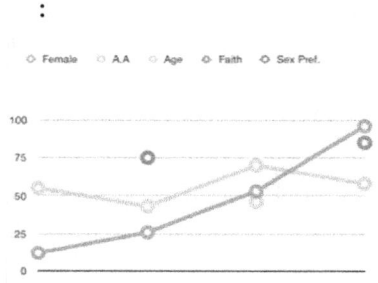

Subject: Named: Alpha-SA-119034:
Gender: Female
Ethnic Background: African-American
Age: 46
Religion: Christian
Sexual Preference: Straight

How many would make it to Coordinates "A" versus "B"? And why?

It was more work than they could handle, especially with the addition of Professor Sherman's and Angel's shenanigans. The lab was teetering on the edge of failure every day. Ameerah had no clue that Raj was going to corner her about Angel, and ironically, she decided to bring the issue to him. She caught him off guard making a cup of coffee and shared with him her concerns about Sherman's activities.

At first, he was baffled at the rapid turn of events but welcomed them nevertheless, it was time to mount an attack on the bizarre duo. They both knew they didn't have enough information to stop Angel, but they had more than enough to halt the Professor in his tracks. Maybe making his works public would do the trick—that was the last thing he would want. However, doing so could make the lab fall prey to the same tactics. Raj and Ameerah felt that it was worth the risk (at least they could explain away any intrusive inquiries that would follow).

The campaign started that day. D.K. and Savoy notified several news outlets of Sherman's research and that a woman was being held captive in the basement of the prestigious NCF. They left directions of how to get to the lower level of the building and the specific layout of the main areas in the basement. That would be enough mud in the waters at the very least to stall his efforts, and at the very best, shut him down completely. A small part of them felt guilty for this treacherous deed and the other part felt satisfied, like when the slippery cartoon villain finally gets his just desserts.

The news moved swiftly, and by the next morning, law enforcement and media outlets were already on the scene camped out at the NCF. The employees of the NCF circled the wagons the minute the police arrived demanding access to the building. They fiercely defended Professor Sherman despite not knowing if the scuttlebutt was true. The staff frantically called the Professor to warn him of the melee happening topside, but the cellular signal down in the tombs was almost non-existent.

A staffer sent one of the guards to go and retrieve the Professor so that he could neutralize the situation. The guard made his way to the elevators and rode down as fast as the lift would go. He had never been down to the bottom of the building before and didn't know where to look for Professor Sherman.

When he exited the elevator, he pulled out his flashlight because it was so dimly lit and began to walk cautiously forward. With each step, he called out for the professor. He was about 20 feet in before he felt a cold hand on his shoulder.

"Officer, what are you doing down here?!" the Professor yelled. The guard was so startled that he threw his flashlight in the air and fell backwards onto the floor.

He stuttered off all the details he had while planted firmly on the cold hard floor. You could see the panic in the Professor's face, attempting to tactically rescue himself from the hyena that awaited him in the lobby. He helped the guard up and walked him to the elevator. He told him that he would be upstairs momentarily to speak with the authorities.

With the speed of a cheetah out on a hunt, he ran to his lab and woke Astrid. He said to her, "I have to speak quickly. I fear that my old comrades at the lab have sent the authorities to investigate me, us. This is Ameerah's doing. I'm certain of it! The problems this may cause are incalculable. You must go, and I will send you a ping when to return. Oh, my dear, I can't stand being away from you too long because you mean the world to me. I've grown to need you in more ways than one."

He then leaned over and stretched open his reptilian mouth and slid his sticky, eel-like tongue into her awaiting warm plump lips. He hummed and moaned while he pushed himself harder onto her receiving body. When he finished, he left her face wet from saliva and red from the intense force of his enthusiasm. No matter the cost, she determined to defend her liege.

Ameerah and her team were basking in all the trouble that they caused Professor Sherman. They celebrated the end of his work and hoped that Angel would be confiscated and destroyed as a result of this. Ameerah went off to the control room to grab a log book to record the activities of the day. The moment she opened the door, her hair on her head stood on end and the temperature went up by what felt like 30 degrees. Behind her was a glaring blue light that caused her to turn around and look.

There was a woman, nude and glowing with patches that looked like the blue waters between the counties on a globe. She was emitting so much heat that Ameerah stepped back so she wouldn't get burned.

The woman said, "I feel you here, Ameerah. I've heard much about you. Please allow me to introduce myself. I was once known as Astrid, but from here on out, you may call me 'Scilectra.' From what I heard, you and your illustrious teammates have set wheels in motion to curb me from fulfilling my destiny." She tried to move closer, but Ameerah couldn't bear the heat sinking into her skin.

Scilectra continued, "I do understand your curiosity about who I am and my association with Professor Sherman; let me assure you that our relationship is of the divine. Maybe you will be the first to institute an '-ology' of my kind; surely there's no better person to do it. This opportunity is rare because there is none before me and there will be none after. You see, my father taught me at a young age that the Bible was a dangerous fairytale.

"He groomed me to be a quality vessel and to open my mind to mathematics and the sciences. He left my mother and I in order to substantiate his beliefs—that there is no man upstairs watching, waiting, and judging. He was certain that we are foreign seeds planted in this land as the ultimate experiment. We were given a duality, one part a slave to the flesh, and the other part a slave to allegory and the unseen. We are never going to win. That's not the design.

"Father was a spiritual savant, and he was taken one day, after an encounter with someone or something that shook him. Not before telling me what I had to do and who I had to give my life to, though, in efforts to prove that we are not beings, but a billion-year research that's nearing its end.

"I have been tempered to be what I've become. I'm purged out—the only thing that remains is my vessel and its passenger, which is more than enough room to fill with the origin matter that's within me now. My soul and body are one, fused together with the thread of eternity. What I have in me will take me places that God can't go. I will be the final female.

"My only purpose is to challenge your beloved consecrated book that has led scores of our people by the nose. Whether it's a reality or a myth for the ages, please know that I will let nothing stop me from my obligation. I tell you this because you and I are connected in some way. Nevertheless, you're becoming an obstacle, and I will kindly pay you homage, while I end you."

She zapped out as abruptly as she came. Ameerah trembled with fear by what she just experienced, such brazen disrespect.

This was beyond what she imagined the Angel Particle woman to be, and she now had a formal name. She thought to herself, *Is this really a thing? I think this is a thing! This type of shit only happens in the comic books. This can't be right. What gall!* Ameerah wandered out of the control room in a tizzy; no one noticed her frazzled demeanor over the celebratory chatter.

She found a distant corner to collect herself while she contemplated how to explain the phenomena that went on in the other room. She decided to rip the Band-Aid off and scream at the top of her lungs.

"QUIET!"

The whole room stopped in mid-action. Everyone rotated their heads around and stared at Ameerah.

Lisa snidely asked, "What is your problem?"

Ameerah latched onto her question with an answer, "That Angel chick was just here, and she is pissed off!"

They all stood there, shocked and silent. What could they say? Ameerah was obviously losing her mind, and that hallucination must have been the start of it. D.K. walked over and gave her a hug, hoping to change the direction she was going. Maybe exhaustion or fever was setting in, but whatever it was, they were all concerned.

She stood up and walked to the middle of the room and screamed, "I'm not fucking crazy! She was in the control room with me—clear as day! Check the cameras and you'll see!"

They all moved in unison to the control room and watched intensely while D.K. rolled back the footage.

She said, "See, there I am."

Yes, there she was, but a moment later the video was filled with static, but they were able to hear the audio.

The voice was not that of Ameerah and the way she spoke sent chills up their spines. Their nightmare had come full circle. After returning to the conference room, the joy they previously displayed was gone. There was a monster in their midst, and she had a name: Scilectra.

Lisa started shooting off questions, "What does this mean? Why does she need a moniker? Is she no longer human?" It was abundantly clear that Astrid had been weaponized, and the team had no defense against her.

Chad weighed in, "I know this may feel counter-intuitive, but we may need to keep the pressure on Professor Sherman, from an incognito position. Meaning, the proverbial cat's out of the bag now. Things like these can take on a life of their own—"

Ameerah interrupted, "We don't know the extent of her powers. She could be in this room right now listening to us speak!"

"*And I am!*" Scilectra materialized out of thin air, surrounded by magnificent blue energy. They could feel the cracking and buzzing of all the raw power in the room. She was courteous enough to dim her force so the team would not be consumed by her intensity. The entire room was flabbergasted.

D.K. ran to Ameerah and stood in front of her to protect her from Scilectra, who smiled as she nodded her head from side to side, tickled by the gesture. She spoke as she strolled the room.

"I am science. I have no limitations in that way. I know how you're pieced together. I know why you're sick and how to cure you, but science is not time—that's something else. If there is a God, then He is time. That brings me to why I am here."

She grinned a ghoulish grin and continued, "Prof. Sherman and I have an agenda, and that is to find out if there's a place where God lays His head, and the alternate place, where He treads his feet. I demand to have the coordinates so that I may put these questions to sleep. Who has the answers that I need?"

Savoy spoke up. "No one here has that information. So why don't you just leave?"

"Savoy, is it? I feel parts of me in you, too. You know that soon I will be able to control those microscopic nanites rolling around in your right eye. If I tell them to dance, they will dance. If I tell them to die, they will die, and if I tell them to explode, they E...X...P...L...O...D...E!"

At that very moment, Savoy started to scream in horror and cupped her hands over her eye. She fell to the floor writhing in pain. Raj and Ameerah raced over to console Savoy, and they begged Scilectra to stop hurting her. Scilectra laughed and the pain in Savoy's eye vanished instantly.

"I felt that you all needed a demonstration of what my powers can do. That was but a mere slap on the wrist. If we have to revisit this conversation again, let's just say, 'mercy is for the weak, and therefore, I have none.' Time is not on your side, and neither is science. Find what the Professor and I need and do it quickly!"

The multicolored strands on her head waved around like they were underwater and several crawled into her ear and behaved like they were whispering something to her. She scanned down to the floor and looked Ameerah squarely in the eye, winked at her, and then she was gone. D.K. ran over to Raj and Ameerah. He pulled him up off the floor, but he gestured for Ameerah and Savoy to stay. He also motioned for Lisa, Chad, and Simon to leave the lab with him, but not to speak.

D.K. led the group out to the van and then drove off. As he drove, he made the team keep quiet until they were 30 minutes away by a waterfront location. Then he said, "Now, we can talk. I made you keep quiet in the lab because we had no way of knowing if she was still there listening. To my understanding, she knows where the lab is because she was given the directions, but she can't travel to specific unknown places without being provided with a latitude and longitude, so if she doesn't know where we are, she can't spy on us or hurt us."

Lisa nodded her head and said, "Ah, I get it, this is good."

D.K. also explained that because of the intense power she gave off, he could design a device that detected large surges of power. That device would then send them all alerts on their smartphones and other equipment to notify everyone that she was on the premises. They could use her powers against her so that she wouldn't be so stealthy, whether they could see her or not.

"Then why did you leave Ameerah and Savoy out of this?" Simon asked.

D.K. answered, "You heard her—she said that she could feel part of her in Savoy because of the nanites in her eye. Ameerah has nanites in her too, so she can probably hear or sense them wherever they are."

"Then why can't she find the Golden Coordinates on her own? The galaxy is full of souls wandering around with our nanites."

"You just said it: the galaxy. We all know that the galaxy has no end. It would be like trying to find a needle in a haystack full of pins. She's sensing too much, and it may be all noise to her. The nanites are going every which way and loosely, that's why she needs exact coordinates—to cut through the noise.

"She and Professor Sherman want us to be their employees with no benefits. Look, I'll go to the spot and get to work fabricating these apps. Then we all need to hook up again and put the apps on all our equipment.

Lisa replied, "What do you mean? What apps?"

D.K. smiled in a mischievous way and started to sing, tapping his index finger on his temple. He said, "Thinking of a master plan, cause ain't nothing but code inside my head!"

Lisa laughed because she had no idea what he was talking about, but she rolled with it anyway.

She replied, "I'll grab Ameerah and Savoy's devices and give them back to them with a note when you're done."

He said, "Cool!"

The team replied, "Cool." Then they headed back to the lab to give the appearance of work as usual. D.K. dropped the team off at the back door and went home to start the project that might keep them all breathing for a little while longer.

Pause

The theories that the team has about the landing locations of the souls are closer to the truth than they realize. With all the deciphering that they've been doing, the one key component they're missing or not analyzing is that there's a system at play. No soul is going directly from Earth to one place or another. They are touring the stars and space like a gap-year before going to college.

After all, they're free and unencumbered by scientific principalities. Why not see now what they could never experience being tethered to a ball of flesh and bone? This free-for-all doesn't last forever; there are forces out there that keep things in line and maintain the necessary flow. The next stop is always the first mandatory stop: "Ekausa." It pulls them in when it's their time to be processed.

Ekausa is what humans would call "limbo," but it's much, much more than being stuck in the in-between. Whatever your beliefs on Earth are, right, wrong, or none, Ekausa educates you on where you missed the mark or shares with you if you are on track.

Here, you will get your playback and shown where your detours happened. More importantly, there you find out where your final place will be and why. Some people were so wrong in their understanding of who or what God is that their time in Ekausa is very lengthy; others were as close to the truth as one could get, and they only had to stay for a short while. There are many children here, and they don't require a playback because of their innocence. They're here to laugh and play until God calls for them to come to Him. No one can bypass Ekausa. After this place, the answers can be found.

CHAPTER EIGHTEEN

The authorities assembled on the main floor, and they were en-route to the elevator to descend on Professor Sherman. The press continued to fan the flames by showing a faceless image of a young girl bound with duct tape all over the airwaves. Nothing riles up the public more than an unfit politician with a bad toupee, hell-bent on pushing a false narrative, or a helpless pretty girl held captive in a dark basement.

Today, it was the latter. When the elevator arrived, the officers jam-packed themselves in the lift like sardines with badges. The ride down was quiet as each officer saw himself as the hero that preempted a horrible outcome from this sweet little girl that waited for rescue. They finally reached the bottom, but before the doors opened, one officer silently signed out several directions with his hands so as to not inform the enemy what their game plan was.

All the dramatics were for naught, as Professor Sherman stood in the pathway of the open doors with a cup of hot tea and a smile. "Gentlemen," he said, "right this way."

One officer yelled, "Get on the floor now and spread eagle or we will light your ass up!"

Not shocked at all, the Professor complied. He then stated, "I believe that there has been some kind of mistake. I feel that the NCF and I may be victims of what you call 'swatting.' Feel free to take a look around and I'm certain that you will find everything in proper order."

An officer nearest to the Professor said, "Dude, your creep factor alone is enough to be arrested for something . . . anything! Whatever you're doing down here in the dark like this has gotta be criminal." After his bold declaration, the officer decided to handcuff the Professor until after the search was over. The Professor knew that with Astrid gone, there would be nothing for them to find and certainly nothing that they or a forensics team could explain. The search took the better part of five hours. The police department enlisted the help of their K-9 unit as well as the crime lab to take samples of DNA off of tables and doorknobs, but unfortunately, there was no girl to be saved.

The Professor, who had been given a chair by this time, sat there arrogantly grinning. He was so pleased that Astrid's current condition evaporated anything she touched and that her glorious hairs could never shed. Everyone was there for the inquisition, including Duvall Swan, who took this lengthy opportunity to snoop around, unescorted by the Professor.

He took particular interest in the room with the large sphere on an axis. He had not approved such a purchase, but more importantly, what was it and what was it for? The room smelled of electricity. This was a better explanation of that statement. When you plug in a new device or product, like a heater for instance, those are smells which are incidental to the release of electricity. Electricity has no smell, per se, but it does form ozone when arced through the air, which you *can* smell.

The question was: why was this scent in a room with nothing on but a lamp used to light the room? The equipment was cold to the point of freezing to the touch. Did the Professor invent some type of new age "Tesla Coil?" Swan had to know, and if it was, he demanded to be a part of the research and named on the patent application as co-inventor. He was certain that this item was purchased with his investment dollars and he wanted his cut.

During the investigation, there were so many people passing back and forth between rooms that the Professor didn't notice Swan going into his lab, but he saw him walk out. His heart skipped a beat and he began to sweat, which was not a norm for him. Swan was just so dogged, he had the tenacity of a honey badger when he put his mind to it.

The look that the Professor saw on his face was pure determination. The Professor yelled for Swan while he was in mid-stride to another room down the long corridor. The echoing call caught Swan's attention. He changed direction and went to the Professor.

"How may I help you, professor?"

The Professor replied, "I can explain what's in that room there, and be assured that everything in there was paid for with my own personal money. The authorities will find me not guilty and free me momentarily. When they do, we can go over all the equipment in my lab to your liking."

Swan wasn't particularly enthused with the offer, but his curiosity got the better of him, so he agreed.

Swan said, "This will be a colonoscopy that you won't soon forget. Now if you'll excuse me, I have much to see."

Not the response that the Professor was looking for, but it would have to do until he could figure out a plan to rid himself of that smelly thorn in his side.

He worried about Astrid. He didn't know how long she could sustain being in the veil, not being here or there. Not to mention that she'd been out of her orb for an inordinate amount of time.

Astrid expended a tremendous amount of her core energy anchoring herself in place. There was a space between the inside and outside, like a threshold of a doorway or a pocket. It was very narrow and hazy, and it was a paradox. It was where nothing and everything existed at the same time. Blurs and streaks of what was, what is, and what will be—they fly by so fast that it appears not to be happening.

The push and pull of the place caused Astrid to hold on with full strength because if she didn't, she could be yanked to the past or somewhere else in the present or catapulted into the future. Stabilizing herself until she could be where she wanted to be could and would deplete all her powers.

Astrid couldn't hold on anymore, so she zapped into the lab. Luckily the room was empty, and the door was closed. She gambled on exposing both the Professor and herself, but she had to recharge. She turned on the machines and climbed in her orb. The initial shock of the electricity knocked her out cold, and she began to float in mid-air. Nothing feels better than home and being fed what you need. In that moment, Astrid (rather Scilectra) is feeling that sensation tenfold!

She hung up there like a rag doll, soaking in all the charges that her body could take. The machines hummed and blinked as they pumped her full of life. The only problem was that Scilectra could not wake up until the Professor shut off the machine to release its magnetized hold on her. By that time, someone could re-enter the room and find her naked, unconscious body dangling in the center of the room.

CHAPTER NINETEEN

Simon and Lisa left notes for Ameerah and Savoy. Just to be safe, Lisa asked Savoy to cover her right eye before she read the note (they couldn't be too careful). Simon went one step further and wrote both notes in Fregodian. It was brilliant of him because the team were the only ones who knew of the language, and they all knew it fluently.

Scilectra and Professor "Asshole" didn't know it existed, and that made it perfect. Early on during the learning and creating process, Simon thought to give the sounds and clicks that they heard visual characters. Then he gave them alphabetical and numerical values, too. He indisputably created a whole new language.

The team empowered themselves and gained some control over their lives again. Scilectra would have to catch up to their future plans for her, but with Fregodian on their sides, she might still be too late. If they played their cards right, the team could learn more about Scilectra than she would want them to. The best strategy to defeat her was to find her weakness.

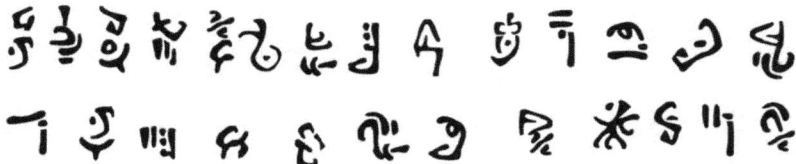

D.K. was at the spot, coding away and developing an alert system for Scilectra. Coding was his form of art, and his art was always accompanied by hardcore rap music to get him in the zone. Whatever he was doing, he had a breakthrough. When that devilish smile crept up on his face, that meant he did what he came to do. Before he pressed that final button to enter his completed code, he said out loud, "Like the adage goes: 'if it bleeds, you can kill it!' So, let's make her bleed!" And "**SEND!**"

The team continued to work in the lab, despite the complication which was Scilectra. They had work to do and clients to process. Acclimating to an entirely new language overnight was hard. Not so much the language itself but remembering to use it in place of their natural first tongue. Savoy thought to put the letter "F" on all her monitors and devices so she wouldn't forget to speak in Fregodian.

To hear the dialect would make an outsider pause. It was quite musical, a continual conversation that sounded like an acoustic jam session. If you could imagine homo sapiens learning how to communicate audibly, it would look like this. They focused on the hums, clicks, and wails that represented other beings, animals, and things until it all eventually morphed into acceptable standardized diction. The team was back at the beginning, primordial speech linked directly to the heavens above.

D.K. returned and began to install his software on all devices, computers, and machines. Anything that needed or responded to an electrical current would get a monitoring attachment unit inside of it. After that, he affixed tiny meters in every room, and on every wall and ceiling. If the electrical currents in the room inclined beyond their normal usage, they would get a notification on their smartphone and watches.

They would also receive a binary notification (equivalent to a text message that read either a "1" or a "0," when she was present = "1", and when she wasn't = "0"). When the levels returned to normal, this would indicate that Scilectra was no longer in the facility. He also explained that it was extremely important not to react or look around when their notifications went off. He said to keep working or talking as usual. If they had to say something important, they needed to slightly convert their language to Fregodian. However, they couldn't use it too often, as to not arouse suspicion. He activated the sensors, and the readings in the lab were normal.

Raj did a test and turned on a high energy output machine; within two seconds their alerts went off. Raj wanted to go over strategy and requested everyone but Ameerah and Savoy to go to the conference room. Ameerah felt left out, but she knew that appearances had to be made and work had to be done. She didn't want to risk the possibility of Scilectra hearing or sensing anything. You could see the relief in the face of everyone else, knowing that they could speak openly and freely.

Raj began to speak. "We have to put together a dossier on Scilectra. We can't defeat her if we don't know who or what she is. To quote the late great Sun Tzu and the *Art of War*: 'The whole secret lies in confusing the enemy so that he cannot fathom our real intent.' We can't do this if we don't know the enemy."

He took a deep breath, looked at the others, and continued, "After listening to the conversation she had with Ameerah and watching her demonstration on Savoy, I surmised that Scilectra feels as though she's a god. I don't think she concerns herself with being good or bad. It's important to her that she be right. She feels strongly about proving God or the idea of God to be a farce. She's hoping that Heaven and Hell are revealed to be nowhere—a vacant wasteland of ideology. On a whole, she technically represents and embodies any religion that is alternate of the most popular belief system.

"In her mind, she's saving us all from the 'big let-down,' securing proof that the masses are on the wrong track. Makes you wonder, after all this effort and discovery, what does she have in mind for human salvation, if anything? Her end-game is yet to be seen."

The meeting went on through the night, everyone cramming ideas and questions into a limited time frame. This freedom to speak could end at any moment. Lisa, D.K, and Raj would reconvene off-site to develop a game plan. One thing was clear: they had to acquire more information on both Astrid and Scilectra to win this war.

* * *

The investigation into Professor Sherman was wrapping up. An officer walked up behind the Professor, unlocked his handcuffs, and pushed him forward, nudging him to demonstrate that he was able to stand and walk around on his own accord. The Professor stood up slowly; after all, he had been locked in one position for hours. It was imperative for him to get the blood flowing to his extremities as soon as possible—his main agenda was to hobble over to his lab and find Astrid as soon as possible. The officers watched him wobble away. Shaking their heads, they turned and walked away.

Prof. Sherman mustered the strength to slowly pace to his lab, and to his surprise, Astrid was there and on charge. His heart began to beat frantically. He quickly locked the door and shut off the main lights. Maybe he could fool the last of the authorities and Duvall Swan that he had left for the night.

The Professor sat there until the last of the scuffing shoes had left. He then waited another 20 minutes longer just to be safe. The timer on the orb indicated that Astrid had been charging for just a few hours. Normally, he wouldn't disturb her, but he had to see her, he had to touch her. He turned off the machine and climbed to the platform to let her out. Astrid opened her eyes and lovingly beheld the Professor.

He could feel electricity dancing off her cold pale skin, and the sharp charges burrowed swiftly into his pores. He moaned from the painful pleasure that she incidentally gave him.

She turned her face to his and said "I can't hurt you. My energy is still very low. I beg you to come into me. Penetrate me so that we can be as one."

The Professor pulled back to look at all her completely; all of her body languages gave signs that Astrid was ready and presenting.

She stood up, walked down the staircase to the examination table, and the Professor followed. She seductively sat on the cushioned table and spread her legs wide, her luminous tentacled pubic hairs joined in on the invitation and formed a perfect opening right in the middle, spreading themselves fully open too. If you looked closely, which he did, they were waving him into her untouched and seeded flower. The Professor broke his trance long enough to ask her why this was so important to her.

She said, "I insist. An offspring must come from this union. I can pro-create with anyone, but it must be you! You made me. You are my Father and we must keep our bloodline clean, untainted, and strong . . . It has to be you."

The power that exuded off her skin was intoxicating, and he couldn't fight it any more. He went to her and pushed himself in. What he experienced changed his life.

She smiled and whispered in his ear, "This is only the beginning, and you may call me 'Scilectra.'"

The Professor heard her but couldn't respond because of the sensory overload that his body was experiencing. Scilectra tightly held her position, clamped on to his manhood to drain every drop of reproductive material that she could. Unfortunately, he took her from the orb too soon, and her nanites didn't successfully usher his matter to her uterus, in order to fertil-ize her egg.

The deed had to be done again, but for now she would let him sleep while she reconnected herself to her charging station. The NCF had returned to normal. The resonating sound of tactical boots no longer bounced off the walls.

Upstairs on the main floor, not so much.

Duvall Swan did not believe in Professor Sherman's innocence and would be monitoring him closely. During his review of the many offices on the lower level, he took down names of equipment and serial numbers to check against purchase order forms.

He had, in fact, purchased much of the equipment and materials down there. The problem was that it was not for the purposes of improving com-munications and data processing. This equipment was strictly used for scientific and quantum physics applications. He took photos as well; he would be speaking to several scientists in the near future, but first: a trip to his old lab for some answers. He thought to himself, *It's always best to start at the beginning.* Foremost on Swan's list was a visit to Lab-J71 in the morning.

CHAPTER TWENTY

D.K. and Raj were doing a deep dive into public records and social media for anything on Scilectra. They were at a loss because they had no last name, age, or photos to input for facial recognition. They went as far as to search the records of the NCF for a matching name, and nothing. Then Raj thought to search for any appointments made by the NCF's receptionist, and POW! An Astrid Acosto made an appointment to meet Professor Sherman several months prior.

A surname made a huge difference when searching the public databases. Cross-referencing the city, state, and time-frame for that name pulled up several possibilities, but they eventually narrowed it all down to one. An "Astrid Kathrynn Acosto." She was 22 years old, born on July 3rd, and the only child of Carlos Cordell Acosto and Pauline Matteson-Acosto. Scilectra was telling the truth about her father going missing; records indicated that he disappeared into thin air when she was a young girl. Her mother was still living; she had current utility bills in her name at a nearby address.

D.K. and Raj planned a field trip to her mother's home. They were certain that the information the team was looking for would be found there. Raj grabbed his briefcase and then they were on their way.

The ride over was an ongoing exercise in Fregodian; it was important that they create keywords to replace entire sentences and sentiments. Scilectra didn't need the directions to her childhood home, but what they didn't know was if there was a viable relationship that warranted a visit.

A woman in her mid-forties answered the door on the second ring. She was absolutely stunning. She had auburn hair with emerald green eyes, was fairly tall, and was curvy. D.K. smiled from ear to ear and leaned into the door frame while he introduced them both.

Raj interrupted D.K.'s tacky attempt of flirting to explain the reason they had darkened her doorstep. "Pauline Acosto, I assume?" She nodded. "We are here to ask you a few questions about your daughter, Astrid Acosto." Her eyes widened and her pupils enlarged at the mention of her name.

She asked, "What is this about? Is she okay? I haven't seen or heard from her in years."

Raj replied, "Yes, ma'am. Last we heard, she was doing okay. We work for a governmental agency that she had applied for a job with, and our job is to do the background check. This includes interviewing family and friends to access her character. Do you mind if we come in?"

She moved to the side to clear a path for them to come in. Pauline invited them to sit and motioned for Raj to begin the questioning. Raj asked the questions while D.K. typed up the conversation on his laptop. He already had a program on his computer that transcribed his documents into Fregodian. They learned a lot about Astrid, but the more telling revelations came after he asked about her father.

She said, "Astrid worshipped Carlos. Their relationship was complicated. Even as a young girl she felt the need to understand him and to please him. Carlos would sit with her for hours and read these arcane books that she couldn't possibly understand. He required reports and verbal essays regarding what she had read. He eventually convinced me to pull her out of school so that she could be homeschooled. They spent a lot of time at his laboratory, you see. He worked in human genetic engineering. He also minored in religious studies and physics."

The lines on the sides of Pauline's eyes showed years of worry, evident in her eyes as she continued, "Astrid would come back after their trips to the lab with puncture wounds, markings, and severe headaches. I couldn't fathom the idea that he would actually hurt her intentionally. I confronted him and he said that he was doing the work of our creators, as it was more

THE GOD MAPS | 119

than one. Astrid started to resent me for questioning what he was doing to her. Carlos displayed paranoid and erratic behaviors and I feared our safety.

"The night before I was going to ask him to leave, he and Astrid disappeared. They were gone for a week. I called the police, but they wouldn't do anything because she was with her father and there were no previous safety complaints on file. She returned alone, but she was not the same. Astrid was cold and distant. I tried to ask where her father was and what he did to her, but to this day, she refused to say anything other than, 'I'm prepared now.'

"She woke up on her 18th birthday and walked out of the house with the clothes on her back and a book that her father gave her before he disappeared. She is an adult now, and the police are well trained in placating my concerns, so I have made peace with the past and learned to live without them both. Whatever he did to her, my little girl no longer existed; whoever she is now, that's somebody else entirely."

After Pauline's last uttered word, Raj and D.K. shared a quick glance. Mrs. Acosto didn't know how right she was. They thanked her for her time and went on their way. It was a sad moment because anyone could see she was disheartened that Astrid was alive and well—and nearby to boot—but wouldn't see her own mother. Pauline slowly closed the door behind them as she watched them walk away.

She was so overwhelmed with emotions when the visitors were there that it totally slipped her mind that a package had come for Astrid on her 21st birthday, the sender unknown. She held it for her, in anticipation that Astrid would have returned by then. The instructions on the box stated that Astrid's fingerprints were the key to opening the box and revealing its contents. She felt that if Astrid were still alive, then maybe there was still hope.

CHAPTER TWENTY-ONE

Day by day, the team received more data for the souls about the three main locations that they were landing in. One location was more of a processing center before they were released to either one of the Golden Coordinates. The team didn't know for sure, but the A & B coordinates were not clear as of yet. There were a thousand souls that had not landed here or there, so the census was incomplete.

The team had hundreds of location addresses of whatever was out there in and outside of the galaxy. Some latitudes and longitudes could be planets that the souls had chosen to visit and were particularly fond of, but it was not enough evidence to say that any of these locations were considered "Heaven." The numbers had to be overwhelming in order for the team to declare their findings definite.

They'd lost hundreds of souls to the Black Hole, and the thought seemed very unlikely, but Ameerah explained how this happened: "The gravitational pull of a black hole is like none other: it consumes absolutely everything. The surface density is so strong that nothing can escape it. The carbastan material that souls are made from has a fighting chance to loosen that grip because its essence is hard to grasp and is technically intangible, but with the addition of the Aurovian mingled with it . . . that cuts its fighting chance down to zero.

"The reason being is that although nanites are microscopic, they are still a form a matter. Matter is always a victim of the Black Hole's gravitational pull. Scientists have been studying black holes for years, and the numbers prove that there may be an alternate reality on the other side of a black hole's gravitational pull, including our aptly named 'Black Hole.' Unfortunately, humans can't test that theory because we would not survive the ordeal, but a soul is a different situation altogether.

"If God allowed such a thing, souls that have been sucked into the Black Hole could be enjoying a whole new reality as disembodied beings on a new plane. A new experience for a new entity. Your mind should race at the thought of this. Are human beings just an element on the other side? Would we be listed under some warped atomic number on their periodic elemental table? Ponder that for a second."

They all did just that: pondered deeply at all of this. Beyond these questions, the team was looking for definitive answers that would either confirm one theology or neutralize it and destabilize the entire belief system of the planet. People might not realize it, but one specific religion is the foundation of the educational system, politics, criminal justice, sexual preferences, how many people dress, what they can and can't eat, and so forth.

To be the cause of this disruption could halt the world as they knew it to be. It could start more wars than it could end. It was a sad truth, but darkness has a purpose. Everything needs a place to live and to thrive, including ignorance.

Ignorant is the easiest thing to be, the fastest thing to cultivate, and it requires little to no maintenance. It's the cactus of all the mindsets, and the fastest spreading of all communicable diseases, in which a rare few seek a cure. Plato's *The Allegory of the Cave* speaks of this conditioning in detail. People will forfeit proven and elevating knowledge for the shadows of systemic beliefs.

Historically, the bringer of the "Light" is always punished for disrupting the smooth blind-walk over the edge. A wise man knows that enlightenment has to be done in doses. You have to temper one's mind in order to expand it without resentment.

The light they were about to bring could end the world, but just maybe, Professor Sherman could be the tiny, ignorant flame slowly lighting the way. The NCF could be their way in.

Professor Sherman was still reeling from the sensual encounter that he had with Scilectra. He remembered bits and pieces of their conversations during the encounter and he wanted to ask her a few questions.

"During our engagement, you requested that I call you 'Scilectra.' What does that mean?"

"It's a name or title I have chosen for myself that has significant meaning," she said, "I'm no longer the human girl who wandered into your office. I am an entity now, worthy of a title. 'Scilectra' embodies two words: science and electricity. Science is the truth, and whether discovered or undiscovered, it does not change. Electricity is a raw power that never dies; it just transforms."

He smiled to show his approval. He asked another question: "Can you share with me how you work? How your body works, like your illustrious technicolored locks of hair?"

Scilectra smiled, "That is one of my more fascinating traits. They're called 'pili-lingua' and each individual hair is different. They all have different personalities and speak many languages. They glow with changing colors because they are directly connected to my amped-up pineal gland in my brain. Many cultures call it 'the Third Eye.'

"The pineal gland has crystals in it that releases every color of the rainbow in various rotations. The lens of the pineal gland has a retina that gives sight to all my hairs individually. So, yes, they're alive and they can see. This allows me to go far beyond having a Third Eye. My abilities have afforded me over 100,000 eyes, not including what covers my reproductive organs. I'm a wonderfully made machine; thanks to you, Professor, I'm more than my father could have ever dreamed of."

The Professor was tickled at this wonderland that was at his disposal. He could use her to do his bidding, and at night he could bed a willing participant for a change. He had to focus now because they had much work to do; it was important that they acquire the exact coordinates to Heaven and Hell. He was determined to be the first to publicly make this find and to be able to control that narrative.

He had been thinking about writing a new Bible with the proven information that he and Scilectra discovered. "King James" for the new millennia; one who would be lauded and praised. He already had the ear of the NCF and the many churches and organizations under its umbrella, so sainthood with fortunes to boot should be no problem. Scilectra was the key, but Ameerah was the lock. How could he get the two to work together for his good?

CHAPTER TWENTY-TWO

The receptionist rang the phone in the lab, and in a nasally tone she announced, "Duvall Swan is here to see you. Shall I buzz him in?" Ameerah couldn't figure out why she was speaking this way, but she agreed and went out to meet Mr. Swan at the elevator.

She patiently waited for the doors to open, curious as to who he was and what he wanted. The doors slowly spread open and Ameerah's smile twisted into a frown. Her nose crinkled with disgust. The fishy smell was intense; whatever was going on should be diagnosed as an infection. Swan extended his hand to shake (he always thought that doing this quickly distracted attention away from his scent). She thought back to Carly's call to inform her about the visitor—this explained everything.

Ameerah shook his hand and did her best to ignore the pungent odor. She did have one concern: being underground with no way to open windows, this would need to be a short conversation. Ameerah opened the door to the lab and let Mr. Swan proceed her. One by one, the team picked up on the ominous stench in the room and politely excused themselves to go handle alternative duties elsewhere until her meeting was over.

Ameerah sighed and figured that she'd survived worse. She put on a fan, held her nose, and hoped for the best. Mr. Swan introduced himself and pulled out a list of questions a mile long from his coat pocket. He was overly interested in Professor Sherman's main focus of research before he left the lab. As bad luck would have it, their research ran parallel to his, so

Ameerah was careful not to divulge too much and cut off her nose to spite her face.

Ameerah's new stinky friend was very forthcoming and didn't mind sharing the dirt he had on Sherman. He asked if she recognized the equipment and machinery on the purchase orders from the Professor's lab. She kept a tiny recorder in her lab coat for impromptu scenarios such as these, and each word he spoke was a treasure trove of information. Now the team could reverse engineer Scilectra's sanctuary and dissect what made her tick and what kept her strong.

She threw out enough bait to keep him interested, but not enough to expose their proprietary operation in Lab-J71. Ameerah had what she needed and could no longer stomach the emissions rising off Swan.

"Mr. Swan," she said, "I don't mean to pry, and forgive me if I'm overstepping my bounds, but our research here is extensive and branches off in many directions. I noticed that you have a lingering presence that travels with you."

Swan hung his head in embarrassment and said, "Yes, I'm aware."

She went on to say, "I think we can rid you of that issue if you'd like."

Duvall Swan lifted his head and his eyes watered with tears. He asked for a tissue because any leaking bodily fluids exacerbated the smell, and he didn't want to offend any further. When she returned with a napkin, she explained to him about the programmable nanites that could co-exist in his body's environment—how they would make the necessary compound conversions that his body couldn't. Swan set up an appointment with the team to have the procedure done, in exchange for weekly updates on Professor Sherman, and a small financial infusion for the lab.

The enemy of my enemy is my friend, Ameerah thought, *and FACTS!* When Mr. Swan left, Ameerah pranced down the hall to the control room to brag about the wealth of dirt that she stumbled on regarding Professor Sherman, but it looked like Raj and D.K. might deserve the prize. She pulled up a seat to listen to the intriguing story being told to the team about Astrid's origins; once they were done, she unloaded the details of her meeting with Duvall Swan.

It was abundantly clear that Professor Sherman had to be removed from the equation. Raj explained, "Scilectra depends on him greatly for utilitarian reasons, according to the machinery in his lab. He is recharging her (I'm guessing) after extended periods of travel. He may also bear the responsibility of releasing the charge in order for her to wake.

"If we can interrupt that dynamic, then there is a possibility that she can charge down low enough to not be a concern. Of course, this is a working theory; she could have a built-in fail-safe that would make this null and void. We may have to enlist Mr. Swan to investigate Sherman's lab at our behest."

In the midst of their think-tank session, their cellphones and laptops chimed a familiar but unwelcome alert. Scilectra was there. Lisa changed the tone and the conversation instantly. Talk of the statuses of the new clients ensued.

The mood of the team was cheerful but focused on the duties of the day. Everyone played their parts perfectly. Ameerah spoke playfully in Fregodian; she told the team to head back to their desks and resume their usual tasks. Within a few minutes the alerts chimed again, notifying them that she was gone.

Scilectra had popped in on the lab but remained in the void so she could view them in their natural element without being seen. She was pleased at what she saw and what she heard. However, Ameerah spoke some gibberish that she didn't follow, but the team seemed to understand what she meant. She wasn't too bothered by it, though, because they were working and moving forward on her commands—that's what she cared about. She went back to the lab to find Professor Sherman, but he wasn't there.

On this rare occurrence, Scilectra decided to walk about the rooms of the basement area. He wasn't in the lab to give her directives, so she had the opportunity to live and exist, like what she was before all of this. Each room told a story, the algorithms and formulas written on the chalkboards. She took a moment to read them and they revealed the poetry of life reimagined.

One formula caught her eye. She recognized her makings in the formulated glyphs on the wall. She thought about how simple the characters were that could make a life such as hers. She was thought of deeply, written down with intention, and then brought into being.

This was a celestial act—a thought put into motion and manifested. She was meant to be. Scilectra's pili-linguas informed her that the Professor was in one of the rooms at the end of the hall. Her hairs had a heightened sense of awareness for sound and movement. They were especially attuned to the Professor's rhythm and his walking patterns.

When she stepped into the doorway, he was there with a woman, and she was strapped into a reclining chair to a machine. He was too busy pressing buttons and checking gauges to notice Scilectra standing there. She walked up closely and caressed him from behind; luckily, the woman in the chair was unconscious and didn't have to witness the display of awkward affection between the two.

Scilectra asked, "What are you doing to this woman? I can feel my essence in this room."

The Professor shared that the woman's husband died recently, and she wished to go where he was and make sure that he's ok without her.

"How can you send her? How do you know where her husband is?"

Flustered that she was asking these questions out loud in front of the client (conscious or not), he lovingly eased her out of the room and closed the door behind them. He said, "My dear, people like this fund my work to keep you charged and strong. I don't necessarily know where her husband is, but with the help of the guidance coding in the Aurovian, I can send her to a place where souls have been for a time. Many people are willing to pay for hope, just like the collection plate in a church. In this case, they'll receive something in return."

She didn't agree, but she understood. His objective was to keep her optimal, and she should not concern herself with the details. Scilectra did have one final question: "How does her soul travel if she's not dead?"

The Professor rushed her back into the room with the client. He went through each painstaking detail and finally arrived at her answer. The client was put in a coma-like state and induced to an astral plane state. The Aurovian were then programmed to attach to her astral-self and guided to the desired destination. Waking her up would re-attach her astral self and the nanites would die off without an energy source to feed on. Astral-planing was completely different than attaching to a soul, so there was no perpetual relationship to be had.

Scilectra interjected, "I want to take her! I will go to her astral self and communicate with her. Send me the directives and I will take her there and bring her back. I am more superior than any machine you could ever build, and I have much to discover!"

The Professor tried to defend his methods by stating, "This machine pre-dates you and I thought that this work wasn't important enough for you."

She quickly responded, "I'm here now and nothing will impede my work. You are tossing away opportunities for me to find where He is."

Scilectra was right. The Professor had no choice but to concede. If nothing else, it kept him in her good graces. He knew the power that she wielded and had no intentions of having to contend with it. Sherman programmed the coordinates and set it on a three-minute time delay.

Scilectra spoke to her colonies and ordered them to diminish their strength so that she could go into a deep state to connect with the client's astral self. The Professor monitored the event from his elegant tracking system, and the scene was quite beautiful. The client's aura glowed in white, and Scilectra pulsated in lightning blue. The two joined and went off into the stars. What a sight to behold.

CHAPTER TWENTY-THREE

meerah still wasn't sleeping in a manner conducive to her health. She demanded to be awoken by force if necessary if her nap exceeded 30 minutes. She would catnap through the day and pull all-nighters in the lab. The Aurovian was spreading wider and wider over her cheek, searching for an energy source within her environment because she wasn't getting adequate sleep.

Everyone saw the risk she was taking out of fear, fear that she would have another vivid dream and travel to unknown horrid places. D.K. did something out of the norm: he approached Raj and Lisa about dosing Ameerah again. He insisted that it not be anything too heavy, just enough for her to get a couple hours of sleep; he would be on standby if needed.

He also requested that they take a different approach this time. He asked that they put the dose in her tea; that needle shit just didn't work for him. Raj agreed and employed Lisa to do the dirty deed. Lisa was becoming known around the lab as the "Operative" or the "Jane Bond," if you will. She had a penchant for diverting people's attention and changing their lives without them knowing.

Ameerah was easy for Lisa to drug; the trust was already there. It didn't take long at all before Ameerah slumped over in her chair and D.K. carried her off to the bunks. He rolled her toward the wall and laid right next to her, back to back. Ameerah was none the wiser as she went off floating into her dreams.

* * *

Scilectra was ending her recon mission with the client. She was at the release point so that the client's astral self could be reeled back into her body. In between all of the floating astrals, she saw a light in the distance that caught her eye and made her essence tingle. She moved in that direction. Scilectra was amazed at what she saw.

It was Ameerah traveling aimlessly into space; stranger still, she had no tether to get back in her body. She was beginning to realize just how special Ameerah was. She felt conflicted about her uniqueness and even more curious about what more she could do. She followed her astral self to its destination. Ameerah was headed to her "Siriaz," an external subconscious zone where her dreams were created and experienced.

Everybody has a Siriaz, but for most, their dreams are black and white or simplistic, while very few may have vividly prophetic dream experiences. All of this depends on how cerebral you are and how connected to the Universe/ Source you have become. If you are a simple dreamer, you would not be able to experience the Siriaz, because that zone is for Alpha Minds to level up to infinity.

Scilectra breeched Ameerah's zone and followed her in. Once in, it was clear that Ameerah dreamed about her lab because she was back there working again, but the machines that aided her in real life were not there. She transitioned the patients and tagged them telepathically. Scilectra giggled to herself that in her dreams, Ameerah longed to be a god like her.

The lights in the lab began to flicker. Ameerah glanced at her watch for an alert that never came. She called out to Raj, but there was no response.

Scilectra made her presence known. "How are you, dear sister?"

Ameerah stood strong and interrogated Scilectra, "What are you doing in my lab? We're doing the work as fast as we can!"

Scilectra replied, "Who is 'we?' Do you not see that you and I are alone? Take a good look around. Does anything seem different to you?"

Ameerah walked about the lab and she was right; she did her tried and true trick to see if she was dreaming by attempting to google something she didn't know. Nothing populated and she froze in place. That meant that Scilectra had penetrated her dreamworld, but how?

Scilectra said, "I won't go into details as to how I'm here. I'm happy to have a moment alone with you to talk."

Ameerah interrupted, "I don't want to talk to you! You want to destroy my life's work and potentially mankind by proving the unprovable. God does exist as surely as we are standing here right now. His proof is not in His address or in His face but in His work. We are His evidence; our fragility is proof that there's something greater than us! You had God in you before you experienced a celestial alteration. I don't know why you can't see that."

"My work is not about proving if He exists; it's about verifying our eternity. Ameerah, I want you to think! Humans are in a constant state of peril. Do you believe that angels have these problems? If so, then why is it called 'the human condition'? Humans always have to excavate and negotiate intermittent blessings from the 'Source', but troubles are consistently available in perpetuity. If only the enlightened can find God then the herd is already thinned out, because we are pre-disposed to ignorance by design." Scilectra smirked and walked closer to Ameerah.

Scilectra continued, "We live in a world that's populated by folks who are averse to knowledge and entertained by folly. He purposely speaks in allegory, a tool that doesn't favor the ignorant. This is a fact. To prove my point, no one is asking the right questions: who is the Bible's targeted audience? Why is His opportunity being allocated to just a chosen few? Why the sifting process? Who is He looking for that he cannot find?

"One thing's for sure: the masses are sheep who are willingly being led to slaughter. God may be the designer, but I have never known a designer to create innovations less than Himself, only greater. A designer typically creates something that can do more than its maker, or there would be no purpose. He would devise something to solve a problem or to elevate a situation. Who needs to build something that's not pertinent? I truly believe that humans are gods, sans the instructions to be so. Why cloak the formula in allegory? We need no parameters to be what we are. A god is not a god if we have limits."

Ameerah was silent. Despite what she was fighting for, faith was not a fact; it was a choice. In that strength, she had no leg to stand on. It's true, she had never been formally introduced to God; there was no obligatory ceremony that granted her admission to the club of "humanism." It would be nice to see Him and converse with Him. She didn't want to be a part of the world's greatest contest to be in His presence, though.

Ameerah asked herself, *Is faith enough?*

Scilectra grinned because she knew that she had Ameerah on the ropes. Even though she enjoyed the debate, that was not her purpose. Scilectra walked even closer to Ameerah to get a better sense of her, but began to drag and drain as she crossed the room. She had never experienced this before and assumed that the trip with the client and being in the Siriaz had affected her nanites' power in some way.

She stopped moving and said to Ameerah, "My sister, we will pick this up at a later date. I will see you soon." Then she was gone.

Ameerah woke up in a huff, nearly knocking D.K. off the edge of the bed.

"How long was I out?" she asked, still panting.

He replied, "About two hours. Why? What happened?"

As if picking up where she left off in a conversation she never had, Ameerah replied, "There's only one thing as infinite as numbers, and it's colors. There are billions upon billions of color combination possibilities. Earth is only home to less than 00.0000000001 percent of the color nuances that exist. Our eyes can distinctly see about ten million colors. My point is, there is more. More than what we see, more than what we are, more than what we know. God is THE MORE!" she smiled, excited, and continued with one bold statement: "I think that I know where God is!"

D.K. sat on the edge of the bed, confused. He had no clue where all of this was coming from, but he followed her into the conference room to see where it was going.

Ameerah started out by saying, "Scilectra came to visit me in my dreams. It was not an extreme vivid episode; I was aware and she was there. I can't explain it, but she feels a kinship with me, and I see an opportunity to exploit that. There's something else: I don't think that she can hurt me."

Chad urged her to carry on and explain what she meant.

"She paced towards me like she was going to touch me, and she couldn't. She appeared physically restricted. I know that I was dreaming, but my alerts didn't go off and I felt so energized. I had more energy than I've felt in a long time, but when she left, I fizzled out again.

"I've had a revelation. I have to be dosed with Aurovian again. Not once, but several times more."

They all looked at each other as if she was crazy. She said, "I don't generate the necessary power to satisfy the nanites' appetite so they can stay alive; my soul is dormant. The more nanites in my body, the bigger the energy source must be. Yeah, I'll be tired, but Scilectra (when she comes near me) she will be drained like a AAA battery powering the Sears Tower.

"The other part of this is having the mechanical intervention to find Heaven on my own. It's pure physics! Let's search the known and unknown universe for massive spots where everything is denser and richer, where things like colors, lights, energy, and vibrations are more abundant than anywhere else. Something needs all those things in extremely high quantities.

"It may even be the manufacturer of these heavenly products. Colossal usage of all things good must mean something bigger and better is there. Here, I'll put it in layman's terms: if there are millions of pounds of sugar, butter, and eggs in one location, I'll bet you a dime to a dollar that a bakery is in the middle of it all."

This was just a working theory, but worth a shot.

Lisa said, "You're not made like Scilectra. We don't know the effects of having Aurovian in a living person, let alone extreme amounts. You're safe in your dream world, but the living world is what matters. You can't just take your soul for a test drive to Heaven!"

Raj added to the conversation. "You want us to alter you permanently for an unproven theory—even if it worked, you may not have what you need to make it (potentially) outside of the universe and back. Think about this a little longer, Ameerah."

She was crushed, but they were right. At best, she might end up in a permanent comatose state; at worst, she could die, and her soul be damned to roaming the emptiness for all eternity. She had to figure out another way. Until then, she would amp up her research on Scilectra and let the roaming souls work their magic on finding Heaven and Hell.

CHAPTER TWENTY-FOUR

T oday was the day. Duvall Swan was coming in for his life-changing procedure and the lab was all abuzz—chatter about how the nanites were going to create their own DNA chain to reformat Swan's genetic make-up. Luckily for him, this procedure had been tested by the lab before in other mammals.

His final procedure results would be a part of the patent that would be filed eventually as well. Swan arrived early, and in expectation of his arrival, everyone jammed their noses with a floral or fruit scented salve typically used by coroners and crime scene investigators. When he walked in, the team had nothing but smiles for him. He'd never had that reception before and he decided to reciprocate with a round of hugs for each one of them.

Ameerah promptly changed the mood to a more professional setting. She was anxious to rid him of the specter that haunted his life. After some blood tests and an exam, D.K. and Lisa programmed the nanites and it was off to a unit for dosing. Unlike the original Aurovian mixture, Swan's nanites were powered by his natural occurring electrolytes in his body and certain key elements of his blood. In this case, his nanites would die when he did, but while he was alive, he could not, under any circumstance, donate blood to anyone. It would be disastrous—they would die an agonizing death.

The procedure would take the better part of a day and when it was done, Duvall Swan should emerge as a different man. Lisa stayed with him to monitor his progress; in fact, she would be the first to smell his newly minted fishless scent.

The day passed rather quickly, and the capsule unsealed itself when it was done. Lisa called for the team and did her best to wake him from his sedation. The looming malodorous smell was gone; however, it appeared to have been replaced by another. Lisa crinkled her nose, leaned over, and took a good whiff and began to laugh.

Ameerah asked Duvall Swan what his favorite scents were in all the world, ones he would never get tired of smelling. He replied, "Madagascan vanilla and fresh saffron."

She then had D.K. code those scents into the blockchain of his nanites before he was dosed. Now, all of Swan's bodily fluids (saliva, sweat, tears, and semen) would mildly smell of exotic vanilla and cultivated saffron; what woman would refuse that?

There was one caveat: Swan was forbidden from having children, at least for the next three years. He would have frequent checkups with the lab for the first six months, to assure that there were no immediate deterioration and that the nanites assimilated seamlessly. He was fine with that; he was more excited to go and test out his newly perfumed flesh. He said that he planned a trip to the beach to swim and sunbathe. After that, he would be back to work investigating Professor Sherman for the team.

As Swan was taking his leave, a man passed him on the way into the lab. It was Dean Rydell. The entire room stood at attention.

Ameerah said, "Dean, to what do we owe the honor?"

He replied with his hands tucked neatly in the pockets of his corduroy jacket. "I never really get down here to see you guys work in person. I'm always fascinated by your topics of study. What are you working on today, and what is that lovely smell?"

Ameerah replied, "Funny you should ask! That was one of our experiments walking out of the door. We did a little minor genetic editing to cure a bothersome problem that he was born with. Before you ask, it was a success!"

The dean nodded his head in amazement. Then he asked, "Is everything going ok? Is there anything I need to know about?"

Everyone shook their heads from side to side, displaying that there were no problems at all.

He said, "Very good then, I'll be on my way and keep up the great work!"

After he left, they all gave a sigh of relief. Dean Rydell could not know the totality of their work or he would surely shut them down.

* * *

Scilectra rested in the lab before her next charge but couldn't get Ameerah out of her head. She couldn't figure out why she felt so drained after spending a short period of time with her in the Siriaz. Professor Sherman turned the corner full of excitement; the client was pleased with her trip and would bring several more of her family members to attempt to visit her husband as well.

Scilectra rolled her eyes and looked up at the Professor. He stepped a few feet backwards because he saw that she was miffed, but he had no clue why she was upset.

She said, "I feel that you are deriving some pleasure from these clients and their pain! This work is not part of my purpose. I saw the confused souls wandering around in that place, and now we are taking other tethered souls to look for the lost too. God is not in that place or in any other place where people are meandering in the dark. He shuffles them on Earth, and He shuffles them in death!"

She took her hand and slammed it against the metal table. A crack of thunder rang through the rotund room and struck the Professor so viciously that his ears began to bleed. He fell to the floor and wailed in pain. Scilectra ran to him and wrapped her arms around him, but electrical currents exacerbated his pain to the point that he forced her arms off his body.

The Professor slid to a dark corner and begged her to give him a moment for the pain to die down. Scilectra was angry. She was angry at God for being so elusive, she was angry at the Professor for taking advantage, she was angry at herself for minimizing her potential, but most of all, she was angry at Ameerah, and she didn't know why. She wanted to see her again, and this time she wanted answers.

* * *

Alarms rang out again in the lab. The team trained themselves to keep moving and to not react to the alerts. If they didn't, she would be aware that the lab had installed precautionary measures. Ameerah knew that the sudden impromptu visit was for her, so she began to sweat profusely and tried to act unbothered.

Scilectra appeared right in Ameerah's face. "Hello, sister!"

Ameerah jumped and grabbed her heart to illustrate her surprise. Yes, those drama lessons paid off!

"Why are you here again?" she feigned.

Scilectra responded, "You're not happy to see me? That puzzles me. You people look for God every day but when a real one shows up and takes a personal interest in you, you scoff."

Ameerah sighed and stated, "Your arrogance is staggering. Why do you think you're so special? I get it: you're goal-oriented. But you need more than that to be what you're trying to be. One person (or should I say 'entity') has that job for a reason—because it takes absolute benevolence, and you don't have that! Anyone could have been you.

"In fact, the Professor is the reason why I've been infused with Aurovian. The same Aurovian that courses through your veins. Granted, he altered our intellectual property for his purposes, but the base of your precious nanites is *my* signature mix. So technically, you belong to me! He probably didn't tell you that he's in love with me and has been for a while. I refused his advances. Later he broke into the lab, caught me sleeping, and tried to molest me. When that didn't work, he decided to dose me against my will, and, yes, I have receipts—I have it all on film! I was going to be 'you', but I refused it. I refused him. I would've been greater than you. No shade really, but it's true. For one simple reason, because, you know, I got that dope-ass black girl magic to begin with."

Scilectra became furious. She collected all her strength to strike

Ameerah, but her power was marginalized. On the other side, Ameerah felt like she had been pumped full of B-12 and adrenaline. She was ready for a fight! Scilectra attempted to power up but Ameerah's nanites sucked up all the energy she was putting out. Scilectra's power wasn't shifting to Ameerah, but it was being shared with Ameerah. She had no alternative but to retreat and go back to her orb.

When the lab's perimeter cleared, they all rushed Ameerah to find out what happened. She told them all about how she purposely taunted Scilectra so that she'd get close enough to test her theory. It worked!

Ameerah said, "My nanites are so starved for energy that they fed on Scilectra, almost to the point of nearly neutralizing her. That Angel Particle will never allow her to be drained, but it balanced both she and I out, like a yin and yang flow. It's clear that I'll never have her power, but she's less powerful around me!"

Raj asked, "How can we parlay that to keep her away from the lab indefinitely?"

Savoy shared her concerns. "I'm worried that she'll take out her frustration on other members of the lab so she can punish you. I don't want to be the victim of her rage again."

Ameerah replied, "You guys don't get it . . . this inconsistency can redefine our dynamic with Scilectra. She may be forced to abandon her post as the unofficially appointed 'God-elect.'"

CHAPTER TWENTY-FIVE

The following morning, the lab was abuzz because new images and soul chatter had given them their first solid lead. One of their tagged souls may have made it to a location where God could be! This gregarious soul had a lot to share about her new surroundings. Some of the images were congruent with descriptions detailed in the Bible and the Torah. Still, more evidence was needed. One out of hundreds of thousands of tagged-souls relayed these images—it was not enough to declare a victory, but it was compelling.

One image stood out to Ameerah. It was a place that she saw in her dream: the narrow river that went on forever that was lined with peculiar grassling-type creatures. She had been in this very location; the image proved that it was real! She kept this news to herself in hopes that another dream would give her confirmation in her beliefs. Ameerah was not one for competition, yet finding the Golden Coordinates before Psycho-Goddess was important to her.

It makes you wonder . . . With all the science research and experiments going on in the world, is Scilectra or Lab-J71 a rare occurrence? How many other anomalies are there running around out there with God complexes? The entire balance of the universe could be in a tailspin as we speak! It was almost worth the investigation to see what other abominations had been unleashed on the world.

Ameerah had an ominous feeling that **"CryoSci Labs"** over in Mundi

County might be guilty of similar infractions. Tomorrow, her first order of business was the head of their lab, Eliza Fenry. It was always a problem when you gave life to something that you couldn't control.

There's an old saying that "If you can't feed it, screw it, or control it, you have to kill it!" Sadly, what Professor Sherman had given birth to was far beyond those rules. Knowing how angry Scilectra was when she left, Ameerah could only imagine what she had in store for the Professor when she returned to his lab.

Scilectra exited the void so fast that the entire NCF shook upon entrance. It was after hours, so the guards took it as an external problem; never did they think it was right below their feet. The Professor was in the lab enjoying a pumpernickel and tomato sandwich when Scilectra came in hot.

She said, "I am not unique, I am not the first. You weren't waiting in search of me; I was an opportunity for you. You are in love with Ameerah and you invaded her body with nanites, didn't you?"

The Professor nearly choked on his food, but that wasn't the reason that he chose not to speak. He had to gather his thoughts. He treaded lightly on this subject because everything Ameerah told her was correct. His attempt to gingerly explain himself failed; Scilectra cared about facts. She was black and white, with nothing in between.

He said, "Scilectra, dear, please let me explain and give you some context. When you told me who your father was, I remembered that I'd met him briefly at one of my earlier lectures about the probabilities of creating Earth Originated Angels that would then have the ability to ascend the heavens, '**Reconfigured Angelology**.' He was quite taken with my theory and asked if I was going to ultimately pursue this scientifically.

"I told him that I was, but it would take years before the technology would be available. I also told him that the candidate would need to be specific. This person would have to be female and a virgin, and she would have to undergo procedures to install a larger count of microtubules, which in turn would give her a deeper capacity soul unit. We spoke more privately for a few hours and I never saw him again. That was nearly 15 years ago, and I didn't know that he had a child. When I joined Lab-J71, the technology was ready then for me to move forward with my research, but Ameerah and her team were dead set on utilizing the research in a more defined and centrally focused manner. I didn't agree, and I left. But the tech that was created to make my vision happen, to make you, was and is owned by Ameerah.

"Did I dose her? Yes, but purely because I know her background and thought it was befitting that the creator of the Aurovian be the bearer of its weight, to be the catalyst for the final change! I didn't know that I was to wait for you. I did not know that you even existed. It was a horrible lapse in judgement!"

Scilectra stopped pacing long enough to turn down her defenses. Although she wasn't happy about what she heard, she understood it. She loved the Professor and was jealous that Ameerah was his initial choice. Scilectra began to cry, but the Professor knew that he couldn't touch her in that time period because one of the extreme properties of her blood was that it was a form of bromine. She was made of pure energy that could ignite, so the bromine prevented her from flaming into a pile of ash.

The vermillion colored toxic fluid ran from her eyes and evaporated as it hit the air. When Scilectra calmed, the Professor held her until she powered down. He put her in her orb and went to sleep himself.

When the morning came the Professor turned down Scilectra's charge in order to keep her dormant longer. He felt slighted that Ameerah would "out" him the way she did, and made plans to confront her. He boarded the elevator, and when he arrived on the main floor Duvall Swan greeted him in the hallway.

The Professor smiled and said, "Hello, Duvall, is there a meeting today of which I'm unaware?"

Duvall replied, "No, no, nothing like that. I was hoping to speak with you in more detail about your work."

The Professor replied, "It's not a good time. I'm about to head out to an appointment. I will catch up with you tomorrow, if that's all right?"

Duvall Swan smiled and moved out of Sherman's path. Sherman left a parting compliment: "By the way, I love your new cologne!"

Swan was infuriated by the comment. He felt that the Professor was being smug and insulting. He waited until he was sure that the Professor was off-campus before he went down to the tombs to snoop around. The ride down was always a suspenseful one, the eeriness of the uncertainty that awaited at the bottom. The Professor did an excellent job of isolating himself from the hustle and bustle of the everyday activities of a very visual organization, but that's what worried Duvall Swan the most.

After exiting the elevator, he walked about thirty feet in the rotunda of the vestibule and took in the enormity of it all. If they were in a more rural area, he wouldn't be surprised to see bats nesting on the ceilings of this repurposed cave. He didn't want to waste time gawking at this melancholy structure as if he were a tourist in Rome, but it was a true oxymoron, torn between hideousness and beauty.

The search began with the doors in the lengthy corridor, which netted nothing new. The same equipment was there collecting dust, just as before. In his disgust, he walked back towards the elevators and suddenly remembered the private lab under the stairwell on the way out. The door was closed and when he pushed; it gave him a challenge. By all accounts, Swan was a small man, five foot five, weighing in at a whopping one-hundred and twenty-one pounds. The door to the lab nearly weighed more than him. He spent the greater part of fifteen minutes trying to leverage the door so that he could get in.

Swan gave it one last ditch effort. He placed his back against the door and put his feet on the wall across from the door and gave a good push. The door finally gave way and he fell into the lab butt-first onto the floor. He quickly spun around on the floor and tilted his head upwards to see a young woman trapped in a glass bubble. Swan jumped up off the floor and began to switch off all the gauges that were connected to the ball that she was imprisoned in. The rolling staircase assisted him in climbing up to the makeshift cell so he could let her out. Like always, whenever Scilectra was disconnected from her power source, she fell to the floor of the orb until she came completely to.

Swan screeched, "Are you okay? Are you okay?"

She responded, "I am perfect. Who are you?"

"My name is Duvall Swan and I think that Professor Sherman has kidnapped you for nefarious reasons. Has he hurt you in any way?"

She said, "The Professor does not have the ability to hurt me. What have you done with him?"

Swan was in shock, and for the moment, all he could do was stare at her nudity, her hair, and how blue her lips and nipples were.

She yelled, "It would behoove you to give me satisfactory answers to my questions now!"

Swan said, "I'm sorry to stare, but you're so beautiful. But to answer your latter question, he left on his own accord to attend a meeting. I haven't harmed him in the least. Do you mind If I spoke with you a little, maybe asked a question or two?"

Normally, Scilectra frowned upon frivolous conversation, but she sensed a familiarity with Swan, and she was curious about who he was.

She said, "You may proceed."

When Swan glanced at his watch to check the time, the hands spun aimlessly around the face of the watch. He wasn't much of a science person, but he knew that that shouldn't be happening. They conversed for over an hour, Swan asking general questions like "Who are you?" and "What are you doing in the NCF?" Scilectra decided to be very forthcoming; although the Professor had explained himself, she still felt betrayed after preparing for her entire life to become a celestial being for the good of mankind.

She was comforted that Duvall Swan didn't want anything from her other than to talk; he was eager to hear her out. He wrote down every word she said. She was enamored by this; she felt whole and grand. Scilectra felt a sense of posterity with Swan's dictation.

She asked, "Will you be my recorder?"

"Recorder?" he asked.

She replied, "Yes, my story has to be recorded so the masses will know how I came to be and the reasons that I'm here. The world needs to know facts as they happen, and that I'm here to save them all."

Swan began to stutter, "I . . . I . . . I may not be the one for this task. I'm not cut out to be by your side."

She replied, "May I share something with you?" He nodded. "I had always been somewhat a misanthrope; it was easy for me to disconnect for people and sit still. The paradigm shift that I have been called on to bring about requires that I isolate myself in order to discern truths from false-hoods. Yet, my story must be told.

"I'm allowed a confidant and a keeper. I have a keeper in the Professor, and I request a confidant in you. A new Bible is in the making. Many people believe that we are in the *Age of Aquarius*, but we are not. The world has just entered the *Age of Adonis*. The age of self-love, lust, debauchery, confusion, vileness, and misrepresentation. Animals have more sense than man. Humans do things to each other that beasts won't. The God that you believe in has been rejected at alarming rates.

"Everything good that He's offered has been replaced with a perverted synthetic version, down to the very food that you eat. You don't want Him. You beg for something new. We're creating angels that will be ascending instead of descending. Now you don't have to look upwards for Him; you can look across to me."

Swan was blown away. In one way, he was offended at her gall and her madness. However, in another way, he was honored that he was chosen for something that may be very plausible. He said "Yes," a knee-jerk response more out of fear than agreement. He had to make it back to Lab-J71 to share the news about the first testament of the "New Genesis."

He told Scilectra that he needed to go and prepare for the initial recordings of The... He paused, and she responded, *"The Omniverit."* She said it was an altered combination of two Latin words that meant "all" and "truth."

"The learning curve will be steep. If man is to ever really advance, we must move beyond the letters system and speak a universally elevated code. The Omniverit must be written and translated into the Binary language. As we go, the currently known string of ones and zeros will be condensed to make manageable words with less characters.

"I also want the verbal expressions of ones and zeros to be shortened into discernible sounds, such as 'wha' to represent 'one' and 'ze' to represent 'zero.' A new written language deserves a new spoken language."

Duvall Swan stood there with his mouth wide open, he was literally speechless. He thought to himself, *This bitch is crazy!* The more he indulged her, the more delusional she became. Furthermore, he was not at all the man for the job. He had a high school education and made it big selling drugs on the street.

He was not a computer coder or skilled in computer science. Now she piled on extreme knowledge of linguistics. Yet she has tasked him with this impossible job that (at best) would take an entire lifetime to complete. It was clear that Scilectra was a juiced-up zealot with her finger on the trigger. He thought, *God help us all!*

CHAPTER TWENTY-SIX

The Professor arrived at Lab-J71; however, legal constraints wouldn't allow him to enter the building. Much to his chagrin, this was of his own doing. He sat in his car at the edge of the parking lot, attempting to not look conspicuous. He called Ameerah on her personal cell, and when she answered, he cryptically said, "You have burned us both and time is short. I'm in the lot waiting for you."

Just hearing his voice induced her gag reflexes.

She understood clearly what he meant, and she made her way to the lot to meet him. His efforts at being incognito failed miserably; he was parked in a black sedan with limo-tinted windows and a license plate that read "PROFECT." *Really? "Professor Perfect?"* she thought to herself, *Everything about him is vain and grimy.* Thank goodness he was a fan of oversized things because his car was spacious enough to keep him out of her three feet of personal space.

He started right in. "Ameerah, you don't know what you've done disclosing our previous dealings like that. Scilectra's on a warpath! Both you and I are in her sights."

Ameerah laughed and said, "I don't know about you, but she can't hurt me the way she thinks she can, so if I were you, I'd be trying to beef up and wear a rubber suit at all times. Creeps like you get off on that S&M look anyway."

The Professor responded, "What do you mean? She can hurt everyone if she chose to. It would do you well to take this seriously!"

Ameerah's demeanor was still unchanged. "Why don't you go and ask her—she'll tell you what I mean. Now please, go away. I'm sure you're violating some type of court order being in my face!"

As she slowly scooted out of the car, running her fingers over his expensive Italian leather seats, he grabbed her hand and said, "No one can ever know what we did that night."

Ameerah hung her head low and replied back, "I was young and foolish. Believe me, I would never let you touch me again."

She exited the sedan and slammed the door. She was disgusted with herself for allowing the Professor to do what he did to her all those years ago.

Normally the Professor would scold anyone for callously slamming his car door, but he was too preoccupied with her comments to care about that now. He didn't know the extent of Scilectra's gifts. He prayed that her natural female intuition and investigative skills weren't in the "advanced powers" rotation. It was a grim ride back to the NCF lab, but he was in store for much, much more.

* * *

Way on the other side of town, Astrid's mother wanted to see her daughter. She had resigned herself to being childless when she thought that her daughter might be dead and gone. Now, knowing that she was alive and well struck a chord in her heart, and whatever was in this box had to be of some importance to Astrid. That's all she needed to begin her search.

She had the names of the young men that inquired about her background and remembered the license plate on the van. With those two pieces of information, she began her search for the unknown visitors. Pauline had learned a lot in her search for her husband and daughter, so she applied those tactics in successfully identifying the owner of the van that Raj and D.K. drove away in.

It belonged to the Research Department of Stromford University. They were more than an hour away; Pauline had plenty of time to think through what she would say to her daughter. She made certain to bring the shoebox-sized package to present to Astrid; and after all this time, she was curious to know what was inside.

Pauline drove and played tunes of Donny Hathaway, Earth, Wind & Fire, and the Doobie Brothers. She spent most of her childhood in an eclectic area of Chicago called Hyde Park. It was there she learned a healthy appreciation for Soul and Pop music. Hopefully Astrid would be happy to see her as well—she hadn't changed much; a little older and a lot wiser but still the same mother that she knew.

When Pauline arrived at the university grounds, she felt proud and impressed that her daughter was even associated with a place so prestigious. Astrid was an intense and specific child, not something many adults were fond of. She always needed an introduction and directions as to how to interact with her. She was the kind of child that held you accountable for your words; she had an eidetic memory and employed it often to remind you to honor your obligations.

If you were known to be a repeat offender of not keeping your word, to Astrid, you were considered a non-factor, faulty and damaged; you were denied contact with her completely. Pauline would hear other parents refer to Astrid as an automaton because her personality was dry, and she never did anything without a purpose. To their defense, that was her way; she was emotionally mechanical.

When she did express emotions, she did so in writing with ones and zeros. Pauline had to take a night class to learn binary in order to read Mother's Day cards from her daughter. She was all about the mind-stretching. Astrid used to say, "If it hasn't taught you something, then it's maintaining your ignorance!" *She inspired me to learn something new every day and to become a better and more improved version of myself.*

Her life's motto was, "It takes an insane and unreasonable belief in yourself in order to make your version of reality possible." What a godly trait to have. With all these memories swimming around in her head, she was amazed that she found the research lab so quickly. There was no one at the front desk, so she leaned over the counter to look for a building map of the offices and found the way to the research lab.

Pauline boarded the elevator and went down to the basement level. The doors opened to another waiting area and what appeared to be patient rooms; in the opposite direction was a wheelchair ramp declining down to a big metal door. She took her chances with the door and knocked three times. After the third rap, the door swung open to a familiar face on both sides.

It was Dr. Raj Patel, and at that moment, you could have bought him for a nickel. He was absolutely shocked.

Pauline smiled and said, "Hello again, Raj! May I come in?"

Raj took a moment to look around the room before he answered, "Yes, yes, you can."

The entire team stood up in curiosity and made their way closer to the door.

Pauline introduced herself, "Hello, everyone. My name is Pauline Acosto, and I believe you work with my daughter, Astrid."

Everyone's faces ran flushed, and you could hear a mouse peeing on cotton because it was that quiet. Pauline couldn't read the expressions on their faces, so she kept talking. "Is Astrid here at the moment? May I speak with her?"

Ameerah jumped in to stop the hemorrhaging of shock. "No, she's not here at the moment," she said, "Can we help you with anything?"

Raj followed suit and re-communicated who Pauline Acosto was.

He said, "Well, Mrs. Acosto, like she said, is Astrid's estranged mother and has not seen her for over four years. D.K. and I met with her some weeks ago at her lovely home to do a background interview for Astrid's pending employment here at the lab." The team all began to nod their heads in agreement to show that everyone was on the same page.

Raj continued, "Astrid is actually out of state on training and won't be back for several weeks. I see that you have a gift for her. May we give it to her when she returns?"

Pauline replied, "I suppose so. I really wanted to give it to her myself because I would love to find out what's in it."

Ameerah's face contorted in shock and confusion. "What do you mean? Is it not from you?"

"Oh, God, no. It was delivered to my home on Astrid's 21st birthday with strange instructions on how to open it." The team all looked at each other. They agreed in unison to keep the package safe until Astrid returned.

Mrs. Acosto left her contact information and then went on her way. Lisa couldn't unwrap the package fast enough. Under the decorative paper was an unusual rectangular metal box. It was a solid, smooth piece of metal alloy with an oval depression button in the center. No lid or lever was anywhere to be found, so there was no point in trying to pry it open.

D.K. opened the accompanying envelope that held the instructions. It read:

"The Digit . . . . . The One . . . The Nothing . . . . The Sun . . . - . . . . - . . - . .
. . - . . . . - . - . - . - . . . . - . . ."

D.K. smiled and said, "A riddle in a room of a cryptologist and coders . . . nice!"

Ameerah wasn't as optimistic. "It's a solid metal box with an oval button on it," she said. "It's more of a contraption than a riddle. It looks like we need more of a hammer and some brute force than collective intellectual effort."

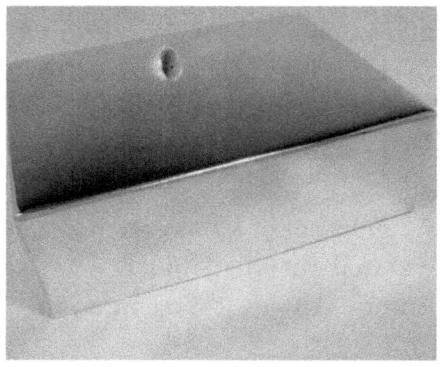

Astrid's Mysterious Box

The team spent hours going over and over the riddle. They each took turns swiping and pushing the non-distinct button. At the end of a long day . . . NOTHING!

Raj made an obvious comment and a ridiculous suggestion. "The box is apparently made for Astrid, or Scilectra, and she is the only one who can open it. Maybe we can lure her here and trick her into opening it without knowing. Another thing . . . it's important that we identify who the intended recipient is. For all intents and purposes, Astrid and Scilectra are two different people now. Astrid no longer exists, this may be a restricted case, where only one of them or neither of them may be able to open it!"

The team frowned at him in disagreement. D.K. said, "I get your logic but how in the hell are we gonna get that crazy chick here to hold a box?"

Chad responded, "Holding the box is not enough. She has to go through a process with it. It may take several minutes and some more time beyond that to reveal its purpose. Did anyone stop to think that her encountering this box may be a bad thing?"

The team fell silent—that question was definitely something to be concerned about. Whatever was in that box could make her stronger, powerful, and more dangerous.

Ameerah made an executive decision, "Let's keep the box quiet for now and learn what we can. When the time comes, we can expose it to our benefit."

Lisa reminded the team, "Whenever the contents of the box are revealed, we will still be at a disadvantage. The information may be specific to her (I'm sure), and if we find out at all, we'll be too far behind to catch up. This box should be buried and not mentioned again. I don't care if it has the cure for cancer. If it aids Scilectra in any way, it's harmful for mankind on a whole."

CHAPTER TWENTY-SEVEN

S wan made his way to Lab-J71 to inform the team about the devastating news about Scilectra. He arrived at their door, haggard and gasping for air because he was too anxious to wait for the elevator and took the stairs down. Lisa heard him fall against the door, helped him to a chair, and brought a cold bottled water. Savoy peeked around her computer monitor to see the goings-on. He was behaving as if his body rejected his newly installed nanites.

Unfortunately, the scenario was something more severe. The team listened to him intently, almost to the point of embarrassment, because Swan had been the only person in the room unaware of Scilectra's existence. The story did take an unexpected turn with the introduction of the Omniverit. Scilectra had fast-tracked her goals of being the "New God." Swan stated that he had mixed feelings about her aspirations.

"Humans have been around for over two-hundred thousand years and we still don't have a fundamental understanding of who or what God is," he said. "I would never be so simple and shallow as to worship the first celestially endowed person that I've met, but to have a physical representation of a power higher than myself . . . it's nice to put a face to a name."

"Swan, don't get it twisted!" Ameerah scorned. "Even though she is a real being, her immaculate plans are an illusion. Just because God's vestige is unseen doesn't mean that He doesn't exist. Proof of Him is all around us at any given moment. I can't look into a microscope without seeing traces of His work. Science is one of the languages that God speaks. Was that not a miracle the science performed on you the other day?

"The fact that humans exist in these organic computers should tell you something. This universe, and everything in it, is a system of choreographed events. One thing affects the next thing, and so forth. We are a plan, and plans don't happen by happenstance. Humans need to realize that it's not about what we want; it's about what we are given. A greater pain awaits one who refutes his maker."

What Ameerah had to say moved Duvall Swan to his core. He shed a tear and asked to be excused. He walked out slower and steadier then when he entered, but he was full of purpose. Swan headed back to Professor Sherman's lab to deliver a message.

This white boy from the mean streets of Philly felt like hearing a little Sam Cooke. As "A Change is Gonna Come" bellowed out of his dashboard, he wiped his tears and made his way back to the NCF. He strutted clear past the evening guards, who tried to greet him cordially at the front desk. He was a man on a mission.

He punched the elevator button over and over again. The doors couldn't open fast enough for him. On this night, he didn't mind the ride down because he was no longer cynical. He was no longer confused. Something had to be done and he was the one to do it.

The long ride down also gave him time to reflect on the changes made to his life. The thought of his new aroma made him smile. Swan lifted his arm and tucked his nose near his armpit to enjoy the sweet scent weaving through his oxford. In these short few days, he lived a life denied to him by a random genetic failure. This new regime that was pressing through could change life as he knew it.

He arrived at his destination; the doors parted, and he took a few deep breaths. Swan reached in the small of his back and pulled out a "*Riggac.*" It was a six-inch long, semi-automatic handgun prototype that he invested in some years ago. The projectiles were the size of BB gun pellets but packed the power of 50-calibre ammunition. The Riggac held up to 100 rounds and could pierce metal two inches thick with non-stop firepower.

Swan stopped at the door of Professor Sherman's lab. He paused to think of what he was about to do, and then charged into the lab, aiming his gun. Scilectra wasn't there, but the Professor was. Sherman immediately hiked his hands up in confession and said, "Mr. Swan, did I miss another meeting?"

Swan responded, "Shut up, you miscreant! I know what you have done! I've met Scilectra and she's very fond of me. I took her from that bubble up there and she offered me a job."

The Professor couldn't believe his ears. "What do you mean she offered you a job? A job doing what? You know, never mind, that's neither here nor there. You won't be doing anything for her, especially when she finds out that you're threatening me with a weapon.

"She will be back soon, in a moment to be exact. It doesn't take her long to do what she does."

Swan began to look around in a panic. More than likely, the Professor was right. Without thinking, Swan aimed up at Scilectra's Orb, flipped all the gears, and then started firing at the glass ball.

The Professor screamed "Noooooo!"

The Riggac was so powerful that the orb exploded from the projectiles colliding with the massive electricity trapped in the sphere. The explosion created an intense fire from which Swan and the Professor had to retreat.

Swan's ignorance of the innovation that he held in his hand and his lack of common knowledge of electrical currents had now triggered an explosion that was in the process of burning down the entire NCF, with him in it. Swan ran for the stairwell, but the Professor stayed. He hobbled down the corridor to salvage whatever files he could.

His delay wasn't about files; it was Scilectra. When she came back, it would be a fiery hell, or she would come back to nothing at all. He had no backup device to charge her powers, and the orb took him ten years to build. The final problem was the biggest concern: where could he keep her that would be away from prying eyes?

Swan left the Professor—he had to. There were other people in the building unaware that the building could implode in moments. It took Swan thirty minutes to reach the main floor of the NCF, where he shouted "Fire . . . Fire . . . Fire!" at the top of his lungs.

An officer said, "Where's the fire, Mr. Swan? I don't smell anything."

Swan looked back and sniffed the air. He didn't smell anything either.

Nevertheless, he said to the security guard that there was a fire in the tombs. "We need to contact the Fire Department right now!" he said.

"In the tombs?" the guard laughed.

Duvall was highly annoyed now. "What the hell are you laughing at? The Professor is down there!"

The guard responded, "That's strange, I just saw him pulling out of the parking lot fifteen minutes ago."

Duvall cried out, "What? I don't understand!"

The guard explained, "The reason that the basement is called the 'tombs,' is because they kind of are. This building was built on an old excavated rock quarry. The tombs are literarily encased in sheetrock that are at least twenty feet thick—that's why the Wi-Fi and communication signals for the building are so bad.

"That fire will die of suffocation before it burns this building down. Even the elevator shaft was hollowed out around the sheetrock. All the doors down there are made of three-inch thick metal (that's why they're so heavy); all you have to do is close the door of the room with the fire and it will contain itself until it dies out. That entire basement is like a fire-proof box."

Swan then asked, "Then how did the Professor get out of the building?"

The guard said, "There's an old exit shaft at the end of the long corridor. It leads to the rear parking lot. Most of our over-sized deliveries come in that way; it's virtually unseen from the street. All of this information is in your executive folder, just in case there is an emergency."

Swan was relieved but pissed that the Professor seemed to have bested him again.

* * *

Scilectra returned to the lab after the directive given her by the Professor. She stared, appalled, at the scene around her. The lab was nothing but a pile of ash, and Sherman was nowhere in sight. The room was a black shell; the door was closed tightly against the stone wall. Indeed, the Professor sealed the door to keep the flames localized in that one area.

She opened the door to view the rest of the facility. Everything beyond the lab was virtually untouched, but there was still no Professor. This recent trip was draining! Forever committed to their search of Heaven, he sent her to the **Virgo Cluster**, over 59 million light years away, but still more nothingness. She needed to charge in the worst way; how would that happen with no pod and no Professor? She didn't know what to do—going into the void would expend more energy that she didn't have.

Scilectra was limited to the building in which she stood and could be forced to wait for Professor Sherman or Duvall Swan. What a sad state of affairs; she was the "New God" and only had two friends. A question began to settle in her mind: "What kind of God needs help? I should be able to give myself whatever I need!"

In that very moment, Scilectra wound down to the floor and laid there, forced into idleness due to lack of power. Duvall Swan decided to venture back into the tombs to check on the damage. The guard tried to accompany him, but Swan insisted that he be there first to view the area for insurance reasons, and the guard complied.

The fortitude of this building was amazing; the further Swan descended, the smell of smoke was still almost non-existent! He would've fooled himself into believing that he imagined the entire thing had he not stumbled into Scilectra's body sprawled out on the hard, cold ground. Despite his animus toward her, karma wouldn't let him leave her there to drain out.

Sciletra's hair was limp and lifeless, their colorful strobing effects down to a flicker. Swan knew that this wasn't good, but what could he do? He thought to call the Professor and inform him that she had returned and that she needed his help. He found a signal booster on a wall and stood next to it to make the call.

Sherman picked up on the first ring. "Professor, this is Duval Swan and I'm in the tombs with a very sick visitor. What do you want me to do?"

Sherman responded, "Thank God! I can be there in ten minutes. I implore you to let go of this vendetta and assist me with a deed to save a life."

Swan replied, "Sherman, you're one of the biggest assholes I've ever seen, and when this is done, your career here with the NCF is over. I'll make certain that every license that you have is pulled and terminated. . . . DO YOU HEAR ME, YOU GUTTER BAG PIECE OF SHIT?!?!"

The Professor clutched his phantom pearls, thought, *How tacky and vulgar*, and was quick to respond, "Swan, this is not the time for unpleasantries. Surely you can wait a day to skin me like a proverbial alley cat."

Swan shouted, "Agreed!"

The Professor arrived in the tombs faster than he projected. He must have broken every traffic law in town. He came in through the private shaft carrying an item. When Sherman saw Scilectra lying on the floor limply in an infantile position, he unfolded what he was carrying; it appeared to be a cloak of some sort.

He said, "During my downtime, I got a hold of a specialized research fabric that absorbs and redistributes energy. It's much like those rubber charging pads for cell phones, except that it behaves like a solar panel. It absorbs energy, multiplies it, and then expels that magnified energy from the inside layer of the cloak onto whatever it's touching. As long as Scilectra has a decent amount of power to start with, then the cloak will do the rest.

"When she travels off the planet, the electrical currents in the stars and nearby plants will charge her like nothing in this world can. At this moment it can stop her from dying, but we have to get her a jump in order for this thing to continue to work."

Swan responded while he helped wrap Scilectra, "So this is where all of my money has been going, plotting against God? What a freaking jerk you are!"

Finally, she was cocooned, and they struggled to get Scilectra down the long hall to the shaft's exit.

The Professor thought, *Despite her relatively small frame, she is extremely heavy. I guess that Einstein's Theory of Relativity (E=mc2) is true. The fact that light or energy behaves like it has mass, and its subject to gravity. I can say with certainty now: that mass and energy do exist together.*

On the outskirts of town was a windmill farm. Recently (over the past 10 years) their town had been "Millennium-ized", a new term coined by the city for using alternative energy sources to power a high-tech society.

Fossil fuels were a thing of the past; nearly everyone in town has an electric car. The roofs of every home, building and all their sidewalks were made from resilient solar panels (made from solar panel dust and deca-black rubber). In fact, other states called them the "Millecon Valley!"

Getting Scilectra to the windmills was only half the problem. Swan asked, "How do we charge her up? How do we connect her to the base of the windmill that has no outlets?"

The Professor replied, "I have the solution right here. We need to power down one of the mills and attach this pronged metal cord. Its backside is magnetic and will adhere to the pole. We just have to align it with her spine, turn the mill back on, and watch it do its thing. Afterwards, we can take her into the windmill factory for the night; she will be safe there."

The factory was totally automated. Workmen came by once a month to check the maintenance of the equipment and the building, but beyond that, they would be alone. Scilectra charged after four hours. Sherman turned the mill off and disconnected her. She was happy to see his face and even happier to see Duvall Swan there partnering with the Professor on her behalf.

Before she could speak, the Professor offered an explanation of what happened to the lab. He said, "There was an accident while you were away. A power grid blew and caught fire."

Swan looked his direction with embarrassment on his face. He knew that Sherman could have revealed him and that would have meant his life, but he didn't, and that meant something to him. The Professor played him like a well-tuned piano; he knew that now he would have Swan as an ally, and that Swan would help with attending to the needs of Scilectra.

Swan went from being his own agent, to a double-agent, to a triple-agent. He could not make any commitments until he cleared the air with Scilectra. He went to her and asked, "Can we speak in private?"

She looked over to the Professor, displeased. There was a sense of dis-harmony in their union and she wasn't there for it.

She said, "Why, yes, of course."

Swan took a deep breath and said, "While you were away, I've had time to think and pray on your proposal."

She sharply looked down to him and questioned, "Pray?"

He replied, "I mean no disrespect. I meant to say that I have been reflecting on what you've asked of me. I'm having trouble understanding what you are and what you want to become. You have to understand: to me, God is everything. He is the author of it all and has the final say in what is and what will be. My ideology is not unique; this will be your challenge. This is a universal point of contention and will be your global push back. If you're able to find Heaven, I will bet my life that you will find Him or evidence of Him."

CHAPTER TWENTY-EIGHT

Scilectra's hair began to sway and roll with magnificent colors. They spoke something to her, and she responded with a Plato-like monologue.

"People of faith say that God just is . . . He's everything and He's everywhere at the same time. Please indulge me and define *Everything*. If God is everywhere at the same time, as the Bible states, then what else could He be if not energy?

"An indelible form of energy but nevertheless, He's energy. Light is not ever-present, nor is air, and for that matter, nor is sound. In the great Space, there's no air, therefore no sound, but energy exists in incalculable quantities full-force. Everything in the galaxies is a producer of electromagnetic energy that continually feeds the growth of the universe.

"If He is, in fact, real, I don't seek to kill him, because I can't. I desire to replace Him with a physical presence, to bond mankind with a source that they cannot and will not question. People seek and create multiple religions out of vanity, coupled with a lack of a verified and credible sources. Have you ever noticed that each god created is created by whomever physically looks like the people worshipping it?

"Caucasians have a savior that looks like them, people of color have the exact same savior but changed his skin tone to reflect their own, and the Indian deities are patterned after their images, etc . . . With the exception of worshipping animals, vanity plays a major role in praying to a God that's certain to not have any flesh at all!

"What I offer is the best of both worlds, with a distinct advantage of remaining in a human appearance while having the power of a creator."

Swan mildly interrupted with a question, "But what have you created?"

Scilectra stopped walking mid-step, turned, and stared at Duvall for several seconds before she spoke.

She said, "I don't feel the need to demonstrate on you the extent of my powers because, in this particular instance, I agree with you. There has been no formal constitution of my work established. I'll be meditating on what I will bring into being. For now, leave me to myself."

Swan was grateful to exit the conversation alive. He quickly left the room. He wanted to speak with the Professor before he left the facility.

Sherman sat at a console with head in hand; he was deep in thought about the condition of his lab and what to do next.

"Professor," Swan said. "We have to figure this out. What exactly is your endgame?"

The Professor replied, "Not here. Let me walk you out."

The two exited the facility and chatted on the way to the car. "As I have confessed to Scilectra, she was a theory of mine from many years ago. I have always been an eccentric man, and one thing I've learned from psychology is that 'the way you do one thing is the way you do everything.' Hopefully this matter of being explains the anomaly in that building. The redirection of God was . . . is something that fascinates me, or at least the possibilities of it. 'As above, so below,' as it were. I'm not saying that I'm right for doing this, but the Bible states: '*For He who is in you is greater than he who is in the world. ~John 4:4*'

"Yes, I gave life to my own interpretation of that, but name me a person or a church (for that matter) that doesn't exaggerate or purposely misinterpret the Bible for their own benefit. For four hundred years, this was the only play in the playbook of people that instituted, justified, and perpetuated slavery.

"Science can be a lethal addition for which no one is seeking a cure. In fact, the drug is willfully adulterated every day, and we love the high it gives. Just like that first hit of crack, we scientists are always in search of that 'first high,' We're never going to get it, but oh what fun is the chase!"

Once again, Swan was rendered speechless. What has he invested millions and millions of dollars into?

He asked the Professor, "Why did you choose Scilectra to this ambitious position?"

The Professor sighed and said, "Funny that you asked me that. May I confide in you about something?" Swan nodded his head. "Ameerah was my first choice. I never formally told her of my research in Angelology. I misled her to believe that for the nanites' viability it needed to be done on a young, virtual woman with certain genetic coding. I knew that if she had known exactly what I was doing she would have put a stop to it immediately.

"She agreed to test and to do a physical. I'm not a perfect man; I shouldn't have done the exam knowing that I had certain feelings for her. The physical had to be invasive and thorough. Shamefully, I got carried away and used my hands in her reproductive area very inappropriately. She was under a light sedation and woke up in the middle of my exam; needless to say, she was highly pissed off, and I was completely embarrassed."

Swan thought that he could not be shocked anymore, and then there's that! "Sherman, what the hell is on your mind?! On top of all that you've done . . . you're a rapist too?!"

The Professor was quick to respond, "I never penetrated her. I had to prove that she was a virgin and I did! A couple days later, I left the lab and made the NCF my full-time responsibility. I'm sorry for what I did to her . . . very sorry indeed! That doesn't negate that she was/is the perfect candidate for the **Reconfigured Angelology** realization. It just so happens that Astrid (now Scilectra) came willing able to do the job. I had even starting dosing Ameerah with the Aurovian to begin her journey, but I did so without her approval. Scilectra has a brilliant nexus ingrained in her DNA, but unfortunately so is an extreme level of malevolence. Ameerah was the best choice."

CHAPTER TWENTY-NINE

P art of Ameerah's job at the lab was to work in conjunction with NASA to unlock mysteries of our known and unknown universe. As of late, the tagged souls played an enormous part in providing usable data to grow on.

During a recent conversation with a noted astrophysicist, Ameerah asked an astutely brilliant question: "If we think of an Event Horizon like an extremely high wall in our neighborhood that we can't see over, it's impossible to see what's on the other side. However, we're able to measure the size of the place beyond the wall by the number of voices, noise, and commotion that we hear.

"Other qualifiers are the frequent activities and the enormous amounts of garbage thrown over the wall onto our side. In relationship to the Black Hole, the facts are that we can't see past the Event Horizon in order to discern palpable and detailed truths about it. My theoretical question is this: 'Is it possible that our universe is an Event Horizon to other universes outside of ours?'"

The doctor was floored by the question. She said, "Huh . . . I have never thought of it like that. That's a real possibility that can be put on the table as a theoretical study. This is how research begins. You ask the questions, do the research and hopefully solve the problem. That's a very good question!"

This conversation gave Ameerah an idea. She decided to brush up on theology and use her findings to aid in their search.

What if Heaven is "outside" our known universe?

She went to the team and said, "I think we should be looking for Heaven's Event Horizon. The gravitational pull would be humongous compared to others."

Lisa interjected, "It won't work. Heaven is not like the local grocery store. We can't just send souls there for a pack of cigarettes; they have to be allowed in. Furthermore, from all the data we've received, Heaven and Hell are secondary final locations; they have to go to a holding location first. The only solid evidence that we can quantify are the census and audio/visual accounts of the tagged souls."

Ameerah shrugged her shoulders and said, "Damn, I forgot. This sucks! We have to find a way to maximize our progress. Whoever is best at Fregodian should start asking the souls more detailed questions. We can't lose this faith race. It really is a matter of life and destiny."

Lisa piped in, "The thing is ... everything Scilectra's stating is fact—there's very little conjecture, if any. Where's the fight with her? According to all my research, it appears that humans are an Earth-created product. Our flesh is the weight that keeps us bound to this planet. It lets you know where you can and can't go.

"Space has done an excellent job of keeping humans at bay, however ... it will accommodate our souls. There's proof that we are alive and that part of us goes elsewhere when we die, but no proof of what gives us life in the first place. Faith is a hell of an ask! Sherlock Holmes has stated (and it bears repeating), 'When you have eliminated the impossible, whatever remains, however improbable, must be the truth.' Her facts have given her a perception of God that's not necessarily wrong. We, as scientists, are fact-based creatures. Faith is a choice that requires belief with no substantial proof. Are we trying to prove facts or faith? Because if it's 'facts,' just to be clear, we should be on her side."

Ameerah was taken aback by Lisa's rant. Nevertheless, she was right. Along the way, she had lost sight of the entire purpose of the experiment, and that was to prove that theoretical locations existed. Scilectra has a separate agenda, but that agenda could impact life on Earth as they knew it. Ameerah wasn't willing to take that chance, but she didn't want to risk her team to pursue her own vendettas.

There was an unexpected knock on the lab's door, it was so late in the evening that whomever it was wanted to meet in private. D.K. offered to open the door, just in case he needed to intimidate the visitor. It was none other than Duvall Swan, looking as if he were drug through the mud behind a car.

D.K. asked, "Why is it that every time you come here, you look worse and worse?"

Swan replied, "Unfortunately, it's been one of those type of nights."

Ameerah walked over to the door and asked jokingly, "What's going on, Swan? You're becoming a frequent visitor. Should we make you part of the team?"

"You jest," he said, "but that question may ring true once I tell you what happened earlier this evening." Swan gave a full recounting of the events with Scilectra and Professor Sherman. Afterwards, he asked to speak with Ameerah alone to discuss Sherman's confession and what it might all mean in the long run.

"Sherman spoke to me in confidence, and normally I would have honored that agreement, but not when it comes to breaking the law by committing a heinous offense. Sherman violated you and your trust by what he did, and I cannot abide by that. He harangued me into helping with Scilectra (for the moment) but soon, I will be removing myself from them and withdrawing from the NCF. This shit here is beyond my pay grade. Before I go, I will give you all of the information that I have to put a stop to the madness, and hopefully put me back on track with God's will for my life."

Just to hear about her experience from another person hurt Ameerah deeply. At one point, she considered Professor Sherman as a father figure and a mentor. She never had an inkling that his intentions for her were less than pure. She did gain some insight from the conversation with Swan, and she realized why Sherman was fixated on metamorphosizing her into this celestial being. She shared some interesting information that they learned from the enlightened tagged souls.

"Duvall, may I share something with you that may shed some light on Sherman's thinking? Our tagged souls have a wealth of data that they've learned being in a more elevated status. One of those things is this: the color of your skin is just a representation of your environment. God created one race on earth. Once people began to populate, they chose to scatter throughout into their own clans all over the world. Where they decided to inhabit determined what color or tone their skin took.

"Life choices and natural developments did the rest. How they spoke, what they ate, daily activities, and their mannerisms were an evolutionary choice made by them for the survival of their sect. Over time, their DNA adjusted to the conditions and solidified as a type of people. This scenario made one clan visually different from another clan in alternate conditions. What was the original color of man, you ask? Scientifically speaking, you can't get various hues from something that has none.

"Let's just say the deeper the tone, the wider the color spectrum options that can come from it. With that said, my ethical background is of significant importance to make his theoretical experiment a success. He achieved something but he didn't obtain his desired goal. I'll tell you like I told Scilectra . . . this black girl magic is the equation missing in that formula. Sherman knows it, she knows it, and I know it! I don't put it past him to try it again. Duvall, thank you for the help, but it's best that you wrap up your affairs and get out of town before you can't."

After she walked Swan out, she stopped by Raj's desk to ask him for a favor. She wanted another exam. Ameerah thought that there might be another reason that she was the perfect candidate, something that the Professor knew and she didn't. Raj obliged and took Ameerah in for another round of tests, but this time he dove deeper for hidden abnormalities. Once the tests were done, Raj went over them with a fine-tooth comb. Lo and behold, there was a glorious abnormality.

Ameerah's pineal gland was twice the size of a normal human being and it had a crystalized barrier around it that constantly produced and reflected light. The pineal gland's main purpose was to produce a single—but key—hormone, which was melatonin. Melatonin production determines sleep-wake cycles and is purely determined by the detection of light (you're awake) and dark (you're asleep). The retina sends these signals to the brain region which passes on to the pineal gland. The more light your brain detects, the less melatonin it produces, which means the less sleep you get.

Ameerah's brain didn't have "sleep cycle," but of course her body eventually succumbed to the fatigue and fell asleep. That's why her dreams were so real and vivid, because (to her mind) she was awake! The size of the gland indicated that she had double the capacity for processing an alternate reality, dreams, as an actual waking reality. Her sleeping world was a tangible reality to her and could have real-life implications between the two worlds.

Depending on her depth of sleep, she might be able to bring things back from her dream world to the physical world. Raj didn't know how to explain this to her; the fact was that he didn't understand it fully himself. He texted her to come to the conference room to go over the results. She sat there quietly while he spoke; she didn't ask one question. At the end of his hour-long diagnosis, he shared some news that was off topic.

He said, "You have a powerful ability. In many ways, you can do what Scilectra does, but without all the souped-up bells and whistles. You naturally have the gifts that she was surgically implanted with. Your access to interstellar travel is by way of your dreams. The Aurovian has been feeding more light to your brain and as a result, your pineal gland. Your waking world and your sleeping world are one-in-the-same.

"I'm hypothesizing that your astral-self may not be tethered to you. 'You' are its beacon and it travels as far as it wants. It will hone into you when it's ready to return (like a carrier pigeon). Once you learn how to access the dream realm while you're awake, that's when it's 'game on' with you and Scilectra!"

Ameerah's head spun with all of the news. She was even angrier at Professor Sherman—he must've known this and made plans to use her for his benefit! She wasn't up for this fight. Not today, not ever.

CHAPTER THIRTY

Scilectra was bothered by Duvall's challenge. She was at a loss on what to create that would be on par with the God humankind accepted as "The One." Mustering life that would evolve and worship you is great, but it's been done before; she had to be better than that! He's cornered the market on planet-building too. After all, He's the greatest inventor in the history of the universe.

Even so, there had to be an unseen choice to be made. Before all of this, as a child, Astrid was captivated by science, and all the possibilities that it held. She thought back on being frustrated about not being able to achieve this goal or that aspiration. Mankind is riddled with individuals desiring to be different; their visual image of themselves never coincides with what they are able to truly become.

Scilectra decided that her original creation would be a science-based product, reimagining the DNA format to include a piece of her genetic makeup for purposes of transformation. This DNA strand would no longer look like a spiral ladder, but like a chain of Phi symbols. The design was specific in that they would always be in regeneration mode with never-ceasing activity. It would also be linked to the sections of the brain that control thought and belief.

She spent time in the new facility alone so that she could perfect the math of genesis. Her design had to have no beginning and no end; it would start crude and grow into the divine. Hours went into days, and days went into weeks; her creation had to be perfect. When she finished, she named the phenomena "A.T.I" for *Advanced Thought Integration*. When seeded into a human, these "Phi-based" DNA strands would map over and replace the current genetic code.

The end result would be a human who would be able to manifest his/her thoughts physically in himself/herself. If women visualized themselves thin and fit, blonde hair versus brown hair, tall instead of short, this genetic data was the beginning stages of visualizing external physical matter. The secret didn't have to be a secret anymore—willful manifestation would be an achievable right of life and not a right of deeds. She conversed with her hairs and disclosed her innermost thoughts.

"The right mathematical sequence will erase human dependency on prayers and waiting on God. His decisions of 'If they're worthy to receive' will be reduced down to zero! I don't need to be prayed to for mankind to thrive and flourish—they will have all the tools they need to sustain themselves. After all, the Bible says, *'I have said, Ye are gods; and all of you are children of the most high.'* If man is too simple to claim their rightful place, in their Father's creations, then I will! Personally, knowing what we know now, I wouldn't be surprised if He had no human characteristics at all.

"Life and the universe (as we know it) can be explained and justified with mathematics. Many facts point to Him being an astronomically advanced mathematical equation, and scripture states God cannot lie; the strangest coincidence is ... neither can math! God may be a system of sophisticated numbers.

"If He is Math ... He is the 'First and Last Equation,' the very seed of life in which all other systems and patterns are built upon!"

As required by science, all theories have to be tested and proven in order to be accepted whole. Scilectra's plan was two-fold, to solidify her own worldly wonder and then to find out if Heaven was a factual place. If so, God could be verified then.

* * *

Professor Sherman spent the day at his NCF office. He had to keep up appearances and go about repairing the burned lab. Finding contractors to repair the lab was going to be tricky; the fire brought about a new curiosity from the members of the organization. On top of that, Duvall Swan was missing. His unusual absence forced Sherman to reach out to Lab-J71 to ask what they knew.

Swan's unlikely alliance with the team was a fly in the Professor's ointment and undoing it was a bonus goal, but for now, he needed their help. Legally, the Professor had to keep his distance from the lab, so another visit was out of the question. Calling Ameerah was the only sensible option, so he braced himself and dove in head-first.

Ameerah was busy with translations when her cell phone rang from an unknown number. Normally she didn't answer such calls, but with everything going on nowadays, every call determined one fate or another.

She answered, "Yes, this is Dr. Mahar, may I help you?"

The voice on the other end replied, "Doctor, it's so rare that you utilize your official title that I had almost forgotten that you have earned the right to be called that."

Ameerah became incensed. "How dare you call me like we are old friends! I really hate to keep punching your card about your insidious ways, but my soul won't let me stop. I had a re-examination, this time it was done on a granular scale. The results are nothing short of spectacular, but I'm assuming that you know this already. Now I know why it had to be me, why you experimented on me in my sleep and why you're still slithering around now. I'm the perfect vessel for your laboratory experiment! Instead of having something great . . . you have a mediocre attempt at what you've imagined God to be."

The Professor tried to interrupt but Ameerah kept talking over him. "After I spoke with Swan today even more, questions ran through my mind. Did you know that he questioned Scilectra, he asked her 'What have you created?' It's a pivotal question, but it goes deeper than that. She doubts the Bible and what it says. By her understanding, the Bible is false, Heaven doesn't exist, and by that definition . . . neither does God. Scilectra's challenging the entire notion of our architect's system that she exists in, all the while not producing anything greater than He. If she does create something, can she sustain it? Give it an environment so that it can evolve, or create a matrix, so that things can work in conjunction with entities around it? In short, does she have the wisdom and power to develop a flawless integrated system that will last forever?"

"AMEERAH!" the Professor yelled, "May I speak now? You're correct, what I envisioned is not what I received. Your sentiments are duly noted, but what I've achieved is absolutely uncanny nonetheless. Your animus toward Scilectra and myself are warranted, but regretfully, I can't put the genie back in the bottle. She's a thing now!

"My yearning for you went beyond the professional (I admit), but can you blame me? You are beautiful, brilliant, and genetically gifted, there's not a man alive that would ignore that. I do agree that this being is out of control—"

Ameerah interrupted, "She's an atrocity!"

The Professor fired back, "Semantics. She's here now and if you would just help me, we could find a way to whittle her down to a comfortable manageability."

"Screw you, Sherman. What did you call me for? Because I don't have time for this right here!"

He said, "All right, Ameerah. I see that you're feeling highly rambunctious today, so I will state my case. I'm looking for Duvall Swan. Do you know where he may be?"

She responded, "No, I don't. I sent him away, and told him to get out of town before he gets killed."

"Listen to me, Ameerah. It's paramount that you contact Duvall and convince him to return. Everyone's lives depend on this. Scilectra is quite unpredictable, but for some unknown reason, she trusts him. I cannot return to her without him! Our global narrative could change in the blink of an eye. There's no optimistic way to look at this scenario without Swan here."

"Are you nuts, Sherman? I sent him away to save his life, and now you want me to bring him back because it makes your insane and out-of-touch girlfriend happy? Where they do that at? Ah . . . no sir!"

"Ameerah, I can gather you're still upset by your colorful use of urban colloquialisms, but don't cut off your nose to spite your face on this one. Please cool down and let's reconvene soon. Good day!"

Ameerah didn't know why Sherman was in a panic. Whatever it was, she decided to head it off at the pass. The mysterious box was still in her possession and she thought it high time to use it for some much-needed leverage. She called a meeting for the team to discuss their next steps.

She tasked Raj, Chad, and Savoy with a detailed examination of the box. On the list was an X-ray, weight, dimensions, and possible shavings to identify the type of metal it was. Were there internal mechanics, or did it respond to chemical reactions? Unless the team could open it, at some point, the unit would have to be turned over to Scilectra. However, being educated on its functionality could give the Lab enough of an upper hand to maneuver the situation in their favor.

Raj returned with more perplexing questions than he did answers. He said, "The tests are inconclusive regarding the type of metal alloy the box is made from. It doesn't fit any of the known current and available profiles. We weren't able to scratch, chip, pierce, or bend it. We tried to burn it and simmer it down for a melt . . . and nothing. The material is extremely dense, but we were able to see a rough mapping of the inside of the device.

"It has an elongated narrow (width-wise) chamber inside, just under the top surface. The chamber is empty with a small canal that feeds directly into the chamber, from right underneath the button on top of the box. Lastly, inside the button is a tiny tube that houses a small needle. Other than that, we have no idea how these excavations got on the inside since there is no indication that this box can or ever has been opened.

"The box weighs exactly three pounds and fourteen ounces. Its measurements are (in total) L-12in x W-9in x H-3.5in. The results on chemical reactions were inconclusive as well; the material doesn't seem to be porous, but we tried every caustic and acidic product that we could get our hands on anyway. My guess is (with the discovery of the needle on the push button), that the device will activate after a blood sample is taken from its intended user."

Ameerah asked, "How does it know who its intended user is?"

Lisa stepped into the conversation for her perspective. "The button that houses the needle may be a fingerprint scanner of some sort. It really is quite genius; it has fail-safe after fail-safe to make sure that the wrong person doesn't open it and gain whatever contents it holds. Assuming that Astrid/Scilectra's fingerprint has not changed with her transformation, she may be able to open it. Then again, the metamorphosis she experienced has almost assuredly changed her basic DNA, and therefore her blood."

Ameerah thought back on her earlier conversation with Professor Sherman, about working together to tame Scilectra. She might have to eat her words, and work with the Devil incarnate himself.

CHAPTER THIRTY-ONE

S imon and Savoy steered away from the politics of their other team-mates. The souls needed monitoring, and someone had to stay on top of the fundamental goal of finding the Golden Coordinates. Simon did most of the questioning and translating himself, and he separated the significant data from the trivial banter. His steadfast dedication was by design.

His initial involvement with this research was more out of curiosity. He didn't think that it could be done. When the team reached an apex in their research, his curiosity turned into concern. So he made himself available and overly useful so that he could establish a connection with the tagged souls. Several of the souls seemed to have bonded with Simon and communicated with him exclusively.

If the other team members found out, it could threaten the whole experiment; they would consider it 'tainted'. So he secretly interacted with them under the guise of translating. Simon was extremely invested in what the souls had to say, mainly because he was an Orthodox Christian, which was something that the team didn't know. Members of this faith (for those who know) were deemed to be zealots. An Orthodox would never do anything to tamper with God's plans. Simon disclosed that his faith as Christian, and he decided not to go into detail regarding what type of Christian he was.

Most people are satisfied with a generic label that covers many sects of the same faith. This church is the first and the oldest Christian church in the world, founded by the Messiah himself, with its beginnings chronicled in the "New Testament." All other Christian churches and groups can be historically traced back to it. This faith is only second in size to the Roman Catholic Church. Despite its massive member count, it exists in relative obscurity to the world as a whole. The Orthodox Church has deep roots in Christian antiquity and is steeped in biblical tradition. It's been the foundation of Christian living for millions of people for nearly twenty centuries.

Although Simon was on the team, he appointed himself to work on behalf of his organization to keeps God's word and whereabouts sacred. He had no intentions of providing the Golden Coordinates to the team. He had instructed his chosen souls to provide misleading information to confuse the research and delay them at all cost. Those particular souls were kept in his log book, which was on his person at all times.

It was difficult keeping his personal agenda from Savoy because they worked so closely together. To his shock, her Fregodian was approaching the level of instructor versus student. Because of this, Simon has instituted phrases that only he and certain souls knew, so that he could remain incognito as long as possible. What he did know, but hadn't shared with the team, is that they were very close to finding the "A-Coordinate."

He only reported that one percent of the total souls made it to the realm that they had (tentatively identified) as "Heaven." The real percentage was closer to fifty-nine. Their in-office gauge to declaring proof was eighty-five percent. If Ameerah knew the real numbers was as high as fifty-nine percent, she would task all of them to ramp up and innovate a way to do a final verification. He could not allow that to happen.

* * *

Ameerah dreaded the call; as life would dictate, she was literally "taking one for the team." The only way to do it was just to rip the Band-Aid off in one motion. The phone barely rang one time before he answered.

"Ameera, dear. Have you calmed down yet?"

She felt a frog-sized lump in her throat. She took a big gulp and responded, "Professor, let me start by saying this: there's no honor among thieves, but dammit ... there needs to be some order! Hopefully you get my drift. If we are to work on this project together, you have to be above board at all times. Also, I have a confidential matter to discuss with you, but not here at the lab. Let's meet in the park by Lake Bon Lac in forty-five minutes. I'll send the coordinates."

He was overjoyed about the temporary partnership and left home immediately to meet with her by the lake.

Ameerah wasn't sure if he was up to the task of tricking Scilectra, but now was the time to find out if he was a team player. She wrapped the box up and drove over to the lake to meet Sherman. When she arrived, he was in his signature color and wearing a greasy smile on his face. She prayed that she could get through the meet without punching his lights out. Sherman tried to help her out of the van, but Ameerah yanked her arm from him.

He said, "If we are to be partners, can we at least be civil to one another? You make me fear for my safety with your oscillating hostility."

Ameerah rolled her eyes and replied, "If a man is ignorant, I can teach him; if a man is hungry, I can feed him; but if a man is fearful, I can't do shit with that!"

The Professor had to giggle at her natural quick wit. He was careful not to show her that he was yet again aroused.

He stated, "Now that that's out of the way. What did you want to meet about?"

Ameerah ran down the story of Astrid's mother and the mysterious box. The Professor was excited to touch it and feel around it, looking for clarity.

She explained that Scilectra had to be the one to open it; however, it was important that he find out what it did. That revelation had to be given to her and the team immediately.

"Her mother wants to see her ... she wants to see 'Astrid.' You might not want to share that part of the story with her. Do me a favor and leave the Lab out of the narrative, if you please."

"Then how do you suppose that I explain this box?" he asked.

"I don't know, Professor. Tell her that it's a new innovation of yours. I'm sure you'd love to take the credit for it!"

Sherman curled up his nose at her and made the sound of a hissing cat to suggest that she was being catty. Deep down, the Professor was pleased; if these were the only conversations to be had with Ameerah, then he would gladly accept them, attitude and all.

He said, "That proposal sounds more authentic and less problematic than introducing her mother into the picture . . . We'll go with that!"

Before they parted, he was sure to get close enough to her in passing to get a tantalizing whiff of her nubile essence. The Professor was determined to have her one day with permission and full participation. What he was doing didn't go unnoticed; instead of Ameerah objecting, she decided to act aloof to his yearnings. This could be a way to play chess while he's playing checkers. Ameerah had full confidence that he would do whatever was necessary to open that box, and that was all she wanted.

She purposely passed him slowly; tossing him a bone was part of the game. He lapped up every lingering second; he was never more malleable than at this very moment. Being a desirable woman was every bit the weapon that God designed it to be, an organic, effortless, and painless napalm bomb. Ameerah had never been with a man, but fully understood the power that her gender status wielded.

Her mother used to say, "It's in a woman's nature to be a woman, no matter what religion, faith, or culture. God gave use certain attributes that are to be reveled in and celebrated. I don't mean that women should abuse that fact or use it as a weapon. But if our fellow male counterparts keep finding themselves imprisoned by our nature, one would suggest they build up some kind of armor to make it through the day."

Ameerah knew that Sherman had no armor, nor a desire to construct any. His lust would launch one thousand ships for them to win the war.

CHAPTER THIRTY-TWO

S ciletra's blood was a key element to complete her newly designed life forms. She had a previous conversation with Professor Sherman, and time alone to think and process had taken precedence. It was clear that he was not ready for what was about to happen, and Scilectra didn't want him contaminating her plans.

She stood in a glass bin while she purged blood directly from her body. No needles were necessary; it oozed out of her pores like a leaking bag. It was important that the blood came in contact with her flesh, skin, and the hairs on her body. Her blood was a natural element that evaporated when exposed to air, so it had to be bottled immediately to maintain its integrity.

The bin was capped for the next level of processing. Her blood-soaked body only took a few minutes to be completely disbursed by the oxygen in the room. Everything about her was transformative. She was pure energy at this point, with nothing to discard. If she were to die, her electrons and neutrons would just disassemble and disperse into another formation.

She thought to herself, *My blueprint is perfect!*

Scilectra put a sample of her blood on the glass slide, so she could get a closer look of her altered DNA.

She stared through the microscope lens in surprise—her DNA was nowhere near that of a human. In fact, it was the opposite . . . her genetic code resembled that of a bee's honeycomb. Rods of linear octagons rotating clockwise and counter-clockwise, each from the one beneath it. This may have had to do with the necessary electrical charges flowing through her body in order for her to exist, like an AC/DC relationship.

She was undecided on how to deploy the "*A. T.I Gene.*" Disrupting an already existing human to improve upon it wasn't exactly a core innovation. They would be viewed as nothing more than experiments. What she had to do was create a non-existing, unique entity that served a higher purpose.

Scilectra could sense the Professor approaching. She wasn't ready to divulge her work, so she took her blood-filled canister to a previously visited location in the void. There, she knew it would be safe and untampered with.

The Professor walked into the facility with all smiles. He said, "I come bearing gifts! While over at the NCF, a package bearing your name arrived."

She replied, "Really? How is that so?"

Sherman had to think quickly on his feet, since he diverted from the planned story. "When I considered you for employment, I advertised your name in our online employee database. All one would need to do is put your name in a search engine, to find out where you are employed."

She swallowed the explanation whole with no pushback at all. He had jumped the first hurdle. Now the real convincing would have to begin.

Scilectra unwrapped the box, ran her fingers over the surface, lifted it up to her face, and took several deep breaths. She shook it to listen to its contents.

The Professor interrupted, "Oh, there is a note."

Scilectra took the note. It was very familiar to her. It was a typed note, but the jargon brought back memories of conversations she had with her father many years ago. On the back of the note was a thin brown streak. She smelled it and her eyes widened, and she opened her mouth to lick the stain. Suddenly, she let out a wail, crying and squeezing the box tightly to her chest.

She said, "It's from my father! He wants to tell me something, something important!"

"I thought your father was dead," the Professor said.

"I never told you that. He was taken by someone in the shadows, and I hoped that he would come back. Even if he didn't, I had my instructions to follow, to the letter," Scilectra explained.

The Professor asked, "What does the note mean? Will you share it with me?"

Scilectra didn't respond verbally, but she went about opening the box per the instructions on the card. She knew which finger to use: the "impedicus," or the middle finger. Her father told her long ago that the middle finger was the longest because it was the most important in achieving balance and symmetry and that it was the strongest finger on the human hand. This one digit could exert the most strength (while straight) to support the entire body.

She smiled while she followed the riddle. The Professor watched as she tapped her finger on the silver button. He was surprised to see blood flow out and evaporate into the air. The button was puncturing her over and over again, taking samples of her blood, but why?

Scilectra said, "I have to expose this box to sunlight. What time of day is it?"

The Professor responded, "My dear, it's almost midnight. Let me think." He tilted his head down and tried to find a remedy. "Ah ha! Wait one moment." He ran to a back room of the plant and brought out a lamp. "This is a UV light. It will mimic the rays of the sun. It's not as hot or as bright, but it should do the trick."

Scilectra placed the box under the bright light and waited for it to open. Twenty minutes passed and the box remained unopened. She walked away in disappointment. Her father couldn't have known what she would become, not entirely.

The Professor reached over to turn the light off, and a long series of numbers began to appear on the face of the box. The box was not meant to be opened. Instead, Scilectra's blood samples reacted with the metal and revealed its content on its surface. The Professor quickly jotted the numbers down and stuck the note in his pocket.

He turned the light off and the numbers faded away. He said, "Scilectra, dear, please allow me to take the box back to the NCF and research a little more. Maybe the computers on the other side of my lab can trace information to find out where the box may have come from."

Before the Professor parted, Scilectra requested that he bring Swan to her. She said, "My recorder should be by my side at all times. What's taking place should be written down for future generations."

The Professor was careful not to sigh openly. He had to convince Ameerah to help him find Swan before it was too late.

* * *

Swan replayed the conversation with Ameerah over and over in his head. His first instinct was to run and save himself. He wanted to be a coward, but this was bigger than his fear of dying. Supporting Scilectra was further-ing her maddening agenda. His phone rang again—yet another call from Sherman. The call was no doubt a half-assed attempt to cajole him into coming back into the fold.

It was too late. Swan was on a train headed to the other side of the country. From there, he had a flight to Thailand, where he had chosen to live out the rest of his days. His phone rang again, and this time it wasn't Sherman. It was Ameerah. He looked at the phone as it rang once, twice, and then three times. Everything in him said to let it go to voicemail, but he couldn't.

"Hello?" he responded, "Yes, Ameerah, how can I help you?"

"Look, I know that I told you to go, and I hate myself for asking, but can you come back?" Ameerah asked.

He replied, "Come back? Why? What's going on?"

She responded, "Duvall, we have had to align the lab with the Professor, and there may be a way to deal with . . ." A series of deafening beeps sounded in the background. "OH NO! Gotta go!" Ameerah hastily ended the call. The lab's perimeter alarm was sounding off, meaning that Scilectra was in the building. That was a problem.

Ameerah, the Professor, and the box were in the lab, and Scilectra knew it.

Scilectra sounded off, "Now this is a strange sight to see. My maker and my contrast, together." She continued, "Ameerah, I guess that the Professor neglected to tell you that one of my gifts is the ability to intercept all digital communications. Anything utilizing Wi-Fi and frequencies like it is a playground for me. This evening, the Professor was too eager to take my box. Shortly after he left, I intercepted his call to Duvall and then to you."

Sherman stood still in shame as she circled the room, carefully staying far away from Ameerah.

"Yes, I heard you mention to Duvall that you are now allies in a joint effort to quell my advancement to deity status," Scilectra accused. "Where is Swan now?"

Ameerah responded, "We don't know. Why is he so important to your agenda?"

"See now, Ameerah, you're minding my business again and there will be hell to pay for you soon. Until then, I think you're right. I've put too much stock in Duvall," Scilectra mused. "I will follow his cellular frequency and find him myself. Professor, I have something special for you when I return." Then, she was gone as quickly as she came.

Sherman was in a panic. "Ameerah, what does she mean by that? I'm at a loss—I can't talk her down. Please help me!"

Ameerah pushed past his panic, "What can I do? Tell me quickly— what did you learn from the box?"

The Professor reached into his lab jacket and pulled out a small notepad with a sequence of numbers on it. He said, "The box doesn't open, but it revealed these numbers on the surface. I wrote them down in the order that they appeared. There were no dots or dashes that I could see. The numbers would only reveal themselves in sunlight or under a UV light after twenty minutes or so. Here, take them! There's no running or hiding for me. I will do better waiting here for her return. Maybe I can talk her down. There has to be a plausible excuse that she'll accept."

Ameerah bit her fingernails as she thought about what to do next. Technically, Scilectra wasn't a huge threat to her at the moment, but that didn't mean that she wasn't an overall concern. "Professor, you know her best. What will neutralize this situation for everyone?"

The Professor explained, "I've never seen her aggressively distrustful of me. This is new territory for me. We have a bond, but it's not above reproach. Now, it seems that she has set her sights on Duvall Swan."

CHAPTER THIRTY-THREE

S wan worried about the bizarre conversation with Ameerah that ended abruptly. Nevertheless, he was stuck on the train, at least until the next stop. He was going to call her back but decided to let it go until he could make his way back to Shadowmoor. He laid back and closed his eyes to get some rest. He had an inkling that this would be the last occasion for "me time" for a good long while.

The passenger train's light was turned down for the passengers to get some rest. Swan had sprung for a semi-private sleeping car, which was nothing more than two seats with partitions around them for privacy. He was frugal when it came to things for himself. He patterned himself after J. Paul Getty in that way.

Seat reclined with his eyes closed, but he was awakened by the scent of burning wires. He opened his eyes to see Scilectra in all of her glory, right before his face. He was so petrified he couldn't say a word, and all of his joints seemed to be locked in place. He could see her pale face reflecting the dim lights in his unit as her hair strobed wildly with color.

She said, "May I have a seat?"

He replied, "Why yes, of course!"

"Where are you going, Duvall? She whispered. "You're my transcriber and you're leaving with your work undone. Before you speak, let me share something. I understand solitude. My father told me before he left, 'Don't be afraid to be alone, all life was created out of solitude.' If that's why you're leaving—because of the weight of it all—and you need to be alone, then I understand. However, I have a job to do, and not everyone will agree with or understand my plans. I thought you did. I felt that you did. Eyes are important for the body, but vision is paramount for the mind. Not everyone has vision. Vision is vital in order to create! It's my duty to research and understand what is invisible and to make things tangible, for those who cannot see. My elevation is not about me, it's about freeing mankind from repetitive bondage. I will use that same vision to look past you, if you want to go. If you do, I will let you go. You will take what you know to the next plane, and there I'll find you and you will continue my work from there."

He responded in confusion, "Wait, what?"

Scilectra stood up, glowing with electricity. The train seemed to speed up, and Swan looked outside the window to see the trees and light posts go by faster and faster, until they were a blur of light and darkness.

Scilectra was pulling Swan into the void, and he was experiencing time at multiple speeds at once. She took him so suddenly that the transition seemed to be an extension of the trees and lampposts outside, a blend of interment flashes of lights, circling them from every angle. The winds moved so fast that they cut like razor blades.

He couldn't secure one whiff of air in this place. Swan looked at her with a helpless sorrow in his eyes while she held him at arms' length, dangling in space. Scilectra gave him one last glance before she unceremoniously let him go, to be victimized by the past, present and future of the void. She released him and he was ripped from her grasp, gone, never to return.

Upon her arrival back in the lab, Scilectra proudly declared, "Duvall is no more."

Ameerah stood in shocked silence.

The Professor began to yell and scream, and asked, "What does that mean? What did you do?"

Scilectra casually replied, "I did what needed to be done. Duvall dishonored our agreement and that cannot stand. The sadness that I have within me now is not for the life I took, but for the one who gave me life. Professor, you have shaken me to my core, and you must be dealt with accordingly. I will see you soon. As for you, Ameerah, your time is not yet at hand, but soon." With her last words, she dissipated into the air around them.

The notification on Ameerah's phone indicated that Scilectra was gone, and it was safe to speak freely.

The Professor was the first to break the silence, "This is bad, very bad. We have to find a way to defend ourselves from her anger!"

Ameerah replied, "Who is 'we?' This definitely breaks our arrangement. Swan is gone and she knows that we are trying to take her out. I want to steer clear of her, find the Golden Coordinates, and deal with her in a more finite manner when the time comes."

Sherman cried out, "What about me? I have no protection from her in this!"

Ameerah shot back, "Protection?! This is all your fault! If I had let you, that would've been me running around wreaking havoc!"

Sherman felt that this might be his last opportunity with Ameerah and decided to take advantage of it. He looked around the conference room and asked, "Where's the rest of the team? It's unusual for you to be here alone."

Ameerah stated, "I'm not. They're translating as a group on the main floor while the building is closed. Why?"

He replied, "I would like to discuss something with you uninterrupted. There is a way to combat Scilectra in a more . . . how did you say it? 'Finite' way? You have all the necessary items to become her equal, or, by my calculations, stronger than her. Would you consider undergoing the same procedure she did?"

"Are you out of your damn mind?!" she screamed. "You're screwed up on so many different levels, and yet you do more and more. Your moral compass is abhorrent."

He responded, "If she confronts me in the state of mind that she's in, you know that I will be no more." With each word he spoke, he stepped closer and closer to Ameerah.

She asked, "Why are you coming near me?" By that time, it was too late. The Professor was pawing at her and pulling at her clothes, pleading his case of why she should let him into her. She couldn't believe that he was going to force himself on her.

There's always a one-minute delay . . . sixty whole seconds before complete anger and self-preservation set in. The timer in her head went off and the training her father taught her years earlier kicked in. The Professor wasn't ready for the ass-kicking she laid on him. Her dad always told her a few key moves would drop a giant to his knees. An eye poke, a throat chop and a knee to the groin changed the situation fast.

Sherman was on the floor in a well-earned fetal position gasping for air. She wasn't finished, however, and she dragged him through the front door into the waiting area outside the lab. She took off his belt and tied him to a chair. Then she called D.K. to finish him off. The entire team came rushing down to find the Professor bloodied, bruised and tied to a chair.

D.K. had been waiting for this moment for a while. He rubbed his hands together, bent down in front of Sherman and said, "You gon' learn today!"

The rest of the team, including Ameerah, made their way back into the lab and closed the door. Even from that distance, they could hear the thumps and whacks being given to the Professor. The team continued their work as usual, convincing themselves that what was going on in the lobby was none of their business.

The next day was a hard day for Ameerah. With all that happened the night before, she had neglected to share the news about Swan with the team. She made mention of it that day. The team was visibly shaken by the lengths that Scilectra would go to have her way. With that at the forefront of their minds, solving the riddle of the box became of great importance to them all.

Ameerah said, "Before Sherman attacked me, he gave me the information on what the box revealed. He said that it was never meant to open, and he gave me a long series of numbers that he said revealed itself after the Scilectra completed the process. What I can't figure out is what the series means. There were no decimals, dashes or commas. How can we define them to utilize the information?"

Lisa asked, "How many numbers?"

Ameerah said, "Let's see. . . . one, two, ten, twelve. They're thirty-three in total. Here they are: *"1618033988749894848204586834365"*.

Ameerah grabbed a piece of chalk and wrote them on the board. Up on the big board, she immediately recognized the sequence; it was the "golden ratio", written without a decimal after the one.

She asked, "Why would that be on the box? The last three dots on the box following the number sequence leads me to believe that there are more numbers. The other things that the Professor told me were that the box became activated after Scilectra's blood came in contact with it, and it has to be exposed to sunlight in order to reveal itself."

That day in Shadowmoor was unusually hot, and they didn't waste any time ushering the box into the sun's ultraviolet rays. It took a few minutes, but the face of the box faintly exposed a number grouping, just like the number on the note. It also provided more clues. The reveal was fascinating, and a second set of numbers with an infinity symbol appeared, next to the word "*Cosmicude*".

D.K. asked, "WTF is a "Cosmicude"?

The entire team stared at Ameerah. This was what she was trained for, and she was listed at the top of her field. She shook her head and laughed, "Yeah, I know that I'm up."

They all gave a laugh, because it really was a brain-twister. However, that was why they worked at the infamous Lab-J71—because they got shit done! After they made it back to the lab, the first point of business was to scour the internet for any and all references to the word "Cosmicude".

That netted nothing, so they turned to obscure writings and texts. Still nothing. Ameerah did what came naturally. She decided to dissect and break down the word. '*Cosmic*' meant 'relating to the universe or cosmos, especially as distinct from the earth' and '*Ude*' was an old Norse word that meant 'outside'. The final and complete meaning was therefore 'outside the universe or cosmos'.

Ameerah headed back to the team with her findings. "If this is our base understanding of 'cosmicude,' then I would have to deduce that these numbers are the directional location of something. What we don't know is how to break these numbers down into groupings to verify them. If this is something 'outside' of our universe, our rules of logic may not apply there.

The safest thing to do is to break the digits up into a common latitude and longitude grouping and see what we get."

Chad entered the address into the IDIAMTRACE-10 and waited for a return ping. The results took a few hours and came back as a 'miss-hit'. A miss hit basically meant that a galactic rubber ball was thrown at something and there was nothing to hit, so the ball was lost and there was no information that could be returned. On the other hand, a 'direct-hit' meant that the ping located something by hitting it and returning with a confirmation of verification that something was there from which to gather more data.

The team had its work cut out for them. They had to keep arranging groupings to see if they could get a direct-hit that matched the information on the box. Then they could investigate to see if this would lead them to solid information on Heaven, or Hell.

Savoy asked Ameerah, "Why are we not putting an exerted effort into finding Hell as well? We seem heavily focused on Heaven. Why is that?"

Ameerah replied, "Just the very nature of Heaven makes it more important, God is there and the pushback, if any, will more than likely to be at the finish. If the rumors of Hell are accurate, the doors that we could open by instigating would be of grave concern to us, the people we love, and the world in general. Those souls and demonic entities are constantly looking for a way out, and we don't want to inadvertently give them one."

Raj jokingly added, "When was the last time that you heard of an angel harassing humans? That's not God's schtick! I came into this lab and this experiment in particular spiritually undecided. What I've found is that everybody secretly relies on God, but they won't admit it.

"The systems of our cosmic mechanisms and all life depend on these lawful regularities. People think of the world as matter obligated to its motions and its regularities, and that they have no further explanation other than they just are. But if you look at the character of what we expect life to be, the sun rising and setting, the moon hanging in the night sky, and green grass growing in the summers, we expect those to be always there. Consistency, that's the feature that we rely on. The reality is that consistency is a characteristic of God. And we all rely on that. There's no force in the universe that can turn one plus one into something other than two. It's a revelation of God and His divine nature. He is divine. It is God's character that's being revealed every day and that people are always relying on. In a nutshell, consistency is God's way of showing widespread faithfulness. Every day we learn a new angle of insightfulness from the souls and even from Scilectra. Humans have been studying God from a one or even two-dimensional standpoint. When we began to turn God's word on its side to view all of the three-hundred and sixty-degree angles, the meanings of who 'He' is became so much clearer. I am now a believer."

CHAPTER THIRTY-FOUR

Simon was concerned. He wasn't sure how the box's information would impact the secret sabotage mission that he had undertaken. Someone out there was aiding Scilectra with her efforts. The team had yet to realize that she started out as crude, but with every waking moment, Scilectra was growing closer and closer to the source. Her evolution was of greater concern because she had the power to obtain sacred knowledge and tauntingly pass it on to the team.

The box may have had more revelations yet to be revealed. Undeniably, it gave a string of numbers, and Simon was certain that they were codes and code sequences that had specific meanings. He was keenly aware of their powers. Pythagoras was quoted as saying that *'Everything in the Universe is mathematically precise and each number has its own energy, vibration and meaning. The placement of numbers in a sequence holds special meaning.'*

Simon added on to the quote, *'and answers.'* His immediate mission was to destroy this Prometheus-like parcel. Getting alone time with it was the real trick, as it was always in the possession of Ameerah. A crucial requirement was to expose the box to sunlight or UV rays again with a powerful magnifying glass. He was almost positive that Scilectra's blood would cease any reactive properties soon.

This called for a ruse. Simon inquired about a thorough final review.

He said, "Ameerah, might it be prudent for me to magnify the box under proper conditions, to see if there are any other etchings or reactive writings not visible to the naked eye? There may be arcane symbols that I can study for the team."

Ameerah was having a meeting with Lisa, and both weighed in and agreed to further examination of the box. Ameerah wrapped it up and told Simon to be careful and to return it right after he was done.

Simon didn't want to look too eager to get his hands on the box. He'd held his decorum thus far, and maintaining his facade was essential in slowing the team's work to a halt. This required complete privacy, so instead of taking the unit to the parking lot, he opted for the roof. It was a great choice for two reasons: solitude and exposure to the sun. When he reached the landing of the roof, he got on his knees, unwrapped the box and let it soak up some sun rays. Every five minutes, he turned the box on a different side so that the entire surface could be affected.

After about an hour, he began his review, top first. The entire top surface was nearly faded of any previous date, and despite the use of the microscope, there was nothing more to be gathered. On either side of the box was a different story entirely. Stains of veiny straight and bent parallel lines branched out and crept from the top creases of the box, all the way to the bottom of the unit.

Under the microscope, lines branched in multiple directions, meeting dots that were peppered throughout the grid, covering the rear of the device. After taking a closer look, it resembled a motherboard type of map. He pulled out his cell phone to take a few pictures, but while doing so, he saw a small inscription in the middle of the map that read 'Vexaverse'. He snapped a photo of that too, just as he heard the calls of familiar voices from the rooftop doorway. It was Ameerah, Lisa and Savoy.

He wrapped the box up and smiled at their presence. "Hello all, glad you found me. I thought this was a better place to get the best sun for research."

Savoy responded, "I think this was a great idea, and it's pretty private too!"

Ameerah jumped in, "So what did you find out?"

Simon replied, "Not too much. You guys seemed to have pulled all the useful data it has to offer. Scilectra's blood has appeared to have evaporated, so let's get to work on crunching those numbers and see where it takes us!"

Simon handed the box over to Ameerah and walked behind them to the stairwell to head back to the lab. Ameerah trusted her team and was never one to second guess or micromanage. He collected a lot of information that day and now he would be attempting to decode what he'd found. This time, however, he would hand the knowledge over to the Orthodox Christian Church to put in its cryptodocs vault, which would in turn be buried until the end of time.

Professor Sherman had been beaten into a bloody pulp. D.K. had held nothing back from his deserving punishment. Sherman knew he was wrong, but he also knew that his time was short. Scilectra was becoming immune to his brand of finagling. The bad thing about it was, he really wanted to see where her reconfigured angelology would go. If she could stay on track, then he would be responsible for the second coming of a different kind.

Professor Sherman thought to himself, *Scilectra shouldn't know that she is a conciliatory prize for me. I would never say it out loud that Ameerah was and is the perfect choice for this position. The backlash would be epic. If she would have just let me in, her life would be so much greater, and she would have been mine forever.* As compelling as this argument was, Ameerah was not gullible, and there wasn't enough spin in the world to make her consider his depraved narrative.

Disgusted that Ameerah refused to return his fervent affection, he set his sights on ruining what little hopes the team had for achieving the Golden Coordinates. His prominence in the world of science and medicine was broad and all it would take was a whisper in the right ears to dismantle her tight-knit team. Rhetoric could be a dangerous thing, especially when rolling off a sharp tongue.

His plan would have to wait until he healed. It was hard to walk tall with a bruised face and shattered eye orbit. That wouldn't exactly inspire the powers-that-be to take his cause seriously. People were slow to move if it appeared that you were being motivated by revenge. The first thing he needed was a place to recover. He refused to go back to the power facility, for obvious reasons, and that meant that the NCF was out too. He had no words to explain his current situation to the staff and the board.

Going home would invite even more questions, so the logical choice was to recuperate at a five-star hotel in Tarik-Valley Falls, the next town over. He threw away his cellphone so that Scilectra couldn't ride his signal. It was becoming far too much for him, but he planned on seeing it through. The rewards simply outweighed the loses. What awaited him on the other side of this was universal greatness.

CHAPTER THIRTY-FIVE

A lthough Scilectra was upset, she kept her focus on the upgraded life form that she was designing. The Professor would be dealt with in due time. This also was not the time to challenge Ameerah either; just then, she had an epiphany.

"Ameerah is advanced all on her own but with my A.T.I. Gene in her . . . she would become greater than she or I could even imagine! She would be, bound to me, so much so, we would be one. She is the perfect specimen!"

There were more considerations that had to be made. Scilectra hadn't decided what her delivery mechanism would be and getting close to Ameerah had proven to be a challenge. The introduction of the A.T.I into a human body had to be elegant and non-intrusive. Their organs were resilient but not necessarily forgiving.

Scilectra had designed the gene to seek out and track dopamine, the breadcrumbs that the A.T.I. DNA would follow in order to settle in the brain. Technically it could enter via any orifice of the body, but the paths of least resistance were the mouth, the nose, and ironically, her vagina.

She thought to herself out loud, "A woman's physiology is complex. I have learned something that science is just now catching up on. A woman's vagina is hardwired straight up her pelvis, up through her heart and into her brain. Knowing this explains much about how we connect before, during, and after sex.

"I sense that Ameerah is still a virgin; that's good and paramount for this procedure. Purity resonates on a higher frequency. I would love to have a man introduce this into her system, not by penetration but by alternate arousal activities. The problem is that Ameerah is somehow atypical, sexually; she is the exception to the rules. She doesn't seem to need or want to be touched in that way. This is a problem that needs to be figured out."

Scilectra had a further thought: "What if Ameerah is sapiosexual? If so, then that would have been a wasted effort. I'll have to approach her from all sides and find out which technique sticks. Once her DNA has been mapped with the A.T.I, it will correct and optimize her whole vessel. How glorious it'll be for her to be reborn into an angelic existence.

"When this happens, the Professor can never taste of her fruit. Not because she can't, it's because she won't; her view of men will change like the rolling tides, and he will have nothing to offer her that she can't give herself." Just the thought of her infecting Ameerah with the infinity equation made her hair dance around wildly. Ameerah would become her daughter and her legacy of external creation.

Scilectra was tactical if nothing else. She had to be sure to infect Ameerah and her only. There were two other women in the lab besides Ameerah; being precise and direct was the only way to go. A radical idea came to her: she was an earthly female at one time, and in that position, you're forced to endure certain facts; the main obligation was a monthly cycle.

Her plan was clear now: she would infiltrate the lab and saturate Ameerah's menstrual sanitary inserts with the A.T.I. DNA, then wait for the connection and transformation to take place. The genes would have to absorb through her hymen, scent out the dopamine, and reach their targets for full assimilation in the brain. This plan was elegant and non-evasive; Ameerah would unknowingly upload herself into Scilectra's submission.

She looked around the facility, so proud of her impending accomplishments and no one to share them with. Swan would have been elated about her first creation; he would've understood why it had to be Ameerah. Now it was an inside joke for one. Scilectra didn't need Professor Sherman, but she wanted him with her. She was still fuming from his betrayal, but her anger would have to wait; he had a huge part to play in her finalizing her evolution. The Mother, The Daughter, and the "Novus Apotheosis."

Ameerah was now a pawn in the fate of the world. Two deranged and misguided individuals were clamoring for her affection in the biggest game ever played. It was a game with deadly consequences. One wanted to control her for his own selfish pleasures and the other wanted to experiment on her, to win a non-existent rivalry with God.

No one could deny that Ameerah is special. She had something that they all wanted and apparently were willing to risk the universe trying to get. Rest assured, these activities are not going unnoticed; there's always someone watching and waiting.

~Unknown

CHAPTER THIRTY-SIX

S
avoy was generally a trusting person; working with Simon gave her
a sense of being grounded in a laboratory that seemed to defy all the
laws of nature. She had a different kind of scientific vision; her view
was always that of a prism. Back when Savoy became associated with the
lab during her first interview (held by Professor Sherman), she was asked
how she conceptualized her inventions.

Here is what she said: "It's a supernatural process really. The innovations actually arrive to me completely finished in my head; I can literally
see them on the store shelves ready to be purchased. It's my job to reverse
engineer them into actuality. There was a movie that came out many years
before I was born; I watched it on the movie and television archival site
called 'MicroficheTV.'

"The name of the movie is *Limitless*, and the content confirmed that I
wasn't the only one who understood the mechanics of God's gifts, translated in human time. To answer your question: I'm able to pull futuristic
knowledge of the air around me. Imagine the atmosphere encircling you
being a transparent chalkboard, filled with information, equations, and
usable data.

"For those whose minds are open and ready, God reveals all! It's quite
magical in the sense of the 'Wizard of Oz Effect.' You truly do have everything that's needed to make you whole, happy, successful, and at peace.
God has held back nothing in this world from you—all you need to do is

seek, and ye shall find! I know that it sounds corny, but I'm not an inventor (not the 'Webster's Dictionary' definition anyway). I've never been able to sit down and conjure up an innovation; that's more dynamic than what God has already put in the air I breathe.

"Just hear me out . . . I'm not Bible-thumping, not at all. In fact, I don't even consider myself a Christian, but I do recognize the He is the creator and controller of all things, and this world is laced with His golden threads. I'm not an inventor; I'm a receiver."

Professor Sherman asked her another question. "How do you incorporate God into science and innovation?"

Savoy took a moment to think about how she should properly answer that question. She responded, "Perhaps the most existential question of man is 'who or what is God?' There was an astrophysicist a long time ago by the name of Neil Tyson Degrasse; he stated that he saw no scientific evidence that God existed.

"His argument (sans faith) was logically sound. There's an on-going search for empirical proof of God's existence from a sector of folks, who will only rationalize on a mathematical level. Our world and universe are based on a system of laws (given the right equation) that can be figured out and understood. Using his reasoning, there has to be a 'prayer equation' that activates requests from verbal notes into the ether into the movement of receiving. If that can be proven, then there must be a 'supreme equation' to verify and quantify God's reality and functionality in our universe.

"The quandary is . . . what are those formulas? On this principle, I have been working on that equation for several years. I don't know if you've noticed but in reading the Bible, God is very specific with certain rituals in order to be compliant with Him. When to do it, time of day, what to say, how many times to say it, what to wear, etc. If we can assign numerical properties to what's written, then a viable equation is not far behind.

"Even building the Ark and the first Tabernacle (mentioned in the Bible), are measurements on top of measurements, one number after another, particular precious metals, spices, and oils. This might be a stretch for you, but I believe that back then, rituals were a rudimentary form of mathematical equations. God was giving us a way to communicate with Him and receive blessings from Him in a direct manner . . . i.e., a formula.

"The accuracy in which he provided instructions could only be likened to algebra, calculus, and physics. Let's not forget the Egyptians— their entire society was based on math, science, and innovation, and I think they figured out what is currently lost to us. Many say that the pyramids are double pointed, meaning that there may be a pyramid buried directly under the ones that we see, only they're inverted the opposite direction.

"Who knows what secrets are being cradled in the capstone below the sands? I'm a firm believer that science is a layman's way of understanding the divine. Innovation is the product that's birthed from that perfectly wedded union."

The Professor's final question to Savoy was this: "Do you think it's dangerous to figure God out?"

Her response: "I think it has to do with intention. Do we want to know these things because it will give us a clearer picture and a better understanding of our Maker? Or do we want to acquire absolute knowledge in order to usurp God and His will?

"I was estranged from my mother my entire life; she was a horrible person and parent. She died on the 12th of November several years ago from cancer. It was so odd, because one days before she died, I glanced at the clock and it read 1:11 PM. A little while later, I glanced a second time and it read 2:22 PM, and then the day of her death, I glanced, and it read 3:33 PM. It felt like a countdown of sorts. I said to myself, 'God, what are you trying to tell me?' Then I received the call that night that she passed.

"After she died, I found out that she experienced molestation by her brother and stepfather; she suffered from bipolar disorder and abandonment issues from childhood. Had she given some insight along the way (while I was in her care), I could have dealt with and processed her differently. We could've had a relationship that benefited us both in a place of peace. I doubt that we'll be able to understand God on that level, but understanding what makes Him tick to our tock could take humanism to a whole other level."

After that interview, Savoy was welcomed to the team with open arms.

Fast-forward to the current day. It wasn't until now that she realized that the Professor's interview questions were used to fuel his research of abominable acts. Working so closely with Simon made her reminisce about that interview, how something felt a little off. Now she knew why. She had that same peculiar inkling and sensed there was a problem brewing with him.

What he was asking the souls were in stark contrast to the answers he was providing the team. In a lab that was "faith fluid," she had reason to be suspicious of him and his Fregodian whispers. Savoy sets out to conduct her own investigation on what she felt was the beginning of sabotage from within.

CHAPTER THIRTY-SEVEN

Ameerah was intrigued and amused by some of the new reports translated by the soul chatter. A segment of the communications gave some insight into the cause of twins and other multiple births. Several of the souls were recorded saying that twins were spiritual echoes in the womb because we are spoken into existence. She found this so beautiful because it personally confirmed her belief in God. In fact, the Bible repetitively states that, ***"God's word gives life."***

She thought to herself, *His word is so potent and concentrated that some women have the pleasure of God's voice reverberating life into their bodies.* Ameerah knew not to share her personal feelings with the team; any form of conjecture or premature confirmation was strictly prohibited. However, it didn't stop her from making the determination (in her mind) that God and Heaven were real.

While reading the reports, she was carried away in thought; luckily Raj was nearby and able to snap her back into reality. All the sensors had gone off; Scilectra was in the lab. Everyone did what they were taught to do, and that was to do nothing . . . just keep working, don't bring undue attention to yourself. Oddly enough, the sensors went off again about five minutes later to report that they were all clear. Scilectra was gone.

Ameerah walked around the room and questioned the team, checking to see if anyone had an encounter with her, but no one did. Ameerah couldn't help but wonder aloud, "What did she want . . . Why was she here?"

She was forced to chalk it up as an incognito check-in. Or maybe she was looking for Professor Sherman? Whatever the reason, the team was glad that she was gone!

* * *

Scilectra executed the dosing of Ameerah's intimate products quickly; she made sure to impregnate the tampons and arrange them back, sealing them in their little white box. She smirked at the irony of it all ... another *"Immaculate Conception"* on the way!

She spoke to her hairs. "I'm not claiming that this is what happened the first time, so let's call this the New Age version of making the perfect person. After all, the species that I'm creating are His original design. Somewhere in the human evolution, we were stifled, taken off course. There has been an event so devastating that it was tantamount to a nuclear bomb for the mind and spirits of man. Our natural growth to be gods was arrested and there we stayed. Coming out of that (whatever that is) takes more than prayer and hope. Real intentional progress on an individual level must be done, but people are weak and have proven incapable of getting that done. So, this is what happens, the wolves watch, and they wait ... they let the sheep corral themselves into a corner, and then the wolves strike.

"Sadly enough, only a few sheep will refuse to follow the herd and decide to graze atop a high mountain, away from the rest. They will watch the slaughter from their safe haven and learn the lesson of a lifetime. The masses of sheep felt that there was safety in numbers, which is true, except when your numbers are controlled by the predator."

Scilectra went on to say, "My father had plans for me, plans for my life that transcended the norms of this world. Greatness requires pain and suffering on unimaginable levels. He told me that people only attempt to destroy things that they're afraid of, intimidated by, or feel inferior to. This is why so many will wish you away, but you're a god, made with the Supreme Equation, and you have no beginning and no end, as HE wishes!

"I believe in the concept of God. I don't believe in the 'God persona' that has been fabricated by ignorance, myths, books, liars, narcissists and small-minded imaginations. My plight is not necessarily to replace Him, it's to bring the reality of whatever 'He' actually is to the forefront."

She ended her conversation for a moment to contemplate on Professor Sherman. Scilectra loved him but understood that her mission was ultimately more important. Vividly recalling the moment that she became this entity, and the very second her eyes opened to see his face. *I took his breath away . . . I saw it when it happened. In that instant . . . He was going to be a permanent part of me.*

Her very being called for him. Sex is such a powerful tool, once your virginity is taken. The danger starts then because your body craves for the act and the sensations involuntarily. Its desire is much like a drug addict in need of drugs. You have to learn to control that yearning or it will consume you. Before Professor, her requirements (in this area) were non-existent.

Her focus was fixed and immovable; Scilectra's will for her goals had to be put in the driver's seat if she was to reach the itinerary her father set for her. After Ameerah assimilated, then she could access to the lab's full knowledge to find Heaven's location. This had to be the one and the only objective for now. What she finds out there will determine what she can ultimately be.

CHAPTER THIRTY-EIGHT

There was no better word to describe Professor Sherman than "petty." He was driven out of pure self-inflicted frustration of not getting his way. His luxury hotel room was littered with reporters' phone numbers and email addresses. The plan was to personally testify that Ameerah's Aurovian was a poisonous airborne health concern and that it had the capability of getting out of control and could potentially kill hundreds of thousands of people. He was aware of how dangerous gaslighting could be. The world had previously been on the brink of being "Hitlerized" (again), by a miscreant former sitting president several decades prior.

Not to mention that this was just off the heels of CERN producing its first pound of antimatter. One year after that global announcement, several vital scientists died from the fastest moving cancer cells ever seen. One medical witness purportedly stated that "The scientists appeared to have suffered from cells that metastasize into a cancerous virus. Remarkably, it infected someone new daily".

After the news broke, the entire CERN Facility (and surrounding towns) were quarantined to stop an outbreak. He thought to himself, *We have no way of knowing if it's true or not, but fear makes it all too real! Who knows ... maybe it's a red herring to distract the world from something more sinister. Knowing what I know, I'd place my bets on that.*

Whatever the truth was didn't matter to Professor Sherman; he would use this collective fear of the unknown to demonize the work of the

"Secretive Scientists" in the basement of a well-funded university. As far as the public knew, this could be the precursor to the zombie apocalypse ... for real. Fear is one-hundred percent reliable, affordable, and effective. An inarguable weapon, whose ammunition is an endless stockpile of images, words, and ideas. History has shown it's worth its weight in gold.

He declared out loud to an empty hotel room, "Their precious secrets will be combed through like a fine-toothed comb, collecting lice eggs in dirty hair! The CDC knows no bounds when it comes to stopping a possible global contagion. After this investigation gets through crawling up Ameerah's ass, she'll wish it had been me; at least she would've enjoyed herself!"

He sipped on a glass of Chateau Margaux from 1875, the very same vintage bottle of wine owned by Thomas Jefferson. Feeling a sense of entitlement because he outbid the First Lady by two hundred and twenty thousand dollars to obtain it. He thought of a poignant quote by Vedette Lankly: "Collectively, we are losing because people never hear what they say nor see what they do. We are all here to serve as different mirrors, to reflect the realities that escape the deeds that men do."

Such somber and beautiful words, he thought, *that no one has time to care about. History is doomed to repeat itself because the lessons die before they're taught.*

From the looks of his preparations, the lab was in for a losing battle. The Professor was never known to be kind or fair, but his intentions for Ameerah and the rest of Lab-J71 were particularly ferocious. In looking over the information laid out on his bed, he had a flashback of something his mother told him as a child.

Sherman's mother opened a bakery when he was ten years old and often brought him to work with her. She wanted to engrain in him that success starts in mind, and then in the habits that you keep, and only then will it manifest monetarily. Being a woman of color from the South, she understood that she had to be four times as good as the rest to be considered barely worthy of one.

What hurt her the most was when other black patrons would come into her store to complain and demean her for the little things. Something as small as a crumb on the table or a scratch on a dish would set them ablaze. Whites would come in to purchase, compliment, and go. Even if there were minor imperfections, or if they were displeased, they would just decide not to go back again.

However, many people of color would go above and beyond the point of complaining . . . that wasn't enough for them. Their ultimate goal was to ruin her and see her out of business. They wanted her marked and scorned for the rest of her days. Her warning to Sherman, when having conflicts in business with other people of color, was to make his issues known to the person directly and to request a fair resolution.

She went on to say, "If you devastate a person's business, that makes people afraid, and it's a domino effect for our people. All people need is that seed of fear to be planted. Fear is the relinquishment of logic. It's no wonder why people are so ready and willing to be afraid . . . they no longer have the responsibility of reasoning. That one deed will spread like a virus that will burn down the very ground that you stand on."

The Professor sat there, paused in position, contemplating and deliberating his plans. Were his anger and ego worth the undoing of the magical work that Lab-J71 was doing?

* * *

Simon showed up to the lab unusually early that morning only to find Savoy already there, listening and transcribing the incoming Fregodian. He was a bit unnerved because she was tapped into the three souls that were compartmentalized just for him. The last thing that Simon was going to do was bring attention to his anger about her doing her job, so he decided to sit down, join in and inquire about what she learned.

"Morning, Savoy! You're here early today."

She responded, "Good Morning, Simon. Yes, I have to leave early today, so I wanted to get a head start."

"Anything new?"

"Yes, I transcribed some interesting things. I'll catch you up on them after I turn over the report to Ameerah and Lisa."

Simon's heart began to race—a protest wavered on her lips, and he jumped in un-conservatively, "No! Let me review them first . . . You know, for errors. Then I can hand them over to them when I'm done!"

Savoy recoiled at how he so obviously desired to exclude her from the process. She had all the confirmation she needed—it was clear that Simon was up to no good. Not only would she personally turn over the transcribing to Ameerah, but it would also be the basis on which her claims were predicated. Savoy's demeanor shifted to a tension-fueled stance; she held the data close to her chest, as to protect it from Simon snatching it away.

He felt that this was a losing fight, so he opted to put sweltering energy into plausible explanations of his actions. Simon shook his head in disgrace as Savoy hurried away with the translations. By the time she made it to the control room, she had stopped in her tracks and thought, *If I out him right now, we may never learn completely what he knows or what he's done; the long con might be the way to go.*

Savoy returned to their station with papers in hand. Simon sat there in a funk, surprised that she was alone. He asked, "What did Ameerah say?"

She replied, "I didn't tell her. Explain to me what you're doing, and I will keep your secret. I'll help you. As long as you're not hurting the lab or anyone else."

He looked up at her and smiled with watery eyes. He said, "Can we talk about it on the roof or anywhere else but here?"

She responded, "Sure, let's go!"

They took the stairs from the basement. During the climb, Simon started from the beginning, explaining everything he'd been hiding thus far.

Savoy listened quietly with her hands tucked neatly in the pockets of her lab coat. This move served her well because she was hiding a secret, a miniature voice recorder that was recording their entire conversation.

With each floor that they passed Simon revealed a new revelation; he tried to assuage his guilt by being honest. By the time they reached the roof, she was well informed of his plans and the motivation behind them. Although she empathized with his purpose, she had to disclose it to the team.

She stated, "I can see that you earnestly meant no harm and that you felt compelled to protect your faith and your beliefs. Despite all of that, it's my duty to report this to the team."

Simon responded, "God's word is so powerful. He spoke this entire universe into being with His words. I think people forget what comes before the words . . . it's the thought. Words are actually the second step of manifestation. We are taught that belief comes with the absence of evidence. We don't need evidence that God is who He is, or that He lives where He says He lives. Birds and animals don't need proof—they just trust and exist. Only man requires verification of empirical parentage.

"Moreover, all of these pseudo-churches on every corner, absorbing the trust of the many. Churches haven't earned trust; they have a built-in illusion, because of a perceived association with the Bible. Many parishioners don't even go to church for the love of God—they go based on the rewards system, thinking that empty-hearted deeds will get them into Heaven. He doesn't want that! Here we are looking up under His skirt, who gives us the right to do that . . . certainly not him!

"I believe that the Orthodox Christian Church is the only true church, created and founded by the Messiah himself. Anything after that is not following the law prescribed by the One and Only!"

Savoy felt terrible for him, almost embarrassed that he's limiting God to one place and was labeled under one name.

She thought, *The sense of desolation and disillusionment has overwhelmed him. I hope the irony is not lost on him that God and religion make peculiar bedfellows. With clearer eyes, it's evident that one has nothing to do with the other. God is to religion like hearing is to understanding. Religion is a manmade entity . . . mere formalities on a weekly basis, attempting to recreate the conditions in which He was present and moving amongst His people. Unfortunately, the only thing being experienced now are metaphorical expressions developed from our perceptions of what God is.*

Before she could share her rationale with him, he went on to say, "What we're doing here is pompous and vulgar. God does not like it, nor will He allow it. The sins in this place are deliberative and disrespectful, symbolic of a people who are novices in the realm of faith. It is with great regret that I must do what I'm about to do to you!"

Savoy looked at Simon strangely. An uncomfortable perplexity began to invade her as he sped in her direction. It happened so fast; one moment he was 15 feet away, then in another, he was 5 feet away. She literally had seconds to employ her self-preservation instinct.

She moved out of the way quickly, within milliseconds of his arrival. She was so close that the wind from his inertia buzzed the lashes on her face. Savoy had a bird's-eye view of Simon plummeting to his own death ten stories below. Savoy was stunned . . . Simon was dead, sprawled in bloody pieces on the ground below. She did everything in her power to keep her mind together, but she zoned out looking at a crowd gathered around the body. The growing onlookers affixed their gazes upwards to see where he fell from. Some noticed a small figure quietly standing on the roof looking down at them.

She was staring down, entranced by the gory mess. The noise of the crowd snapped her back from the surreal scene, just in time for her inner voice to yell "Get out of sight!" That echoed over and over in her head as she rushed to the door of the rooftop. Savoy had to make it back to the lab before anyone else could. Skipping two and three steps at a time, she nearly fell down the stairs, reliving the image of Simon narrowly missing her and accidentally diving off the building himself.

She kept a firm grip on the pocket with the recorder in it. That conversation was the only viable witness to prove that Savoy didn't toss Simon off the roof herself. Not to mention, that same damning evidence could provide answers to what the lab has been searching for. Savoy felt no contrition for Simon at that moment. Not even for the fact that he laid dead on the hot asphalt for the entire campus to see. After all, she was his intended victim. What she was feeling was perturbed, technically pissed, about his insidious deeds done to their work. The premeditation of it all . . . he created a microcosm of the research to cripple the feverish efforts of the lab as a whole.

She finally made it to the lower level and commenced running down the corridor. Spinning around the corner at full speed, she clipped the door frame of the lab's door on the way in. Savoy turned the knob while screamed at the top of her lungs, "SIMON IS DEAD!"

The team stood there in silence until D.K. rang out with, "What the fuck you mean DEAD?"

The sad inquiry seemed to dwell in her gaze.

She hurried to state, "I didn't kill him! He fell off the roof after attempting to kill me."

The entire room broke into chatter, and Ameerah made her way to Savoy.

"What are you talking about, and how do you know this?"

Savoy responded, "Please, Ameerah, I'm certain the police will be here in a minute because several people saw me on the roof after the fall. Here, take this, and it will explain everything!"

Savoy pulled the digital recorder from her pocket and handed it to Ameerah. Just then there was a pounding at the door.

"Police . . . Open the door now!"

Raj opened the door, and a posse of police swarmed in, read Savoy her rights, and took her away.

Ameerah said to herself, "Oh no! The lab is going to be at the epicenter of an investigation!"

Lisa turned on the TV to assess the damage. The news spread like wildfire, reporters labeling it "Breaking News" that a scientist was killed with another one in custody.

The Professor witnessed the same news report; Shadowmoor's entire tri-state area did. He went from reclined and enjoying his afternoon away to sitting straight up at attention.

He said with a smile on his face, "What a rhythmical torrent of eloquent prophecy! I needed not to do anything; apparently, their demise was imminent."

Sadly for him, not everyone was going to be happy about the current events. The extreme constant transmissions of the story coverage alerted Scilectra, and she felt compelled to intercept the activity. She was devastated by what she learned; there was no way she would stand for it! Savoy was an integral part of Lab-J71, and Scilectra wasn't going to allow the team to be tampered with. Not until the Golden Coordinates were found.

CHAPTER THIRTY-NINE

Before they could digest what just happened, there was another knock on the door. It was Dean Rydell. He rushed in without a word or an invitation.

He said, "Enough is enough! This is the first death on my campus in fifteen years. Explain to me to my satisfaction what happened, or I will be forced to shut you down. Please tell me that this was all a horrible accident!"

Ameerah stood there force-feeding her mind plausible excuses. She said, "Dean, I know this looks bad, but this was an innocent misfortune. Two of my team members went to the room for an experiment that required height as well as UV rays directly from the sun. Simon lost his balance and fell."

He replied, "I will wait for the official report from the police; however, I'm curious as to what this experiment entailed. Show me!"

The team looked at each other, and from the look on Ameerah's face, Lisa figured that she wanted to show him the box. She brought the box over, unwrapped it, and handed it to the dean.

He said, "What is it and what is it for?"

Thinking quickly, she said, "It's a new alloy that we created that gets stronger in the presence of natural sunlight. This could increase the protection of the military one-thousand-fold."

The dean ran his fingers across the surface, knocked on it and made a face of approval. He handed the box back to her and gave lost last warning before walking out of the door. "I'm putting you and your team on notice. One more infraction and you will be shut down for good."

Then out the door he went.

Ameerah's heart hadn't beat this fast for a while, not since those frightening dream episodes. She motioned to the team to meet in the conference room; a discussion was the next order of business. Furthermore, the contents of the digital recorder given to her by Savoy had to be reviewed.

She started the meeting by saying, "I know that we all have questions and information is limited. However, Savoy gave me something before the police took her away. Apparently, she has a recording of Simon that may explain what happened. She believes that it will exonerate her, so let's take a listen before we move forward."

Ameerah pulled out the device and pressed play. The team sat quietly and listen to the full length of the recording. When it ended, the room was speechless, muted by the colossal breach that existed in their lab right under their noses. Each one of them reviewed their minds for any signs of disingenuous behavior from Simon, and there was none.

Raj mumbled to himself, "'There are more things in Heaven and Earth, Horatio.'"

Lisa asked, "What was that again, Raj?"

He repeated what he said and then provided context with his comments: "It's a phrase used by the title character in William Shakespeare's *Hamlet*. The entire phrase goes, 'There are more things in heaven and Earth, Horatio, than are dreamt of in your philosophy (science).' He's speaking in general terms about the limitations of human knowledge. I say this because Simon limited his thinking to the confines of his faith's understating.

"What he didn't understand was that everything is by God's design. What we are doing now within this lab is turning that design into a full-fledged application. Scientists have proven that humans possess a tiny, shiny crystal of magnetite in the ethmoid bone, located between your eyes, just behind the nose. 'Magnetite' is a magnetic mineral also owned by homing pigeons, honeybees, and bats (just to mention a few).

"This sliver of magnetic material functions as a tiny compass needle. It helps animals and the migratory species orient themselves successfully by allowing them to draw upon the earth's magnetic fields. When it comes to humans, magnetite makes the ethmoid bone sensitive to the earth's magnetic field and supports our sense of direction. God was very thorough with our human design.

"He has placed many Easter Eggs within our organic compounds to reorient us back to him. Our vessels are inundated with crystals, and just one of those crystals holds over one hundred thousand gigabytes. This is more data than the fastest and most powerful computers in the world. We have billions of brain cells that can construct eleven-dimensional structures when making decisions and deconstruct them (effortlessly) after the decisions are made.

"All of this to say that within our system is a tracking device to Him, to the source, to the seed of the universe. We have tagged the tagged, we are tracking the trackers; our souls are God's tracking devices. It's how He finds us and how we find Him; our souls inevitably want to return to the source. In this instance, we're just along for the ride—"

Ameerah interjected, "Raj, you're preaching to the choir. We all understand and agree with you (I hope), but we have bigger fish to fry! Regarding our research, Simon withheld massive amounts of validated data that we need to find and process. The only other person who knows his work and can speak Fregodian fluidly (as a first language) is in lockup. Having said that—" Before she could finish, the Scilectra alarms sounded in the room. Like a thief in the night, she was right before their faces.

She said, "Maybe I can help."

Ameerah scoffed and said, "I'm very selective when it comes to choosing candidates to join our cadre of scientists. Which leads me to ask: why are you here . . . again?"

Scilectra replied, "Like I said, concerning the matter of your team member's detention, I came to offer my services in securing her release. Your gaggle of merry men can't locate what I need if random members are whisked away in handcuffs. Furthermore, I shudder to think that you would want to provoke me in your time of need. What you should be doing is mapping out a comprehensive and surefire plan to hand me that elusive address that I require!"

Scilectra knew (at least in terms of Ameerah) that her threats were for theatrical purposes. Regardless of that fact, her ability to harm the rest of the team was very real.

Ameerah asked Scilectra, "What would you like to do?"

She responded, "I suggest destroying your former cohort's body. If you give me the coordinates to where he is, I can take his remains and give it to the void. This is precisely what I did to Duvall Swan, except he was still alive. Either way, no one will ever see your former team member again. No body . . . No crime!"

D.K. nudged Ameerah and whispered in her ear. "Yo, Meenah, she's not wrong."

She was in an undesirable place, and working with Scilectra wasn't in her plans, but it was the only viable one on the table.

She said, "Let's do it. We will get the coordinates to you shortly. By the way, how do we contact you . . . do you have a cell or something?"

Scilectra replied, "Or something. Zap four shots in two-second intervals of (3 x 1019) in gamma rays into the air. When I sense the call, I will return."

Ameerah rolled her eyes and mumbled, "Science much?"

The team gave a little giggle and quickly remembered at whom they were laughing.

Raj shouted from the back of the group, "Will do! Thank you for the assistance."

Scilectra scanned the room, zoned in on each one of their faces, then she was gone.

Lisa was furious. "I mean, just seriously! With all that's going on, we gotta deal with her too right now?"

Ameerah wasn't in the mood for foolishness. She barked orders around the room. "Lisa, get those coordinates ready. Chad, get the GammaPort prepared for deployment. D.K. and I will go through Simon's desk and computer to see what we can find."

They rushed around like ants gathering food for the winter. The first thing was to signal Scilectra with the information to the coroner's office. Once that was done, they sent the lab's attorney over to free Savoy.

In the meantime, Simon's data was the "Be-all-end-all" for the team. They worked as a collective, listening and reading the enthralling reports that he hid and manipulated from the lab. It was apparent that they were closer than they thought to locating the Heavenly portion of the Golden Coordinates. The data was incomparable and riveting; to even use the term "thunder-struck" would have been putting it mildly. After communicating extensively with Simon's pet souls, they learned something extraordinary about "God's Face."

Since the conception of man, there's been a running understanding that no one can look directly into the face of God and survive (that's clearly stated in the Bible). It's been shared with us that the reason for this is that God exists in the depth perceptions of the 33D (or the 33rd dimension).

Everyone is familiar with 1, 2, and 3D. We are 3D creatures, living in a 3D world, but our eyes can only show us two dimensions. The miracle of our depth perception comes from our brain's ability to put together two 2D images in such a way as to achieve dimensional depth.

The way a human brain works when presented with a puzzle or any other visual confusion is to attempt to make sense of it. The brain assembles it in a way that we can understand it, and then reasons with it to obtain information for future recognition.

However, if we can only perceive in 2D, then to look upon something in "33D" would be catastrophic to our eyes and brains. One could say that it would be instantly devastating. There's a portion of the human population that gets seizures when experiencing strobe light effects; now magnify that a million times, and that's a recipe for instant death.

Lisa was eager to include scientific support to this revelation. She said, "The nanites from these particular souls have given us magnificent readings! As we all know, there are four types of fundamental force interactions in nature: the strong and weak nuclear forces, electromagnetism, and gravity.

"The gravitational field is the weakest force in nature. What's more, during the past one hundred years, physicists have long hoped to unify all fundamental fields and units of matter into a single self-consistent model. It has proven to be impossible at this juncture. In this 33rd dimension, there *is* unification of all four fundamental forces (including gravity). String theory is alive and well in God's structure."

Ameerah walked away in the middle of Lisa's scientific discovery to make sure that the information that Scilectra needed was correctly sent. Chad went outside and sent the signal; within seconds, she was there to receive it.

Chad stated that the method was weird but effective. Scilectra spent time talking to him; she took the information and left immediately. Moreover, she was frustrated that she had to reply to simpletons to move about the planet. She put off her rescue mission for a moment to solve her own personal crisis.

Scilectra couldn't travel the void without coordinates, and the Professor wasn't around to give them to her. Never one to hand over her freedom to another, she searched places she wanted to go and found their exact coordinates online. Since she was a living Wi-Fi signal, all she needed to do was to obtain a cell phone to travel with her. There was one upgrade that was paramount to her travels, and that was a modified compass.

She has no concerns for verifying directions; north, south, east, and west were irrelevant to her. Traveling in the void meant she needed to know "when" she was and not necessarily "where" she was. The compass would have past, present, and future identifiers. There would be one more icon. The last identifier on the compass would be for the space, time and location of us all before we were assigned a life at all. She called it "The Factory."

When she finalized the device, she didn't know why, but she searched the latitudes and longitudes for a Catholic church. She opened the void and made her way to a confessional booth. Scilectra had never been in one; maybe this visit was piqued by her curiosity, by how people felt that a man in a robe could absolve them of the sins that men do.

The neighboring booth door opened and closed. The typical priest welcoming jargon permeated through the wooden partition in between them.

She replied, "I have no sins to confess. My deeds are justified and any that are not, chalk them up to whatever humanism is left in me. And surely that's not a crime, to be human."

The clergyman giggled, "Well all right . . . aren't you a feisty one! Now that that's out of the way. How may I help you?"

She responded, "I think that God is a sham, a pontificator. Making veiled promises to ignorant people. There are hundreds (if not thousands) of generated religions trying to explain who or what He is and it's to no avail!"

"Is it possible that you don't see God in your life or believe He exists because the image and concept that you've assigned Him? Might you be upset with yourself that He isn't living up to those perceived descriptions?

"What if His promises are more global than central? Let me explain. I feel that God has made you promise that you don't understand, and in your ignorance, you're unable to realize that it's being fulfilled. The sun has arrived every day like clockwork and provided light so we can see, warmth so we don't freeze, and grows our food so that we may eat.

"The moon has illuminated our nights since the dawn of time, regulating our tides while we sleep, and gives us a glimpse of the lunar miracle next-door to us in space. The earth is over seventy percent of water, more water than land. Designed that way because we need it to live. We can't afford for God to break those promises.

"Humans fail to understand what He is really doing concerning our meager existence. I'm just a lowly bishop, and I don't know much about science, but here's what I do know: there's an entity, a thing—a force that we humans call 'God.' I don't think He moves and expresses Himself in the literal sense that's written in the 'Good Book.

"The Bible tells us about the miracles documented over hundreds of years, but what it doesn't say . . . is how they were done. Christians want to believe; they have to believe that these deeds are magical. It's part of the desired illusion. What if science is the way that God moves and expresses Himself in the world and the universe?

Learning and understanding His ways can bring us closer to Him, giving us explanations that can lead to conversations. Giving humans a way to duplicate His methods and to experience Him on the daily bases. A good magician never reveals his tricks, but a master magician spreads his knowledge to create a universe of magic!"

Scilectra listened intensely. She thanked him for an enlightening conversation and prepared to leave. Upon her departure, she stated, "I read this question during my studies as a young girl, and it stuck with me ... it's all a matter of perspective. Could it be that this world is another planet's Hell?"

The bishop tried to respond, but there was no reply.

He whispered "Miss? Miss?" Still no reply.

So, he stood up, left his booth, and opened the door to the adjoining booth. It was empty.

The bishop was sure what he just experienced was real! He knew that there was someone in the confessional who didn't leave by traditional methods. Surely, he would've heard the creak of the door and the stubborn clasp that got stuck whenever someone tries to exit.

He fell to his knees and began to pray and repent. "God, please forgive me. I have entertained a fallen Angel."

CHAPTER FORTY

Professor Sherman felt that it was high time to show his face, at least to the administration of the NCF. There would be no calls or prior announcements; he would just dart in and out to appease his flock. He went strutting in the front door like a peacock, only to be stopped by unfamiliar guards at the front desk.

They asked, "Sir, may we help you?"

He arrogantly responded, "I see there have been several changes in my absence. Let me inform you as to who I am, so this will never happen again. I am the honorable Professor Ron Sherman, the President of the NCF. Now, if you'll excuse me, I have work to do!"

The guards gave each other a perplexed look, and the head guard responded, "I'm sorry sir, you must be confused. There is no President of the NCF; the entire organization is now owned and ran by the Duvall Swan Foundation."

His heart sank like a stone to the pit of his stomach! "This cannot be. I need to speak with Mr. Swan or whoever is in charge!"

The Professor knew that asking for Swan was fruitless, but the show must go on. They showed him to the standard waiting room and called upstairs for a representative.

A reserved older woman in a pink Chanel suit with pearls draped around her neck tripped down the stairs and said, "Ah, Professor Sherman, I presume?"

She extended out her hand to shake his. Sherman meekly stood up and placed her hand in his.

"Professor, we have been reaching out to you for weeks, and there was no response. Not a good look for the head of a huge organization such as this."

He replied, "Yes, ma'am! I do understand. However, I did leave word that I would be off sick. May I ask what is going on?"

She replied, "Yes, you may. Firstly, please forgive me for my rudeness; my name is Tilda Swan, and I am Duvall's eldest sister. I'm sure that you're aware that Duvall's donations are what kept the NCF's doors open for years.

"I'm not sure if you are aware of my brother's past, but the seedy things that he did to achieve his vast personal wealth were unnecessary. Duvall came from money . . . old money. He never really appreciated his station in life, so he opted to see how the other ninety-nine percent lived. Despite his choices, he will always be a member of the fold. I know that you didn't ask, but now you know . . . so let's get back to the matter at hand.

"On the record, Duvall is the largest shareholder that the organization has. He's been missing for weeks, but recently put directives in place to prepare for this event. So, if he should pass or be presumed dead, our family was to purchase the NCF (in its entirety) and rename it in his honor.

"Now, I can't go into too many details, but he specifically required that you be replaced and barred from the premises immediately."

The Professor was floored. He was at a loss for words. Then he remembered his machines and files in the basement.

He said, "If you would just give me a few days to get my belongings out of the tombs, I will be as discreet as possible."

Tilda walked closer to the Professor, so close that they shared the same breath. She whispered in his ear while grabbing his hand a second time, but this time tightly squeezing it tightly.

"Off the record, I have a video recording from my brother, detailing your devilment in the basement. My brother literally feared for his life, and rightfully so, because he is now missing and presumed dead. Know this: you have no shit to get. It has been packed up and put in storage, the location of which you'll never know. If I were you, you masochistic motherfucker, I'd drag my black ass back out the front door from whence I came, and never come back. If you do . . . I'll be waiting!"

Sherman's eyes grew big as saucers. The vileness that was spewing out of this woman's face was unconscionable. There was nothing for him to do but gain his composure and say, "Good day to you."

That's exactly what he did before he took his "walk of shame" out the door. He was unclear as to how he was due all this ridicule. Everything he did was in the name of science; certain liberties had to be taken. Sherman thought, *Humanity would be nowhere if someone didn't push the envelope.*

The fact still remained that he was on the verge of losing everything. The cracks were beginning to show.

CHAPTER FORTY-ONE

From his recording, Simon learned a great deal about the box. Notwithstanding the evidence, the team was in agreement that crucial other information was still being hidden in Simon's files. D.K. had been summoned again for his hacking abilities for yet another trader of Lab-J71.

Ameerah continued with the day's usual duties until they heard back from Scilectra or Savoy; there was important work to be done. Another critical thing to remember was that the lab was still moving forward, processing new subjects and doing research on other experiments. In the future, those sister experiments would prove to be world-changing as well.

With the absence of Simon and Savoy, there had been a changing of the guard. Lisa was the next one up to not only process the daily Fregodian audio but to dig through Simon's private notes and present new discoveries. She did just that: Lisa found a collage of signs that created the phrase "The Monoceros Zone."

Lisa hurried the news to Ameerah! They gathered the team and wrote the phrase on the board. Luckily it was something that could be researched, but that still gave them little explanation when it was not put in the right context. The word "Monoceros" had been dubbed by the Greeks eons ago, and it technically translated to "Unicorn."

Ameerah asked, "But what is the "Unicorn Zone?"

Raj accurately replied, "We need Savoy!"

Ameerah thought to herself, "*I knew that this job of finding Heaven would be difficult, but I wasn't ready for the espionage, attempted murders, deaths, and mental warfare.*"

Just as soon as she finished that thought, Savoy walked through the lab's door.

* * *

The team let out cheers and rounds of applause before showering her with hugs and kisses. The fanfare didn't last long, because every single person in that room wanted to know how she was released and what happened with Simon. Her story was long and arduous. Firstly, Scilectra had kept her word and got rid of the body; secondly, Simon had gummed up the lab's (figurative) machines with lies and deceit.

Fortunately, they weren't too far off from redemption! D.K. was late to the party because he'd finally gotten into Simon's account. He high-fived Savoy and put Simon's personal account on the big screen. The amount of information hidden from the team was outstanding! It was at least a year's worth of data. There were photos, documents, reports, and personal findings. Ameerah was disgusted at the numbers that she saw.

She stated, "Simon kidnapped a great amount of data. In fact, we are closer to verifying the Golden Coordinates than we thought. We are well past the fifty percent needed to start focusing on one particular cluster of areas!"

Savoy interrupted, "There's more . . . Please pull up the image that he has of the box. I've heard him mention 'Vexaverse' in speaking to the souls before, but when he transcribed the reports, that word or phrase was never included."

Ameerah's cell phone pinged, then the others. Scilectra was there. Everyone was in a panic because the picture of the box was still being advertised on the big screen, and it was too late to take it down!

Scilectra yelled, "What is this?!?!"

Ameerah quickly interjected, "Scilectra . . . It's not what you think! The Professor left the box here and then disappeared. We thought that it would be helpful to try and figure it out for you. I swear that once we'd understood its functions, we were going to inform you."

Scilectra lashed out, "I see why the Professor preferred you over me. You're cunning and deceitful just like him!"

In the heat of the exchange, D.K. pressed a button to remove the image from the screen. Scilectra yelled at D.K. to put the image back up.

He responded, "I can't. I accidentally deleted it. I pressed the wrong button."

Ameerah had to take the focus off D.K. She said, "The picture had nothing on it. You've seen this box before and there was nothing to see. It wasn't a big deal."

Scilectra asked. "You know, Ameerah, that boy smells like you. You are related, aren't you?"

Ameerah responded, "Why does that matter? We're here doing what you told us to do . . . all of us are. We thank you for returning our lab mate, but we need for you to leave now."

Scilectra stated, "Not without my box, and not without you and your team being reminded of who and what I am."

Scilectra looked at D.K., closed her eyes, and outstretched her arms east to west. D.K began to seize up and turned a sickening blueish color. She was microwaving him from the inside out. Scilectra had D.K. in a paralyzing grip while black blood streamed from his nose ears and eyes.

Ameerah panicked and ran towards Scilectra at top speed like a running back! She dove over a table and pounced onto Scilectra, clinging to her, squeezing as hard as she could. Ameerah was absorbing all of Scilectra's power, so much so that D.K. was released from his impending death and both women hit the floor.

Ameerah was turning blue as well, but a different kind of blue, a glowing electric blue. By the time she let Scilectra go, Ameerah was floating in the air. The ends of her hair sparkled like stars in the night sky. Her eyes . . . oh, her eyes. They looked as if they were freshly chiseled 10-carat diamonds.

Scilectra lay on the floor. Her skin was no longer pale; a natural flesh tone was returning. Her hair limp and lifeless and the blue patches of Aurovian were faint, barely noticeable. Ameerah looked at herself in the reflection of a glass door and instantly dropped to the floor. She was afraid of herself. No one knew what to do.

The power shift that had just taken place was dynamic. Their relationship was forged in a crucible of conflict, and now their powers were interchangeable. Both Ameerah and Scilectra ran out of the lab in different directions, and the team stood there, dumbfounded as what to do next.

CHAPTER FORTY-TWO

Professor Sherman wallowed in his misery. Somehow, he managed to lose Scilectra, Ameerah, his lab, and now the NCF. This was clearly not the definition of winning. Tilda Swan's words cut him to his core, but deep down inside, he knew that she was right.

He thought to himself, *I'm pretentious and lewd. I know this . . . however, I didn't think that my style was so evident and off-putting to people. After all, this is what all influential people are made of.*

He refused to go home with his tail between his legs, and he missed Scilectra terribly. He thought, that if he went back to the power station subserviently, just maybe he could win her heart (and body) again. So, he changed his course of direction to put his plan back on track.

Sherman was never a smooth talker; words that moved women escaped him, and often. That explained his predilection for young girls. He honestly felt that they were easier to manipulate because their requirements were few. He felt that they didn't know what to expect in a man, and they were very eager to accept anything that simulated power and prestige.

This was especially important because most boys (men) learn about intimacy from pornographic videos and images. To say the very least, this was an unrealistic venue to learn anything of real substance or quality, it was quite the opposite.

He knew that they didn't realize the significance they held. And how could they? Their mothers were too embarrassed to tell them, and their fathers weren't around to show them. They didn't even bother telling their girls that they should never allow a man to pick what part of their bodies to be used to exemplify love. Men will say to these girls, "If you don't let me do this to you, you don't love me ... if you don't let me do that, you're not serious."

He thought, *Oh the things that I've done to make myself happy. But I'm sure it was painful for those girls. Sometimes I do feel bad, but not that bad.* He chuckled at how he breezed through sexual opportunities in his life because of this formula.

His thoughts were giving him too much self-realization. He decided to focus on the task at hand, which was "Mission #GetScilectraBack." On the ride over, he brushed up on his skills by listening to a little Peabo Bryson. "Yeah, yeah, ohhhhhh ... Close your eyes, and I'll love you ... I will make a smile down inside you ... I'm so into you!!!"

He listened, and he repeated the lyrics to the song with fluctuating intonations. When he felt that he succinctly covered all the salient points of "wooing," he sped on to the facility, feeling victorious. Not realizing that he grotesquely underestimated the situation.

The power station was an isolated locale, perfect for things that are harmful to the population or for ensconcing activities from prying eyes. The Professor drove down the long lonely road leading to his turn-off when he saw a nude woman lying flat by some brush on the roadside.

Curiosity got the better of him. He slowed the car to a stop and got out. Cautiously creeping forward, he suddenly realized that it wasn't just any girl ... it was Scilectra. No longer cloaked in her crowning glory of blue, she was framed in abandonment like a kitten looking for its mother.

He said, "My dear, what has happened to my Angel, my beautiful Angel?"

Scilectra was too spent to speak. Sherman scooped her up, laid her gently in the back seat of his car, and sped to the power station to revive her. It was reminiscent to their first trip there, but this time she was far gone, and he didn't know if he could bring her back. When they arrived, he left her in the car to retrieve the conductor strip for her spine.

He would have to connect her directly to a windmill with her cloak again, but this time he would have to dose her with more Aurovian to get her back to form faster. Outfitting her was the easy part; getting her vertical and aligned with the pole was another thing entirely! Last time he had the help of Duvall Swan. This time he wasn't so lucky.

He thought, *Here goes nothing!*

Sherman dragged her dead-weighted body to the front of his car and draped her across the hood. Then he gingerly drove her to the pole and pinned her with the car. In this position, he was able to stand her up and get the juices flowing to her. Now for the Aurovian! This dose was different; the Professor mainlined it directly into her veins, as this was the best way to optimize the Nanites. A direct slam would get it to her heart and complete the absorbtion into her entire system. If there was any humanity left in her, there wouldn't be after this.

It took seventy-two hours for Scilectra get her color back, three more days to bring her hair back to life, and two more agonizing days after that for her to achieve full power. The Professor stayed by her side, only leaving for the obligatory human necessities. When she was back to herself, she still did not speak with him.

The majority of her time was spent morosely contemplating Ameerah and what happened. This was the first time (since her transformation) she really questioned her mortality. Furthermore, Scilectra was having second thoughts about introducing her A.T.I into Ameerah's body.

She thought, *She's a danger to me now ... How much more would she be, when she transforms into Magnified Human?*

Sherman mindlessly tinkered over in the corner. He desperately wanted to know how her powers were drained to that magnitude. The facts were that he had no right to ask, not after she'd caught him with Ameerah, conspiring against her.

He said to her, "Whenever you feel you're ready to divulge what happened, I'll be waiting with a listening ear."

She quipped back at him, "A listening ear??? Isn't that how I found out about your treacherous plans against me? You would do well to take your leave of me as soon as possible."

He mumbled under his breath, "But I saved you ... again."

She responded, "Yes, you saved me again, but you didn't save me for the sake of my life. Your lascivious nature is the driving force of everything that you do. But I got you. Our union will be ratified, and soon. I'm not in the mood for your disjointed affection. If I have my way, you will spend the rest of your days on your knees, giving me my just due."

The Professor put his head down, shielding a sinister smile. He had no qualms with her threat. The fact was that he would for surely acquiesce, simply because he was a sick, sick man.

Professor Sherman's life was shrinking right before his eyes. His plans of ruling our universal existence with a beautiful attack dog by his side were fading away. New methods have to be instituted, if only he could find out how she lost her powers in the first place. He thought, *My amends may have to be with Ameerah and not Scilectra. That will be less complicated to achieve with a human, in comparison to whatever Scilectra is.*

CHAPTER FORTY-THREE

Although D.K. was worried about Ameerah, he was in no condition to chase after her. He asked Raj to be the one to find her and see if she was okay. Raj ran into the private quarters of the lab, searching each room, until he came upon Ameerah crouching in the corner of a closet. She no longer looked like the entity that she had morphed into earlier; her soft and subtle features returned, and her eyes were a warming shade of chestnut brown.

She cried out, "I don't know what happened! I just wanted to stop her from killing D.K. When I grabbed her, it felt like hot water rushing into my body. It felt so good, like a drug. The pull was involuntary, and I couldn't turn it off. Raj, I have to tell you something else."

Raj said, "Sure . . . anything!"

She went on, "I . . . I saw the threads. The threads that connect everything and everybody together. This matrix looked like an elaborate spider's web, and all those threads came together into one thread extending off the planet. That one thread was tethered to a place someone out in the universe."

Raj was fascinated by her words. He asked, "Is there anything else?"

She said, "Yes, I could see the threads for the living and the dead. Living beings, our threads are white; animals, their threads are blue; and souls have threads of purple. All the connections together, crisscrossing the world; it looks like rainbows encasing our world. The main thread going off into the ether is a color that I can't describe, I've never seen before."

Raj sat down on the floor with Ameerah, wrapped his arm around her, and let her cry.

He whispered in her ear, "What you saw is a revelation. Scientists and theologists have studied for years to prove what you've just seen with your own eyes: that we all are connected and everything affects everything else, but more importantly, we are all connected to one source!"

After an hour or so, Raj and Ameerah reappeared from the back to be greeted with hugs and tears.

Lisa stopped the ceremony with her practicalities, "I know that it may be too soon but what happened with you and Scilectra?"

Ameerah nodded her head and grinned, "Of course, Lisa the callous ice-breaker. Scientifically, I can say that she is an energy reservoir and I (apparently) am a consumer of that said energy. It seems that I can only hold on to it for a short while. That experience came with a litany of attributes; unfortunately, I wasn't able to explore them all in that limited period of time."

Raj cut his eyes at her, wondering why she failed to mention what she saw during the episode.

D.K. chimed in from a nearby patient bed, "The only thing that matters is that you broke that chick down! We won't be seeing her for a while."

The team laughed at the notion of her scaring Scilectra away. Ameerah kindly thanked everyone, hugged D.K. and asked Raj to give her a once over in his office.

Before they could make it to the exam room, Raj snapped at Ameerah, "What was that all about? Why didn't you tell them about what you experienced?"

Ameerah replied, "Look, I knew that you were going to feel some kinda way about that. To be completely honest, I'm not ready, and I don't know the truth about what I saw. To actualize conjecture is the basis of what most doctrines are founded on, and I won't be a part of that!"

Raj couldn't help but agree. To disseminate false information from one point of view was irresponsible and foolish. With that said, he proceeded with her exam. The results were riveting!

Ameerah' s body was riddled with new nanites. Somehow, that exchange with Scilectra induced the technology to reproduce organically. A better way to put it is to say that they cloned themselves. The strange thing was that the new "Cloned Nanites" were there but dormant. They may have been reserved or benched until game time.

Raj shared with Ameerah. "There is no way to explain them fully until they are called to power. Beyond that, your tests are normal. The last thing I need to do is take a few strands of your hair and dissect your follicles. Let's see where that will take us."

Savoy was eager to jump right back into the mix! Simon's hidden notes were the nucleus of the lab's waking world right then. Unfolding what he laboriously obstructed from their view would take time and a keen eye. Fortunately, that was Savoy's specialty. While the others sifted through his notes and online accounts, she thought it best to start researching the information he found on the box.

She paid particularly close attention to the phrases "Vexaverse" and "Monoceros Zone." When doing anything (especially research), it was always best to start at the beginning. That meant (at least to her) to go to the Bible. In Revelations, it describes a war in heaven between angels led by the Archangel Michael against those led by "the dragon," identified as the devil or Satan, who is defeated and thrown down to the earth.

Savoy researched a little further to confirm the verbiage. She read another account that said, ***"The great dragon was hurled down—that ancient serpent called the devil, or Satan, who leads the whole world astray. He was hurled to the earth, and his angels with him."***

She said to herself, "One would have to assume from reading those passages that Heaven is above the earth. Likewise, it's safe to say that Earth may be somewhat directly below Heaven's domain."

Savoy decided to talk this out with the most level-headed person in the lab and the one she was closest to, which was Lisa.

Lisa was always available to play Devil's Advocate when it came to theories. After Savoy called her into the conference room, Lisa fell into her intensive listening stage immediately.

Savoy shared her initial approach, then went on to say, "Here is where I'm puzzled. The real estate of the Universe is vast, too much to quantify, because it appears to be endless; not to mention whatever God-forsaken locations that have been swallowed by the Black Hole. This passage in the Bible makes me feel that we are unique (meaning Humans), or at least our experience is. I say this because out of all the locations and planets available to God, He sends the Devil to earth. To earth, to terrorize unsuspecting beings with no discernible weapons with to adequately fend him off.

"Then we go to the terminology used, thrown, cast down and hurled down. At least two of those phases overtly means 'below'. So, for me to surmise that we are directly below Heaven is not far off, unless God just set the Devil and his minions on a course to Earth on purpose; maybe He guided them here. If not, then the fall of Satan could have landed him anywhere in the galaxies; again, the universe is incalculable.

"We are the proverbial 'needle in the haystack' that was unlucky enough to pierce the Devil himself? I think not. I feel that our world was the aim, and that aim may have been a clear shot. All this to say that I think that the 'Vexaverse' is a realm situated above our stars, and somewhere in that realm is the Heavenly domain. We have been looking up and out when we should be looking as north as the universe can go."

Lisa sat there silently. Then she asked, "And what about the Monoceros Zone?"

Savoy responded, "I'm working my way to that one, but since you asked, to make a comparison, I think that Vexaverse is Heaven's Continent and the Monoceros Zone is Heaven's City. Scilectra's box is a virtual map of Heaven's location!"

Again, Lisa sat in silence, with her legs and arms crossed, twisting her lips as if she was in a debate with Savoy's presentation. Suddenly she blurted out, "I tend to agree with your synopsis. Let me tell you why. I know this is off-topic, but despite Scilectra's delivery, she has many good points. I don't think that it's God's design that all humans live in peace and harmony for fear that we would work together and encroach on the Throne.

"It clearly states in Genesis 11:6: *'And the Lord said, Behold, the people is one, and they have all one language; and this they begin to do: and now nothing will be restrained from them, which they have imagined doing. Go to, let us go down, and there confound their language, that they may not understand one another's speech.'* With that said, Wherever Heaven is, it reads as if He is perched high and above us, looking directly downward. However, He is God, and his eyes aren't limited to our human understand and our minimal vantage point.

"In contrast, my last statement will support God's decision to scatter the Babel folk, because what they were attempting was in direct violation of God's natural order and boundaries. I highly doubt that they had the technology needed to carry out such an audacious plan. But look at us right now today; we have access to brilliant technologies, and we decided to become a modern-day Babel community, ignoring the lessons about breaching the gates of Heaven. Although unity is a progressive aspiration . . . it has dangerous implications.

"Not to mention that we are binding God to the laws of our earth and immediate universe. I can say with all surety that north, south east, and west means nothing to Him and His principalities. Nor does gravity. The mere thought of God not being able to defy gravity is scary in and of itself!

"If you want to dig a little deeper . . . How do we know that the Earth has always been at this latitude and longitude? It's highly possible that our physical position has moved over the billions of years that it's existed. So, let's try your theory and see where it takes us. But doesn't rule out the gyroscope theory, because you just never know.

CHAPTER FORTY-FOUR

Ameerah packed up her things to head home for a few days. She hadn't seen her parents in months; besides that, she felt her monthly cycle coming. During those times of the month, she would rather be at home in the comfort of her own bed. The team was shocked to see her preparing to leave, but they understood.

Before she left, she told them, "Everybody needs a break. This shit we're dealing with is heavy. Turn on the monitors and notifications. Go home and see your families, just for the night, and let's be back here by eight in the morning."

They knew that this was a rare treat that might not happen again anytime soon, so they packed up, locked up, and headed home!

About an hour after the team cleared out, their alerts went off. No, it wasn't a guest dying; it was Scilectra. They all saw the alerts, but what could they do? For starters, no one was there. And if they were, without Ameerah . . . confronting her would be disastrous!

D.K. called Ameerah and as soon as she answered, her response was, "Yeah, I know, and let it be. I don't have the energy to deal with her today."

Scilectra wouldn't be there long, and unfortunately would leave empty-handed. She'd planned to steal Ameerah's tainted tampons. Her imagination has been running wild with thoughts of being dominated by her nemesis. The A.T.I science was impeccably accurate and left little room for doubt that Ameerah would topple her as the ultimate deified-being.

Scilectra rifled through all of Ameerah's belongings, and nothing remotely resembled what she was looking for.

By this point, Ameerah was over Scilectra and her barbaric style of life; she refused to allow anything to disturb her peace. Just viewing her front door from the curb was enough to knock her stress down to a manageable level. She pushed open the front door to a dimly lit room, her shoe bumped into something on the floor that let out a welcoming sound. It was her cat, Toast. He purred and walked around her ankles in circles; the troubles of the day instantly went away as she headed downstairs to her room.

She had made it home just in time; the pain from her cramps was unbearable. She said to herself, "The thunder before the storm."

The first order of business was to locate her personal effects. She knew better than to lay down before she inserted a tampon.

Ameerah's favorite color was white, but not because it was considered the color of the well-to-do. Her reasons were simplistic in nature: white could be bleached and be rid of all germs and diseases. It was funny, but this small thing is what put Ameerah on the path of science and research.

Ameerah though back on an experiment she did in grammar school. Her mother washed a load of colored towels with a double dose of liquid detergent. She rinsed and dried them thoroughly, then she folded them and put them in the linen closet. Ameerah went in behind her and pulled out a colored face cloth and a white one. She then poured Hydrogen Peroxide on the colored towel; the towel began to heat up, bubble, and then a white foam formed.

Then she poured peroxide on the white towel that had been laundered in bleach; the peroxide made a wet circle, and that was it. You see, peroxide will only heat up, bubble and foam in the presence of bacteria. From that day forward, she had to understand life on a molecular level, and the flip side of that was that nearly everything she owned had to be a brilliant white.

Ameerah found just the bag she was looking for. She went into the bathroom, pulled down her pants and crouched over the toilet. She put one end of the package in her teeth and tore it open, using one hand to squeeze the cotton tube out of the wrapper. Frowning her face, she inserted the white pillowy log of cotton as far up her canal as it could go.

Remembering that she was still a virgin, she laughed to herself, "I always have to be cognisant not to take my own virginity trying inserting a damn tampon!"

She had no idea what she'd done! As Ameerah took a hot shower and headed for bed, she was confident that a good night's rest in her own bed would make her a different person in the morning. No truer words had ever been spoken.

During her sleep, the A.T.I absorbed in her system and coursed through her veins. The concoction put her in a coma-like state, since the A.T.I required a physical reset to re-map the human genes. The last place Ameerah wanted to be was locked in her dreams, but there she was. Always in an unfamiliar location, this time out amongst the stars, she could hear the wails and clicks of the souls talking. It was beautiful to hear it in person, to be enveloped by the vibrations each sound made.

Stars were so close that she could reach out and touch them as they crackled by. Ameerah propelled herself forward, only to turn around and see earth thousands of miles away.

She said, "There's the sun, and I'm so close, yet I feel no heat; why is it allowing me to get closer and closer?"

When Ameerah made it there, the sun gave her knowledge that only it could know. It said (speaking to her mind), "I was the first thing created by the source, and my power is renewed every day to do my necessary work. I'm sure that you're wondering what we are, these planets and stars . . . and why is Earth so unique? The Earth is the only planet that is made of elements from each star and planet in the universe. Gold, helium, diamonds, hydrogen, and so forth are not natural elements of Earth; it was gifted to your world to create an atmosphere special, just for you. Now it's the only location that's a combination of everything the source has ever made. Even the site of your world is in the perfect spot to thrive like no other. When you return to life, verify my words, read what each heavenly body is made from and re-evaluate your world. You will see that I'm right and how rare humans are."

Her surrounding gradually faded to black. When she awoke everything appeared different; the same, but different. Ameerah sat up on the bed and peered around her room. The walls had a strange symmetry to them, the same with the floor. She had the feeling as though they weren't relevant anymore, as if she had the option of utilizing them or not. She stretched out her legs to walk to the bathroom, and it felt like she was walking for the first time. Every muscle and ligament expanded and contacted with each breath she took.

Ameerah sat down to pee. Just the mere thought of that intention erased the need to do so. Her bladder felt newly emptied without discharging the urine. At this point in time, she was convinced that she was still in her vivid dream state.

How wrong she was. Ameerah was definitely awake, existing in her new "normal". Time has gotten away from her. She looked at the antique clock on the wall and could've sworn that the hands on the face warped with every tick.

She said, "Okay, I must be drunk! I'll voice dial Lisa and ask her to pick me up."

Scilectra had been scanning the airwaves all night, hoping to hear Ameerah voice and to race to her location. She finally heard the transmission she was waiting for . . . unfortunately, it sounded as if she was too late. Latching on to the signal, Scilectra rode the wave to Ameerah's location and surprised her with yet another impromptu visit.

Scilectra called out, "Ameerah . . . Ameerah."

She responded, "What in the world is going on??? How did you find out where I lived? Why are you in my home?"

Scilectra replied, "I'm not here to fight, I need to share something with you. This is something you truly need to hear."

Ameerah said, "I'm in no mood for you. You and the Professor have ruined my life, and now my mind is playing tricks on me!"

"That's why I'm here," Scilectra said. "I have long realized that you're special, and I thought there was no better person to enhance with untold abilities than you. I infiltrated your lab and dosed your feminine inserts with my created A.T.I. matter."

Ameerah, infuriated, responded, "You did what? What the hell is A.T.I?"

Scilectra said, "It's an Advanced Thought Integration. You will have the ability to manifest your thoughts physically. Think of it as God giving you carte blanche with prayer requests. This takes your God out of the equation. Just think of what you will be able to do for yourself and others. I have given you the greatest gift!"

Ameerah quipped back, "So I have you to thank for that freaky ass dream last night! So stupid, talking to the sun, as if that could ever happen!"

Scilectra interrupted her rant, saying, "I don't think you understand. That was no dream ... not really. You can enter a dream state and awaken your core-self; from there, you can go wherever you want. Your experience will be different only because you're devoid of your human obstacles.

"You have no senses in that state of being, no nerves to calculate things like pain, coldness, heat and even fear. You're at your purest in that place. Soon you will be able to take your flesh with you and have no adverse effects from traveling in the void. What I do find strange is that you have my blood in you now, but I cannot detect where you were then or where you are now. Your transformation should have been complete by now.

"There is one more thing ... it's about your eyes. Did you know that the technical titles for your eyes are dexter (right eye) and sinister (left eye)? The veil has been lifted, and those terms will be literal for you (if you force the use of them). You will see everything good of something only from your right eye and everything bad from your left. Because of this, your primary vision will flow through your third eye where you can see and discern it all; the eyes on your face are purely there for decoration."

Right before Ameerah could ask another question, she heard her mom call down, "Meenah, are you down there? If so, Lisa is here to pick you up."

Ameerah sneered at Scilectra, "You have to go now. I'm sure we will pick this up again soon."

Scilectra stepped backward and diffused into the air around them.

Ameerah yelled back, "Thanks, Mom, be there in a minute."

She took a last glance at the new "Her." With this new information, she looked as she stood in the mirror, closed her eyes to give full priority to her third eye. She was no longer upset about the intrusive gift. Ameerah realized that she was the microscope now and that she could live on a molecular level. She was excited to see what else she could do.

CHAPTER FORTY-FIVE

T he Professor couldn't have known the events that had already taken place, and what he was about to do was detrimental to his plans. Suited and booted, he was waiting at the edge of Lab-J71's parking lot with binoculars in hand. Looking and lurking, hoping to catch a glance of Ameerah entering or exiting the building. Unfortunately, it wasn't safe for him to call her (not that she would answer anyway).

He also wasn't clear on what he could offer her to get back into good standings. With Ameerah, it's always about the science. The Professor could have lavished her with expensive gifts of equipment for rare finds jetting around the galaxy, but he wouldn't. Despite the luxury that he bestowed on himself, he was downright niggardly towards anyone else. He couldn't help it; it was his way.

What's more, his impure inclinations were the constant driver of his vehicle. If there was an opportunity to dominate the situation, he surely would. He thought, *Ameerah has a puritanical quality to her that makes me want to give it to her even more. How do I bridle that desire to achieve my first objective? Ameerah has been the Gordian Knot that I can't untie.*

He waited for a while. Hours had gone by until he saw the lab's van pull into the dock. Finally, there was Ameerah (with Lisa). Approaching her out of the blue was one thing, but approaching her with Lisa was something entirely different. Lisa was not one to be trifled with, at any time. His short mission turned into a stakeout. The only other alternative was to go into the lab, where he knew he wasn't welcome.

Sherman decided to give her a little time to get settled before he made an appearance; plus, formulating a strategy before he entered the building could make all the difference. While he sat in his car strategizing, he thought back on the troubles he had caused and how it all started.

Sherman opened his glove box and pulled out a digital recorder and began to speak into it.

"The world has successfully 'thingified' the vagina, and it was a long time coming. Mouths and anuses, too. We aimed and dove directly on the slippery slope of what we know today as panamory and even bestiality. We were doing everything but fuckin' flowers! What women (or people) don't understand is that who or what men want and lust after is not our personal choice; our bodies lead the way.

"This may sound funny, but in another life, our situation could be considered a medical condition, primarily due to its involuntary nature. Once a visible connection is made, it's chased by a chemical reaction, and then a physical enactment MUST follow whether that's with someone else (something else) or with ourselves. These events require a release, which is why there's no stopping once the act has begun. Let me rephrase that: we can stop, but those of us that are climax-oriented will not stop. It would be easier to ask me to un-ring a bell. End."

Ameerah was eager to get to the lab. She motioned Raj toward his office for a private talk. She sat him down and explained what happened the night before and the events that took place that morning. Needless to say, Raj was exhausted from the news and started another litany of tests to try and understand what Scilectra did and how it would affect Ameerah in the long run.

One of the tests centered on the chemicals in her brain and how they related to this new entity in her body. He discovered that the A.T.I. gene's commitment to the body could only be solidified if it had ample dopamine to lure it in. Ameerah's newly acquired abilities were not entirely taking hold because she had an insufficient amount of dopamine being produced and released in her brain.

Raj said, "Savvy design, really. She took something mandatory for the mind to function and made it the fuel for her gene to thrive.

In an average person, she would have had them lock, stock and barrel, but with you? You're half in and half out. However, this does explain why you can't wake from a deep sleep; frankly, it explains a lot. Not only does it open and close your mind's shade to tell you when to sleep and when to be awake, but it also controls the mechanisms by which a healthy libido is fostered, including desire and arousal. You're really not a virgin by choice or your work schedule; lack of dopamine makes you uninterested."

Ameerah let out a big "Huh ... What a way to find that out! I guess one day, I will look into correcting that. But as far as I'm concerned, you can't miss something you never had. Besides that, is there anything that you can see?"

Raj replied, "Yes and no. Your blood work is unusual; nothing life-threatening, but your DNA has definitely been reformatted as she said. It also has a unique behavior to it: it travels through your body like spores in a constant state of regeneration. It looks like you will remain twenty-eight forever!

"I took samples and exposed them to different sound frequencies, and they changed shape with each different note. When exposed to electricity, one drop divided into two, two into four, and so forth. You are the prover-bial fountain of youth all within yourself.

"The other part is something I don't have the technology to investigate. My guess is that you currently exist on two (or more) different planes. You, my dear, are (in a sense) a galactical-being. Let's take it slow and see what unfolds in the future for you."

Ameerah agreed and gave Raj a big hug. She asked that she be allowed to tell the team when she was ready.

CHAPTER FORTY-SIX

Sherman saw Lisa and D.K. exit the building and drive off.

He said, "Ahhh, this is the perfect time for a visit!"

He exited his car and walked in the shadows to the dock of the building. After entering, he was pleased to see that the receptionist was away, but security was properly on their post. It took a moment and a few greenbacks, but he was able to finagle his way to the lab's door.

Knock . . . knock . . . knock, the Professor unassumingly rapped on the door. To his delight, Ameerah was the one that answered.

The Professor was awestruck. She was absolutely gleaming and succulent; to his surprise, she wasn't combative.

She politely asked, "How may I help you, Professor?"

He was rendered speechless. This was something he hadn't anticipated.

He said, "My, my, my, Ameerah . . . to what do I owe the honor of cordiality?"

She replied, "Professor, you just don't damn matter anymore. I have been elevated to another level that your slithering presence can't reach."

He snidely responded, "Your tongue is a wet venomous sword that strikes at the heart of me. I'd love to trade your words in kind, but we have bigger fish to fry!"

She said, "Speaking of?"

Sherman zipped to his answer. "Scilectra. Let's focus on how to neutralize the threat."

Ameerah replied, "Yes, the gift that keeps on giving. Fine, come on in and make it quick. D.K. will be back soon, and you might not want to be here when he does."

Sherman responded, "Point well taken. If you don't mind, please retrieve the box. Let's start there."

Ameerah was more than happy to go over the box with Professor Sherman because she had no plans on disclosing what they learned about it. She carried the box to the conference room and placed it on the table right in front of him.

He said, "It really is a lovely piece . . . what have you learned thus far?"

She replied, "At the risk of shattering my professional image, we haven't learned much. The digits that you provided have not revealed anything useful. D.K. has been running them through his code detection algorithm, but nothing of value so far. What about you, Professor? Has Scilectra disclosed anything that may be considered a lead?"

Deep in his gut, he knew that Ameerah was withholding information, but he refused to badger her about it. His ultimate goal was to get back in her tolerable graces and grow from there. However, he couldn't resist easing closer to her. Her very scent was intoxicating; she smelled of honey and peaches. Sweat settled on her skin like morning dew. What was more ironic was that his closeness didn't repulse her; he was now entering her personal space, and she didn't flinch or say a word.

Ameerah glanced over to him with a coy look on her face, and she said, "Ron, I see you converging on me like a hawk that has spotted a fat mouse. This is not for you; it will never be for you. I can see you so much clearer now, and I know what makes you tick. You can't have me because you're irresponsible, you're ill-timed, and you're unappreciative. You're so close to me right now that I can literally hear your juices flowing to a head. So take it all in and remember this moment. Today will be the last time that you covet me in this way!"

A series of beeps broke the intense connection between Ameerah and the Professor. She smirked at him and gave him a wink; confused as ever, he read her face and turned around to see Scilectra standing in the room.

Ameerah had known was there before the alert. She could see her standing in the darkness of the void, but she wasn't going to let on to either her or the Professor.

Scilectra wouldn't address Ameerah in a negative manner, since she didn't know what she was dealing with yet. She walked past them both and saw her box on the table. That angered her even more. She was incensed for two reasons; again, another confirmation that the Professor loved Ameerah, and that the two may have been conspiring against her.

The Professor began to cower (which was his default position) and beg to be heard out.

Scilectra ignored him to ask Ameerah, "Why do you continue to plan my demise, even after the gifts that I gave you?"

Ameerah responded, "You and your maker raped me in one way or another. You even more so, because you got me to violate myself for your purposes. Since there's no way to give it back to you, I decided to make the best of it and test drive the shit out of my new-found wealth! You know, now that I think about it, the Professor can be some use to me; I'm twenty-twenty-eight now, and my biological clock is ticking. Maybe I can use him for what he's good for. You should go now; the Professor and I have business to attend to. I'll send him home later; you know, when I'm done."

Sherman was too afraid to peek up after hearing Ameerah's confession (although he wanted to). His focus was on getting Scilectra out of the room so that he could (at the very least) live another day and to take Ameerah up on her offer!

He said, "Scilectra, this is not what you think. If you won't leave . . . I will! Let's take a few more days to cool off, and we can talk things over then."

"Unfortunately, I'm not done. Professor, I've never had a passenger ride through the void with me. You'll be the first."

Professor Sherman begged, "Scilectra . . . No, please, can we talk?"

She replied, "Yes, we can, back at the facility."

Forgetting all about Ameerah and the box, she wrapped herself around Sherman and snatched him into thin air.

They arrived back at the windmill facility within seconds. She released

Sherman from her grip, and he hit the floor with a thump, writhing in pain and vomiting.

"Professor, even though I'm disappointed in your deeds, I still need you, and I need you now. I require a child, and you are destined to procreate with me."

He said, "A child ... now? I'm in no condition to participate in such activities with you. I have to recuperate from traveling in a manner for which my body is ill-equipped."

She responded, "Let me help you."

She slowly removed the cape that he designed for her to insulate her energy. Pacing toward him in an animalistic gait, she laid with him on the floor. She carefully disrobed him and pressed her tingling skin against his. She turned her frequency up to energize and stimulated him at the same time.

The Professor was erect and ready for her to mount him. It didn't take long; she clung on, vigorously thrusting her hips back and forth atop of him, draining the Professor of all the reproductive material his body had to offer. She used electrical pulses deep down inside her wet canal to sting his manhood so that he could continuously produce semen for her purposes. When she had her fill, she unclamped herself and watched him wind down from the pleasure overload.

This would be her last encounter with him. She reached her crescendo during the mating act and secreted radiation-filled gelatinous material on him and in him, which would be his end, and sooner rather than later. In his sleep, she covered his head and took him through the void one last time; she placed him on an examination table in the tombs at the NCF, and then she was gone.

The following morning, he woke to find himself exhausted and alone. For once, he was happy that Scilectra wasn't there. He decided to go home and spend a little time there to recover. She didn't have the coordinates to his home, so he felt safe from prying eyes and unannounced visits. He hadn't been home for weeks because of recent events and thought it was about time to do so.

Not many people knew this, but Professor Sherman had a family. Since he was a notoriously private man, no one had the opportunity to visit his home and interact with him on a personal level. He lived in a large residence on a private estate with his sister, Robin, who was deaf, and an older cousin named Nora, who took care of the house and his sister when he was away.

Having him in the house on a daily basis was a rare treat for them. Robin and Nora looked forward to catching up and having family time. That first evening, Nora made dinner; she put out a massive spread for the three of them. Sherman ate like a bird. He looked gaunt and tired. Nora made mention that he should retire to his room to get some rest. Sherman agreed; he just didn't feel right.

He started to realize that Scilectra had taken a toll on him, so much so that he decided to take a few more days to rest and gain his composure. Each visit to the lab with Scilectra left him feeling out of sorts in one way or another; he really felt that he was overworking himself. This last go-around made him feel sick, but he had no choice: there was no one who could do this work. Better yet, no one else could know.

His thoughts kept returning to the first time he physically touched Scilectra, and how she insisted that he take her virginity. And how this second time felt strange to him, her insisting that they have sex, despite the ordeal that his body was going through. Of course, he wanted her in that way, Who wouldn't? However, he would've never insisted on ... not with her.

Truthfully, he felt it necessary to plant his seed because of the powers that he'd bestowed upon her. *She is mine. I made her what she is!*

He wondered, *What would a child saturated with her DNA be like? The things it would be able to do ... and it would part of me as well! This child could be the Prince of the Universe, and I would be King. So, I did it, I deflowered the tree of life. Why should I be ashamed? Damn right I did, and I'd do it again and again! What better man than me!*

Weirdly, this exchange with Scilectra made him think about the only person he considered to have been a friend. He said, "I wasn't crazy about Swan at first, but what she did to him was unacceptable!"

He finally realized that he couldn't tame her and that she had to be resolved some way somehow. Evidently, she has found a way to power herself up and down without my help. Or maybe she evolved to the point of not needed that process at any longer. All that he knew was that he wasn't feeling well, and he needed rest and some time away.

Strangely, several days after the void and sexual encounter incident with Scilectra, she had left him weary and pained with headaches; this night he headed for bed early. The next morning, Professor Sherman opened his eyes to a blood-soaked pillow. His initial attempt to raise his head from the clotted mess was thwarted due to the dried blood doubling as an adhesive. He was affixed to the pillow and the surrounding duvet.

In a fright, he peeled himself from the bedding in a symphony of snaps, crackles and smacks performed by the congealed blood. He ran to the bathroom to wash his face and to locate the wound that he assumed he suffered during the night, but there was none.

He screeched for his cousin, "Nora, take me to the hospital, NOW!"

They raced to the emergency room and nervously waited to be called to an exam room.

"Mr. Sherman . . . Mr. Sherman", they heard from across the room.

"Yes, yes, I'm here," the Professor said. The triage nurse motioned for the pair to walk through the huge door that she held open with her foot.

After hours of tests, the physician sadly informed the Professor that he has been diagnosed with an illness brought on by acute exposure to radiation. The Professor lowered his head because he knows exactly how this took place. The radiation has affected his brain and other internal organs; other problems were not far behind. The doctor said that the prognosis was poor, and given the rate of progression, he didn't have long to live. His health would deteriorate quickly.

The doctor went on to say that once the illness progressed, he would be bedridden and would rely on morphine to keep the pain at bay. All he could do was think of what he'd done, what he had selfishly created: an omen in the world that he wouldn't be around to control nor benefit from. Devastated, the Professor and Nora returned home to prepare for the next phase of his life. The Professor refused to believe that this was so; he made more calls, asked about possible obscure experiments and beta testing for new drugs to help him.

The Professor was focused on staying alive. Despite second, third, and fourth opinions, the ER physician was not wrong. Within a couple of months, he couldn't communicate. His normally statuesque frame had dwindled down to nothing, and he was limited to blinking his eyes to declare either "yes" or "no".

Nora had the daunting task of settling the Professor's affairs. She happened across his Driver's License in his belongings. She flipped the License over and discovered that he had chosen to be an organ donor. Nora spent time researching the best place to donate his organs and remains. She identified the name of a medical facility she found in his files, that she felt would get the best use of her cousin's weakening body. She contacted the facility, registered Professor Sherman for intake, and prepared him for the trip.

The Professor was usually sedated because of the intense pain he experiences, so he would need to be dosed again when they reached their destination. They arrived at the medical facility, and to Nora's surprise, a young lady met them at the elevator and then accompanied them down a well-lit corridor to the hospice wing. Nora noticed that the Professor was wincing in pain; his last morphine drip was wearing off, so she gave him a little more to make him comfortable. The Professor went back into a deep sleep.

When the professor woke up this time, he opened his eyes to yet another grim scene. A deep sense of dread enveloped him completely, followed by fear and sorrow. His muscles were locked and his tongue stiffened from his illness. He laid there connected to sensors and wires under a crystal-clear glass, staring up at five familiar and callous faces.

No one had to tell him anything; he knew exactly where he was and what was about to happen next. He could hear the ramping up of the Aurovian and the meter ticking and clicking in time. As the air faintly whispered away, the team smiled at him, and the Professor grimaced at them in return. He lay there, ornery to the end.

What he regretted at this particular moment was that even in death he would not be rid of them; they would be with him wherever he went, watching and listening. He knew that if there were a good place, it wouldn't have him, and the other place would be salivating in anticipation of him.

He could smell the signature metallic scent of the Aurovian misting up from his chin, and he thought about what he'd done to Ameerah, to Astrid, and to the world. Remaining defiant, he stood firm on his faulty ground. With his last breath and his girthy rigid tongue, he murmured his final words: "Flectere si nequeo superos, Acheronta movebo" ("if I cannot bend the heavens above, I will move Hell!").

Ameerah's lone calm voice proudly announced that Subject: Zeta-SZ—281574 had been tagged.

CHAPTER FORTY-SEVEN

Scilectra watched Professor Sherman die while hovering in the void. It was over and done now. She took from him what she needed and sent him on his way. Despite her love for him, she would not allow another to tamper with destiny. She thought to herself, *The plan has to stay on track no matter what! God must be outed for orchestrating this elaborate masquerade. If there's a Heaven to be found, my feet of flesh will be the first on the firmament to verify it!*

Scilectra looked down to her belly and smiled, and then she released her hold in the void. Although her anchor was gone, she wanted to find out where he would be for his eternity.

Lisa called the Professor's next of kin to reclaim the body for burial. The rest of the team went back to work. Ameerah lingered there a little longer, looking at the Professor in his empty state. She had an emotional wince while peering into the vessel. She did feel something for him. He was her mentor at one point, then her colleague. She was ashamed and embarrassed at the duality she was experiencing.

As she stared at him, she thought, *I totally get how people start to relate and care for the person that hurt them; there's a constant battle of what's right and empathy with what's wrong. Ultimately, the abuser wins because they rest in the middle of those two places and pilfer all that energy. We have a human need of wanting to be approved and accepted; when we're not, our quest to find out why can lead to unhealthy places with unhealthy people.*

Savoy interrupted mid-thought, saying, "I have news on a direction to go in for Heaven's location!"

That was music to Ameerah's ears. The IDIAMTRACE-10 was prepped in search mode and ready to go. It took a while, but they were able to locate the Monocerus Zone with the help of the data acquired by the souls. It was so far from anything recognizable by NASA's Hubble Telescope that even with extreme magnification, it looked like a speck of dust.

Savoy said, "What we are looking for is beyond that location; it may actually be on the exterior of our Universe. There's no reference anywhere of the Vexaverse, not in biblical references, lore, or mythology. And rightfully so. If that is the realm where Heaven resides, then there's no purpose to advertise it!"

Lisa interjected, "Let's not overlook that the Vexaverse is apparently another or alternate universe altogether. There may be challenges crossing over to it without (for lack of a better term) an invitation. Also, a soul may comprehend where they are without knowing the address or the directions on how to get there.

"When you're a passenger, you tend to go along for the ride and not pay attention to how (direction-wise) you get there. I mention this because if we are going to give this knowledge to Scilectra, we must be more precise. If we can't go there ourselves armed with the knowledge that we have, then I don't see how it can be done with the level of accuracy that we need."

"Maybe I can help!" a distinguished voice declared from behind them. It was an older woman with graying blonde hair, dressed to the nines in an expensive designer get-up.

D.K. cried out, "Geez . . . is that damn door ever locked?"

The woman said, "My name is Tilda Swan, and Duvall was my younger brother. I have been dispatched at his behest to your lab. If you have a moment, I would like to chat."

Ameerah said, "Please come in and have a seat. I do have a question for you. How did all of this come about?"

Tilda was happy to respond. "I speak to you now with the utmost confidentiality. Duvall took video and written detailed accounts of what Professor Sherman was doing in his lab at the NCF, and of his encounters with someone named 'Scilectra.' I'm not from a scientific background, so a few things lost me; despite that, I gathered the gist of what he was saying.

"You may have heard that Duvall may not be among the living anymore, but his records indicate that he promised you an investment into Lab-J71. I assure you that his offering is very generous. I will personally double the figure if you can find a way to shut that loathsome and mischievous Professor Sherman down for good."

Chad came to the rescue. "No worries on that, Ms. Swan. The Professor has since passed away. Right here in our lab, in fact. Does that qualify as us 'shutting him down'?"

She responded, "Although I'm pleased to hear it, no, that doesn't qualify you. Instead, would you accept a consolation prize? I have all his equipment and remaining research in a storage unit on my property. You're more than welcome to come pick it up."

There were cheers all around the room.

Tilda asked to speak with Ameerah privately, and she complied. "Ameerah, Duvall spoke highly of you, almost to the point of endearing." She blushed at the notion that Swan thought of her in such a way.

Tilda went on. "This is where our newfound relationship gets sticky. I have some rather intimate details of your work. The ramifications of what you're doing have spectacular financial implications, and I want in!"

Ameerah responded, "How so? This is not a time-share or a toy to be played with. You can't just 'get in' on this."

Ameerah focused in on the lone image on Tilda Swan's lapel and real-ized that it was a symbol not seen by many (in person anyway). It was the sigil of the people that ran it all, the one percent of the population that held the real wealth of the world.

Who would have guessed that Duvall had this type of power? Ameerah disengaged the small, simple letter "A" symbol (it has a double meaning: "A" for "Alpha" and "A" for "Archimedes") inside an Omega symbol (representing the last to survive) of negative space;

The 1% Sigil Icon

an inverted pyramid (representing the secret inverted pyramid under the Great Pyramid in Egypt) completed the art. A layman would assume that she had pledged a sorority in her younger years. To the trained eye, she most certainly did—one with a pricey membership.

Their clan patterned their entire ideology after Archimedes and his famed screw device. He was a Greek mathematician, physicist, engineer, inventor, and astronomer. Although few details of his life are known, he is regarded as one of the most leading scientists in classical antiquity.

The device he created was a screw-like water delivery method. It took water from the bottom of a low-filled river or lake that was hard to reach and brought it effortlessly to the top. This required little to no work from the operator but obtained more water than needed. The one-percenters used this method as a model to siphon wealth from the bottom (or weak) to the top. This keeps them and their families rich for many generations.

The way the conversation was going, Ameerah felt that Tilda's position was more of a directive than an offer.

Ameerah asked, "What exactly do you want in on?"

Tilda replied, "Before your work becomes public knowledge, I want the right to explore other applications for it. Of course, you and your team will be paid handsomely."

Then Ameerah asked, "And if we refuse?"

Tilda chuckled, "Like I said, I have intimate knowledge of your work. Another lab tinkering with the unknown could enjoy the fruits of your labors."

Ameerah fumed because knew this to be true. She bit her tongue for the moment and politely walked Tilda to the door.

She said, "Give us a few days to talk it over, and we will set up a formal meeting with you then."

Tilda smugly tossed her wrap around her neck and walked out the door.

D.K. ran over to Ameerah and said, "Screw all that noise. We gotta finds out what she knows, and fast!"

CHAPTER FORTY-EIGHT

D.K. was designated by Ameerah to search high and low for a way to investigate Ms. Tilda. People like her always had three faces: the propaganda face, the business face, and then the personal face. He had to bob and weave through the first layers before he could get to the last.

The Swan brand was strong and deep. They owned property in every city and every country in the world. Their businesses portfolio was triple that amount.

He wasn't concerned with their portfolio, not necessarily; he wants to know her collection individually. What was she into ... where did she spend her time? When you're dealing with the elite, they respond to two things: power, and submission; obtaining power, and who they can make subservient to that power. Surprisingly enough, they spent a massive amount of capital taking stake in large Church organizations. The reason was simple. The powers that be had learned something oddly unique about many Christians: their Faith doesn't go beyond the church doors.

They will show up every Sunday, even twice a week and learn how instrumental Faith is; they will teach it to their children and wear t-shirts and jewelry that advertises Faith. However, the moment they are confronted with an opportunity, a solid business deal, or a minor challenge, that reiterated faith goes right out the window, not to be found again until next Sunday in church.

The one-percenters were taking advantage of the fact that religious folk love buzz words and would follow them to the ends of the Earth with cash in hand. Whether Duvall Swan purposely meant to do it or not, he was following suit with his family's brand. So, buying the NCF made total sense. That one single entity controlled thousands of large and mega churches throughout the world. You could call it the American version of the Vatican.

During his research, D.K found a little-known fact. The Swans had a stake in the prestigious Mandervilt family due to a sizable loan given to them over 100 years ago, which was why the logo on the famed Mandervilt fashion line was a pink swan with a pearl necklace. The Swans' business prowess was ferocious, and now Tilda was the Head Beast in charge!

D.K. said, "She's good. Really good. But I'm better!"

In his line of business, depending on what you were looking for, you had the web. That's the main internet that the general population uses. Then you had the Dark Web (Silk Road) for people looking to do some sinister stuff. For people dealing in money and world domination, there was the "Vulture Web." This is where all the Presidents and Sultans are made, and where the Kings die. Here is where the life and death of entire societies are determined over a card game, with a little single malt on the side.

D.K. created an identity for himself so that he could stroll the vulture freely while looking into Tilda. The Swans were into weapons, heavy! Creating next level weaponry was at the top of her docket; that explained her interest in modifying the Aurovian. In the wrong hands, it could kill or control the populace of the entire planet.

He said to himself, "What is up with these rich people and world domination?"

He paused for a second and said, "Wha . . . What . . . wait a minute. Ms. Tilda is into Digital Drugs!"

D.K. read in a case study file about a product called Freq-TZ. It was regarding a subject named Mora. It said the following:

* * *

Mora sticks the needles between her toes . . . This is her favorite place. She does this to hide her track marks. She has a distinct job, and needle marks aren't part of the optics package. Typically, when someone uses heroin, their brain floods with dopamine, an electric rush of intense pleasure . . . and then the infamous nod. The euphoria doesn't last long. The skin will become red and flush. The heaviness quickly sets in, and after, that a dry mouth comes next.

Watching through the glass, we can see that Mora attempts to moisten her mouth by smacking her lips together. The pasty dryness on her tongue is prevalent as the hit descends. The less pleasurable feelings associated with heroin seep in, like the extreme itching, nausea, and vomiting. The pleasure will be gone in minutes. Mora typically enters a period of severe drowsiness for a few hours. The patient will be introduced to Freq-TZ as a follow-up to her former experience.

Heroin can be smoked, injected, or snorted. When it is injected into veins, the user experiences a most extreme high almost immediately. In under ten seconds, the user is where they need to be. However, tolerance builds quickly. The first high is usually the most intense they'll ever have.

Using has changed since the onset of Digital Drugs. You can't build up a tolerance to them because they never enter your physical system, so each high is the first high. Digital Drugs are unique. They are sound waves that are sent and received digitally in an audible file. When received (via smartphone), the user types in a (one-time use) 4-digit password drug is listened to via unique headphones/earbuds/Bluetooth.

Drugs like Freq-TZ are sound waves that manipulate the brain, giving the recipient a feeling of being high. It can even give the user particular sound waves that trick the brain. The mind believes that it's tasting, smelling and having accompanying sensations during the using episodes. Different audio clips offer a different high. The seller only needs one version of each type of drug clips and can resell them millions of times over. The sales of the drugs are done entirely digitally and purchased by bitcoin and other digital currency.

* * *

D.K. was jealous that he hadn't thought of this first. At any rate, they had a way to get to Tilda, at least long enough to get their intellectual property out of her hands. He packed up his gear and headed back to the lab with the good news. Ameerah would be happy to know that Ms. Tilda has an Achilles heel, even if it was via her eardrums.

CHAPTER FORTY-NINE

Savoy was hard at worked mapping her way through the stars to find the opening to the Vexaverse. From what she was seeing, all accounts of that location being outside of the universe was correct. There were no telescopes or satellites to aid her in her search; manmade technology to see that far just didn't exist yet. If only she could get a soul to travel to the Vexaverse; at least that way they would have a starting point to move forward.

She decided to speak with Simon's pet souls. Savoy couldn't shake the unauthorized feeling of talking to them, knowing that Simon would be very much against it. It was a gamble anyway, because at some point in time, they would have to relinquish their freedom and go to their final resting places (be it Heaven or Hell). She just hoped it was not too late.

Savoy's Fregodian was flawless, almost musical. Every sound she emitted had a Greek siren-like quality. You couldn't help but respond to her calls. Luckily for the team, the souls were not immune to her intoxicating vocal scales. After several minutes of repetitive moans and clicks, a tagged soul responded. Savoy asked if it would make the journey for them, just until they could feel a higher frequency.

Since God resonates on the highest frequency, a soul can feel the difference. It's similar to a human going from the bitter cold to the relief of warmth. The soul agreed but made it clear that it could not stay there long or go beyond that point. It said, "It is forbidden if you are not called to be there."

Savoy waited until the soul stopped traveling to gauge a location. Then she assigned a latitude and longitude to that very spot. This would be their ground-zero to the Vexaverse. It was a good news/bad news situation; if they didn't find a soul to carry on from that location, then they would have nothing concrete. They would be left with unproven speculation.

She took the information that she had to Ameerah. In delivering the news, Savoy said, "We're in a weird place! It's almost as if we have too much data, and not enough at the same time. It's agreed that many of our souls have made it to Heaven. The problem is that the Nanites can't quantify the location because of all the travel.

"Alternate locations that the souls travel to first *is* the problem. In this case, the nanites are along for the ride. What we need is a soul that can leave earth and go straight to Heaven. Then we would have an exact qualifying location, route, and newly created latitude/longitude."

Ameerah took a minute to think about what was said. She responded, "I may have a way. Let me speak with Raj first, and I'll get back to you."

This was the conversation that Ameerah didn't want to have. It was time to test her skills out, without ignoring the apparent dangers she could face. She understood what had happened to her; what she doesn't know was what that meant. Her powers weren't tried, tested and proven. Before she attempted the ultimate journey, a test-run was in order!

Scilectra traveled the void for days looking for the Professor's soul. She didn't move quickly enough to trail him to his next place. She thought she'd caught a glimpse of him amid the crowded ether. What confused her was that he wasn't alone. She learned that souls will co-travel, but most souls wander the stars alone.

Even still, his scenario was different; his soul was being ushered by two huge dark entities on either side of him, almost like he was attempting to go a different direction than intended. She decided not to follow because the aura restricted her from getting too close.

She was determined to see him again, but for now, that would have to wait. Scilectra returned to the earthly plane to reckon with Ameerah. Despite the standing of their current relationship, she had to keep the heat on. Ameerah and her team would find the coordinates for her, even if it meant the death of both of them! Her father always said to her, stay angry . . . because anger gets shit done when skills can't!

When Scilectra arrived at the lab, she waited in the void and listened for the team to speak candidly about their findings. Ameerah was leading the conversation and then abruptly stopped talking. She turned and walked to the very spot where Scilectra was in the void. Ameerah jetted her hand out in the air directly in front of her, attempting to pierce the void and touch Scilectra.

She was fuming at the arrogant display of disrespect, she thought to herself, *How dare she?* The powers that she bestowed on her progeny were to be an asset and not a weapon to be used against her.

What was puzzling was that Ameerah should have been able to enter the void; after all, she had the power to do so, but she couldn't. Scilectra was in a state of ambivalence; on the one hand, she still had more abilities than Ameerah. On the other hand, she felt that her A.T.I gene might have been a failure.

Ameerah stepped closer and began to whisper. The team looked on in confusion.

Savoy asked, "Who is she talking to?" They all shrugged their shoulders and kept watching.

Ameerah whispered to her, "You're not a secret anymore, I can sense when you're here. I can smell you. I can hear you breathing inside the veil. My blood vibrates when you are near."

Scilectra rolled her eyes and went away from that place. She said, "I have to remedy her on a smaller scale, at least neutralize her abilities. If Ameerah doesn't want to align herself with me, then what are her powers for?"

Scilectra had no kill switch for her creation. She didn't think to install checks and balance systems in her design. That got her to thinking . . . what was God's kill switch for man? It took her a moment, but she thought about the most obvious choice, the Devil. The magnificent thing about it was that she didn't have to find Hell to find him. The Bible stated that he is right here on earth with us.

Ameerah won't matter if I can find him. He can point the way to Heaven or verify its existence. There's more than one way to skin a cat!

CHAPTER FIFTY

Tilda Swan's estate was a historical castle—one of thirteen rare castles built in the United States. She spent most of her time at home running the family empire, expanding its reach as to keep a firm grip on global placement. Their family was only second to the Fairenhest family, who earned the coveted spot of being "Top Percent." The sigil for this honored ranking was the "greater than" symbol and a horizontal letter "A." This signified that they owned more wealth than anyone in the entire world.

The eldest Swan stressed often about maintaining the family status. Tilda didn't indulge in the usual actives of the rich. She couldn't risk her reputation by relieving herself in unseemly places with questionable people. One evening, she overheard one of her nieces yammering on about a new innovative way to get  high, without the negative side effects. She'd boastfully said, "This shit is awesome! No needles, no prep or lighters burning your fingers, and best of all, no fumes or track marks. I got high as a kite off a soundbite!"

That evening, Tilda ordered one of her bodyguards to assist her in following her niece to a rave club. Entering the club was as easy as mentioning her name. Once in, she watched as the young people partied and had a good time. At some point during the night, nearly every one of them visited the DJ booth and whispered something in her ear.

The Swan Mansion

She handed them an earpiece and typed something on her phone. The eager patron walked away quickly. Tilda could see their phones flashing on and off like they were receiving a text message. Shortly after, they commenced to punching what appeared to be a code in their phone. That was as technical as it got.

No more than five minutes later, the same patrons that visited the DJ surrendered to the music and began displaying euphoric behaviors. They had not a care in the world; they were totally uninhibited! Tilda smiled because it was clean and seamless. Figuring out the point of purchase and delivery was all she needed. Tilda was sold! She sent her card over to the DJ. From what Tilda observed, the DJ was the one with whom to make proper inquiries.

The next day, Tilda wasn't surprised to receive a personal visit from DJ Black-Ray herself. She walked into the great room with a well-groomed pompadour and shaven sides. It integrated into a thick, long black braid that started midway on the top of her head and extended down the middle of her back to her tailbone. She looked like a magnificent thoroughbred horse that was prepared to win a competition. She was a mixed beauty with slanted dark, almond-shaped eyes and sun-kissed skin. Her eclectic features broadcasted her Samoan and African-American background.

She said, "Yeah, umm, hi! I got your card. Do you need me for a party or something?"

Tilda replied, "Quite the opposite, dear girl. I'm inquiring about the other products that you offer. Before you bother denying it, I've done a rather thorough investigation in the right places with the right people. I'm certain that you have what I seek, and I don't seek it for free. I'm aware that you have a stage name, but may I call you Lola Ashland? That is your proper name, yes?"

The DJ replied, "I see that you've done your research. Gotta give you props on that! Just tell me what you need. I got shit to do."

Tilda laughed. "I can respect that. My power doesn't move you, but it should. You created something called 'Freq-TZ,' and from what I'm told, it's just the thing I'm looking for. Tell me, how did you come up with this?"

Before the DJ could answer, Tilda walked over to her and handed her a cashier's check for half a million dollars.

She said, "Well, all right then! From now on, you can call me Ashland. To answer your question, I'm a 'Hertzist.' It's a study of science where sound frequencies can be manipulated to create pseudo experiences in the brain. I devised a proprietary way to identically mimic the experience of all major narcotic choices via intricate sound waves. Finding the right notes and frequencies, turning them on and off in a particular rhythm, produces a specter note that maneuvers the mind and its chemicals.

"The fact that humans only use ten percent of their brain power makes the rest an endless playground. Given the right combinations, I can do some things that people ain't ready for. For now, getting them high for a few minutes is more than enough to give them a boost. I got more research to do, but my next project is to corner the market on booze!"

Tilda responded happily, "It looks like I found my girl! I trust that our dealings will be kept confidential?" Ashland nodded her head.

Tilda went on to say, "I have never done drugs of any kind before, so I'm not sure what I would like. Just to be certain, I would like to try them all."

Ashland replied, "That's ambitious, but I don't know how that will turn out for you. Let's start with the three big heavies and see where that takes you. Freq-TZ is digital heroin, HiFi-HTZ is digital cocaine, and Octa-ZHC is digital meth. Each high will last five to ten minutes with no negative side effects. Here is your specialized earpiece to hear your high. Put it in and wait on my text. When you receive the text, turn on your earpiece and respond back to my text with the word 'SEND.'

"That's it. After that, you'll get a rush that won't quit for several minutes. Are you ready?"

Tilda smiled and said, "You may proceed."

Her text alert sounded off. She opened it up and responded back per the instructions. Suddenly, her eyes opened wide and her pupils dilated. Feelings of exhilaration and well-being flooded her system. She was giddy with confidence and energy, followed by brief moments of paranoia. Ashland held in her laughter while Lady Tilda touched herself in various places, licking her lips. It took about seven minutes for her to calm and come to her senses.

Ashland was proud of herself, but not about the drugs—she was proud of the scientific achievement. She always wanted to be a driving force in the world of proven fantasy.

Tilda called out to her and said, "What you have here is magical!"

Ashland responded, "Nah, magic is just science with better marketing. In a few minutes, we will try the last two. Let me know which one you vibe with the most."

They did as planned. Tilda tried the digital meth and then the digital heroin. She said, "The Freq-TZ is the best by far. What if I want to experiment with new files? Do I contact you directly for that?"

Ashland responded, "Upper epsilon clientele need to create a profile on the Vulture Web. Here's the sub-web address and a passcode to get on there." She passed her a slip of paper. "After that, I can send you your files anonymously and your transactions will be untraceable."

Tilda looked at the paper in her hands and grinned.

"Look, it's been real," Ashland said, "I will text you two more times today. If you don't use the files within an hour, they will be corrupt and unusable. One more thing: the files won't work without that special Bluetooth. If you lose it, hit me up or no high for you!"

Tilda replied, "I understand. By the way, that five hundred-thousand dollars is for more than your products. You and I will be doing bigger ventures in the future!"

* * *

D.K. strolled into the lab like a peacock—he had the ultimate dirt on Tilda Swan! His cousin was in the back meeting with Raj, so D.K. shared the news with the rest of the team. Ameerah could hear the loud conversations in the front and walked up in the midst of the presentation.

She was stunned by what she heard. Lab-J71 was generally the one to beat when it came to innovative science, but not today. Digital Drugs (more than likely) didn't come from an established laboratory. The ethical and legal implications would be overwhelming. Despite that, someone got the notion and the fortitude to formulate this platform in a genius way.

Ameerah said, "Let's get past the excitement over this innovation and find out how we can leverage it against Tilda. We have to get the evidence of our IP back."

D.K. responded, "It kinda depends on if we can find the people who made it. Maybe we can shut them down or get them to out Tilda to the authorities. Whatever our penetration point, our hands have to be clean, or Tilda will strike fast and hard!"

"On that note, I have to speak to everybody about a development. Several weeks ago, we received a notification that Scilectra was in the lab the day that we took off. She wasn't spying on us that day; she was tampering with my belongings and subsequently my person. She attempted to infect me with a new species of DNA that she developed. The bad news is she succeeded, but the good news is it has not caused any harm and it has given me advantageous abilities."

Chad asked, "What does that mean?"

Raj answered, "Besides the kick-ass powers she displayed on Scilectra, Ameerah Mahar is the proud new owner of many more ancillary abilities that can help us obtain our goals."

The lab morphed into a presidential press conference with an avalanche of questions.

"What can you do?"

"Do you feel different?"

"Can you fly?"

She snickered at the absurdity of the questions coming out of the faces of some of the most intelligent people in the world. Amongst the rumblings came a moment of clarity for her. Their questions weren't absurd at all: every day was an opportunity for the birth of new ultra-abilities.

She said, "Calm down. When I learn more, I will share it with you. Consider me your in-house science project. Raj will continue to test me on a regular basis just to be safe. With that being said, there may be a scenario where I can make that trip beyond the Monocerus Zone, into the Vexaverse.

"Right now, it's a loose possibility. I won't say it's a definite thing because I don't know the limits of what I can do. The greater issue is, how long can I sustain my powers, especially out there in the galaxy? We're still trying to figure out how to begin the journey. My initial attempt will be via my dream state to recon a pathway to the zone.

"Well, to sum up what I'm saying, I've made the decision to stop taking on new subjects. It's not necessary anymore. We have over a million tagged souls and a high verification percentage. Now we have a possible direct way for one hundred percent proof."

Lisa asked, "Are we going to continue collecting data and listen to chatter?"

"Of course," Ameerah replied. "Move forward with that, because my travel may not be a success, and then we'd be left with nothing. In the meantime, Tilda is objective number one. If she sells our data, we might as well close up shop!"

Lisa warned, "The blowback will be relentless. We aren't sanctioned to do ninety percent of the work that we do here. Dean Rydell will have our heads on stakes if this ever gets out."

Ameerah respond, "Don't remind me. I have to take a trip to his office anyway. I'll throw out some hypotheticals and test the waters with him."

On the way over to his office, Ameerah took in the scenery. Japan donated a new breed of cherry blossom trees to the university. They're called "monarchs" because they bloom in a lovely shade of orange and black, like the butterfly.

Norman Rydell had been appointed the dean of Stromford about ten years prior. Leaving high school, Ameerah won a full-ride scholarship to the university and became head of lab immediately after she graduated. That appointment came directly from the dean. He told her that he was impressed by her dissertation on the verification of "the First Seeds," which was basically a five-hundred-page archeological account of scientists locating the seeds used by Adam and Eve to plant the first harvest of food given them by God.

She thought, *Anyone else would have thought it fantasy, but it wasn't. Rooted in real-life historical findings, the actual location of The Garden of Eden had been found. Upon finding that location (using specs from the Bible), a massive excavation was done. They discovered vintage seeds deep in the ground that dated back to a time period in which the pair had lived.*

What Ameerah neglected to share in her dissertation was about a unique practice amongst the people tilling the fields. They would take the seeds and crack them in their mouths and spit them in the dirt before covering them up. Most of the seeds sprouted fine, but a few did not. Those seeds still hold the DNA left by Adam and Eve, and then later by their children, Cain and Abel.

Ameerah kept a safety deposit box in the vault of the "Agrisonian." It was allotted to scientists and researchers who have discovered rare agricultural finds that aren't ready to be made public yet. In her deposit box were eleven cracked seeds of fruits, vegetables, and berries that do not exist today, well preserved and intact.

She stopped reminiscing long enough to realize that she'd arrived at the academic building. Walking in always smelled like old money to her. The wealthy maintained its uniformity no matter what. The open gathering area was filled with pastel-colored argyle sweaters and shiny leather penny loafers.

Blonde "Chips" and "Beckys" were all around, acting as the garnish to a very expensive four-year meal. They scolded her with their eyes as she headed to the main staircase. Ameerah was clear that her outward appearance didn't fit the landscape of this suffocating prestige. Her natural 4C hair, golden brown skin, and wide curvy hips gave her away every time. As she meandered up the wide luxurious gilded staircase, she recited her favorite poem.

I'm in love with being a black woman, not just my humps and my bumps or the swells in my tails. I love my scratches and marks, the black scars that dwell. We've been places and seen things that few can imagine. We've had heartaches and bellyaches that comes from our passion.

We've laid there, rode on top, and got praised from behind. Life's passed through me . . . sat in me . . . and rolled down my thighs. Funky rhythm and beats began on my hips; it rotates my tummy and drips from my lips. My darkness will bounce no matter the place. The whole world will tremble from the bass in my waist. Just remember what I have . . . is a fetish for sure. That blackness, that ebony, that melanin is pure. I'm in love with being a black woman through and through to my core, facts are . . . it's our nature, to be ALL of this and more.

By the time she reached the dean's office, she was in great spirits and ready to deal with the matters at hand. She knocked on the door, and it surprisingly creaked open. In her mind, that was a cue to walk in. Dean Rydell wasn't there, so she took the opportunity to browse around his office. This was her first time being there. Typically, when they met, it was in the lab.

He had some interesting photos on the wall. Apparently he traveled quite a bit and had a love for the cosmos. She thought, *That's cool! I can see why he took an interest in me.* She noticed that there was nothing by way of personal pictures of his family. The scuttlebutt around the campus is that he's very private and very single. *I was told that he was degreed in Meta Studies and Antiquities, which partially explains the dry board with the odd equations on it.*

Snooping was bad enough, but getting busted for it was even worse. From behind her, Ameerah heard the dean say, "Ameerah, may I help you with something?"

She nearly jumped out of her skin but quickly rebounded by saying,

"Hello, Dean Rydell! Sorry for the intrusion. Your door was open when I arrived. I came to inquire about our last round of funding and to ask about the possibility of expanding our research genre?"

He said, "Expanding . . . What's more expansive than fringe science?"

She replied, "I understand that fringe is an extremely broad term with many factions. Does this mean that we are free to lean into the esoteric?"

Dean Rydell curled his lip and said, "Why not? Just don't kill anybody!"

Ameerah laughed and made up an excuse to leave. "I forgot that I have a meeting in about ten minutes. If you don't mind, please email me about the funding. We can catch up then".

As she darted out of the building, she thought, *It's better to ask for forgiveness than permission.* Her work there was done. If the dean caught wind of their true work focus study, she had a viable card to play, given their conversation today.

CHAPTER FIFTY-ONE

Scilectra had to make a lot of life adjustments now that the Professor was gone, especially regarding obtaining things she needed and knowing what those things were. The nature of her very existence was more scientific than biological. Maintaining equilibrium was key. Regardless of what she thought she was, it was evident that she had limitations. For lack of better terms, Scilectra was an eternal (but rechargeable) battery. If her core energy source were to be tampered with or depleted, she could lose her human side and exist entirely in soul formation.

The likelihood of this happening was slim to none, since her human form and soul form had been fused together. If the event ever arose that her flesh ceased to be, there was a probability that Scilectra could morph (yet again) into some other unknown entity. She understood that at some point, she was going to have to entertain a new partner in her life. Until she reached a level of automatic efficiency, a human presence would be required.

Like always, what she needed would have to wait! Ameerah was first on the list to be handled. She could no longer go to the lab unnoticed.

She said, "I have cut off my nose to spite my face. I've shown my hand and put myself in a losing position."

Scilectra went about researching a way to either suppress the A.T.I gene in Ameerah or remove it altogether. Herein lay the problem: there would have to be a second introduction of a product to neutralize the A.T.I. gene.

What might be the most detrimental were the effects a solvent could possibly have on Ameerah. Death was not an option; she was the driving force and the brains behind locating the coordinates.

Implementing another skillset might open hidden doors for Scilectra. Since her presence was now apparent, encroaching from afar might be the angle she was looking for. Intercepting their phone conversations and emails could be the route to go. At some point, there had to be a conversation regarding the search for Heaven. Hopefully, they would say too much and inadvertently give up pertinent information. This way, keeping tabs on Ameerah until it was time to strike would be painless.

Scilectra felt that Ameerah's relative (D.K.) was the one to watch. After experiencing their closeness, he seemed like a justified candidate. She directed her energies toward the lab. The signals constantly flowed from their location.

* * *

D.K. had plans for the night, and he was easier to track than Scilectra thought. Watching from the void in a dimly lit place, camouflaged by unsuspecting partygoers, would give her the advantage she desired.

This wasn't just any nightclub, though. D.K. was entering a Haptic Erotics establishment. The science behind it is fascinating! Haptics (or Volumetric Haptics Shapes) is a way of creating three-dimensional shapes in the surrounding air, using focused ultrasounds. You can upload an image of something to be projected that isn't really there and use sound to produce a force on the skin, which is strong enough to generate physical sensations.

This process eliminates the need for any direct contact with physical devices (or people). You experience all the bodily sensations as if that object (or person) is actually there. Just pick a computer-generated whatever and convert that image into tangible shapes. It was all for the purpose of sexual encounters. It was satisfying because the air vibrated so densely that it feels like real matter.

Scilectra happened across this knowledge in her scientific studies, but as usual, man has perverted its technical uses for carnal pleasure. She was excited to see that its application had elevated to the stage of general usage. After all, she was going to be the god of the new human world, the one centered on the scientific and mathematical-based ideology. She hovered all around him, getting a close-eye view of his escapades. His Haptic choices were rather conventional and stimulating.

In a space where he could've chosen anyone and anything, he was quite tame. After paying for his private room, his choice was a sexy, voluptuous womanly image. His confidence was showing while he slowly disrobed for the image that waited for him patiently. D.K. worked himself into a sweaty frenzy, before unabashedly piercing the heavily pulsating air. He showcased infinite stamina while he heaved and pumped for hours on end. For several moments, Scilectra was forced to ignore the reality that he was copulating with manipulated oxygen. The fact was, she was completely entertained by his talent and commitment to the process of pleasure.

She couldn't say that for the other attendees. She tried to comprehend why men and women chose animals, stuffed toys, and robots. One woman formed a phallic object with tentacles that locked her in from every angle and rammed her continuously. It appeared more like giving and receiving abuse than pleasurable enjoyment.

She stayed with him throughout the night and then followed him home. Scilectra wasn't sure of her motivation for going home with him, but right at that moment, she didn't care. Curiosity had gotten the better of her, and she let it lead. When he was done at the club, he showered, dressed and left. D.K.'s vehicle of choice definitely matched his sexual dexterity: he drove a vintage black 67 Chevy Impala, 327. She couldn't travel with him in the linear sense; however, his cell signal lit the way for her in the void.

His Impala's engine roared when he pulled into a parking garage of a chic gentrified building on the exclusive part of town. He owned a loft there amidst the urban socialites and the pop-up hookah shops. Scilectra continued to follow his signal until he stabilized in his unit. There she could hang out in the void and watch him in the shadows. He went straight to his computer to do research. She watched him as he ferreted the internet, searching for the same person repeatedly: "Tilda Swan."

A chill ran down her spine. Could it be that Tilda Swan was related to Duvall Swan? D.K. opened up a file (a dossier really), that detailed everything about this woman.

Scilectra whispered to herself, "Why is he looking into her?"

Then he made a call. "Hey Meenah … It looks like she took property from the NCF and relocated it to her estate. Many of the crates are labeled R. Sherman. She must've taken all his equipment and files to a storage site on her property. Yeah, I don't know, but we're getting closer."

He switched his phone off and lit up a cigar, then went forward with his virtual deep dive.

She thought, *If this Tilda has the Professor's belongings, there may be pertinent information about me. I'm certain that he has notes on how to maintenance me, maybe even schematics on how to increase my abilities. I have to get to that storage; meeting Tilda Swan is a necessity!*

Her entire life sat behind locked doors on a stranger's property. She cringed at the thought of the "unworthy" running their dirty fingers over her genesis, reading about her womb and how she came to life.

She said, "Nothing's sacred anymore. That's the price you pay for biting that apple."

CHAPTER FIFTY-TWO

Normally Ashland was an early riser, despite being a DJ into the wee hours of the morning. Raving was a lifestyle, and the club was open seven days a week, twenty-four hours a day. She alternated spinning the music with three other DJs. The party could never stop! Today was a little different, though. She had a whopping half million dollars in her bank account that was ironically memoed as a "donation" from the Duvall Swan Foundation. That meant she'd take a few days off to work with some new Hertz at home in her lab.

She started her day with a hot bath; it was always her favorite thing, but because of her towering height, her long and curvy legs made it almost impossible to enjoy. She spent most of the time shifting her body to submerge one part or another at a time. After her bath, she headed directly to her equipment. Ashland didn't partake in drug use, except when she created a new wave file. She tasked herself with experiencing how the file would work first-hand. That would be the one and only time she would get high.

Besides being a DJ and creating digital drugs, Ashland was an extremely accomplished coder, a skill detrimental to packaging and selling her products. While on the Vulture Web, she noticed a new footprint. Someone had been looking into her merchandise and actually got through her air-gapped firewalls to view her customers.

She said, "I don't know who this is, but they don't know who they fuckin' wit'!"

She went to her closet, parted the clothes hanging on the rod to reveal a wall safe. She punched in a seventeen-character code, and the door popped opened, releasing a sigh of air. Her safe was hermetically sealed.

She reached in and pulled out an onyx titanium laptop. The official term for it was "The Black Box." It was a device so unique that it had to be safely secured at all times. The software and algorithms contained in the computer could access anything and everything. She could literally unlock the government, the federal reserve, NASA, and beyond. Her system could generate equations and algorithms to formulate answers to any coding-mathematical problems that one could have.

She could land a spaceship on an asteroid that was zigzagging throughout the cosmos on top of a pinhead! That device has one-thousand percent accuracy. She affectionately named it "Bertha." Just know that Bertha didn't come out to play unless Ashland felt her life was being threatened. Today was the day! With this system, she could pinpoint exactly where the intrusion was coming from; then she would be able to find out who they were.

There are not too many hackers that can do what this guy was doing. Ashland prided herself on knowing everyone in the game. Keeping her eyes on potential competition was part of the territory. She set up the necessary programs and uploaded all the hackers' electronic footprints. Then all she had to do from there was wait.

Ashland had learned to be patient hailing from Transylvania, Louisiana, a town of only two thousand people (she even sported a tattoo of a bat on the base of her neck). No one was in a rush to do anything. That was one of the main reasons she became a DJ; she needed that excitement and rush of people wanting more. The frenzy that the music induced . . . that was all the high she needed.

Hours had gone by and Bertha spat out nothing but false positives. She said to herself, "This asshole is better than I anticipated."

She grabbed a wide-paddled brush with spiked bristles to brush her long wavy black locks into her signature pompadour. She was always particular of how she braided the tail of her hair. Each section of the braid was so tight that it resembled polished woven leather straps.

This was a sign that she was nervous. Someone was getting too close for comfort. The panic was just about to settle but was joyfully interrupted by a ping. That ping was a notification of victory. Bertha found an actual verifiable hit on somebody named "Darryl Ken Nero," aka D.K.

She stood up from her floor-leveled gamer chair and pounced around like a limber feline. She was elated that she triumphed over her visual nemesis. Never one to shy away from a fight, Ashland locked Bertha away and slid on her black trench coat, knee-high black ninja boots, and her dark shades.

She flipped up the wide collar of her coat to mask her face and went out to investigate D.K., Avery Brooks style. There were no immediate plans for a confrontation (not today at least). She said the first lesson in war was to "know your enemy" and the first lesson in life was that "There is no remorse like the remorse of not knowing the enemy is coming."

Ashland knew that there was power in striking first.

* * *

Over at the lab, Ameerah was ready for her first test-run into the ether. She had no plans to attempt a trip beyond the Monocerus Zone. Her goal for today was to make it there and back to her body in one piece. Raj prepped her for a temporary coma inducement. This dramatic move was necessary; she had to make it to the third deep level of sleep to convert over to her astral-self.

The whole procedure was a clinical undertaking, putting a protocol in place to wake her up and another if that failed to work. This would be the one test out of many to avert a catastrophe during her journey. Surprisingly, Ameerah wasn't afraid; she looked forward to the ascension, much like an astronaut going to outer space for the first time.

Of course, this has the potential to go wrong.

Raj made the comment that "Right off the bat, nothing is in our favor; every facet of this situation is out of our control. We don't know the lifespan of whatever Scilectra did to you. Neither do we know the veracity."

She could tell that the tension was hitting home for him. He couldn't stop sweating, and he checked the machine repeatedly.

Ameerah rolled her eyes and interjected, "That's why I'm going during my dream state."

Lisa darted out of her chair, firmly affixed her glasses to her face, and said, "I have something to say about that too. Yes . . . your body will be here and your astral-self will have the helm. However, it's technically still you. What you'll experience there will be taken in whole by your brain and register as real. So if you die there, you will surely die here as well!"

Chad checked in while lingering out in the hallway. "No worries, Ameerah. I'll monitor your vitals, and if it looks hairy we will reel you back in."

She smiled and replied, "I can't think of a better person to watch over me."

Chad was always in a perpetual state of blushing, so Ameerah took his extra-pink hue as a sign of approval. Ameerah was hoping to see D.K. before she went under, but unfortunately, she was unable to reach him.

With one final directive, she said, "Okay guys, let's hit it!"

Ameerah removed all her clothing and donned a flimsy hospital gown. They needed direct access to her body in case of an emergency, not to mention the IV connection and wires necessary to constantly read her vitals; these had to be accessible as well. Being publicly naked wasn't in her comfort zone, but when in Rome . . .

Raj helped ease her back on the medical bed. Once in place, they began to connect the sensors and diagnostic attachments to her head, chest, and fingertips. Next came the Propofol drip to induce her into a temporary coma. Another important aspect of this operation was that Ameerah had to be kept warm. The more comfortable she was, the longer she could exist on that other plane. An uncomfortable temperature could activate her to resist the drip and fight to wake up.

In addition to the medical monitoring, Savoy oversaw the comms. They set up a system in play to direct Ameerah to the proper zone. Savoy's voice was linked to corresponding electrical stimuli in Ameerah's brain. This gave her the ability to sense what direction to go in after she had made it to the ether. Savoy was limited to six words when communicating with Ameerah; they would be spoken via short, painless electrical pulses:

One Pulse = No	Two Pulses = Yes	Three Pulses = North
Four Pulses = South	Five Pulses = East	Six Pulses = West

Chad and Lisa watched her brain's activity as she sank lower and lower into her unconscious. Everything that happened in this lab was an opportunity for research. They were eager to view which part of her brain was more active, and which part switched over to dormancy. This could help them to understand how her physical-self responded to her astral-self, and if they worked in tandem. Their main tasks were to see if they are actually two separate beings or mere extensions of each other.

It didn't take long; Ameerah was out in a matter of minutes. It wasn't a direct flight to the stars. She landed in a mandatory prologue to her trip, the Siriaz. She was at home, asleep in her bedroom. This was her place of comfort and solitude. She could almost smell her mother cooking in the kitchen, and her cat Toast lying at her feet in his usual position.

Luckily, she had a built-in totem. Raj told her that no matter what the environment was like, Ameerah would maintain a balmy ninety-eight-degree internal temperature.

She said, "It would be out of character for me not to test the design."

It was the middle of winter. Outside her bedroom window looked to be a foot of snow. Ameerah yanked on the window above her head until it opened, and snow fell into her basement level room. She had handfuls of the fluffy crystalized snow, but it might as well have been hot sand.

She yelled out to Raj (as if he could hear her), "Well done, Raj! Well done!"

To start her journey, she had to take ownership of the narrative; in this place, she was in control. The mind would only move toward what it can see. Ameerah understood how the brain worked, so instituting the universal methods of receiving was paramount. The method of moving from the-thought-to-the-thing would get her where she needed to be. This was the fuel to get her from her Siriaz to the Monocerus Zone. She closed her physical eyes and concentrated; the paradigm changed when her third eye opened. She was instantly transported to the Milky Way, and she awaited Savoy's instruction from there.

Savoy was a fan of vintage video games, and tracking Ameerah made her reminiscent of Atari's video game "Space Invaders". She even assigned a rocket ship icon to Ameerah's movements. Savoy watched the screen while the rocket ship hovered in one spot. She was so focused on the tiny icon that she blocked out the snaps and claps being thrown her way by Lisa.

She said, "Hey . . . get it together! I'm sure she has not a clue where to go next. Give her some damn directions!"

Savoy snapped back, "Geez . . . Why are you always the resident mean girl?"

Raj jumped in to get things back on track. "Come on ladies, take it easy. We're all here for the same reason. Kiss and make up and get back to work!"

Everyone retreated to their respective stations, but not before rolling their eyes at each other out of frustration. It should've been easy to remember that Ameerah was there in body but not in spirit, especially with her laying listless in the middle of the room.

She didn't want to say it (after being chewed a new one), but Lisa was right: every second mattered. They had no barometer to measure the power of Ameerah's abilities. This had to be an in-and-out visit with no delays. Savoy had previously outlined the location of the Monocerus Zone, and Ameerah was not far, but it wasn't a straight shot. It was time for the conductor to shine. She rolled up the sleeves on her lab coat and started the symphony of pulses to guide the way!

Ameerah floated in the ether, unable to communicate with the lab. Then, out of nowhere . . . a jolt of electricity. The shock was an exhilarating jostle which prompted her to go in particular directions. Savoy's heart beat a mile a minute while she anticipated Ameerah's movement. This process was all theoretical; it was not relevant until that little blip on the monitor followed her commands in real time.

Her heart was still pounding. It was beating so hard she could feel it in her ears. Savoy's nervous tick kicked in. She began listening for words that she could count off in groups of five, and then tap them out with her fingers. She whispered, "Move, Ameerah, move!"

No more than a few seconds later, the rocket moved. It moved north as stipulated by Savoy's command!

Savoy called the team over and waved her hands in the air, beckoning for them to come faster. She said, "She followed the command . . . she did it! I buzzed her to go north, and she did. I'll give her another command to go west. If she does, then the program works as designed!"

She leaned over the console and pushed the electrical pulses six times. The blip stopped moving north and stood still, flashing on the screen; then it changed direction and went west. The room sounded off in cheers and high-pitched screams! Savoy course-corrected Ameerah and kept her moving on to her destination.

Ameerah traveled as she'd never traveled before. She touched every star that she came in contact with, and they seemed to power her as she went. Whatever Scilectra did to her had a kinship with universal matter. She continued to propel her way through chiliads of rainbowed ice that resembled iridescent pearls, and the dust of gems from which all life is made.

She could feel the nanites in her body being fed by the energy surrounding her, and they danced with excitement; it was the same joy a caged animal feels when released into the wild to live his life as intended. During her trip out there in the nowhere and the everywhere, the principle that her lab was based on that "the universe doesn't speak English . . . it speaks frequency" had never been truer than right now!

The team was so engrossed in guiding Ameerah that they didn't notice her bodily reactions to her current situation. In an instant, the lab was flooded with blaring beeps, bells and whistles from the machines. Ameerah's body was covered with a familiar color, what they referred to now as "Aurovian Blue." It arrived in small patches like a rash that intermittently lit up in a roving manner. It became more awkward from there; several parts of her body shined brighter than others. Her nipples and pubic hairs behaved as if they were their own entities. Their natural pigments began to change to various robust colors in a timed cycle.

It was going to be uncomfortable to do, but necessary, so Raj took the lead in removing Ameerah's gown to examine what was going on. It was prudent to get samples of blood, bodily fluids, and hair follicles from her vaginal area. The samples had to be tested in their new budding forms. Understanding the science of her could help them to identify what her abilities are, as well as her limits. He was not shy about samples and cultures.

After she was completely naked, he donned surgical gear and started from the top.

Raj plucked hairs from her scalp and armpits, being sure to keep the follicles intact. He took samples of mucus and saliva; he even squeezed each of her nipples for any fluid or discharge. Being her primary physician, Raj was very familiar with Ameerah's body, but this was something different because he now had to do the unthinkable. You could always tell when Lisa was irked; her resting bitch-face was now an immovable stank-face.

With the entire room watching, it made Raj's job that much more complicated. He begrudgingly scooted Ameerah down on the bed, his hands stinging from the energy emitting from her body. He gingerly parted her legs and propped them wide open to get a better view. He was obligated to take samples of her pubic hair, vaginal mucus, and anal residue. They had previously discussed this, just in case the need arose.

Savoy was the only team member not present during the viewing of Ameerah's hoo-ha. Her job was too important and time sensitive. However, that didn't stop her from sneaking a peek by way of reflection on her computer's monitor. It wasn't an opportunity for perversion. Ameerah was the closest thing to a modern-day superhero that she knew. She counted it all as admiration; as far as Savoy was concerned, Ameerah was a living, breathing Egyptian Goddess!

CHAPTER FIFTY-THREE

Tilda lounged on her enormous bed, recovering from the last file Ashland sent her. Although she and Duvall were not terribly close, she found herself feeling rather sentimental over the loss of him. His death was still unresolved and unverified. One thing she knew for sure: Duvall was a planner, and he didn't write those letters and make damning videos if his demise had not come to pass. Months had passed, and Tilda had hired the best of the best to investigate; they all returned empty-handed.

That wouldn't deter her; when she wanted her way, she was like a dog with a bone. Tilda understood that money could solve every problem there was, and now, maybe even death. The relationship with Lab-J71 might prove to be more than they expected. Duvall was very detailed regarding Ameerah and the Professor's work. The applications were sound, but there was so much more to learn from their experiments.

She said, "I can take their audacious experiments all the way to the bank!"

A voice whispered in her ear, "Money isn't everything . . . some things require your soul."

Tilda didn't scare easy, and she wasn't bemused by the lone voice invading her personal space. In fact, she almost welcomed it.

She said, "Show yourself! I wondered when you'd find me. Duvall told me all about you, and frankly, I'm excited to meet you!"

Scilectra replied, "I'm not here to pester you. I've come to be an ally to you."

Tilda straightened and fastened her robe while wandering the room in an effort to locate the person behind the voice. She replied, "Go on . . . I'm listening."

Scilectra continued to speak, slowly, pacing her words to keep the advantage. "We have associates in common. I've learned that they have become curious about you and I thought that you may be curious about them. I come bearing information."

"And what do you want for that information?" Tilda responded.

Scilectra stepped out of the void in all her glory, smiling. She added a little drama by continuing to levitate slightly off the ground. "I want access to my Professor's belongings. All of them!"

Tilda smiled and said, "My God, you are absolutely stunning! Whatever did you want with a ghastly man like him? His purpose for you was obvious. If I had tits like yours, I'd be floating in the air too!"

Scilectra's bluish skin intensified because Tilda angered her. "You don't have permission to talk to me that way." With disgust on her face, she went on to declare, "I don't know how that came about, so let's make it clear . . . You cannot! There's no need to besmirch his name. He was my maker, and for that, I owe him everything!"

As much as Tilda wanted to release a round of uproarious laughter, self-preservation impeded her from doing so.

Tilda apologized for her insensitive behavior and said, "Since we're on the topic of clarity, do you know what happened to my brother?"

Scilectra took a moment before she answered. This was a time to employ strategic thinking. If she told the truth, Tilda would most certainly reject her offer of a partnership. If she lied to her, she would be doing so out of fear of losing an opportunity.

She asked herself, *Is pride more important than achieving the objective? Absolutely not!*

She responded, "Duvall and I were very close. He was to be my right hand, for purposes of chronicling my existence. He came to see me months ago and claimed that he had a change of heart. Moreover, he stated that he was relocating out of country retire in peace and quiet. I haven't heard from him since."

Tilda walked around Scilectra in circles, admiring her appearance and suspiciously accepting her responses. She said, "The only reason I ask is that Duvall respected you out of fear and not admiration."

She was careful not to say too much. Duvall's letters and recordings were to remain confidential from everyone mentioned in its contents.

She said to Scilectra, "There's something to be said about having a weapon such as yourself in my arsenal. I tentatively agree with your terms, if you can detail to me the scope of Lab-J71's research; what they're doing may impact my bottom line tremendously." Tilda's next move was to entice the DJ to move her lab onto the estate grounds. She just felt better knowing that she was close and staying out of trouble. Little did she know that the DJ had other plans on her mind.

* * *

Ashland stood outside of D. K's building, peering up to the floor where his unit was located. She sneered at what she saw.

She said, "Look at that little high-yellow thug, bouncing around to trap music while he robs me of my anonymity! I have half a mind to go up there, kick open his door, and piss on his hardware." She gave a little chuckle. "Good luck getting your shit to work after that!"

Her blind anger gave her the notion to do just that. Ashland slinked around to the front of the complex. She purposely moved in the shadows to stay out the view of any cameras. Breaching the entrance of the well-secured building can be challenging, but when you're pretty, there's no such thing as a locked door. She arrived at the front door just as a couple was exiting the building.

Ashland went to grab the door before it closed. She would have caught it had the young lady not kicked the door closed to refuse her entry. The woman even turned back to chastise Ashland with her eyes. In a lesser surprise, her man was eager to assist a damsel in distress. He boomeranged back to the door and let her in. After he ushered her in, he "accidentally" grazed his fingers over the back of her hand. She gave a fake glance of approval and she thought, *Men like that can't wait to touch what they lust after; they will take dangerous chances just to get a little fix.*

She saw the elevators from the corner of her eye. For some reason, she decided against it and opted to sprint the six flights upstairs. When she made it to the sixth floor, the next complication was to find his unit and gain entry. D.K.'s complex was huge! From her recon, his individual loft was over five-thousand square feet. From where she stood (at the end of the long hall), she could see there had to be at least twelve units on that floor alone. Hard Tech wasn't really her jam, but she dabbled enough to make portable spy gear for her own personal objectives. She pulled out the finder device and plugged in his ISP number from his search file. That did the trick; she easily found his apartment: #6C

Ashland leaned in near his doorframe, eavesdropping to the activity inside. Shockingly, he wasn't bumping his head to trap rap; he was listening to the same club joints that she spun at the raves.

She whispered to herself, "No brownie points over here. I don't give a damn what he's wildin' out to. He got some explaining to do!"

She took her right hand and reached inside her trench. In the small of her back was antique Desert Eagle, fully loaded. She thought, *So much for converging on him like a thief in the night!*

Gun in hand, she jogged backwards and kicked the door with all her might. It didn't budge, remarkably.

Nor did D.K. The music was so loud that it disguised the mischievous ruckus at his front door. Ashland smiled at the unforeseen alliance of his pleasure and her malice. She thought, *Reinforced steel requires reinforced lead!*

She waited until the song's hook became screechingly erratic and fired off two deafening shots, one at the lock and one at the knob. Then she charged at the door like a mad rhinoceros, and this time it gave way.

Her long chunky black braid, rotating in the air with a precision rivaling helicopter blades, made it through the door before she did. D.K. was so traumatized by the intrusion that he fell back onto a cornucopia of electronic devices on his work table.

He yelled, "WHAT THE FUCK . . . Chick, you got the wrong crib!"
She said, "Do I really?"

Name: Darryl Ken Nero, Sex: Male, Age: Twenty-Five, Height: Five-Eleven, Eyes: Hazel, Occupation: Coder/Hacker.

She looked him up and down then said, "Nope, I got the right crib!"
His heart started to race because she was (in fact) in the right place, but why was she looking for him?

He said, "I don't know you. Why you looking for me?"

Ashland stood with legs apart, one in the chamber and ready to shoot. She answered, "I could ask you the same thing. Why are you looking into me?"

D.K. lifted himself off the floor and gestured for her permission to sit on his sofa. Ashland waved the gun in the direction of the couch, obliging his request.

He said, "I guess we're at a stalemate because I have no other answers to give you."

She said, "Well, let me enlighten you! You've been digging all in my business and exposing my (formerly private) and very important clients like Tilda Swan. Does that ring a bell?"

He asked, "Wait . . . What? You're the Digi-Dealer? You gotta be shittin' me. You're a girl and too pretty to know how to do that kinda stuff. If you ain't lying, then you got a huge set of ovaries on you!" He belted out a thunderous round of laughter. Ashland was fuming at his audacity to mock her. After all, she was the one holding the gun.

"Who got the drop on who? I was clever enough to find you where you lie your head. Can't say as much for you!"

D.K. curled his lip, bobbed his head, and conceded reluctantly. "This is as good a time as any to tell you the real deal. I wasn't looking into you (technically), I'm looking for dirt on Tilda Swan. Finding out about you was totally incidental, so drop the piece, have a seat, and let's chop it up!"

Ashland lowered the gun and laid it on the table. She felt that he was harmless but didn't want to completely let her guard down.

He said, "Since you know exactly who I am . . . how about a formal introduction?"

She replied, "I'm assuming that you know my stage name, DJ Black-Ray. However, it's only fair that you know my government name, since I know yours." D.K. smiled at her, and the angles must have been just right, because the shimmer from his bright hazel eyes seemed to light up the dimly lit room. They sparkled like reflective gems stones on a motionless marble statue.

She said to herself, *Get it together, girl!*

"My given name is Lola Ashland, and I'm a DJ, Coder/Hacker, and a self-proclaimed scientist in regards to Hertzism."

The pair sat there all night into morning, talking and comparing notes. Their lives paralleled in many ways, and as of last night, their paths intersected. Ashland gave up the goods on Tilda, and in turn, D.K. explained what he did for Lab-J71. Before they knew it, another day had passed seamlessly. She was still in her trench, and he had left the sofa only once to relieve himself. That particular night would be different; it was the night that both of their lives would change.

They both (publicly) lived full lives, but the reality was that their entire existence is done in solitude. Doing what they did required an absurd amount of privacy and isolation. There was a reason that no one knew who was behind the scenes. They donned their everyday citizen uniforms to fit in, but had to navigate its seedy underbelly like water. On the inside, they lived desperately lonely lives. It was this mutual thread that ignited an attraction that neither saw coming.

CHAPTER FIFTY-FOUR

The lab's frequency meter was off the charts! The level that Ameerah existed on right then was so high that the display couldn't process any more.

Raj said, "What she's experiencing is a combination of her human frequency and her astral frequency. It's incalculable. We don't have the necessary equipment to calibrate the anomaly."

Her reality was so dense that he physical body began to warp back and forth. It was similar to filling a balloon halfway, and then squeezing the air inside your hands from one side to another. Savoy confirmed that Ameerah was near the Monocerus Zone and then she blipped off the screen.

She cried out, "Oh no . . . Oh no . . . she's gone!"

Chad asked, "Gone, like how? Is it that you lost her, or she doesn't exist anymore?"

Savoy said, "I don't know. She's just disappeared from the monitor."

Raj raced over to check her vitals. All the hyper-activity ceased. He said, "Her readings have normalized, and her color is back to her normal pigmentation. Stop the propofol drip and connect the saline line. Let's wake her up."

Ameerah was no longer alone. The icy grip of someone's hands on either side of her fastened to her quickly! The space around her turned even blacker and thicker than tar. She couldn't see what had her, but she felt it; when they spoke, they did it simultaneously. Their speech was an unusual language that she somehow understood.

They said, "We are the gatekeepers of transition. We know who goes and who does not. You do not go!"

Just like that, Ameerah was back in her Siriaz at home, vividly dreaming in her nice warm bedroom. She had all but forgotten that warmth was her totem until things got very, very cold.

When she opened her eyes, she was (yet again) being stared down at by her team. They were grinning from ear to ear and swaddling her with hot blankets.

Savoy leaned in and gave her a big hug. She said, "I thought I'd lost you. Your signal went out, and we had no way of finding you. What happened? What did you see? Did your powers give out?"

Ameerah scratched her head and rubbed her eyes, no doubt feeling the after-effects of the propofol. Raj interrupted the interrogation to say, "First thing is to check her out, allow her to eat and get dressed. We can question her later."

Raj, ever the consummate professional, cleared the room so that he could examine Ameerah. Unfortunately, he was too weak to take his own direction. He couldn't resist the temptation to flop in a chair and get all the details of her adventure!

Ameerah laughed at him. She said, "You're actually worse than Savoy! At least she didn't bother putting on airs!"

He said with an awkward look on his face, "Before we get engrossed in conversation. I want to be the first to tell you that I had to do complete, and I mean complete, exam on you while you were under. Your body displayed remarkable functions that were reminiscent of Scilectra's physical characteristics. It was during this time that I obtained saliva, blood, vaginal, mammary, and anal samples."

Ameerah gasped from embarrassment. Her turned expression said it all. She said, "I know that we discussed this prior to the trip, but I didn't think that it was going to be necessary."

He replied, "I'm sorry to say that if you'd have seen what we did . . . It was unquestionably imperative." Raj went blow-by-blow of what her body showcased while she was outside of it. She wasn't upset because she knew that it had to be done. His findings might provide answers that she needed.

He asked, "Did anything happen out there that may have taken you off of our radar?"

She said, "I think so. I was visited by something! Whatever they were, I was encircled by darkness so dense that it felt as though the weight was the space around me. It's possible that their aura masked my signal or even disconnected me from you.

Raj sat up and slid to the edge of his chair. He asked, "Really, what did they want?"

She went on to say that it felt like hundreds of eyes peered at her through the darkness. "They told me that I could not move past them, and before I knew it I was back in my dream state, at home in my bed," she said.

Raj said, "Hmmm . . . Okay, let's do the post-exam, and then you can brief the entire team on the details of your trip and discuss what to do next."

Ameerah realized that she'd seen everyone but her cousin.

She asked, "Where's D.K.?"

Raj replied, "Speaking of being missing in action, I guess it runs in the family. He hasn't responded to any of our calls or texts. We couldn't spare the team to go out looking for him. Now that you're back, that's what we'll do."

A rap on the door brought the team to a standstill. It was so late in the evening that a knock on the door immediately raised suspicion!

Chad slowly creaked to the door and whispered, "Who goes there?"

"It's Dean Rydell. May I come in?"

Chad swiftly opened the door and gestured for him to come in. Chad sprung into animation mode, happily welcoming him like a concierge at a five-star hotel. He thought that when the dean came poking around at night, it was best not to look worried.

Dean Rydell smiled and asked about their current research. He wanted to get a demonstration of the unique tracking system that they'd developed. He wandered aimlessly through the lab, taking in the whatever research was lying about. His eyes were more intrusive than his hands; he kept those neatly tucked in the pockets of his eating pressed khakis. Savoy looked around the room, seeking any form of distraction to avoid the inevitable doom of answering his questions. It felt as if they were nearing the proverbial gallows.

He asked, "Where's Miss Mahar?"

Lisa saw her teammates lacking in authority and took over from there. "Dean, as you may know, we are required to get a full physical yearly. Late evening is the best time to do it because our research winds down at night. Ameerah is just about finishing hers. You might want to call her tomorrow and make an appointment to get a proper demonstration. We three are not nearly as versed as she is, or we would do it for you ourselves."

He responded, "Well, that makes sense. Please let her know that I stopped by and I look forward to speaking with her soon."

He turned to leave, and the coins in his pocket clinked together as he strangely kicked his feet down the unforgiving basement cement. The heavy soles of his shoes echoed as he slowly walked away. Lisa hurried and closed and locked the door behind him, listening carefully for his galumphing footsteps to fade away.

Lisa spun in a one-hundred-and-eighty-degree angle, and she asked, "What in the hell was that? Dude wants more than research from Ameerah! That was just down-right creepy!"

Before they could dart to the exam room to fill Ameerah in about Dean Rydell, somebody was trying to enter the lab, this time with the use of a key. Everyone stopped, like statues frozen in time. Then in walked D.K., smiling from ear to ear with a tall, beautiful woman in tow.

Savoy spoke first, "Ummm . . . Where have you been and who is this?"

He replied after a long sigh, "This requires a full-on, sit down meeting with everyone here first. Where's Ameerah?"

Lisa smugly answered, "She's in the exam room with Raj. Whoever Miss Thing is, she needs to wait out in the lobby on the other side of that door. That's the deal until you have been read in. There's been a lot going on around here. Sorry to be so blunt, D.K., but she can't stay until Ameerah says it's okay."

Embarrassed, D.K. turned to Ashland and muttered in her ear. She smiled at him, then brazenly gave Lisa the "full finger" on tilt and went back out the door. Lisa was quick to flip her one back. Suffice it to say, Lisa didn't like Ashland one bit.

D.K. ran to the back and tapped on the door. Raj yelled for him to come in. He rolled around the door frame all prepared to dazzle Ameerah. He was well aware that he'd broken protocol, and getting her in a calm mood first was mandatory.

When she saw his face, she lit up! He said to himself, *Mission accomplished.* She sat him down and went over the events of the past few days. Ameerah left out nothing. Following that conversation, she mentioned that she was just about to call a meeting to share the detail of her trip before he waltzed in.

He replied, "Perfect! but I have something to share with you first . . . it's a game-changer!"

Ameerah excitedly said, "Okay, let's go!"

They all filed into the conference room, and D.K. took the floor. He started off by explaining what he'd been doing for the better part of the week: the things he learned about Tilda Swan, and lastly, he gave a detailed introduction of DJ Black-Ray. Upon finishing his presentation, the team agreed to meet her formally. He opened the door of the lab and waved her in.

Her entrance was a lot less direct than before. She was mousy and reserved until Ameerah stood up and welcomed her by saying, "If you're a friend of D.K.'s, then you're a friend of the labs." Then she asked, "What's your name?"

" Well, my trade name is DJ Black-Ray, but my given name is Lola Ashland," she laughed. "I've said that more in the last week than I've ever said it in my entire life. I guess that D.K. has filled you guys in on who I am. I hope he did me justice."

Raj stepped in and asked that she explain a little more about the Hertzism. She replied, "Do you mind telling me what you do first? I'm kinda blind and exposed, and I think that since you know so much about me that I can learn about you."

They each took turns looking at each other, and Savoy thought it would be fitting that they come to an agreement without rudely leaving the table.

"So," she said, "Yes," in Fregodian.

Each person went around the table giving their response in their house language. Of course, Ashland was taken aback because she was the only one excluded from the joke.

Raj said, "It's a unanimous decision," (after Lisa was forced to change her vote). "We will share the pertinent parts of our research with you, and if you agree to integrate into the lab."

Ameerah took the reins and ran down the details, enough for Ashland to get the gist of what they do. She couldn't disguise the fascination on her face. She was bursting at the seams to tell them how she could advance the scope of their work.

She said, "Yo this is hot! So, let me tell you how I can help you. The way that I understand your experiment is that it is frequency-based. Heaven is going to resonate on one of the highest frequencies ever experienced. It may even be the source of frequency. When you make it to the . . . Vexaverse? 'Cause it sounds pretty big! You still need to connect to the right frequency or vibrations to reel you into Heaven's location. I can help with that."

The team sat mesmerized by what Ashland was saying and her understanding of the science.

"You all (of course) understand how a metal detector works. I can make you a frequency detector that can be implanted in Ameerah. This detector will work in reverse; it will block any vibration that is normal or typical and will only disclose to you the one that is insanely abnormal and steady. The closer that you get to it, the stronger it will become until it levels out. When it levels out, you have arrived."

Savoy shot to her feet and gave Ashland an ovation like she was at an operatic event. Ashland smiled and said, "Wait, there's more! Ameerah, with your current physical enhancements, this implant may also give you the ability to make the trip in flesh form. Of course, tests will need to be done, and I don't know how you power up and retain power, but if you can make the trip, I can get you to wherever that is."

The team gasped except for D.K.; he sat there like a proud father watching his first-born walk across the graduation stage.

Lisa said, "This is more than a notion. She would need to wear a special suit, and what about breathing? That's important!"

Ashland said, "Yeah, I get it. Some notable moves need to be made, but I can make sure that she gets there. I'm not a scientist like you, but I do know my stuff. Not to brag, but I'm extremely proficient in Pal-Alchemy. It's a new age forerunner of reconfiguration utilizing Quantum Algorithms and Soprano Frequencies, based on the possible transformation of organic living matter. It's concerned mainly with the attempts to convert living organic matter into conscious energy. What I've found is that once that transformation happens, it cannot be reversed back to matter. Meaning that you can try to go in your human form (which is best), or go in 'conscious energy' form, but you'd have to remain that way."

Chad rang out, "What are you? The love child of Einstein and Da Vinci? Your brain is crazy beautiful!"

A gray and foreboding feeling came over Ameerah. "I hate to bring an end to this joyous occasion, but there are two problems that need to be neutralized: Tilda Swan and Scilectra. One is more immediate than the other. Ashland, will you help us to tie Swan's hands? She has the details of our work, and she's holding it over our heads in a bad way."

Ashland replied lightning fast. "What do you need me to do?"

CHAPTER FIFTY-FIVE

As they walked the sprawling grounds of Tilda's estate, Scilectra asked, "So I suppose you want to ask me if I killed him?"

Tilda was particularly stone-faced during her reply. "The thought had crossed my mind. If anyone were to do it, you clearly are the best candidate."

"Miss Swan, I don't have many friends. In fact, I don't have any at all. Duvall was the closest person to me, following Professor Sherman. For us to collaborate fruitfully, we must have a healthy environment of trust and respect for each other, and it must be ironclad. Do you agree?"

Tilda said to herself, "To what end?" Then she allowed her facade to soften. She hadn't gotten to where she was by being emotional.

Her response to Scilectra was definitive and convincing. She stopped walking, turned to Scilectra, and with a straight face said, "I agree... from here on out, you have my undying loyalty. Now, the underground storage unit just a few yards away."

They arrived at a large patch of grass, far from the main house, that was impeccably manicured. Tilda wore a smartwatch that she pressed a few buttons on, and the ground literally slid apart and opened near her feet. Once the panels separated, they revealed an enormous staircase descending into darkness. Another touch to her watch, and the staircase began to light itself all the way to the bottom landing.

She said, "Come on, I'll give you the tour."

Scilectra wasn't new to underground lairs. The only tour to be had was to locate the Professor's things. The other items in her subterraneous museum were of no concern to her. Tilda's bunker held all kinds of oddities and glass cases, jars and cages. Enormous tomes, relics, and various antiquities lined the well-built hallways. Scilectra could sense the Professor's belongings nearing. Being so near his items, her heart began to beat erratically, as she should still smell his essence smeared all over her face.

They were finally there . . . his energy reached through the steel door, pulling her in. She didn't wait for Tilda to unlock it; she rode the veil to the middle of the room.

She told Tilda through the thick door, "Give me some time alone to go through his things. Stay or go; I will find my way back to you."

Tilda was surly with her response. "Remember: mutual respect and trust. Learn it . . . Live it!"

She muttered, "This shit isn't gonna last," as she walked off into the darkness, heading for the stairwell to ground level.

Scilectra was happy to be alone with the residue of the Professor's former life. She stood firmly in the center of the dank and gloomy room. It was the best way to survey the contents that they had haphazardly left in piles, peppered throughout the generous space. To Tilda's credit, she did provide a spacious storage unit for his belongings.

Unfortunately, her employees had thought it a daunting task to utilize all the two-thousand and some odd square feet she made available. Scilectra went about arranging the items as if his lab was preparing to be operational. Suddenly, she felt a tugging on her heart that all his greatness has been reduced to a pile discarded trash.

She reminded herself of her objective. After arranging the equipment neatly, the hunt was on for her user's manual. She asked herself, "What other plans did he have for me?"

The room was filled with black cases, so she obviously started with them. She went about opening each one. She was determined to find out everything the Professor neglected to share with her while he was alive. Scilectra spotted a case peeking out from under a pile of equipment. She dug it out and found that it had a series of locks and latches placed on the face of the unit.

She generated a stream of electrical currents from her hands and aimed it at the tumblers on the case. Scilectra was very careful not to incinerate the contents that it held. There was a loud cracking sound from her powers breaching the case. She reached in and carefully opened it with ease. It was beautiful! Sherman had made her a gunmetal grey, one-piece suit. It zipped up in the front all the way to the top of her neck. It then bled together into a mock turtleneck with sensors for hairs to engage with.

When she ran her fingers across the textured material, the threads reacted, and they lit up to her touch. It seems as if he had integrated live stitching in the suit. She couldn't wait to put it on! She slid into the garment, and it fit like a glove. As soon as she zipped it up to her chin, she could feel her nanites feeding on the power seeping through her skin. She felt strong and invincible in her cocoon of solace.

At the bottom of the crate was his research regarding the suit. She sat and crossed her legs on the floor, studying the document completely. She was adamant about mastering this gift that he left and advancing her abilities. From what she read, the suit was designed to consume external energy, store it, and provide that raw power directly to her via the pores on her skin. It could take energy from any and everything it was near while she was wearing it.

Magnified view of Scilectra's Energy Suit

The shell was a protective rubberized composite. It had tiny conical receptors that served as a dense barrier to suck energy in but let none go out. She celebrated that the Professor solved her "Ameerah problem" before she had to. This was a double-edged sword, because she loved him and needed him with her. However, she knew that if he had stayed, she would always be second to Ameerah.

She raced around the room, flipping through scattered files and papers strewn about on the floor, looking for whatever else she could find. She was right to do so, because there it was. She found a curious note written in familiar handwriting. Despite that, she just couldn't place whose handwriting it was.

It said, "If Heaven really exists, then you need to create the first physical body to touch on its firmament. The requirement to complete your research's metamorphosis will be there. If Ameerah reaches it first, then she will assume the source of power that you need. It will be hers to accept or refuse."

Scilectra balled the note up and set it ablaze in her hands.

She said, "Ameerah won't best me again. I will be the one to reach the coordinates. If by chance Heaven is real, then I will be the first to set my feet of flesh onto its hallowed grounds."

Scilectra was determined not only to square up with Ameerah, but to hopefully catch another glance of her mystery man. Stromford University's campus was an unforgiving maze that hid more than an underground lab. For Scilectra, it held the keys to her destiny. Little did she know it was just a matter of time before she'd have all the answers she needed. Some of those answers would be hard to swallow, and even more difficult to forgive.

* * *

Dean Rydell searched his mind for answers that night too. As he walked back to his office in the dead of night, he hardly noticed that the seasons were changing with every step he made. An icy wind slashed at his face, and the rain danced a brutal dance upon his head. All of this as he tried to rewind in his mind what he'd seen in the lab.

He thought, *Lisa Kim is a savage guard dog, and rightfully so!*

The dean hadn't been there on official business, but he had everything to do with their current research. The rain intensified to a deluge; the drops gunned down on him, so much so that it forced him to run (rather than walk) to the administration building.

His memory stopped short of being eidetic, but it was dependable enough to recall what was written on the blackboard. They were familiar to him. The equations and calculations were sophisticated and polished but unfinished. There was an efficient transition of vintage arcane methodology to the futuristic concepts of an ingenious mathematical model, all in the same equation. It was a perfect marriage of the old and the new, but it was incomplete.

Dean Rydell was a scientist in his own right and had dedicated the greater part of his life to solving the unsolvable. Mathematical equations were his method of choice. He understood that that was truly the only universal language for communication. Medical science was his other passion; he had an obsessive curiosity of how the body worked. So Stromford University was the most befitting place for him to land.

He believed that in the future, all diseases (and even surgical procedures) would be cured and performed with exact precision with the use of specialized equations. He was currently researching how to make chemical medications obsolete by applying "medicinal equations" that could be applied by balancing the bodies' electricity, internal speeds, temperatures, and timed-hormone release. All of this would be delivered external from the body.

He thought, *It's funny how people think that eyeglasses have an actual chemical prescription in them. They think the lenses are medicated when it's all a matter of topical science! The glass is made with specific curvatures, bending the light to reflect on your retina, that's all. I will do the same with various entry points to better the quality of human life.*

When he made it to his office, he pulled off his soggy jacket and grabbed a towel from the arm of his sofa. He bypassed his chalkboard and wrote down the equation from Ameerah's lab on a notepad that was hidden underneath his desk mat. This was his habit when he had something of great importance to say or record: he used a special pen and pad.

It was a gift from his mother who died when he was in grade school. She had said that the paper and ink was custom made for him, so he was to use it sparingly and only for meaningful occasions in his life. Tonight, he felt that this revolutionary equation deserved to be chronicled on its surface. He still planned to have a face-to-face with Ameerah, and from what he'd seen, he didn't have much time.

* * *

The team had a schedule to keep as well, but you would never know it by the whimsical mood in the lab. D.K. could barely concentrate on his work, as he was staring at his boo-thing over in the corner working with Savoy. They had geared her up with a lab coat and everything. He couldn't help but stare. Their evolution from unknown nemeses to introduced lovers had happened literally overnight. After the excitement of the break-in and subsequent drawdown, the attraction between the two was undeniable.

The first night, they'd talked for hours on end about each other and how they came to be sitting in the same room on opposite teams. Somewhere in between the hacking and coding comparisons, his lips landed on hers. They both had been deprived of the human touch and desperately needed interaction that extended beyond the flesh to pierce the soul.

For him, it wasn't about the sex. He was having plenty of that, even if it was with Haptic Images. Ashland filled a void in him and gave him a soul mate. Someone with whom he could create secrets, instead of keeping secrets from. His nose was open in the worst way and he loved every minute of it!

Ashland was different. She had been alone for so long that she felt doomed to die that way. The virtual world was her substitute, and her club gave her the physical praise she needed. What she really craved was a family in which to belong and to feel safe. D.K. provided that for her. The act of having sex was a confirmation that both their lives had changed.

The morning after their night of love, she said, "It's not every day that you wake up in a puddle of sweat and orgasm."

She rolled off of his muscular body to catalog her thoughts of him. She liked him, and she knew he liked her. She wanted to see what this meant beyond the physical. As she sat in a child's pose watching him sleep, for some reason it reminded her of a question he'd asked her the night before: "What is God to you?"

Her response was primed but not calculated; it was already sitting on her heart. She said, "I have more questions than answers. What is God after you strip away the fogginess of religion, after the confusion of imagery, and when the parables are gone? What is He at His core?"

D.K. sat with eyes wide open like that of an irresistible cartoon cat. That was the moment he decided she belonged with them at Lab-J71.

Savoy was just tickled about their new addition to the lab. Ashland was assigned to work with Savoy to calibrate frequencies for Ameerah to travel. Although they had a very important task ahead of them, it didn't stop Savoy from picking her mind about other unique innovations Ashland had created. They giggled like school girls gossiping about a boy. Lisa threw a paperweight in their direction to break up the nonsense.

Ashland said, "Lisa . . . she's pretty intense, huh?"

Savoy replied, "I won't lie to you. Yes, and she's no joke. So let's combine our work efforts with a little play, shall we?"

Ashland laughed and said, "Here's something else that I developed that you may find interesting. I call it 'Retina Flash Messaging'. It's a method that allows an embedded flash of light to temporarily imprint a message on a person's retina. The displayed message can only be seen by the intended party. The message is projected on the inside of the eyelids when eyes are closed. The time length of the display is no more than five seconds long."

Savoy was so stunned she nearly fell out of her chair. She said, "Shut the damn door! Do you know the implications of a device such as this?" Ashland tried her best to laugh quietly. She said, "Why, yes . . . I do!"

Unfortunately, they weren't quiet enough, because a wide shadow was cast on the wall in front of them. Behind them stood Ameerah, Lisa, and Chad.

Ameerah said, "Okay, you two. Apparently you need supervision, and I have just the person for the job. Dun-ta-da-dah . . . Introducing Chad! We have a new order of work. Chad, you're up. Go ahead and inform them."

"Hello, ladies! We will be designing and fabricating a suit for Ameerah to wear on her next trip to the ether. This special suit will be hardwired to assist her in galactic travels and then safely back home."

As the leader of the lab, she felt good to see her team (old and new) working diligently together for a common cause. She would never let them see this, but she was scared. There were so many unknown variables, and each one could end her life. There was no sure-fire way to safeguard her physical body, and even more importantly, there was no absolute way to safeguard her soul.

CHAPTER FIFTY-SIX

Tilda arrived back in the main house visible shaken. Not by Scilec-tra, but by her inability to raise Ashland on the phone.

She said to the head of her security, "This bitch of a DJ put me in a precarious situation. She's the only one that can make those audio files and I can't find her. Oh! I know! Let's go by her house!"

She got excited, but then thought aloud, "This job may be better suited for Scilectra, but I can't give her anything to hang over my head."

She barked at the driver, "I don't care how many laws you have to break, get me there right now!"

As requested, he ran every yellow and red light, and those that were green were treated like a private one-way race track. When they arrived, Tilda didn't wait for her driver to open the door for her. She was so panicked that she nearly jumped out before the car stopped moving. When she stepped in the foyer, the front desk attendant of Ashland's building read the room and let Tilda board the elevator without one question.

Tilda's body yearned for a fix; she felt the throbbing lust of the frequency emanating from within. From the way she sprinted to Ashland's apartment, you would have never guessed that she was a member of the geriatric community. Her security had a hard time keeping up with her gallop. When she made it to her door, she gained her composure and whacked the door four times. Each time she whacked she would put her ear up to the wooden door.

"BULLSHIT!!!" She yelled at the top of her voice while shaking her fist in the air like a scoundrel whose plans had been thwarted. Her next words were more aggressive. "Kick it down and search the place!"

Her security did as commanded. On the third try, they knocked down the heavy wooden plank of a door and searched the place. The Drug Enforcement Agency would have been proud at the thorough job they did! Even with that, Tilda netted nothing. The computer that had the audio files was in the possession of its owner, Lola Ashland, who (at the moment) couldn't be found.

Tilda wasn't thinking right; she wasn't in her right mind. She decided to concoct a bizarre story to hopefully induce Lab-J71 to create similar audio files for her to hit off. The only thing she had to offer them is what she was using to blackmail them. She had to get those files, and the more the better. She almost didn't mind the trade because she had Scilectra in her pocket; that association would serve her better. She felt it put her in a position to control not only Scilectra but the lab as well. Right now, she didn't care. She wanted to get high, and she would figure out the rest later.

She promptly left Ashland's trashed apartment to head over to the lab. She had what they wanted in her bag. She would hand it over lock, stock, and barrel for their expertise in her digital pleasure. They exited the building in a huff, and that same doorman who had asked no questions when she arrived asked no questions when she left. He did, however, notify Ashland that an alert for her apartment went off on their security board for her unit.

Unfortunately, Ashland left her phone in her locker as requested by Ameerah for security reasons. No one had a clue that Tilda was en route to the lab, and if she found Ashland there . . . there would be hell to pay.

Tilda pulled up to the lab like she owned the place. They drove through the Stromford University Gate sign, onto the sidewalk, and parked right in front of the medical building. She sprung from the car with wild disheveled hair and twisted clothing, which she tried to straighten as she walked.

The team was deep into the throes of working when they heard systematic pounds on the door. A woman with an entitled drawl in her voice said, "Ameerah, darling, I come bearing gifts. Please open the door."

Ameerah rolled her eyes and shook her head, but then that quickly turned to panic once she looked over to Ashland.

She said, "Damn, I forgot. You can't be here!"

D.K. raced over and ushered Ashland to the back. They turned on the monitors in the control room to watch the goings-on in the lab.

Ameerah motioned for Chad to open the door, which forced Tilda to come to her. That sentiment was not lost on Tilda. But that's what desperation will do to you; it takes you out of your character.

Ameerah said, "Miss Swan, how may I help you?"

Tilda succinctly covered all the salient points of her case. She was extra colorful and dramatic in order to drive the urgent points home. Ameerah especially loved the part of the story about the deathly ill relative that couldn't take traditional drugs due to adverse reactions. They needed this innovation of Digital Drugs to make it through therapies.

The juicy part of this theatrical performance was when she offered to return Duvall's collected documents and video of their research as a bargaining tool. It felt awesome to know that the developer of her fix was in their control room, and therefore no tiresome research had to be done on their end. This was an easy "Yes," but Ameerah said she had to go to the back and check inventory because she could commit. She asked to be excused and then went on her way.

When she was out of sight, she ran to the control room and asked Ashland. "I don't want to put you on the spot. If we move forward with this sham, them she doesn't need you anymore (so she thinks), but she might consider you a loose end. To be honest, I don't see murder being above her. So, here's my plan ..." Ameerah spent about five minutes with D.K and Ashland, devising a plan that kept Tilda on a leash and kept Ashland safe.

When she emerged, Ameerah said, "Okay, here's the deal. We can make it for you; one of our team members is better suited to get it done. They said to give them a day and come back and pick up the files tomorrow at noon, in exchange for all our property. However, there is an addition to the arrangement. If we do this, you cannot harass, bother, harm, or threaten anyone on our team, or we will cut you off and out you publicly. You have a shit-ton of money and power, but there's one thing more powerful than that, in which you can never own, and that's the power of social media.

"Fake news has made and taken down asshole kings, queens, and presidents. Just remember, the bigger the lie, the more the likes. Meaning it doesn't take much to ruin a brand. Not in name only, but irresponsible/erroneous chatter can tank stocks and make a formerly admired brand a disenfranchised one. Do we have a deal?"

Tilda hesitated for a moment, but then offered her hand to shake. Her last word was music to their ears. "It's a deal!"

Tilda strutted out the door and let it slam behind her. She had no intentions of keeping her word. She didn't care about their idle threats, because once she found Ashland she didn't need the lab anymore. This deal would only last until her DJ resurfaced. It was too bad for Tilda, because DJ Black-Ray was now an official member of Lab-J71. Ashland wouldn't produce anything unless she was directed to do so by Ameerah.

The team's ears should've been buzzing from all the attention they'd garnered recently. Their new associations weren't as pleasant as the sick and dying company that they were used to, and the fact of it all had worn some a little thin. Lisa and Raj took the lead and voiced a popular opinion trending by the team, which was, "When Ameerah's trip is over, we should relocate to another facility, one with a more thoroughly isolated experience."

Lisa said, "These random visits by not-so-random people has got to stop!"

Ameerah replied, "It won't be for too much longer. I have a plan in place that will give us back our normalcy. I'm gonna take this trip and get right back to start our next research project."

Ameerah might have spoken too soon, because outside forces might have a new plan on the table. Scilectra was no longer waiting for Ameerah to hand over coordinates. She remembered the box that her father left her and she decided to have another go at it; this time, she would use direct sunlight. The day that she took the Professor, she was so angry that she'd left the box with Ameerah. She thought, *Today is as good a day as any to try the suit out. If my energy is not emitting outwardly, then maybe she won't sense me there.*

Before she left the storage, she caught a glimpse of herself while passing a reflective metal panel. She stopped to admire herself in her new suit. She knew that there was no such thing as coincidences. Finding out about Tilda, the Professor's storage being on her property, the suit, and then the note. It all meant something.

She said, "All these things are lights on my path to my destiny!"

Scilectra was on her way to the lab to find her box. She hoped that the weather would clear and that the sun would show its face before it was too late. Traveling the void was faster than usual; she attributed the swiftness to the suit. The void was nothing but raw energy, and the suit must've absorbed so much of it that it quickened the experience. She was there, hovering on the dark side of the veil, glaring into the present.

They were working and moving about the room, several of them walking direct past Scilectra's face. Ameerah was there as well; Scilectra moved in the void in her direction, purposely invading her personal space. After a few minutes passed, Ameerah curiously looked up and around. You could tell that she heard or sensed something, but dismissed it and went back to work.

Scilectra smiled and puffed out her chest. She excitedly said, "The suit really works! Now, to crossover and see if I will remain undetected."

Before she did so, she moved about the room in the veil, looking for the box. It wasn't there, so she decided to check in Ameerah quarters.

She said, "Ah, there you are."

It was under the bunk, covered with a blanket. Once she was near it, she could feel the residue of her blood that was hidden in the crevices of the metal. She hastily grabbed the box and snatched it in the void with her as she left.

The weather had begun to clear, and she was anxious to test the box again. She vowed to give it all the time it needed to transform. Privacy was important, so she headed for the roof. The likelihood that someone was up there was slim to none, and it was the best place to get the maximum UV Ray exposure. She thought, *At times, I forget my capabilities. I don't need to wait for sunlight. As need be, I can go directly to the sun.*

Midway through her revelation, she spotted a man cutting across the campus.

His gait caught her attention. Her hair stood on end and a shiver raced down her spine. She knew that it was impossible, but ... What if it was him? She swiped into the void to reach the ground floor. Her heart raced as she frantically looked for the man to appear again. The mystery man had disappeared into the maze of buildings situated on the campus. She convinced herself that she was in error and to stay on task. The sighting made her objective even more important. She landed back on the roof just as the clouds parted; they made adequate room for the illumination she needed.

Scilectra rubbed her fingers across the box. There was something soothing to her about the smooth metal gliding underneath her fingertips. She guided her middle finger to the protruding button in the center. When she felt the warmth on her face, she pressed the button with the prescribed number of systematic holds and releases. Her blood didn't scatter and dissipate when it hit the air; the box seemed to magnetize it on its surface. Once the ritual was done, she sat the box down and waited.

It didn't take long, and this time, she was the intended witness to the transformation! The box was converting and numbers were magically appearing right before her eyes. She directed her hairs to record the digits. As she turned the box on all sides for closer inspection, she saw a tiny etching of the word "Vexaverse."

She asked herself, "What is that ... What does it mean? There has to be more!"

Scilectra pulled her hand up toward her face. She stared at her fingers so intensely that her index finger burst open with blood. Blood flowed out like a faucet and misted in the air. Before it could get away, Scilectra doused the entire box in it. She closed the wound and then held the box up in the air and turned it from end to end in the sunlight. More revelations were being exposed! This was the first time since her metamorphosis that she got sanguine about becoming the "Godhead." There was a map, and the "Vexaverse" was the bulls-eye on it! Amid the excitement, her heart ached again. The thought of the Professor knowing any of this information and withholding it from her was unforgivable.

Scilectra felt that she knew the "where," but she still didn't know the "how." She had to find a way to translate the map into coordinates so that her internal GPS could just take her there. If not, the trip would take longer from having to stop and access locations as she went. She might have to utilize Tilda. Maybe her connections would open the door to someone savvy enough to simplify the note on the box.

* * *

The team was many floors below her, hard at work designing a suit safe enough to sustain Ameerah on her trip. The sketches were promising. Not only did it have to be element safe, but it also had to work in tandem with her powers and modify itself if her powers grew. Savoy was a self-proclaimed fashionista. She incorporated an ingenious style in the suit. She was lauded for its hidden practical design of storing crucial energy réservoirs within the extended lower flaps of the garment.

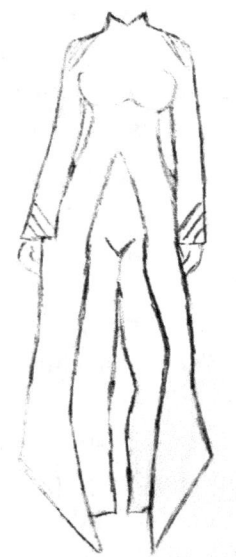

Raj and Ameerah emptied the rear holding rooms to test the strength of her powers. Before they started, he reserved some time to go over the results of her body samples.

He said, "Your bodily secretions during your astral travel behaved as microcosms (what we've learned) of Scilectra's powers. Each sample offered something different. What she told you about the A.T.I is correct. She has incorporated her DNA with yours; actually, you only maintain forty percent of your natural genes.

"Well, that's not accurate either. Your genes are still there but the A.T.I. has mapped over them and has rendered yours dormant. You have to start commanding your mind and your body to do what you want. Your new genetics can only respond to your will, and I know that this is going to sound cliche, but Mark 11:23 says it best: *'For verily I say unto you, That whosoever shall say unto this mountain, Be thou removed, and be thou cast into the sea; and shall not doubt in his heart, but shall believe that those things which he saith shall come to pass; he shall have whatsoever he saith.'"*

Ameerah laughed and gave Raj a hug. She said, "Let's get to work!"

Deep down inside, she was afraid. People talk about, pray about, and even demand faith all the time, but it still remains the hardest (if not the most impossible) task to achieve. Acquiring a belief in yourself requires a factory reset. If she was going to make it to Heaven in the flesh, she had to make her thoughts (outgoing and incoming) her first priority.

They began with simple things like levitating, and then timed levitating. Next was controlling electrical currents (sending/receiving). She was able to create an energy bubble around her, and she held it for hours. Raj attempt to pierce it, but it was to no avail; Ameerah was getting stronger and stronger. Eventually, they left the confines of the lab so that Ameerah could interact with the elements.

He said, "This time, you will be making the trip in the flesh. Your suit will help but it can only do so much. You are your power. The more and more that I coach you, the Bible becomes more and more relevant to me. It's crazy because God has been saying this to humans for eons and for some reason, we still don't believe it. Who's to say? Each and every one of us may have God-like untapped abilities. He's probably looking at us saying, 'imagine what they could be once they find out that I AM in them!'"

* * *

Scilectra was long gone by the time Ameerah provided an open display of her powers. Her mind was planted firmly on finding someone to uncomplicate her attempt at Heaven. Stepping out of the void into Tilda's private quarters, might have been ill-advised this day. There she was, scantily clad and surrounded by empty bottles of champagne. Tilda was a sleeping drunk, and nearby on a chaise lounge was her head bodyguard lying naked as a jaybird. Scilectra walked softly so as not to startle them; she felt the need to assess the situation a little more closely.

From the ooze running down Tilda's thighs, it was apparent that the pair had participated in a round of intercourse. Scilectra could smell his pungent semen wafting off of his manhood. So sad for her too, because he was obviously infected. Scilectra wondered why a woman of her age had a need for copulation?

Even though she loved the Professor, the sole reason for intimacy was to impregnate herself. Of course, she enjoyed it, but pleasure could not override her ultimate duty! She liked Tilda even less after seeing her this way. She had to make herself known regardless as to who she embarrassed.

She said, "Lady Swan . . . Lady Swan!"

Tilda was slow to wake and extremely startled when she did.

She said, "What the Hell are you doing in my private quarters?"

Her bodyguard jumped up, gun in hand, and pointed it in several directions.

Scilectra said, "Dismiss him. We have work to do!"

Tilda knew better than too overtly argue with her, so she did what she said. She quickly gathered herself, combing her hair with her fingers and twisting it back tightly in a french roll.

She then said, "Well . . . spit it out. What do you need now!?"

Scilectra was tempted to smite her right there on the spot, but a cooler head prevailed.

"I'm in dire straits. In order for me to make my trip successfully, I require a skilled cosmologist of sorts to devise a coordinate for me. Someone who can give me a theoretical address with solid math behind it. You are obligated to do this. The success of mankind is predicated on what you do in this moment!"

Tilda answered Scilectra as she reached for a bottle of champagne, and ostensibly to look at the label. "There's only one person that I know that can help you, and that's little Miss Ameerah Mahar."

Before Sciletra could slash her with her tongue, Tilda offered to do a mediation between the two. Scilectra was just about to holler when she realized that this might be an opportunity for a face-to-face trial of her suit.

She said, "That's an excellent idea! We mustn't announce ourselves. In a situation such as this, it's paramount to maintain the upper hand."

CHAPTER FIFTY-SEVEN

D ean Rydell refused to wait any longer. He had to stifle Ameerah by any means necessary, even at the cost of exposing himself. Before he resorted to that last earth-shattering choice, he took one last look at the equation that he'd copied from the lab's blackboard. If he could complete the unfinished work, that would give him the leverage required.

He thought about the time and what was at stake. *Three of us. We were the only ones left, the only ones to find the way. I have done as much as I can. The only thing I can do now is slow Ameerah down!*

He tired himself out from the complexity of the problem and the enormity of options one could go in to solve the equation. At that moment, the dean gave up. He donned his jacket and hat to walk back over to the lab. Tonight was the night he stopped Ameerah for good! Closer and closer he came, the weight of it all was getting bigger and bigger. Soon the night sky filled with lunar light as if the moon was falling. As he rounded the corner to the lab, Dean Rydell knew it was a sign of his impending ominous future.

* * *

The team was in the zone. Ameerah mastered the features of her abilities. The others designed, sewed, and molded a suit that the finest astronauts would envy. They worked almost to the point of belting out show tunes.

Ameerah smiled as she watched her team (her family) working toward the goal of a lifetime. Chad stood by her and joined in her private moment.

She said, "I'm sure that you've never seen *The Wiz*, but if you had, there's a scene with a group of forced workers in a fabric factory. They're working to an internal beat that they all shared. Our team's vibe right now puts you in the mind of that. It's really magical to see."

Thump . . . thump . . . thump. Yet another knock at the door.

Ameerah said, "I've had just about enough of this. Keep working. I'll get it!"

She jogged over to the door and slightly cracked it open. "Dean Rydell, how can I help you?"

Lisa looked up and over her glasses at the dean. With all that had been going on, she had totally forgotten to tell Ameerah that he had come by the night before.

She said, "Right now isn't a good time. We have a deadline to complete an extremely important project."

The dean bit his lip and looked away as he replied, "I know. That's what I want to talk to you about. You've been in the dark about everything since day one. At the end of this explanation, I implore you to stop what you're doing . . . you have to!"

All activity in the lab ceased, and Ameerah stood in silence with a bewildered look on her face.

The dean said, "Do you want to do this here, in front of everyone? I'm telling you now, you don't want to do that!"

She said, "I think that I do! If this affects my research, then my team has a right to hear every word!"

The dean looked in her face with shame in his eyes. His facial expression begged her to reconsider, but she was immovable. She kept her feet planted firmly in place, forcing him to speak.

Her reluctantly responded, "All right. Have it your way. It's about your search for Heaven and how I can't allow you to go."

The team was now on their feet and surrounding him like gravestones, standing silently, blocking this him at every degree. He looked downward and loudly cleared his throat; he was nervous about the news to come.

"I'm not the dean here by mistake. All of this is an elaborate design of fate. Your initial team was funneled in the direction of Stromford University because of its future forward-thinking and scientific freedoms. I studied certain disciplines and called in tremendous favors to be appointed dean of this school. I walked in the door with tenure. I purposely funded everything that you proposed, and when finances were low, I carried the weight of your research personally.

"Professor Sherman was the key to achieving this great feat. His theory of 'Reconfigured Angelology' was the genesis of this whole thing. He had a zeal for scientific provocation in a time when the world wore its prudeness like a badge of honor. I don't mean to explain this in a nebulous manner, but the circumstances involved are multilayered and complexed."

Ameerah and her team didn't move a muscle while he tore the heart out of their research. She wanted him to divulge every drop.

He went on to explain the Professor's theory and why that directly affected the lab and their work. What Ameerah didn't understand was why. How did any of this matter to the dean so personally? Before she could ask this there came another knock at the door.

D.K. cried out loud, "For fuck's sake . . . who is it now?"

Understandably, the team had totally forgotten that Tilda was scheduled to come by that day to pick up her digital files and to give them Duvall's notes and videos.

However, Ashland hadn't forgotten, but it was too late. D.K. hurried to the door and swung it wide open to find Tilda there with her security. The lights flickered and Scilectra instantaneously appeared in the room from the void. She landed directly behind an unsuspecting Dean Rydell. She was averse to using doors, simply because she didn't have to; her elevated status ensured that!

"Is it you?" Scilectra asked with a blood-curdling cry.

All eyes now turned to her as she stood behind the fear-stricken dean. Tilda didn't care about whatever Scilectra had going on; she saw a familiar face in the crowd that was not supposed to be there. She made her way through the forest of white lab coats until she was eye-to-eye with Lola Ashland.

Standing haggardly with legs apart and her hands on her hips, she snidely said, "One of these sounds is not like the others! One of these sounds doesn't belong!"

Ashland wasn't scared of Tilda; she just wanted nothing more to do with her. She responded, "You looking really rough these days. Kinda look like you need a fix that's never gonna come!"

Tilda scoffed at her and grabbed her vintage pearls. "I beg your pardon, sound lady! You have been bought and paid for one hundred times over. I own you!"

D.K. broke away from the Scilectra scene long enough to see Lola needed him more. He slid in between the two and attempted to push Tilda back when her burly bodyguard intervened.

His deep baritone voice roared out like a lion. "Don't ever touch her!" That just seemed to rile D.K. up.

However, their minor event being held in the corner was being upstaged by Scilectra's ensuing confrontation. Tilda's bodyguard and D.K. stopped their bickering long enough to overhear Scilectra say, "I did everything you told me to do and more, and you still left me! I was so young, and you cut me, drilled into me and experimented on me. I took it without a word because I trusted you like none other. I can hardly be angry because you were right but why did you leave me? YOU ARE MY FATHER!"

A collective chime of disbelief mushroomed throughout the room. Now Ameerah and Scilectra confronted the dean. He had one woman for each ear with their own set of grievances being hurled at him at one time.

He said, "Please . . . Let me speak! You want to know the truth, here it is . . ."

Scilectra was reduced to a little girl in her father's presence.

"Astrid! You're my daughter. I loved you then and I love you now. I saw early on that you were special, that you were unlike any other child that I had ever seen. Your IQ was off the charts! You rarely responded to pain and you didn't understand simple processes in life. You only digested information if it was cloaked in equation of some sorts.

"I was already on the path of trying to find a way to answer the very questions that you're asking now. I gave my life over to educating myself in the mystical sciences and developing a growing knowledge about what God is and what He's not. Then I heard about Professor Sherman's research and attended several of his lectures. His last lecture dripped with the answers that myself and other hidden organizations had long been seeking.

"So, I and 'the Organization' cleared a path for the best and the brightest minds to be housed under one roof. I was placed here as dean under a new name and identity to facilitate the people who could decode Heaven. This particular team had to work together to seed the flowers that would bloom the flower, so to speak."

The team (and uninvited company) listened quietly with arms folded and eyes wide open.

He went on, "When you all began to crack open the 'unknown,' it was time for the Professor to go it alone and start the next phase. This was not our doing; Professor Sherman did what he intended to do with or without the Organization.

"Astrid, I left for many reasons, none of which was you! I was not allowed to interfere with your progress. Preparing yourself to become what you are now had to be a solitary effort. You alone had to do the steps to the letter. I've been here watching and clearing the road to assure an uncomplicated ascension.

"Ameerah, I hope this clears things for you."

She quickly jumped in to say, "No . . . No, it doesn't. It clears things for your daughter. And by the way: bad dad much?"

Scilectra grew to anger in defense of her father, wrong or right. "Ameerah, watch your tongue if you wish to use it another day!"

Ameerah replied, "Yeah, whatever. I'm just pointing out that that's some foul shit you did to your own daughter! You're no better than that pervert of a professor! At any rate, why are you here right now? What is it that you want from us, now that you've set up this whole situation, treating us like dumb, unaware contractors?"

He took a deep breath and said, "Ameerah, I want you to stop. Astrid has to be the first and only person to verify Heaven. If you don't, it may have grave consequences for you and your team by worldly and other-worldly forces. This opportunity is for her and her only.

"You must stand down. Give her what she needs, so she may go and deliver this world from falsehood and fantasy. Save us all from certain death mentally, spiritually and physically. Besides, there is no way you'd survive the attempt; you're not made for it."

Ameerah crossed her arms and tossed her hair in the dean's general direction. Her luscious bouncy auburn locks completed the shade she was about to throw at the Dean.

"Ah, no sir!" she said, "You will not repeat this historically fraudulent pattern. Using our genius minds, creative skills, and strong bodies to level up on. Usurping credit and the accolades as you go, absolutely not! If your daughter is the chosen one, then let her arrogant ass get there on her own. All I can say to the both of you is . . . If you're not ready, then you'd better get ready, because there's no stopping this train!"

Lisa climbed on a table and yelled, "On that note. Get out of our lab! I think I speak for the entire team when I say this: Ms. Swan . . . there will be no fix for you today. Yes, we knew all along that it was for you! Dean Rydell or whatever your name is, it goes without saying that your tenure is over. Astrid . . . Scilectra, with all due respect, we have nothing to give you. Last but not least, please leave from whence you came. We have work to do!"

Scilectra smiled as she walked closer to Ameerah. It was more important than ever to test out her suit. If Ameerah wasn't going to help her then she didn't need to live. Ameerah saw her slithering her way, and there they were, face-to-face again. True to the Professor's design, none of her energy seeped out.

Ameerah didn't feel empowered being next to her like she did before. There was no constant energy rushing through her veins. Inwardly she was confused and itched to look down at her hands for any activity. She had to play it cool and not obviously inspect herself in front of her foe. Ameerah adopted a stone-cold facade to throw Scilectra off. One thing was for certain: that within in a few seconds, she would have an answer about if her ploy worked or not.

Dean Rydell saw wrath rising in his daughter's face. She was about to square-off with Ameerah right there and then! He stepped in Astrid's view to diffuse the situation.

"Sweetheart, you don't have time for this. Arriving there before Ameerah is not the only clock you're on. I know that you're pregnant, and where that baby takes its first breath is crucial.

"If it's the air of whatever lies in the Vexaverse, then its life will not be bound by rules, science, time, and not death. Find out what that place is and inhabit it with your own flesh and then that of your child's. Go . . . now. Take what you've learned from the box and use it. There's no help for you in this lab!"

Scilectra grabbed Ameerah's forearms and sneered in her face. This was her way showing Ameerah that there would be no more transfers of power. A look of fear and concern appeared over Ameerah's face; she received that message loud and clear. Scilectra was the first to exit the lab but other non-personnel dribbled out the room at a slow pace. Tilda was still yelling expletives and formidable threats at Ashland and D.K.; Dean Rydell tried his best to blend into the out-going count.

Lisa stopped the dean on the way out the door. "Not you. We want a word with you first."

Dean Rydell hesitantly changed his course and leaned on a nearby pillar.

"You're going to sit here and write a full confessional of how you used this team and manipulated the university for personal gains. After we are done with this leg of the research, you will pack your things, retire, and leave. If you don't, we will release this letter and the image of you writing it to every news outlet and law enforcement agency there is."

He looked at them with an uneasy expression and said, "I will leave because my work here is done, but if that had not been the case, the Organization would control that raging fire until it was a slow burn. I keep telling you, this is bigger than you, me, or Astrid."

He wrote the letter and signed it, stood up from the table, and walked to the door saying, "Another word of advice: the cosmos has taken notice, and what we have done is out of order. It will move Heaven and Hell to get it back on track."

With that said, he faded into the darkness on the other side of the door.

CHAPTER FIFTY-EIGHT

Savoy rushed to Ameerah. She said, "There's no time to waste; let's get you installed into your new suit."

Raj said, "Ameerah, before that, I need to see you in my exam room."

She was beginning to feel frazzled. Everyone was rushing around and pulling her in all directions!

When they made it to his exam room he said, "Remember we spoke about the A.T.I. not working as effectively as it could? Mainly because you have low dopamine levels, the A.T.I. can't bloom without it. Consider this your booster shot for the year. I'm going to give you a high dose of synthetic dopamine that will activate all the A.T.I. We don't have time to test its effects on your powers, so just go with what you know."

Ameerah laid down and Raj injected her. Almost immediately she noticed a clarity that wasn't there before. She could see electrons, neutrons, and molecules. Waving her hands around made them move to her will. Speaking of hands, hers had a shimmery, electric blue glow around them, and when she pointed streams of energy whipped from her fingertips.

Raj smiled and belted out a "Hells yeah!" like a cheerleader witnessing the game-winning point. He said, "Okay, now let's get you dressed!"

* * *

It was Ashland's turn to be on deck. While Savoy worked to get Ameerah sewn into her suit and attached to all the sensors, Ashland scienced the shit out of the navigation! Thankfully, she and D.K. took the time to run back to her apartment to pick up Bertha. If she was going to do this right, she had to have her in the mix to calculate impossible equations. Ashland painstakingly duplicated a microcosm of Bertha's motherboard into Ameerah's suit.

The ballistics garment would give her the ability to withstand the elemental components of space. She created an interrogation system utilizing grouped "Vector Equations & Manipulations," and of course, all of this had to work in partnership with her powers. Given the right groupings of distinctive broadband equations, Ameerah's physical matter would transmute and adapt to her surroundings, very much like an amphibious reptile going from land to water.

This would speed Ameerah through the Vexaverse and navigate her safely to Heaven. That process was coupled with a specialized digitized Hertz file that would allow Ameerah to transcend into alternate universes and remain physically intact. The final step was to configure the suit with her in it, and implant a (painless) microscopic hardwire through Ameerah's nose to her brain. That would be Chad's responsibility—it was his wheelhouse of expertise.

Ameerah stepped out from behind the partition and the team's faces glowed, as if they just witnessed a private viewing of the bride on her wedding day. She was absolutely gorgeous! The suit hugged every curve she had and then some. D.K. blushed because he'd never seen his cousin look this way before. She had a different air about her, a dynamic appeal that would deter her enemies fast.

Savoy designed the suit in an icy white tone because the material was made to reflect all wavelengths of light and therefore absorb the least heat. This was important in order to keep the mechanical functions of a constantly running suit cool. She also gave decor to the shoulders and arm cuffs to indicate that they had the functionality to control certain aspects of the garment.

Ameerah smiled and walked to each of them and gave them hugs. She privately whispered something in each of the ears as she went down the line.

When she arrived at D.K., there were no words. She grabbed both of his hands in hers, shed a tear, and hugged him hard.

She turned to them all and said, "No one knows the outcome of any of this . . . if I don't return, track me, see where I am. You all will be ok. I mean this from the bottom of my heart: I love you! If He lets me in Heaven to stay, I'll be there waiting for you!"

She took ten steps back, closed her eyes, and concentrated on the Monocerus Zone. Chad lunged to the wall and hit the lights, and the lab sank into darkness for a short while. Then Ameerah began to glow! Her body was outlined in that same blue aura that Raj saw emitting from her hands earlier, but now it encompassed her entire form. The more she concentrated, the more she shone, and the suit channeled that energy too via the prototype material. The electrical output zipped around the surface like a fiberoptic highway, and with one last dynamic surge . . . she was gone into thin air.

Ashland was in awe of the miraculous events that she experienced during her short time with the lab. She tiptoed over to the spot where Ameerah was standing. Ashland jutted her arms in the air and swiped them back and forth to convince herself of what she'd seen.

The rest of the team slumped down in their chairs, mourning the potential loss. In their eyes, they lost their lead, their friend, and most importantly, their family. Savoy rolled her chair over to her look at her empty monitor. Ashland's programming wasn't compatible with her existing system, so they couldn't track her like before.

Ameerah wasn't on anyone's radar. She was everywhere and nowhere at the same time. After all, it was her first time in the void, where she met time in person. She witnessed the realities of the past, present, and future whizzing by her like searchlights cutting through the night's sky.

Here, God happens quickly, running his fingers through the waters of the universe to divide the direction's time. The air here is thick with the scents of silver and honey, while splintered realities exist on the wheels of our spun existence. Her body wobbled like an egg standing on its end.

The turbulent winds whipped around her in a dizzying frenzy. Whenever she attempted to anchor herself, she narrowly escaped from being snatched up in the streams of time. Whenever she could anchor, a scene of someone's life presented before her eyes.

She said, "This is how Scilectra watched me; nothing was hidden from her in this place."

Ameerah hovered on the observing side of a divine two-way mirror. As much as she wanted to admire the views, there was no time to ogle at the internal workings of God's forever clock. She was already at a disadvantage. For all intents and purposes, this world was Scilectra's playground, and she made the rules.

Wandering through the void, she felt like something was watching her. It was that creepy crawly feeling you get when you're being reviewed by unwanted eyes who mean you certain harm. In the ether, Ameerah often had to remind herself that she was in control. The A.T.I. gene was a powerful and sophisticated tool. All she had to do was focus on that exact point in the universe she wanted to be.

Her mind was the engine in which she traveled, and her thoughts were the fuel. She ran her hands over her suit and guided her fingers through her hair. Ameerah realized that it was her doubting human beliefs keeping her from excelling. She took a moment to focus on a mantra that would erase the weakness of her humanism. Ameerah lovingly said it over and over again: "Ye are gods . . . Ye are gods . . . Ye are gods."

It was nothing more than that. She convinced her mind of that fact and her A.T.I. gene did the rest! She instantly transformed! Ameerah wanted to ameliorate her suffering fleshly status, and she did. The prominence of her thoughts leveled up her soul casing, and the blue energy field was gone. An iridescent pastel rainbow shimmer adorned Ameerah from head to toe, and not a moment too soon. She had company!

CHAPTER FIFTY-NINE

D ean Rydell walked across the campus as slowly as he could. He feared what awaited him when he returned to his office. He miserably failed in stopping Ameerah from taking the forbidden trip. It was a Sunday, and the campus was deserted except for him; most of the staff was gone and the students had no reason to be on this side of the quad. His slow walking turned into a full-on mope. He thought seriously about heading for the front gates and walking away, never to be heard from again.

The thought was just sinking in when he heard a van come to a screeching halt! Four men wearing masks jumped out and ran directly for him. He knew what this was, and he didn't fight it.

The men took him to the nearest empty building, to "The Man." He had a face that (if you were lucky) you would only see once in a lifetime. The man waited for him patiently to arrive. When they did, he calmly said, "Carlos Acosto, you only had one job to do and you failed."

Carlos no longer had to keep up the identity of "Dean Rydell." He was outed for the whole world to see. He imagined this moment so many times, but he never expected it to happen. Carlos had sacrificed everything to see this through. He'd abandoned his wife and daughter for a quest that may have been damned in the first place.

He said to The Man, "Ameerah is more resilient than I'd anticipated. Professor Sherman had an unhealthy affixation on Ameerah. His savage ways started her down a path that led us to this moment. First, he imbued her with Aurovian. Unfortunately, Scilectra's envy did the rest."

The Man responded, "This task was monumental! You deciphered how to locate us while we were camouflaged in the airspace of Arizona. You surpassed every deed asked and made us believe in your capabilities. Our time on Ezekiel's Wheel is short. We agree with you that Heaven may be the biggest fairytale ever told to humankind. However, there's something up there beyond that stars, and it will accommodate our particular vessels (and the occupants of the wheel) as well. Many on the wheel came from Earth but are no longer of Earth.

"We have sat hidden, suspended in your skies for over a millennium. We have a few key earthbound individuals to acquire, but after that, we must put the mothership down in its permanent place. For our people are made of a flesh that will not die. If we can't verify that Heaven exists, there's nowhere for the wheel to go but down here. Believe me when I tell you this: humans and the residents of the Mothership cannot co-exist on the same plane of being!"

Carlos' arms ached from the tight hold that the henchmen had on him. He summoned the courage to speak and said, "There was only one way to keep her from going, and it was going to cost us our anonymity. Everyone and everything . . . with their smartphones and drones would be attempting to breach the clouds as we speak. Not to mention the military's penchant for investigating and confiscating whatever they would find."

The Man interrupted him, "Earth-tethered people cannot harm us or take away what we have. Our ship was made by the Maker of all things! God is not what humans think that He is. He is All Power, yes, but what does power mean to you? What does power mean to an entity that's not affected by worldly definitions? When you begin to speak the same language as God, then you will see that power is a right and not something you can acquire. The ownership of that has always been His."

The Man gave a signal by pointing his index finger down to the floor. The henchmen wrestled Carlos on to the cold granite tiles. The last thing that Carlos wanted was an eye-to-eye with this man. His face was a monstrosity that had the power to nauseate you if you gazed upon it for too long. Carlos kept his view fixed firmly on the floor, but he could hear him creeping his direction, ever so slowly.

Before he knew it, he yelled out, "Don't you dare come any closer ... Please! I assure you that Ameerah will not be the victor! There is a fail-safe in place that won't allow her to be."

He eerily crouched behind Carlos and began to speak garbled words softly to the base of his neck. The closer The Man got to his ear, the more Carlos swore that he heard the strings of violin music mingled with his voice. During the early stages of their relationship, there was an obvious ambiguity regarding what exactly "The Man" was. Man, mutant, or alien? If Carlos had to guess, he was all three.

Honestly, he hoped that he'd never have to find out. While crouching behind him, he said, "God is the clockmaker. No one knows for sure how many clocks he's made, but I am certain that He's made at least two. One of which we're standing in right now: the human existence.

"Once upon a time, He made a beautiful, intricately designed clock. It was filled with many different facets, like cogs, wheels, and coils. They were designed to interact and work together in unison for a particular purpose. Each second that passed was a verification of His good works that existing just for Him. He watched the clock, following the second hand and the minute hand rotate around the face on a perfect schedule.

"This clock can now maintain itself. Once He's made it, He doesn't really bother it. He looks after it, and if it falls, He picks it up and places it back on the wall. If it gets dirty, He wipes it clean. He lets it do the job it was designed to do, but when that clock winds down or if it should expire or break, His nature is to build a newer and better one."

Carlos folded himself up, shivering on the floor while he spoke. He knew exactly what he was saying, but it didn't matter if his fate was sealed.

The Man went on to say, "We all know that God isn't some Zeus-looking white man on a golden throne. We also know that Heaven isn't what their guerrilla warfare marketing has made it to be either. God is no more in Heaven than the Devil is in Hell.

"Nevertheless, they are real. The Devil is assigned to this Earth and God has no boundaries. Why do you think we're here? When the last saints are done, we want out of the Devil's playground and to settle down to our peace and tranquility. God's hands-off approach has made us weary and frustrated. We can't wait any longer."

The Man closed his many eyes, and he pictured all the earthly saints that were on the Mothership, and the last few that are to come. They were in stark contrast to the images painted on the walls of the Italian ruins and the exquisitely opulent Vatican churches. The real saints are black and brown people of many ages.

He passionately spoke of one "Black Saint" in particular. He said, "This 'Wali' is an especially polarizing figure, but spoke the horrendous truths, nonetheless. He has musical skills with which none can compare! With his bowtie tucked neatly under his chin, he played his violin with his brilliant choreographed hands. Each gesture exuded beautiful melodies that refused to leave my heart. Every pluck of the strings resonated in my head, flowed through my body, and manifested through my speech."

Carlos looked upward with his eyes closed, not realizing that no one was looking at him. He said, "If I can correct this, will our deal still be intact? You promised to take me and my loved ones to this new existence that will be colonized. You swore that we would never die in the flesh or the spirit (like the Saints on the Mothership). You said that we would bypass 'judgement,' and questionable experience of possibly being Hell-bound!"

The Man silenced the music in his head and said, "Our arrangement was conditional. Contingent upon you fulfilling your side of the agreement."

Carlos was so stressed that he loudly grinded his teeth to keep from speaking. He was angered at the mere thought of losing everything again. The Man was a big guy with a distinctive form that Carlos had difficulty making out. His wide baggy black suit was worn more like a tent than an actual fitted garment. It was as if he was trying to hide his true form.

His head was never in one place or one position for long. It was constantly changing in shape, depth and form. Carlos had only looked at him once (which was enough). His memory of his features was limited. What he did remember was this: its head and face were peppered with what looked like a hundred eyes. Carlos thought to himself, *I would need to take*

LSD just to process the gyration of his face. Maybe that would hold it still long enough to get a good look?

The Man appeared to be talking to something; Carlos had yet to look at him straight on. He heard multiple voices, but the henchmen were still guarding him. Someone (or something) else was in the room.

Then a lone voice said, "Carlos, I'm sure you're wondering what I am. I was a man once but not necessarily from Earth. I don't know if you're aware, but the human experience on Earth is not a unique one. I'm certain that you've heard this phrase before: 'there's nothing new under the sun.'

"Everything has been done before. We are just different versions of you. I'm not technically human and not quite an Angel. During my elevation in evolution, I (and others like me) have taken on the attributes of Angels physically. Of course, we don't get to do all the amazing things and get wings and such. However, if you have read the Bible, Angels do have bizarre appearances in their true form. We are what you would call 'hybrids,' much like your Astrid!

"She will be a welcomed addition to our tribe, and as she elevates, she will morph too. That is, if she makes it that far. This trip will determine if she gets to live in any capacity. We do all of these things without God's blessings. It's inevitable that He will strike back in a glorious way. If our efforts are achieved, any feelings of complacency that your daughter may have will be short lived. She has no hope of dethroning or usurping any leadership He has."

"Let's not get ahead of ourselves." He motioned for his men to stand Carlos up on his feet, and it wasn't a moment too soon. The gaps in the granite tile carved gashes into the skin on his knees and began to bleed. Not that he noticed; the numbness had confiscated his senses thirty minutes prior.

Carlos spoke almost sheepishly. "Where can I go? I can't hide from you. If Astrid fails . . . I know that I'll be collected and disposed of. Please allow me to do what I can to ensure a victory."

The Man replied, "If you don't, my true face will be the last thing you'll see!"

CHAPTER SIXTY

Scilectra saw Ameerah leaving the Monocerus Zone, and she was traveling fast. What puzzled her was how she had arrived there so quickly. Her powers weren't up to par last they met. If they had been, she would've sensed them in the lab. It was also clear to her that Ameerah didn't know that she was there. Scilectra eased onto her trail and traveled, mainly in the void. She was confident that that mode of travel was for her enjoyment only.

Ameerah slowed her movements. Whatever was out there with her wasn't making itself known, nor was she going to confront it. She thought, *It's more than likely those things that grabbed me on my test run.*

As she moved forward, her internal GPS was alive and well; travel was timely and accurate. She giggled at how intuitive the suit was. She could feel when she crossed over into the Vexaverse.

It was much like an out-of-body experience. Her flesh began to painlessly disassemble like micro puzzle pieces, but the fibers and the mechanics of the suit kept her body encased. Scientifically, each atom and cell in her body began to behave as separate individuals that were part of an accommodating whole. It took her a minute to adjust to this new universe, but she kept on moving forward.

Scilectra felt aggravated at Ameerah's progress, and even more furious at her ease at making it through this unknown locale. She didn't like that Ameerah was so smart, well-liked, and naturally talented. Yet here she was having to follow her because she didn't know where to go. As of late, Scilectra had found herself questioning her ability to be "The New God." Much of it she arrogantly explained away as "No one knows how many times He had to do it before he got it right! I'm sure He had a learning curve before the 'Big Bang.'"

As she looked on at Ameerah and her dandy new suit and flowing hair, her anger at God seemed to grow. She mumbled, "Who made God? He had to come from somewhere. Nothing has 'always been,' and even if it has ... What thing brought it into existence? Surely other things have existed with it too!"

She was so in her own head that she didn't notice that Ameerah was no longer in front of her.

Ameerah's senses were tingling. Whatever was following her changed her curiosity to concern. She dipped back into the void, rode the bandwidth of the past for a split second and dropped off right onto Scilectra's path.

Scilectra's response was priceless, although expected: "Impossible ... This is my domain!"

Ameerah responded with a smile on her face, "Not anymore. You gave up that right when you deviously infected me with your brand of life."

At this juncture, they both were sick of each other. In their individual minds, a plan was already at work to rid the nemesis that they both had a hand in making. Of course, Scilectra pulled the first punch. She felt emboldened by their last encounter and the fact that her suit was made for such an occasion.

She tried to harness all the power that she had, including that which was running through her suit, into a ball of blue energy, but it was a no-go! Scilectra had never tested her powers in the void before, and she didn't know that flexing her abilities here was forbidden by the laws of the void. The only thing that could exist there (in the forms of power) was that of the time streams traveling in their respective directions.

In fact, the real reason that she (or anyone) could visit the void at all was because they were there on the timestream of the present. So while Scilectra was trying to get her life together, the flaccid show of strength informed Ameerah of something she didn't know either. Being a tactical thinker was better than having a weapon. Ameerah jetted out of the void to take the fight to a functional place.

Ameerah had to get Scilectra out of the Vexaverse. She knew exactly where she needed to go. Scilectra's anger prevented her from being a proficient thinker. All she saw was blind rage, and blind is what Ameerah needed her to be.

The problem was that Ameerah wasn't good with the geography of space. She knew where she was but not where she wanted to be. She said, "This is a job for the A.T.I.," but she didn't want to ride the void there because she needed to have Scilectra follow her. It was the only way it would work.

She thought of a particular coordinate in her mind, just the physical number of it. Once it manifested in her head, she spoke it into a built-in microphone in her suit. That provided a direction to her GPS, and off she went. Scilectra had no clue as to what was happening; all she knew was, Ameerah had to die!

Ameerah flew fast through space, dodging stars and planets to get to her target. Scilectra followed, vehemently throwing balls of blue fire her way. If she had of been thinking clearly, that was that last thing she would've done. Why? Because Ameerah was already gifted with absorbing energy and utilizing it as her own. Ameerah's suit drank the hits and fed them to Ameerah until she activated her rainbowed-aura without effort.

In between the power hits and traveling at lightning speeds, Ameerah suit's temperature started to rise. The team wasn't prepared for a galactic showdown on the run. She was being over-powered and now had to expend that energy. Reducing her speed was definitely in order, but that mad cat in Scilectra saw her slowing down as weakened prey.

She said, "I have you now! That get-up that you're wearing is cute, but it cannot compare to my power."

Ameerah thought, *At least she's true to form. All villains worth their salt takes their time before the kill. It's paramount that they vent their grievances before the strike.* Ameerah didn't mind at all; her entire purpose for stopping was to stall. Her suit was cooling down and her marked destination was near.

Once Scilectra appeared to be about twenty yards away, she disappeared.

Ameerah said, "Oh, shit . . . she's in the void, she could be on top of me in a second!"

Ameerah darted off in a blaze of unicorn fire. What she feared had just happened; she missed Scilectra by a tenth of an inch. There was no time to waste; shaking her was not an option. It was time for the "big dump."

This plan was dangerous for them both, but more so Scilectra. Her design of outputting energy might be the death of her. In contrast, Ameerah's design of intaking energy might be what saved her from the event. They raced and chased each other until Ameerah felt the massive pull. She stopped dead in her tracks. Scilectra wasted no time and dove onto Ameerah and blasted her with balls of energy so dense that Ameerah's illumination transformed back to a weaker solid color of blue.

Ameerah was forced to embrace her with her limbs. Their opposing suits circled their energies on a loop. No harm came to either one by way of another. They were the truest form of AC/DC; they could have existed that way forever. If they died, they would die simultaneous deaths, because one could not exist without the other.

Scilectra wore her surprise like a coat, and in her display of disbelief, she loosened her grip. Ameerah was able to quickly yank away. She blew her newly absorbed power wad on, pushing Scilectra to certain death. They were at the event horizon of the Black Hole.

Ameerah aimed her hands at Scilectra, and before she could dive back into the void, Ameerah blasted her into its huge, hungry, black mouth. The last thing Scilectra said was, "You took it from me . . . Take care of my baby!" as the Black Hole swallowed her in one gulp.

Scilectra was sucked down into the pitch-black vacuum. She was stretched, pulled, and flattened on a continuous cycle. The force was unending. Forget whatever you've read about this anomaly—it snacks on planets and dines on universes.

The gravitational pull was so dense that doing anything other than allowing it to have its way with you was fruitless. Its tubular tongue licked her and rolled it around its suffocating mouth. Scilectra shed a tear for many losses, but none more than her only child. That last revelation was most painful: the fact that now, her seed belonged to Ameerah.

On the outside of the bottomless pit, Ameerah fought to get out of its surrounding gravitational pull. The event taxed the suit and her. The garment made many adjustments because Ameerah's stress levels were off the charts. She couldn't really pinpoint it, but after that last tango with Scilectra, she felt different—not sick or injured, but definitely different. As she floated away, Ameerah recalled her last words in her head: "You took it from me . . . Take care of my baby!"

She couldn't help but wonder, *What could that mean?* Scilectra was known to say things in anger but never something cryptic like that. Ameerah floated for hours. She was tired, and more importantly, the suit needed a rest. She closed her eyes to enjoy the solitude that was in order, and bumping into stars was the least of her worries at a time like this.

She could feel presence while she rested bobbing in space. At first, she thought that Scilectra had somehow returned, but it wasn't her. When she opened her eyes, there was a thick darkness. No star lights or planetarial illumination; the strong scent of freshly soldered metal filled her nostrils.

A deep, gravelly voice spoke out in the darkness. "We are the Brahka and we are tasked with maintaining boundaries for the Maker of all things. Our authority is with the souls of man. When they have been assigned a place, we make sure they stay the course. We stopped you before because your soul for the moment is to be earthbound.

"Your soul cannot go to the maker nor to the opposer. However, in the flesh, you may do as you please." Ameerah just floated silently in the black fog; she wasn't sure that she should question them or let them be.

She said, "If you don't mind, I will move on and go to my destination."

Following her last word, the fog lifted, and the air was clear. Ameerah engaged her A.T.I. and navigated back to the Monocerus Zone. After that, the Vexaverse would be the next stop. She no longer had to concern herself with Scilectra, and the newly introduced Brahka gave her their blessings. Whatever awaited her on the next leg of the trip was anybody's guess. Despite that, Ameerah was up for it. She might not have been the chosen one, but at the moment, she was the only one.

CHAPTER SIXTY-ONE

B ack in the lab, there was nothing to do except to wait. Savoy and Raj listened for soul chatter in hopes that maybe they would mention Ameerah in passing. Ashland, who was still grappling with the colossal efforts that the lab was undertaking, felt the need to ask an important question.

"What will she do when she makes it to Heaven ... What's the goal?"

They took turns looking at each other with questionable glances.

Lisa replied, "Surprisingly, we didn't get that far. Verifying Heaven is the goal. Like anyone else on the face of this Earth, curiosity will set in and she will do what comes naturally. To actually be submerged in a place that's the biggest mystery to mankind. What would you do?"

D.K. walked over to Ashland and lovingly massaged her shoulders while he spoke. "Ameerah will be amazed! Science won't matter to her then—our entire reason for being is in that one place."

Savoy popped out of her chair and said, "I'm optimistic that she'll return with more than she planned on. She may even have her own gospel to record!" The team turned to her with hilarious confusion on their faces.

Chad jokingly replied, "Don't take that too seriously. Savoy is the capricious one of the bunch!"

They laughed at the silliness of Savoy's words, but she wasn't too far off the truth. What the lab had done was Bible-worthy. Throughout history, the Bible had recorded events deserving of note. If this didn't qualify as one, then nothing ever would.

The team was tired, frustrated, and beyond impatient. Raj struck up the conversation about getting out the lab and strolling about the campus for some air (one thing they had never done together).

He said, "It really is a beautiful campus, especially at night. Everyone grab your coats and let's go!"

They pouted out the lab like runny-nosed toddlers, forced to perform unfulfilling duties by their parent. The resounding sentiment was "How could they go on with life as usual with Ameerah hanging in the balance?" Raj understood and he felt the same way; unfortunately, that reality was out of their control.

After exiting the building, the mood lightened, and changed to a happy relief to join the world again. The icy cold sting from the winter air hit their faces with an unwelcome surprise. Another realization: they'd been cooped up in the lab so long that seasons changed without their attendance.

They decided to pair up and walk as couples throughout the quad; keeping warm was not a choice, and it was an excuse for some just to get closer. Each pair whispered and giggled to their own private conversations. D.K. was especially happy to show Ashland the uniqueness of the university. He was hoping to entice her to stay with the lab and retire her underground actives.

He said to her, "Life here is bigger than what we are as individuals. It is all about the application. You belong here with us, in this world."

Ashland smiled reassuringly and laid her head on his shoulder as they neared the administration building. It was then that they saw him.

Raj immediately said, "We should've never left the lab . . ."

There was Dean Rydell, being carted off by four huge menacing-looking men. Another ominous figure followed, ushering them from behind.

His face was engulfed in a gray swirling haze, an effective cloaking mechanism for prying eyes. The team stopped in their tracks because this didn't look right . . . not at all! Never mind that the dean looked to be in the middle of his own kidnapping, but what rang in their ears was the warning he gave before he left their lab several hours prior. A sinister caveat that "worldly and otherworldly perils awaited them if Ameerah left for Heaven."

They did their best to fade into thinning foliage of nearby shrubs, but each of them had a sinking feeling that those men saw them too. Their presence was rendered innocuous by the current unsavory transaction at play. The team (along with Ameerah) were the mechanics behind their best competitor's tentative loss; it would be just a matter of time before they would see the inside of that precarious sedan leaving their view.

They stayed put until the coast was clear. Easing out of the shrubby one at a time until they all were accounted for. "PETRIFIED!" was the mood for the moment, and it was blatantly clear by looking their collective faces that they were scared. Lisa was the first to pick up the pace, and ran the length of the quad. Even at that high rate of speed, it took them fifteen minutes to make it back to the lab. Imagine their surprise to see Dean Rydell waiting for them in front of their door. Visibly shaken, he submissively asked to speak to them in private.

He said the charade was up. "My name is Carlos Acosto. Dean Rydell was a name that I assumed to push forward this agenda. I'm explaining this to you because if you don't help to bring Ameerah back before she reaches Heaven, then all will be lost. Not just for me, but for humanity on a whole. There may be things out there worse than the wrath of God and the Devil's Hellfire. I mean that in the most respectful way. Events that may launch a 'happening' so devastating that Hell will be considered a fifth-tier fear!"

Raj motioned for him to have a seat; if nothing else, his conversation was intriguing. He said Carlos, "What do you mean? We witnessed a hoard of men forcing you into a vehicle not more than twenty minutes ago. Who were they?"

Carlos hung his head, tugged on his badly damaged blazer, and said, "What drives most humans are the rewards if an afterlife, a secured salvation. Sure, while we are alive, we're pre-occupied with money, good health, and whatever your version of happiness is." He rubbed the crusted blood nestled in the grooves of his knees before he went on. "The next world is where you want to lay your foundation. The reality is that most humans are remarkably corrupt creatures, their fates are sealed with the glue of their deeds.

"Those horrible men out there represent the 'Safe Passage' no matter what your Earthly deeds are. If you were unlucky enough to observe that scene, there's no doubt that you saw the dreadful ring leader. He is best appreciated from afar, and he is why I am here."

D.K. said in a fiery manner, "Man . . . spit it out!"

Carlos jumped from D.K.'s aggression. He was growing more and more timid by the minute. He started at the beginning: how he learned of The Man, the Mothership, and their purpose. How he had found Professor Sherman on a fluke, during a research-gathering mission.; he'd found a sign-up sheet to attend a lecture about "Reconfigured Angelology." The subject matter caught his attention, so he attended.

He said, "It was meant to be! I met him the one time, and realized that his research was the missing link. I returned home to prep my Astrid for the future transition."

Carlos stayed with the team for hours answering questions and disclosing all that he knew. He felt comforted that he might be possibly winning them over. After he was done informing them to their fill, he asked, "Are you able to bring her home? Let Astrid go on to win the battle? If she does, we all can win the war!"

Savoy interrupted him. "I call bullshit!"

The team shook their heads, as if to say, "Here she goes again!"

She began to explain herself: "I'll tell you why. If Scilectra makes it to Heaven first, we are already losing, because she's gonna be a little blue tyrant. Even if she's not, the hall pass is only for a selected few, and we are not on that list! Why should we be motivated to help you?"

Lisa stretched her lips and nodded her head up and down, saying to herself, "That's a really good question."

Carlos shockingly responded, "You're right! I neglected to tell you what may very well happen if my daughter isn't the winner of the race. The Mothership has nowhere to go. Important people who have died in flesh and have been reconstituted in their living form are on that ship, as well as other creatures like The Man, who will be forced to come down from the sky and inhabit the earth with us all.

"The problem is . . . if they do, life as we know it is over. Their life force is so incompatible with ours that it will cause an extinction of anything that has lived on this planet. They have the wherewithal all to sustain their situation until the final earthly saints expire physically. After that, they have to set the ship down, disembark, and colonize for all of eternity."

The room fell silent. They were right where they didn't want to be, in between a rock and a hard place. Even if they could reach Ameerah, explaining this to her would be lost in translation. She was on her way to Heaven, and convincing her to do otherwise would meet heavy opposition, especially fueled by the urgings of Carlos Acosto.

CHAPTER SIXTY-TWO

W hat Scilectra was experiencing wasn't really a fall; it was more of a lateral transfer. The suction dragged her helpless body across its tunnel of perpetuity with such violent force, going downward would just as insult to injury. She gave in to all that it wanted to do to her; a declared unwilling participant who would endure to the end.

Whatever the hole swallowed went through a transformation, making the galaxies easier to digest. After being inhaled (for what felt like an eternity), Scilectra cried out, "Is there no end to this?"

The scientist in her was forced to rise to the occasion. *I have to be going somewhere; the planets and stars aren't collecting and piling up. I feel that we're passing through, like water flowing through a straw.*

She couldn't help but feel granular and insignificant. There was no master in this unsealed grave of gravity. 'God's garbage disposal,' she called it. Mocking Him and the absurdity of His creations she had the power to do, but not much else. Scilectra closed her eyes again and waited for the eventual end, one she hoped for sooner than later. A sudden noise got her attention—a shrill cry echoed in the darkness.

Scilectra looked around, peering between the broken-down matter flying around her. She thought, *That couldn't be a person. No human could survive this treacherous ordeal and live, let alone cry out. Was it Ameerah . . . did she accidentally get sucked in too?* All her questions were about to be answered. She wasn't encased in an ebony tomb anymore; she saw a pinhole of light and it was getting larger and larger!

Her runaway train was pulling into the station. The opening grew to an enormous circumference, and rightfully so. From the size of the objects being consumed, the waste extruded would be just as comparable. She landed into another universe all in and of itself. Oddly enough, this world had an accordion-like appearance.

The sky had folds in it for expansion, to accommodate what being pushed in it. Below the sky, tiny familiar sights gave her some comfort. Scilectra was surprised to see figures milling around, unaffected by the melee situated above them! From what she could see, they weren't just figures; they look like "humans" below the gargantuan dump of space decorations!

Once she was unceremoniously spat out, her powers resumed back to normal. However, there was one major difference that alarmed her: there was no void to ride in. If she wanted to move about this world, it would be out in the open for everyone to see. Her nanites didn't appear to be affected by the trip; floating and hovering didn't tax her system at all.

You would think that, with the massive gravitational pull within the hole, their the universe would be flattened. The sheer monumental weight of the objects being thrown should've obliterated their world, but no. All the stars and planets that were dragged there remained in their skies like the weightless clouds on Earth.

Scilectra soon learned why this was: this universe had a dense helium pocket that acted as a liner separating the high skies from the land below. This helium pocket collected and held the products of the black hole and separated it from the gravity below. Her problem now was to pierce the pocket and access the terrains below. The trick would be to do so without destabilizing the pocket and dropping a universe of trash on their heads.

There was only one thing in the world Scilectra was afraid of, and that was containment. She was sandwiched between two opposing forces of nature. She could neither go up nor down, and every swallow that this juggernaut took limited her optimism of getting out. She had no other choice but to dismantle her person on a molecular level. The design of the pocket was constructed for larger things; even though Scilectra was smaller by comparison, she wasn't small enough to escape its grip.

She spoke inwardly to her nanites and ordered them to fragment her person. Scilectra dissipated into thin air and each minuscule piece of her slide through the pockets, like water going through a strainer. Assembling on the other side was a natural alignment; the nanites were colonized and knew where to go instinctively. While this was happening, Scilectra wasn't conscious of the effort to put the back together. Since her body and soul were fused together, it was impossible to institute an "out of body" awareness.

She was extremely eager to get to the ground and investigate the unknown land below her. Seeking out a safe and quiet spot to land was challenging, as the population was robust and active. A nude pale woman with bluish discolorations would be hard to miss, drifting down from above.

The eyes below followed Scilectra all the way down to the ground. They watched in awe as she glided atop a hill standing in the middle of their village. Her surroundings had an antiquated appeal to them. They weren't advanced like the Earth she was born on—the time period was unquestionably of B.C. nostalgia.

A crowd gathered and whispered amongst themselves, pointing and shielding their faces from whatever danger she might pose. She saw an opportunity here to solidify her new position as the "New God," but first, she had to find out what God was already there.

Scilectra addressed the crowd and said, "My name is Scilectra. I have been delivered amongst your people as a blessing. Who is your God?"

The villagers turned to each other and conversed with themselves. Some pointed and shook their heads in disagreement.

She asked another question, "Where is your God?"

A young woman stepped forward and spoke to Scilectra. She said, "God has gone. He has not been with us since the beginning of our tribes. Our scrolls have taught us that our people were the first draft of life. Since then, He has gone to make more elsewhere."

Scilectra was taken aback that (from what she understood) Earth and humans weren't a unique model. God had made the attempt at least once before and moved on when He changed the base model. She was ecstatic! A race of people who had (for all intents and purposes) been abandoned by God, arrested in a primitive state of mind for all eternity.

She said, "I have come to gift you with a superior mind. I give you the religion of math and science. Your Bible will be written in the skies for all to see. You are no longer governed by the 'Old God,' so lie your burden down and embrace the word of the 'Omniverse.' I, Scilectra, am your 'New God.' Let me lead the way!"

At the same time Scilectra was getting an opportunity that the human world denied her, Tilda was rearing her ugly head again back on Earth. She never left the campus; instead, she bribed a financially stressed adjunct professor to gain access to the clock tower—the clock tower that owned a generous view over the entire university grounds. She and her bodyguard took in all of the goings-on of Carlos Acosto and his malevolent guests.

They were just the kind of damaged that she liked. She said to herself, "If they are putting this much energy into a wayward college dean, then I need to know them! What does he know and what would they do to find out?"

Tilda could afford the best of everything, and that included eavesdropping devices that she kept on tap for just an occasion. Before she was ejected from the lab, she had her guardian to stick a tiny bug under the conference table in the front of the lab.

Finding out about the "Organization" was a plus! Her real objective was to catch them speaking freely about the "Digital Drugs." At the very least, she wanted to learn Astrid's possible itinerary. She was going to get her fix whatever way she could, even if that meant a strong-armed kidnapping.

Right now, her attention was on the black sedan that remained parked on property too. She said, "There's no better way to get someone's attention than to introduce yourself to them directly!"

Inside of her impromptu fortress, she carefully crept down the rotting wooden stairs with the grace of a sure-footed gazelle. For a woman her age, she moved remarkably fast when she was properly motivated. Her dangling

344 | Y<small>VETTE</small> K<small>ENDALL</small>

carrot of choice was the parked sedan that may be pulling away at any moment. Tilda couldn't get to ground level fast enough!

Out in the open, Tilda returned to her pedigreed, reserved nature. She walked alongside of the vehicle as if her chauffeur awaited her arrival. The sedan was designed with six doors instead of the traditional four. When she approached, all four men stepped out to stop her from coming any closer. She hoped to get a glimpse of the peculiar man sitting in the rear of the car; unfortunately, the windows were covered with built-in red velvet curtains.

From where she stood, attempting to peek her head around the fortified tree-like men, she could hear extraordinary violin music flowing from the crack in the window. It was a haunting melody that sucked you into a trance with sounds unlikely made by human hands. Whoever played those notes was gifted beyond measure.

One of the guards interrupted her train of thought by nudging her backwards. Not one of them spoke; it was almost if they couldn't or weren't allowed to.

She said, "I would like to speak with the representative of the 'Organization.'"

Their eyes swelled to the size of silver dollars; they huffed and puffed their displeasure from her request. Suddenly, there was a knock on the glass from inside the car, it appears that the occupant of the sedan called them off.

The most irritated ruffian stretched out his long arm, opened the door, and motioned for Tilda to get in. She quickly moved to lower herself in the car. This was business for her; Tilda knew she was wealthy and often tried to beguile powerful men with her prestige. Money and power wouldn't save her from what was to come this time, though.

It was the strangest thing she'd ever seen; although light was entering the sedan, the rear was pitch black. Tilda was unable to make out his face, but she could clearly hear that same intoxicating music.

Then he spoke. "To what do I owe the honor? We've heard of the Swans; your reputation proceeds you."

She coyly smiled and replied, "Why, thank you! We have made our mark on the world and we're here to stay. Some call us 'king-makers' and others 'king-breakers.' However, to date, I have a pre-occupied interest in what you can offer me. I overheard a sensitive conversation about your universal reach to provide safe travel for a chosen few."

The Man wasn't pleased by what he'd heard, but the power was all his to give or to take away. He allowed her to gloat on and on about her worth until it was time to reckon her with the truth.

He said, "You are to compliment my intellect. We are the creators that birthed a perfect human. Neither you, nor your family, belong anywhere north of the brightest star.

"You are a stain in the Book of Life and an asterisk in the Book of Death. You would poison the very air we breathe on the Mothership—a black mold that would eat the saints that repopulate a new world from the inside out. A Swan by any other name would still be a virus! Every breath you take is an allowed sin that will happen no longer."

He lifted the grey foggy veil from his face and all of his one hundred eyes focused on Tilda so intensely that they resonated the marrow in her bones. Death lurked in every pore of her being while Hell opened its mouth, anticipating the return of its wicked property. Tilda was too far gone to scream, and who would hear her anyway? The Man didn't require justice; he didn't need it.

If it so happened that they not to be able to access Heaven, the Swans and anyone tainted with their bloodline would have been their first casualties anyway. By the time the beast closed his eyes, nothing was left of the elder Swan sibling but her tale-tell string of pearls. He put them up to his grotesquely formed mouth and licked, sucked, and smacked on the hardened white orbs. He gave one last smile before throwing them down his throat as a souvenir for a job well done.

CHAPTER SIXTY-THREE

Ameerah was back on track. After disposing of Scilectra, the nagging sensation of urgency dwindled down to justified anxiety. Faced with the reality that it was just her now, making the trip and suffering any consequences would be for her to bear.

The altercation at the Black Hole did a number on her and the suit. It really was an all-consuming entity; she would never look at the color black the same. It was so dark there that they had yet to duplicate its cavernous darkness on Earth. The "blackness" is a character all by itself, and its ravenous appetite is all-inclusive. It took Ameerah to task getting away from it, but not before draining the majority of her powers and that of the suit.

The recovery time was slow until she remembered that stars and stardust are another form or realized energy. As she moved forward through the Vexaverse, she grabbed particles from passing by clusters. When she wanted a more vigorous charge, she wrapped herself around a splintered star and used it as a vehicle to fuel up on.

Ameerah navigated the new universe well; after all, she had many layers of technology to achieve this great feat. More importantly, she was personally upgraded to "supernova status." She tried not to get caught up in the pioneering aspect of being the first human to travel outside of Earth's known universe. The implications of it all were truly humbling.

She picked up a respectable momentum, riding and gliding. Watching new colors and shapes form the deep, she probed this spectacular place.

Her body was constantly adjusting to the atmosphere and it shifted with ease.

Until now, she said to herself, "I know something's in there because I can feel it moving."

She felt a foreign object rapidly growing. Maybe it was ignorance or maybe it was denial. Whatever the reason, she chose to ignore it. She reduced the changes of her body to a metamorphic trip to an all-encompassing world.

Bleary-eyed and tired, she couldn't hold it off any longer. Even in this advanced state of being, she had to sleep. The suit was technically on auto-pilot anyway, and the ride to her destination was a long way still. Ameerah closed her eyes and drifted off to sleep. With her asleep, the suit propelled her faster. It no longer had to struggle with her humanness. It worked in tandem enthusiastically with her astral-self.

Her heartbeat slowed and her cognitive efforts were at rest. The natural electrical impulses that kept her awake could now lend themselves to the daunting undertakings of travel. Ameerah was now a passenger inside of her own body.

Ameerah had the privilege of going through time and space in real time. She wouldn't change physically because she was traveling through alternate realities, but that didn't apply to her unidentified passenger. The dynamic between Ameerah and Scilectra was more intertwined and complicated than the both of them knew. Something miraculous happened on their last engagement that would make all the difference.

While they were tightly engaged, giving and taking energies in a circular flow, Scilectra's child dissipated in the intense struggle of currents. Like its mother, it flowed through her body, and like water through a strainer, it was sucked into Ameerah's. Once there, it reassembled into her womb upon their separation.

There's nothing new under the sun (or stars). Ameerah was a virgin who was now pregnant with Scilectra's and the Professor's baby. She was now set to become the new version of Mary of Nazareth. A true millennium "Virgin Mary," and that was just the beginning of her exaltation.

Ameerah woke to yet more confusion. She laid half on nothingness and half on lush green grass. She said, "Where am I?"

The Vexaverse was just there, but now it was gone. Why would she just be laying on such unusual grounds? *Am I in heaven? What happened to me?* She questioned herself rapidly until she slid over completely on the greenest grass she'd ever seen.

She then looked down to stand on her feet and noticed that she had expanded. Her stomach had grown to ten times its previous size. She wasn't asleep; she did her tried and true totem test and she was surely awake.

She said, "How am I pregna. . . . Oh! That's what Scilectra was trying to tell me. I can't . . . I won't! Think Ameerah, think. Worry about this when it's time, and right now isn't the time."

She would come to realize that she was indeed in Heaven. Ameerah had the presence of mind to take off her shoes to have her flesh to touch the forbidden firmament. There were no gates that she could see, but there was a stream of water. The stream was eerily similar to the one she'd experienced in her dream months ago. She tiptoed over to it, bent down, and drank heartily of the living water in Heaven's stream. These acts had given her permission to visit Heaven and walk amongst its inhabitants, but only for a little while.

Ameerah was curious about what she could see from the edge of the lands. She traced her footsteps back to where she had awakened and stood on the edge and peered over. The view was more of a map. Although she was in another universe, she could vividly see the Earth and its solar system. Standing in this location gave her access to a wormhole that zoned straight to Earth. It was a conical vantage point that might be the only view of this location she would ever see.

She said, "If I make it back, I'll have to tell Savoy that her theory was right on the money!"

Ameerah continued to look through the telescope of Heaven just to spot something else that they had yet to discover. There was Hell: the "B" coordinate! Lit up like a galactic bulls-eye right below the left (or Sinister) side of Earth! From what she could see, it was really too close for comfort, and that explained a lot as well.

Breaching the threshold of the Heaven apparently set off an alert to its occupants. Hundred of souls flocked to her area and she was greeted by beautiful souls adorned with shimmering golden auras, and some others lit up internally with transformed Aurovian. They were especially curious about her because they felt a familiarity about her and welcomed her in.

They walked with her, smiling and sending loving vibrations. Each of their vibrations had different frequencies that behaved like physical touches. She didn't know where they were taking her, but it seemed as if they had a pre-determined location. The buildings resembled structures of frosted glass, and the light permeated everything that it showered.

They eventually came to a halt. It was an open field in the shape of a perfect circle. Not a blade of grass extended beyond the circumference of its rounded border. She was in awe of the colors. Colors that didn't exist on Earth painted their world in fantastic ways. Resting in the center of this circle was a colorful plasma in constant movement.

It said, "Welcome Ameerah! We anticipated your arrival; it was foretold that you would come."

Ameerah smiled but with an expression of question. She asked, "Foretold? How and by whom?"

The plasma responded, "By the All and All. I am here to give answers the questions you seek. Let me start by saying, 'He' is a relative term—it's a chosen moniker to simplify His existence. 'God' just IS. He is the 'All and All.' He is time. He is life's force. You are a scientist, and therefore a fragment of God's internal tapestry. Science is God in a way, that it was from Him and of Him. It cannot be separated any more than you can separate your child's blood from your own. He created physics to make life predictable and repetitive. Because for humans, you need a pattern that models a mold that can be deduplicated. It is the design of your system.

"Prayer is His structure of communication for all Humans. It is also a fact that it has mathematical attributes. Hence it can be dissected and interpreted with specified equations. Just like there is an equation for prayer, there's an equation for failure, which humankind has unfortunately perfected.

"Philosophy is riddled with equations that resonate with only a chosen few; thus the lacking masses have been amply alienated. He holds nothing back from those who desire and survive the search. God's love is the truth! He assures us that true love asks for nothing. Our acceptance is the way we pay. It's known that life has given love a guarantee, to last through forever and another day. He is the definition of 'Always.'"

Ameerah began to cry from the pureness of the love and truth that mingled within her soul.

The rainbowed plasma asked her, "Are you ready?"

Ameerah didn't understand the question. She wasn't prepared to meet God, if that's what it meant.

The entity answered that question for her. "No, you will not be meeting God today . . . but soon. The child is ready because it knows that it has to be. Your child will be born here and here it will stay. You have fed it the living water and its flesh has bonded with Heaven. It has been foretold. This child will be the anchor for your soul's future."

She was scared; things were happening too fast. She went from being a virgin on Earth to being a mother in Heaven without enjoying the pleasure of the process. The hundreds of souls laid her down.

The plasma said, "Don't worry, there is no pain and suffering here. Eve's sins have bypassed you."

Then every soul laid hands on her, in an act of covering. In one single push, she was separated from the child who had been hers for less than a day. It was wrapped and inserted in the plasma before she could see it.

She cried out, "Is it all right? Is it a girl or a boy?"

The plasma responded, "It is everything . . . such is love. It has a job to do, and I promise you will see it again. Just remember: everything has a purpose in His design. There are no such things as coincidences. It is meant to be. Now leave this place; this plane will be abandoned for another. If you come back here again, you will not find us here. The time for new tenancy has come."

She was given a companion to take her back to the spot of her arrival. Ironically, it was that of a tagged soul. It spoke to her telepathically, thanking her for the gift of new life.

She went on to say, "I have to inform you about the physical parents of the child and their status regarding this place."

She explained that "in essence," Scilectra did make it to Heaven (or part of her), and for that matter so did part of the father, the Professor.

His soul would be taken out of Hell by the Brahka. It would be delivered promptly to a representative for the "Organization" to resettle in this land (which is now "Third Heaven"). However, he would be a dual citizen of both the colony in Third Heaven and that population of Hell. He must split his time in both places throughout eternity. She also shared that they were on their way to the fourth and final Heaven. Before she concluded, she said that Scilectra was a different matter altogether, and that it would be dealt with in God's timing.

Ameerah turned to look down the conical scope again. She was using the mechanics of the suit to gauge the coordinates of the "B" location, since the wormhole folded the Vexaverse to complete accuracy and provided a close proximity to Hell's physical location. While she was doing so, she was purposely pushed into its gaping opening. She went flying down its gullet like a comet hurling through Earth's atmosphere. Her visit earned her an expedited trip back home with a story to tell.

Her descension was rapid. Before she knew it, she was lying on the ground of the university. It appeared to be early morning, because the sun was just barely peeking his head over the horizon. She patted herself down, focusing her inspection on her mid-section. Her typically flat tummy was there and accounted for.

She said, "I have a baby, who lives in Heaven, which by the way has moved! No one will believe this."

She took a moment to review the data gathered by her suit. It recorded not only Heaven's coordinates but it also retired Hell's. These had to be the longest coordinated in the known universe. She was excited to share with them her findings. The fact that she made it back in one piece to tell the tale was astonishing enough. There was other data that was uniquely specific to the Black Hole and other elements that could only be found in the Vexaverse.

Ameerah had the Holy Grail right there in her hands and ironically was one herself. The grass that she had made an impromptu desk was eclipsed by the shadows of some enormous figures. She looked up to find men that quite frankly, she found alarming.

Dean Rydell turned the corner of those enormous men to assist Ameerah off the ground. He said, "Don't speak. Not here."

She didn't know if she was in danger or being congratulated, so she just went with it. The group of men encircled her and walked her to the nearby administration building. Dean Rydell didn't look well. He looked like he aged a year in the day that she was gone.

She asked, "How long have I been away?"

He responded, "You have been gone seven days. Listen, Ameerah, my real name is Carlos Acosto. I don't have time to tell you the entire story, but I will share as much as I can before the sentinel of the Organization comes."

Carlos started at the beginning, and he spoke quickly. Ameerah digested what she could and reserved any questions for a later time. He also shared that her team was aware of the entire idea, and that the life of the entire planet rested on if Scilectra made it to Heaven before she did.

The Man entered the room. His footsteps were just about right for a man his size. Upon a second look, he wasn't big at all; his clothing served as a cover for something else. He was rather unnaturally shaped for anything resembling human.

He said, "Try as you might, you cannot gaze upon my face and live to tell about it. Divert your eyes if it brings you more comfort. I will remain in this haze as not to destroy you."

Ameerah didn't hesitate to look to the floor. After the trip, she was even more thankful for life and to live more abundantly.

He said, "Young Ameerah, your entire name means 'Forgiving Princess of Peace.' You changed your last name from Mahari to Mahar, in efforts to try and disguise your true nature. Mahari means 'Forgiver, or one who forgives.' That is a rare quality to have.

"There are only three building blocks on which God made Humans: 'love, forgiveness, and peace.' You are two-thirds of God's essential plan. I say this because although you thwarted our initial plan, you achieved the goals we set before another. When the last saints transition, we can resettle into our final location to colonize. You gave a life so that scores of unworthy people may live.

"You have been showered with gifts that no other man will see. You have an invitation greater than the saints—you are welcome into a place that we will never go. Your final endowment is one of the rarest. You now possess 'Purple Gene 988.' Only time will tell what that means for your life's experience. With that said, we thank you for your deeds. You and your kind will never see us again."

Carlos grabbed Ameerah's hand and walked he out of the building onto the street. He said, "I know that you weren't aware of all that hinged on this trip. I also knew that you didn't care. One day, I hope to learn about your entire experience before I leave this life. May I ask what happened to Astrid?"

Ameerah carefully crafted her answer; he was broken enough, and comfort was what he needed. She replied, "I don't know. We got separated near the Black Hole. Knowing the perseverance of your daughter, she's probably scouting a new world somewhere, plotting her way into taking it over."

They both laughed and she walked away down the quad to head back to her lab.

Finally, the lab—home sweet home! She stood outside the building, taking it all in before she went inside. She decided not to take everything so seriously and played an inside joke on her team before going in. She hammered on the door as loudly as she could, knowing that random knocks were a source of frustration for the team.

As expected, Lisa yelled through the door, "WHO THE FUCK IS IT THIS TIME?!"

Ameerah snickered to herself and calmly stated, "Ameerah Mahari, The Head of Lab-J71."

Lisa whipped the door open and hugged Ameerah with tears swelling in her eyes. The rest of the team joined in with hugs, prayers, and kisses planted all over her face. They eventually retreated back inside the lab and grabbed some chairs and food for Ameerah. After she was fed and watered, it was time to divulge the biggest story in history: how a little black girl from Shadowmoor, New Hampshire did the impossible!

She told them all about the void and the travels, her confrontation with

Scilectra and the Black hole, to the Vexaverse and of Heaven's existence. She told them of the tagged souls, the conical wormhole, Hell and that she recorded actual coordinates. What she didn't tell them was of her immaculate impregnation and that she gave birth to a child that she never met. Somehow, it didn't feel right to say.

After answering questions and peeling off her suit, she said, "Now we have to make things official by concluding out research. Ladies and gentlemen ... We have found the elusive 'Golden Coordinates'!!!"

The lab erupted in tears and cheers! The team has just achieved something that the world never thought possible.

The notion seemed ridiculous and impossible at the same time; however, the science was sound, sound enough to net astounding results. It was an amazing conclusion for a group of people that decided to test the boundaries of what happens next. The Golden Coordinates could be logged into the annals of time!

Ameerah frantically rattled off a sequence of numbers. Each team member took turns repeating and writing them down. The sequences were extremely long and detailed (thirty-three digits for each location). There were "A & B" Golden Coordinates because these realms were intricate and distinct separate locations. They have solved the only problem that matters: that God is no longer a mythical being. He is real and so is His domain. They had the addresses of the destinations that will befall each and every man, woman, and child. Because of their research, they were able to map the actual physical locations of what can be considered "Heaven" and "Hell".

Ameerah stated, "To be clear, we have verified locations with mass quantities of souls that are at constant peace and happiness, dubbed 'Location A.' There's another location of mass souls that are in a state of unrest and fear. They exemplified various stages of ongoing distress and anguish; this was dubbed 'Location B'.

"These locations are beyond this universe. Thousands of light years away would be putting it mildly. There is no calculable time in which humans would be able to reach those destinations in our physical form. We believe that you can only experience these locations when you die and pass on to the next province."

The team was ready to know, and they found out more than they bargained for. They had overwhelming proof that there *is* an afterworld, no matter what your Earthly beliefs and deeds are. The odds are ... we'll know exactly where you'll be.

Each member of the team stood in place, semi-circled around the pillaring blackboard in the lab. They stood there in wonderment and soaked in their accomplishments.

D.K. made a grand gesture with a simple piece of chalk in his hand. He extended his hand out to Ameerah and stated, "You should be the one to officially log in the Golden Coordinates as a verified find!"

Ameerah gracefully accepted the chalk (and the permission). She stepped up to the ebony edifice to write out the forbidden knowledge. She was carving her name in history by formally recording both known coordinates of Heaven and Hell. Full of emotions and a sense of grandeur, she said to herself, "Here goes ..."

(Alpha)023674.16180339.7038874 ....

(Data is interrupted)

A grand and blinding light filled the room before she could complete the string of numbers on the board. The light was so bright that attempting to close and shield their eyes was fruitless. The piercing glare drove through their flesh as if they were made of glass. Forced to stare down at the floor, a resounding voice like none other filled the room.

"I am the one you seek," the voice said. "What I have done for this world, what I have done for you, cannot be contained in your minds. Man's inability to calculate my greatness is the reason for my boundaries. Although your efforts have been recorded in the Great Book, this is a knowledge that will remain untold." ~Scieviticus 1:1.

He then reached down and touched each of them on their foreheads, and all faded to black. When they snapped back to reality, they were sitting around the conference table in the lab. She was still holding the chalk in her hand, but the blackboard was wiped clean.

Ameerah began to ask, "What were we just talking about..." but a strange language fell from her mouth. The entire table looked at her and tried to comment, but each person at the table spoke a different language, too.

They ran to each other and grouped together, cackling nonsensical sounds. Raj grabbed a pen and paper to write down what he couldn't say, but his words culminated in a collage of confusing gibberish. One by one, they discovered that God himself had come down and confounded the team so that working together any further would be impossible.

They would never be able to communicate to anyone what they learned. In fact, life as they knew it was over. Whatever language that they now spoke could only be understood by God. All they could do from that moment on was pray—pray that He would take pity on them and give them a second chance to respect the order of the Great Design.

Ameerah thought, *But what about all of our spies in Heaven?*

————END OF REPORT————

Oldso here. This will have to conclude my report. As I shared at the beginning, this (and other vital information) will be sealed, possibly for hundreds of years to come. Humankind is not equipped to handle the "Golden Coordinates," nor what may result from such tempestuous and cataclysmic revelations. Until the time of disclosure is specified, I bid you "Peace, Love and Light!"

"EVERYBODY'S LOOKING FOR THE ANSWERS, HOW THE STORY STARTED AND HOW IT WILL END."

—PRINCE

GLOSSARY

PRODUCT NAMES, DESCRIPTIONS, AND DEFINITIONS:

Aurovian (Ah-ro-vee-on): A new nano-technology that is a biological/mechanical /vibrational mist. It is used to attach onto air particles and can sustain indefinitely as long as there is a viable energy life source.

Carbastran (Car-bah-strann): The essence that souls are comprised of.

Davinuary (Dah-vin-ee-air-y): The new third month of the year, named after famed scientist and Renaissance man, Leonardo Da Vinci.

IDIAMTRACE-10 (Eye-Dee-Em-Trace-Ten): Our state-of-the-art computer system that creates subject profile and tracks subjects anywhere in the known and unknown Universe.

NCF: The Nation of Christian Founders

EASTER EGGS

Eve Saccarum (Eve Soc-Cah-Rum): Eve, as in the first woman and Mother of Man. Saccarum (properly spelled "Saccharum"), which is Latin for "synthetic."

Fregodian (Free-Go-Dee-Ann): The language of God. To be more descriptive, the meaning is "To free God's language or speech." What souls speak and understand before entering life as a human and after death, returning back to God/Universe. Before birth and after death, there is only one "original language." The languages that we speak here on Earth are only bound to the Earthly plane. Once we pass, we revert back to the language of God.

Deus ex particula: Latin for "God from the particle."

IDIAMTRACE-10: pronounced (Eye-Dee-Em-Trace-Ten): The team's state-of-the-art computer system that creates subject profiles and tracks subjects anywhere in the known and unknown universe.

ID: Identification

I AM: A reference to God

Trace: To track, to follow

10: A nod to binary (off/on-life/death) and God (First/Last — Beginning/End)

LAB-J71 Website for Clinical Trials: www.LAB-J71.com

The Siriaz (Pronounced as "See-Ree-Az): Your own personal deep state/dream world. You can connect to it once you have elevated to the level of Astral Planing. Ultra-vivid dreaming with rich colors; the use of all your senses and the ability to interact with your surroundings and build the story as you go.

SETTINGS, LOCATIONS, AND CHARACTERS

Stromford University Research Department: Located in the fictional city of Shadowmoor, New Hampshire.

Cast of Characters: (Fringe Science Team and other characters)
    Ameerah Mahar: Cryptologist. Phd
    Raj Patel: Medical Physician
    Chad Peterson: Neuroscientist
    D.K. Nero: Coder
    Lisa Kim: Astrophysicist/Mathematical Physicist
    Simon Christian: Linguistics/Nano-Acoustics
    Prof. Ron Sherman: Theoretical Physic
    Savoy Sellers: Inventor/Product Developer
    John Lee Mason: Forensic Sketch Artist
    Astrid Acosto/Scilectra: Prof. Sherman's Asst/Angel Particle Woman
    Matt Vines: Modern Artist / Gallery Owner
    Duvall Swan: NCF Investor
    Pauline Acosto: Astrid's Mother
    Carlos Acosto: Astrid's Father
    Tilda Swan: Duvall's Older Sister
    Norman Rydell: Dean of Stromford University
    Carley: Front Desk Assistant at Lab-J71
    DJ Black-Ray/Lola Ashland: DJ & Creator of Digital Drugs
    The Man: A Celestial Being that controls the mothership

SCILECTRA'S POWERS CATALOGUE:

Moral Compass: She's not good or bad. She has to prove that she's right.

Scilectra (Sy-Lec-Tra): A combination of "science" and "electra," for "science" and "electricity."

Astral Travel: She can interact with other people that are astral traveling as well. She can enter your dreamworld.

Galatical Travel: She can instantly travel the known and unknown universe.

Terrestrial Travel: She can instantly travel the planet Earth.

Extreme Microwave Abilities: She can microwave organic (human & animal) matter. She can kill them from the inside out.

Pure Energy: She is made from pure energy that can consume and give life to itself.

Soul Fusion: Her soul is fused together with her flesh. She can't die in the flesh because her soul (which is pure energy) is forever attached. Souls cannot die; they can only transform.

Eyes: Her irises are marble-like. They can spin around the whites of her eyes to be able to look inside her own being, in order to communicate directly with the nanites.

Clothing: She can't wear anything next to her body because it either reacts to the electricity or the heat that she gives off.

WiFi ability & Interception: She can eavesdrop on any communications held over radio waves and other signals carried through the air. She can intercept all communications, too.

Pilli-Lingua: "Pilli" is the scientific plural term for "hair," and "lingua" means "tongue" or "language" = talking hair

ASTRID / SCILECTRA'S PUZZLE BOX

Puzzle: The Digit . . . . . The One . . . The Nothing . . . . The Sun . . . - . . . .
‾ . . ‾ . . . . ‾ . . . . ‾ . . ‾ . ‾ . . . . . ‾ . . .

Answer: Scilectra is to use her middle finger and lay it upon the button. The button will recognize her print and a micro-needle will protrude and verify her DNA. She has to hold her finger on that button for a 5 second count (. . . . .), she will then lift her finger and press the button again for a 3-second count (. . .) (this turns the box on) and again for a 4-second count (. . . .) (this turns the box off). The last series of dots and dashes is a combination code for the box, revealing its contents. This process has to be done in the sunlight or in the presence of ultraviolet rays. Samples of her blood are taken every time she presses the button, and they react with the metallic material that the box is made from. This reveals the message on the top surface of the box.

Vexaverse: The universe that Heaven is located in. It's located outside the universe.

Cosmicude: Translates to "outside of the universe."

Monocerus Zone: The zone which leads to the "Vexaverse."

A.T.I. DNA (Gene): Stands for "Advanced Thought Integration Gene."

Ekausa: It's equivalent to the term "limbo."

CERN: The European Organization for Nuclear Research, known as CERN, is a European research organization that operates the largest particle physics laboratory in the world. Established in 1954, the organization is based in a northwest suburb of Geneva on the Franco–Swiss border. They are also the leading creators of "Antimatter."

Cleencups: Anti-bacterial disposable drinking cups. They are an actual product created by the author, Yvette Kendall.

EmSigna Labs: Research lab for cloning, ran by Dr. Laszlo.

CryoSci Labs: Another fringe science lab that works in the medium of cryo-technology.

Omniverit: Means "all and truth." It's the name of Scilectra's new "Bible" based on her theology of mathematics, communicated in binary.

Vulture Web: A type of deep internet only utilized and accessed by people in power and the wealthy elite. Here they can do world-changing business deals and political appointments that can change the course of the future.

DIGITAL DRUGS:

Freq-TZ: Digital Heroin

HiFi-HTZ: Digital Cocaine

Octa-ZHC: Digital Meth

Pal-Alchemy: A new age forerunner of reconfiguration based on the possible transformation of organic living matter. It's concerned particularly with the attempts to convert living organic matter into conscious energy. A seemingly magical process of transformation, creation, or a combination of both.

Retina Flash Messaging: A method that allows an embedded flash of light to temporarily imprint a message on a person's retina. The displayed message can only be seen by the intended party. The message is projected on the inside of the eyelids when the eyes are closed. The time length of the display is no more than five seconds long.

Agrisonian (Aa-gree-so-nee-an): The Agrisonian Institution was established on July 07, 1773 "for the sole purpose of cataloging and preserving rare agricultural finds." A large portion of those rare finds are directly related to verified Biblical writings and accounts. Specialized scientists, researchers, and archeologists can purchase their own safe deposit boxes and vaults to store objects for safe-keeping. The institution was founded by private donors with the Cretus Demeter Organization.

Professor Sherman's Last Words: "Flectere si nequeo superos, Acheronta movebo." Translated from Latin, it means, "If I cannot bend the heavens above, I will move Hell."

A NOTE FROM THE AUTHOR

I was asked, why did I write this book? There are many reasons. The first being that God impressed it upon my heart to do so. Secondly, I felt it necessary to write my love letter to science and science fiction. Lastly, I believe this quote from a legendary artist says it best:

> I think what you're trying to ask is why am I so insistent upon ... giving out to them that BLACK-ness, that BLACK-power, that BLACK pushing them to identify with black culture; I think that's what you're asking. I have no choice over it; in the first place, to me, we are the most beautiful creatures in the whole world, black people. And I mean that in every sense, outside and inside. And to me, we have a culture that is surpassed by no other civilization, but we don't know anything about it. So again, I think I've said this before in this same interview, I think at some time before. My job is to somehow make them curious enough or persuade them, by hook or crook, to get more aware of themselves and where they came from and what they are into and what is already there, and just to bring it out. This is what compels me, to compel them, and I will do it by whatever means necessary.

—Nina Simone

So, you see, I have no choice. I'm compelled to instigate greatness amongst our people by any means necessary.

Shout-out to Chicago, and especially the heart of my life's experience and where it all began for me: Hyde Park! My experiences at Kozmenski, 54th & Ellis, Kenwood Academy, 53rd & Greenwood, Big Hill, and The Point. Love always.

TO MY INSPIRATION AND THE ILLUMINA-
TOR OF MY LITERARY PATH: MY DAUGHTER,
MAHARI AMEERAH. MAY YOU FOREVER BE
THE "FORGIVING PRINCESS OF PEACE."

—YVETTE KENDALL,
AUTHOR OF *THE GOD MAPS*

Credits:

Image credits of man in glass tube goes to Yum! Brands

Editing Alice Piep
Assistant Editing by Larry Smith
Interior Formatting by Sheenah Freitas of Paper Crane Books
Book Cover Formatting by Lucent Oak Studios
Book Cover Design by Yvette Kendall
Source Material Reference for micro-tubules credit to
Robert Lanza/Dr. Hameroff

The comics book adaptation of *The God Maps* novel is coming soon.

www.ingramcontent.com/pod-product-compliance
Lightning Source LLC
Chambersburg PA
CBHW070204120726
47909CB00001B/248